THANKLESS IN DEATH

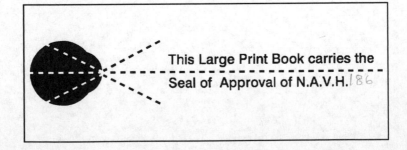

THANKLESS IN DEATH

J. D. ROBB

WHEELER PUBLISHING
A part of Gale, Cengage Learning

GALE
CENGAGE Learning·

Detroit • New York • San Francisco • New Haven, Conn • Waterville, Maine • London

GALE
CENGAGE Learning

Wheeler Publishing Large Print Hardcover.
The text of this Large Print edition is unabridged.
Other aspects of the book may vary from the original edition.
Set in 16 pt. Plantin.

LIBRARY OF CONGRESS CATALOGING-IN-PUBLICATION DATA

Robb, J. D., 1950-
    Thankless in death / by J. D. Robb. — Large print edition.
        pages ; cm (Wheeler publishing large print hardcover)
    ISBN 978-1-4104-6145-2 (hardcover) — ISBN 1-4104-6145-9 (hardcover) 1.
Large type books. I. Title.
PS3568.O243T475 2013b
813'.54—dc23   2013019816

Published in 2013 by arrangement with G. P. Putnam Son's, a member
of Penguin Group (USA) LLC, a Penguin Random House Company

Printed in the United States of America
1 2 3 4 5 6 7 17 16 15 14 13

How sharper than a serpent's tooth it is to have a thankless child.

—WILLIAM SHAKESPEARE

A man that studieth revenge keeps his own wounds green.

—FRANCIS BACON

1

He was sick to death of her nagging.

Bitch and complain, bitch and complain, and nag, nag, nag every time she opened her damn mouth.

He'd like to shut it for her.

Jerald Reinhold sat at the kitchen table, while his mother's never-ending list of criticisms and demands rolled over him in dark, swollen clouds.

Every fucking day, he thought, the same thing. Like it was his fault he'd lost his stupid, dead-end job. His fault his girlfriend — another bitch who never shut up — kicked him out so he had to move back in with his whining, mouthy parents. His fault he'd dropped a few thousand in Vegas and had some credit card debt.

Jesus! His fault, his fault, his fault. The old bitch never cut him the smallest break.

Hadn't he told her that he wouldn't have lost his job if his prick of a supervisor hadn't

7

fired him? So he'd taken a few days off, who didn't? So he'd been late a few times, who wasn't?

Unless you were a work-droid like his idiot father.

But God, she made it such a big fucking deal. He'd hated the job anyway, and only took it because Lori badgered him into it, but he got all the blame.

He was twenty-six, for Christ's sake, and deserved a hell of a lot better than working for chump change as a take-out delivery boy.

And Lori gives him the boot just because he's out of work — temporarily — and goes batshit on him because he lost a few bucks on a trip with some friends?

He could, and would, do a lot better than Lori wide-ass Nuccio. Bitch threatened to call the cops just because he gave her a few smacks. She deserved a lot more than a couple love taps, and he wished like hell he'd given her just what she deserved.

He deserved more than a room in his parents' apartment and his mother's incessant hammering.

"Jerry, are you listening to me?" Barbara Reinhold fisted her hands on her hips.

Jerry lifted his gaze from the screen of his PPC where he was *trying* to relax with a game. He spared his skinny, flat-chested, know-it-all mother one smoldering glance.

"How can I help it when you never shut up?"

"That's how you talk to me? That's how you show your gratitude for the roof over your head, the food we put in your belly?" She lifted a plate that held a slice of bread, a thin slice of fake turkey. "I'm standing here making you a sandwich since you finally dragged yourself out of bed at noon, and you sass me? It's no wonder Lori kicked you out. I'm telling you one thing, mister, you're not getting a free ride here much longer. It's been almost a month now, and you haven't done diddly about finding a job."

He thought: *Shut the fuck up or I'll shut you up.* But he didn't say it. He wanted the sandwich.

"You're irresponsible, just like your father said, but I said, he's our son, Carl, and we have to help him out. When are you going to help yourself, that's what I want to know."

"I told you I'd get a job. I've got options. I'm considering my options."

"Your options." She snorted, went back to building the sandwich. "You've gone through four jobs this year. What options are you considering while you're sitting here in the middle of the day in the ratty sweats

9

you slept in? I told you they're looking for a stock boy down at the market, but do you go and see about it?"

"I'm not a freaking stock boy." He was *better* than that. He was somebody. He'd *be* somebody if people gave him half a break. "Get off my back."

"Maybe we haven't been on your back enough." She layered a slice of bright orange cheese on top of the turkey, and her voice took on the soft, reasonable tone he hated.

"Your father and I scrimped and saved so you could go to college, and you flunked out. You said how you wanted to train so you could learn how to develop those computer games you like so much, and we backed you on that, put the money to that. When that didn't work, your dad got you a job at his office. He went to bat for you, Jerry, and you screwed around and mouthed off, and got fired."

She picked a knife from the block to cut the sandwich. "Then you met Lori, and she was the sweetest thing. A smart girl, a hard-working girl from a real nice family. We had such high hopes there. She got you working as a busboy in the restaurant where she works, and she stuck with you when you lost that job. When you said how you could get a messenger job if you had a good bike,

10

we made you a loan, but that didn't last two months. And you never paid us back, Jerry. Now this last job's gone, too."

"I'm tired of you throwing the past in my face, and acting like it was all my fault."

"The past keeps repeating, Jerry, and seems to be getting worse."

Her lips pressed together as she added a handful of the Onion Doodles he liked to the plate. "You're out of work again, and you can't afford a place of your own. You took the rent money and the tip money Lori had saved up and went off to Las Vegas with Dave and that no-account Joe. And you came back broke."

"That's a damn lie." He shoved to his feet. "It was my money, and I've got a right to take a break with my friends, to have some goddamn fun."

There was a sheen in her eyes — not of tears, not of anger, but of disappointment. It made him want to punch, punch, punch that sheen away.

"It was the rent money, Jerry, and the money Lori saved up from her tips. She told me."

"You're going to take her word over mine?"

On a sigh, she folded a napkin into a triangle as she had for him when he was a boy. Her dented heart came clearly through the sound, but all he heard was accusation.

"You lie, Jerry, and you use people, and I'm worried we let you get away with it for too long. We keep giving you chances, and you keep throwing them away. Maybe some of that's our fault, and maybe that's part of the reason you think you can talk to me the way you are."

She set the plate on the table, poured a glass of the coffee-flavored drink he liked. "Your father and I were hoping you'd find a job today, or at least go out and look, make a real effort. We talked about it after you went out with your friends again last night. After you took fifty dollars out of my emergency cash without asking."

"What are you talking about?" He gave her his best shocked and insulted look. "I didn't take anything from you. You're saying I'm stealing now? Ma!"

"It wouldn't be the first time." Her lips compressed when her voice wavered some, and she came back with the no-more-bullshit tone he knew drew a deep, hard line.

"We talked it over, decided we had to take a stand, Jerry. We were going to tell you together when your father gets home, but I'll tell you now so you'll have that much more time. We're giving you until the first of the month — that's the first of December, Jerry — to find work. If you don't get a job, you can't stay here."

"I need some time."

"We've given you a month, Jerry, and you haven't done anything except go out at night and sleep half the day. You haven't tried to get work. You're a grown man, but you act like a kid, and a spoiled, ungrateful one. If you want more time, if you want us behind you, you eat your lunch, then you go out and look for a job. You go down to the market and get that stock boy job, and as long as you're working and show us you're trying, you can stay."

"You don't understand." He forced tears into his eyes, a usual no-fail. "Lori dumped me. She was *everything* to me and she threw me over for some other guy."

"What other guy?"

"I don't know who the hell he is. She broke my heart, Ma. I need some time to get through it."

"You said she kicked you out because you lost your job."

"That was part of it, sure. That asshole at Americana had it in for me, from day one. But instead of taking my side, she flips me over because I can't buy her stuff. Then she tells you all these lies about me, trying to

13

turn my own mother against me."

"Eat your lunch," Barbara said, wearily. "Then get cleaned up, get dressed, and go down to the market. If you do that, Jerry, we'll give you more time."

"And if I don't, you'll kick me out? You'll just boot me to the street like I'm nobody? My own parents."

"It hurts us to do it, but it's for your own good, Jerry. It's time you learned to do what's right."

He stared at her, imagined her and his father plotting and planning against him. "Maybe you're right."

"We want you to find your place, Jerry. We want you to be a man."

He nodded as he crossed to her. "To find my place. To be a man. Okay." He picked up the knife she'd used to cut his sandwich, shoved it into her belly.

Her eyes popped wide; her mouth fell open.

He hadn't planned to do it, hadn't given it more than an instant's conscious thought. But God! It felt amazing. Better than sex. Better than a good, solid hit of Race. Better than anything he'd ever felt in his life.

He yanked the knife free. She stumbled back, throwing up her hands. She said, "Jerry," on a kind of gurgle.

And he jammed the blade into her again. He *loved* the sound it made. Going in, coming out. He loved the look of absolute shock on her face, and the way her hands slapped weakly at him as if something tickled.

So he did it again, then again, into her back when she tried to run. And again when she fell to the kitchen floor and flopped like a landed fish.

He did it long after she stopped moving at all.

"Now that was for my own good."

He looked at his hands, covered with her blood, at the spreading pool of red on the floor, the wild spatters of it on the walls, the counter that reminded him of some of the crazy paintings at MOMA.

An artist, he mused. Maybe he should be an artist.

He set the knife on the table, then washed his hands, his arms, in the kitchen sink. Watched the red circle and drain.

She'd been right, he thought, about finding his place, about being a man. He'd found his place now, and knew exactly how to claim his manhood.

He'd take what he wanted, and anyone who screwed with him? They had to pay. He had to *make* them pay, because nothing else in his life had ever made him feel so good, so real, so *happy.*

He sat down, glanced at where his mother's body lay sprawled, and thought he couldn't wait until his father got home.

Then he ate his sandwich.

Lieutenant Eve Dallas strapped on her weapon harness. She'd had a short stack of waffles for breakfast — something that tended to put a smile on her face. Her husband, unquestionably the most gorgeous man ever created, enjoyed another cup of superior coffee in the sitting area of their bedroom. Their cat, who'd just been warned off the attempt to sneak onto the table, sat on the floor washing his fat flank.

It made a nice picture, she thought: Roarke, his mane of black hair loose around his wonderfully carved face, that beautiful mouth in a half smile, and his wild blue eyes on her. The dishes from their meal together on the table, and Galahad pretending he didn't want his nose in the syrup added to the "at-home and liking it" ambience.

"You look pleased with yourself, Lieutenant."

"I'm pleased," she said, and added that musical murmur of Ireland in Roarke's voice to her list of morning enjoyments. "I've had a couple of days without a hot one so I'm nearly caught up on paperwork. The quick scan of the weather for today told me I won't be freezing my ass off, and I'm heading out with a belly-load of waffles. It's a good day, so far."

She hooked a brown vest over her shirt — both Roarke approved — then sat to pull on her boots.

"Generally you'd prefer several hot ones over paperwork," he pointed out.

"We're heading into the holidays, end of year 2060. You start on that season, you get the wackies. And the nearer I am to finishing my year-end report, the better. The last couple of days have been a walk, so if I get a couple more like that, I —"

"And now you've done it." Shooting her a look of pity, he shook his head. "You've jinxed any chance you had."

"Irish superstition."

"Common sense. But speaking of Irish and holidays, the family's coming in on Wednesday."

"Wednesday?"

"That's the Wednesday before Thanksgiving," he reminded her. "Some of the cousins are switching off so those who couldn't come last year will. You said you were fine with it."

"I am. No, really, I am. I like your family."

He'd only recently found them. He'd lived most of his life, as she had, without blood kin — and the comfort or problems family bring. "I'm just never sure what to do with so many people in the house who aren't cops."

"They'll be busy enough. Apparently there are many plans in the works for shopping, sightseeing, theater, and so on. You're unlikely to have all of them at once except on Thanksgiving itself. And then there'll be all the others."

"Yeah." She'd agreed to that, too — and it had seemed like a fine idea at the time. All the people who'd come for dinner the previous year, in addition to her partner, Peabody, and Peabody's main man, Mc-Nab, who'd opted not to travel this year.

"It worked okay before." Shrugging, she got to her feet. "What is it — the more the crazier?"

"I believe it's merrier, but either way. And with that in mind, I'd like to add four more."

"Four more what?"

"Guests. Richard DeBlass and family. Elizabeth contacted me just yesterday. He and Elizabeth are bringing the children into New York for the parade."

"Talk about crazy. Who wants to jump into that crowd?"

"Thousands, or it wouldn't be a crowd, would it? They've booked a hotel suite along the route. I thought it would be nice to invite them to share Thanksgiving dinner. Nixie, especially, wants to see you."

Eve thought of the girl, the lone survivor when her family had been slaughtered in a home invasion. "Is it a good idea, bringing her back here, to where everything happened over a traditional family holiday?"

"She's adjusting well, as you know, but she needs the connection. They've made a family, the four of them, but they don't want Nixie to forget the family she lost."

"She'll never forget."

"She'll not, no." And he himself would always carry the image of the little girl in the morgue with her head resting on her father's unbeating heart. "It's not like you going back to Dallas." Now he rose, stepped to her. "Revisiting, reliving all that pain and trauma. She had a family who loved her, and was taken from her."

"So the connection's important. Okay with me, but nothing's going to induce me to go to that parade."

"So noted." He drew her in, kissed her. "We've a lot to be thankful for, you and I."

"And a houseful of Irish relatives, plus a ravaging horde after turkey and pie are part

19

of that?"

"They are indeed."

"I'll let you know on Friday if I agree with that. Now I've gotta go."

"Take care of my cop."

"Take care of my gazillionaire."

She left the house resigned to the coming invasion.

What was it with people? Eve wondered. Clogging up her streets, flooding her sidewalks, jamming on glides, swarming crosswalks. What made them pack into New York for holidays?

Didn't they have homes of their own?

She fought through three nasty knots of traffic on the trip downtown to Cop Central while ad blimps blasted the news from overhead of:

BLACK FRIDAY MEGA-SALES!

GOBBLE UP BARGAINS WHILE THEY LAST!

DOOR-BUSTER HOLIDAY SALES AT THE SKY MALL

She wished to God they'd all *go* to the sky mall and get out of her city. Snarling

20

with equally pissed drivers at yet another tangle, she watched a quick-fingered street thief make hay with a gaggle of oblivious tourists crowded around a smoking glide-cart.

Even if she hadn't been packed in among Rapid Cabs and a farting maxibus, the odds of catching him were slim. As fast-footed as fingered, he zipped away, richer by three wallets and two pocket 'links by her count.

The early bird catches the loot, she supposed, and a few less people would be hitting the sky mall.

She spotted a thin fracture in traffic, gunned it, and ignoring the rude blat of horns, wound her way downtown.

By the time she walked into Central, she had her plan. She'd hit the paperwork first, clear off her desk — righteously. Then she could spend some time reviewing the active cases of her detectives. Maybe she'd toss the expense reports to Peabody, let her partner handle the numbers. There might be room to pull out a cold case, give it another hard look.

Nothing much more satisfying than catching a bad guy who thought he'd gotten away with it.

She stepped off the glide — a tall, leanly built woman in a leather coat — turned toward Homicide. Her short, choppy brown hair framed an angular face accented with a shallow dent in the chin. Her eyes scanned, as cop's eyes always did, long, golden brown and observant as she strode down the busy sector to her department.

When she turned into her bullpen she spotted Sanchez first, his feet propped on his desk as he worked his 'link. And Trueheart, spiffy and innocently handsome in his uniform, industriously at his comp. The room smelled of bad cop coffee and cheap fake sugar, so all was right with the world.

Jenkinson strolled out of the break room with a giant mug of that bad cop coffee and a lumpy-looking doughnut. He wore a gray suit the color of tarnish with a tie of nuclear blue and green curlicues on a screaming pink background.

He said, "Yo, LT."

"That's some tie, Jenkinson."

After setting the mug on his desk, he flipped it. "Just adding a little color to the world."

"Did you steal that from one of the geeks in EDD?"

"His mama bought it for him," Sanchez said.

"Your mama bought it for me, as a thank-you for last night."

"It's so she can see you coming from two blocks away and get gone."

Before Jenkinson formed a witty repartee, Baxter walked in, slick in a dark chocolate suit, expertly knotted tie that picked up the color with minute checks of brown and muted red.

He stopped as if he'd hit a force field. "Jesus, my eyes!" He pulled out a pair of fashionable sunshades, slid them on as he studied Jenkinson. "What is that around your neck? Is it alive?"

"Your sister bought it for him." Still quietly working at his comp, Trueheart didn't even look up. "A token of her esteem."

The kid was coming along, Eve thought, amused, and left her men to their byplay.

In her office with its single narrow window and miserably uncomfortable visitor's chair, she aimed straight for the AutoChef. Thanks to the Roarke connection she didn't have to settle for bad cop coffee. She programmed a cup, hot and black, settled with it at her desk, prepared to be righteous with paperwork.

Her communicator signaled before she'd taken the first sip.

"Dallas."

Dispatch, Dallas, Lieutenant Eve. See the

officer 735 Downing Street, Apartment 825.
Two DBs, one male, one female.

"Dallas responding. Will contact and coordinate with Detective Peabody en route."

Acknowledged. Dispatch out.

Well, shit, she thought, gulped down coffee — burned her tongue — she *had* jinxed it. And grabbing the coat she'd just taken off, she headed out.

Others had arrived in the bullpen, and Jenkinson's tie remained the topic of the day. Peabody, still wearing her coat, added her opinion that the tie had jazz.

But then Peabody loved the neon-sporting McNab.

"Peabody, with me."

"What? Where? Already?"

Eve just kept walking so Peabody had to trot after her in her pink cowgirl boots.

What was her department coming to, Eve wondered, with pink ties, pink boots. Maybe she should ban pink from Homicide.

"What did we catch?"

"Looks like a double."

"A two-for-one start of the day." As she waited for the elevator, Peabody took a scarf out of her pocket, looped it around her neck.

Pink and blue checks, Eve noted. She definitely had to work on the logistics of

24

banning pink.

"It's a totally gorgeous day, too," Peabody continued, her square face wreathed with a smile, her dark eyes shining.

"Were you late because you grabbed morning sex?"

"I wasn't late. Two minutes," Peabody amended. "We got off the subway early to walk it. You won't have many more days like this."

They squeezed into the elevator with a boxful of cops. "I love fall when everything's all crisp and breezy, and they're roasting chestnuts on the carts."

"Definitely had sex."

Peabody only smiled. "We had a date night last night. Just on the spur, you know. We got dressed up, went dancing, and had grown-up cocktails. We get so busy we forget to do the 'just you and me' thing sometimes. It's nice to remember."

They corkscrewed out on the garage level.

"Then we had sex," Peabody added. "Anyway, it's a really nice day."

"Too bad the two DBs on Downing can't enjoy it."

"Well . . . yeah. It just goes to show."

"Show what?"

"You should get dressed up, go dancing, drink grown-up cocktails, and have sex as much as you can before you're dead."

"That's a philosophy," Eve said as she slid behind the wheel of her vehicle.

"It's almost Thanksgiving," Peabody pointed out.

"I've heard rumors."

"We had this tradition, my family. We'd write down all the things we were grateful for, and put them in a bowl. And on Thanksgiving, everyone would pick out a few. The idea is, it reminds you of things you should be grateful for, or what other people appreciate. Like that. It's nice. I know we're not going out to be with the family this year, but I'm sending them my grateful notes."

As she battled downtown traffic, Eve considered. "We're murder cops. That must mean we have to be grateful for dead bodies or we wouldn't have a job. But contrarily, the dead bodies aren't likely to be grateful."

"No. We're grateful we have the skill and the smarts to find and arrest the person or persons who made them dead bodies."

"The person or persons we catch and arrest aren't going to be grateful. Somebody's got to lose."

"That's a philosophy," Peabody muttered.

"I like to win." Eve pulled up behind a black-and-white on Downing. "I appreciate winning. Let's go do that."

Hefting her field kit, she started for the entrance, badged the cop on the door.

"We're on eight, Lieutenant."

"Yeah, I got that. Building security?"

"You have to buzz in, but you know how that goes. Cams on the door, but none internal."

"We'll want the door discs."

"Building manager's on that."

With a nod, she moved to the elevator. Decent building, she thought. Minimal security, but clean. The floor of the cubbyhole lobby shined, and the walls looked recently painted. And the elevator, she noted with some relief, didn't clang or clunk when it opened.

"Easy to gain access," she commented. "Follow somebody in, or get someone to buzz you in. No lobby security, no internal cams."

"Easy out, too."

"Exactly. The place is well maintained, so that says decent tenants and responsible management to me."

She stepped out on eight, approached the cop standing in front of 825. "What have we got, Officer?"

"Sir. The woman in 824 gained access to 825 at approximately seven-twenty this morning. She has a key and the code."

"Why did she go in?"

"She and the female victim had a regular Monday trip to the local bakery, leaving sharp, according to her statement, at seven. She became concerned when no one answered the door or the 'link, and let herself in where she discovered the bodies she identified as Carl and Barbara Reinhold, listed as residents of this unit."

"Where's the wit?"

"With a female officer in her apartment. She's pretty broken up, Lieutenant. It's rough in there," he added, jerking his head toward 825.

"Keep the wit handy." Eve pulled a can of Seal-It from her bag. "And stand by." She switched on her recorder.

With their hands and boots sealed, Eve and Peabody went inside.

Rough was one word for it, Eve thought. The living area remained tidy. Sofa pillows plumped, floors whistle clean, magazine discs neatly arranged on a coffee table. It made an eerie contrast to the smell of death — far from fresh.

A few steps in the room jogged slightly to the right where a table served as a demarcation between living area and kitchen.

And where the line between tidy life and ugly death dug in deep.

The man lay beside the table, his head, shoulders, and one outstretched arm under it. In death he was a bloody, broken mass in what had been a dark blue suit. Blood spatter and gray matter bloomed and smeared the walls, the kitchen cabinets — and the baseball bat that lay in the congealed river of blood beside him.

The woman lay facedown on the floor between the opposite side of the table and a refrigerator. Blood soaked through her shirt and pants so their true color had become indiscernible. Both were ripped and shredded, most probably by the kitchen knife driven through her back to the hilt.

"They've been slaughtered," Peabody stated.

"Yeah. A lot of rage here. Take the woman," Eve ordered, and crouching by the man, opened her kit.

She let the pity come, then let it go. And got to work.

2

"Victim identified as Reinhold, Carl James. Caucasian male, age fifty-six." Eve scanned her Identi-pad. "Married to Reinhold, Barbara, nee Myers, age fifty-four." She glanced over at Peabody.

"Yeah, female ID confirmed."

"One offspring, male, Reinhold, Jerald, age twenty-six, address listed on West Houston."

Carl Reinhold still had both parents, she noted, who'd migrated to Florida, and a brother with a Hoboken address. The data listed the victim's employer as Beven and Son's Flooring, with offices and showroom just a handful of blocks away.

"Victim was beaten severely, head, face, shoulders, chest, extremities. Injuries are consistent with the baseball bat handily left on scene, and coated with blood and gray matter. Erased his face. That's personal."

"I can't count the stab wounds on the

female, Dallas. She's been hacked to pieces."

"I'd say we've got the cause of death. Let's get the time."

Eve pulled out her gauge. "He's been dead for about sixty-two hours. That puts it at Friday evening. Around six-thirty."

"She has almost six hours on him. TOD Friday, twelve-hundred-forty."

"Nearly six hours between kills." Eve sat back on her heels. "Kills the woman in the afternoon, then what, waits around for the man? No sign of struggle in the living area. No sign of break-in."

She pushed up. "Go ahead and call for the morgue and the sweepers."

Solid middle-class couple from the looks of it, Eve thought as she began to wander the apartment. The woman lets someone in, middle of the day? No struggle. Both killed in the kitchen.

She set that train of thought aside once she stepped into what appeared to be the main bedroom.

"Somebody tossed the bedroom," she called out.

"It's pretty strange and vicious for a burglary," Peabody began, and stopped, frowning into the bedroom. "It looks pretty tidy."

"Pretty tidy, not perfectly tidy like the living area. Things are out of place here. The bedcovers aren't smooth, the closet doors open, some clothes on the floor in there. That desk there — one of the drawers isn't closed all the way, and where's the comp? No comp or tablet on the desk."

Eve pulled open a drawer on the bureau. "Everything's jumbled in here. No, she kept a neat and clean house in a neat and clean building. Whoever did this was looking for something. I bet the wit's been in here, and would know if anything's missing."

"You want her to walk through."

"Yeah, after they take the bodies." She walked out. "Second bedroom, not so tidy either. Rug's askew. Furniture's got some dust on it. Why didn't she clean in here? Closet's empty," she added, after pulling it open. "Who has an empty closet?"

"Not me. If you have storage, you end up using it."

"Somebody was staying in here. Dirty dishes scattered around, empty containers." She walked to the bed, yanked the cover down, bent over to sniff the sheets. "Sleeping here. Tag these. We could get DNA."

She turned a circle. "Someone staying here, someone they know. She's in the kitchen, maybe fixing lunch that time of day. We'll run the log on the AutoChef. Maybe he wants something, and she won't give it to him."

Letting herself see it, she walked out again, back to the kitchen. "He's pissed, oh, he's so fucking pissed. The knife's right there, just takes it out of the block and lets her have it. Over and over. Bet that felt good."

"Why?" Peabody wondered. "Why do you say it felt good?"

"He didn't run, did he? He hung around, waiting to do her husband. Another overkill. So, yeah, I'm thinking it felt just fine. Note for sweepers to check all the drains. He had to clean up, he'd be covered with blood. But he's got hours before the husband gets home. Hours to clean himself up, to change, and to go through the place. She probably had a couple pieces of decent jewelry, easy to hock."

"They'd've had emergency cash somewhere," Peabody added. "It's what you do, sock some away in case."

"Okay. Jewelry, cash. Male vic's wallet's gone, and he's not wearing a wrist unit. When we find her purse, her wallet's going to be gone, too. Electronics — that's something we're not seeing in here."

"Easy and portable."

Eve looked at the victims again. "And an

afterthought. You don't kill like this for trinkets. You don't kill people you know like this for some spare cash. You do it for a lot more. Maybe they had more. Let's see what the neighbor has to say."

Eve headed for the door, glanced back. "Run the son," she told Peabody.

"You think somebody could've done that to his own parents?"

"Who pisses you off more than family?" She stepped out. "It's clear for Crime Scene," she told the uniform. "And the wagon's on the way. What's the wit's name?"

"Sylvia Guntersen. Her husband's Walter. He's in there, too. He stayed home from work."

"All right." Eve knocked on 824. The female officer answered, a young blonde with her hair pulled back tightly at the nape of her neck.

"Hey, Cardininni."

The blonde smiled, her frosty blue eyes warmed. "Hey, Peabody. Some morning, huh?"

"You could say. Officer Cardininni and I walked the beat together a few times."

"Before you went Murder on us. Lieutenant. It's good meeting you. More or less." She glanced over her shoulder. "The woman's taking it hard. The husband's holding on, but not by much. They were tight with the vics. Lived across the hall from each other for about a dozen years. They hung a lot, took some vacations together. Close buds."

"Got it."

The apartment layout mirrored 825. The decor was less fussy, but the tidiness factor meshed. The Guntersens sat at the square-topped black kitchen table, cups in front of them. Eve judged them to be about the same age as the victims.

The woman wore her hair short, stylishly spiked, while the man went long and pony-tailed. Both sets of eyes were red-rimmed, swollen. The woman took one look at Eve and began sobbing.

Eve only had to glance at Peabody to get her partner moving forward.

"Mrs. Guntersen, we're so sorry for your loss. This is Lieutenant Dallas, and I'm Detective Peabody. We're going to do our best for your friends."

"They were my friends, our best friends." She choked it out as she reached for her husband's hand. "How could this happen to them?"

"That's what we're going to find out." Eve took a seat at the table. "We need your help."

"I just worried when she didn't answer, so

35

I went in. I found them. I found Barb and Carl."

"I know this is hard," Peabody began. "But we have to ask you some questions." She measured the woman, decided she'd do better with a task. "Do you think we could have some coffee, ma'am?"

"Oh. Yes. Of course." Pulling herself together, Sylvia stood up.

"When was the last time you spoke to or saw Barbara or Carl?" Eve asked.

"I talked to Barb Friday morning. Just a quick chat before Walt and I left. We went to see our daughter and her fiancé in Philadelphia for the weekend. They just got engaged."

"Carl and I met up and had a beer after work Thursday," Walter put in. "That's the last I saw him."

"When did you get back from Philadelphia?"

"Sunday night. I called Barb, but I didn't think anything of it when she didn't answer. I just figured she and Carl went out. They like to go to the vids." Her chin wobbled, but she managed to set two cups of coffee on the table. "Most Friday nights we go to a vid together, but we were going to see Alice and Ben, so . . ."

"Who was staying with them?"

36

"Oh, Jerry. Their son. God, I never thought! I don't know where he could be, what might've happened to him." Her eyes, full of fresh horror, darted toward the door. "Is he . . . is he in there?"

"No, he's not."

"Thank God for that."

"When did he move back home?"

"A while ago. About three weeks ago — no, nearly four — after he and his girlfriend broke up."

"Girlfriend's name?" Eve asked. "And the names of anyone you think he might be staying with. Friends?"

"Um Lori. Nuccio. Lori Nuccio," Sylvia said. "And he didn't have a lot of friends. Mal, Dave, Joe — Mal Golde, Dave Hildebran, Joe Klein. Those are the main three."

"Good. Coworkers?"

"He, well, he lost his job, so he moved back in until he could straighten it all out. Jerry's, well, Jerry's a little bit of a problem child."

"He's a lazy bastard."

"Walter!" Appalled, Sylvia sat down hard. "That's a terrible thing to say. He's just lost his parents."

"It doesn't change what he is." There was gravel in Walter's voice now, as if hard little pebbles blocked his throat. "Lazy, ungrate-

37

ful, and a user." Grief and anger spread over his face like a haze. "I met Carl Thursday night because he needed to talk about it. He and Barbara were at their wit's end. That boy had been out of work for over a month, maybe a month and a half, but he hasn't so much as looked for a job. Not that he'd keep it for long anyway."

"There was friction between him and his parents?"

"Barb was upset with him," Sylvia said, plucking at the tiny Star of David around her throat. "She wanted him to grow up, make something of himself. And she really liked Lori — the girlfriend. She thought Lori could help Jerry grow up some, be a responsible man, but it didn't work out."

"He blew the rent money — and what he stole from Lori — in Vegas."

Sylvia let out a sigh, patted her husband's hand. "It's true. He's immature and impulsive. Barb did tell me Friday morning he'd taken some money out of her house cash."

"Where did she keep that?" Eve asked.

"In a coffee can in the back of the kitchen cupboard."

Another glance had Peabody rising, stepping out.

"They were going to give him until the first of the month." Walter picked up a spoon, stirred his cold coffee. "Carl told me Thursday, he was going to talk to Barb, but he'd made up his mind. They'd give him until December first to get a job, start being responsible, or he had to go. Barbara was upset all the time, there were arguments every day, and it just couldn't go on."

"They argued a lot," Eve prompted.

"He'd sleep half the day, go out half the night. Then he'd complain the water wasn't wet enough, the sky wasn't blue enough. He didn't give them any respect or appreciation, and now they're gone. Now he'll never be able to make up for it."

When he choked on tears, Sylvia leaped up to put her arms around him.

"Do you know how to get in touch with Jerry?"

"No, not really." Sylvia soothed and stroked her husband. "He probably went off with his friends for a few days."

I don't think so, Eve mused, but she nodded. "I'm sorry to ask, but would you be able to tell if anything's missing across the hall?"

Sylvia closed her eyes. "Yes. I'm sure I would. I — I know Barb's place, her things, as well as I know my own."

"I'd appreciate it if you'd take a look. I'll let you know when we're ready for you to

39

do that." Eve rose. "We appreciate your help."

"We'll do anything we can." Sylvia pressed her face to her husband's shoulder, and they rocked each other.

When Eve stepped out into the hall, Peabody stood talking to Cardininni.

"Coffee can's there, and it's empty."

"See my shocked face."

"And the sweepers are on their way up."

"Okay. Officer, when the scene's clear, I want you to walk Mrs. Guntersen through, make a note of anything she says is missing."

"Yes, sir."

"Peabody, let's go find the lazy bastard son."

"Keep it legal," Peabody called back to Cardininni.

"When I have to."

Eve stopped long enough at the elevators to brief the sweepers when they unloaded, then stepped on with Peabody.

"Tell me about the son."

"Lazy bastard probably fits," Peabody commented. "Flunked out of college, second year in. He hasn't held a job for longer than six months, including one at his father's place of employment. His last job was delivery boy for Americana restaurant. He's

had a couple minor pops for illegals, one
for drunk and disorderly. Nothing big, nothing violent."

"I think he graduated."

"He did that over what they had stuck in
a coffee can?"

"He did that because his life's in the toilet
and they'd decided to stop pulling him out.
That's how it strikes me. See if he's used
any credit cards, debit cards, in his father's
or his mother's name."

She stopped off to get the security disc
from the uniform in the lobby. "Start
canvassing the building," she told him.
"Find out if anybody saw anything, heard
anything. And when and if anyone saw Jerry
Reinhold. Start on the eighth floor, but
cover the building."

"Yes, sir."

In the car, she slid the disc into the dash
unit. "Let's see when he left."

She programmed it to start Friday morning, then moved it fast forward. She saw the
Guntersens leave with big smiles and suitcases, and others move in, move out.

"That's our vic coming home from work,
eighteen-twenty-three on Friday night."

"He looks tired," Peabody commented.

"Yeah, he thinks he's going to have an
argument with his son. It's going to be a

41

whole lot worse."

She ran the disc through Friday night into Saturday morning.

"He stayed in there?" It horrified Peabody. "He stayed in there with his dead parents."

"Plenty of time to get whatever he wanted, think things through. There he is, there he comes, twenty-twenty-eight, Saturday night. Over twenty-four hours in there with them. And he's hauling two suitcases. Let's check on cabs picking up at the address or on either corner at that time. Lazy bastard isn't going to drag those suitcases far."

"He's smiling," Peabody said quietly.

"Yeah, I see that. Keep running it, see if he comes back." As she spoke Eve pulled out into traffic.

"Where are we going first?"

"We'll try his last known address."

While Eve drove, Peabody multitasked. "No activity on either of the vics' cards."

"So he's not completely stupid."

"And he didn't go back to the apartment."

"Got what he could get."

"But how far can he get on the contents of a coffee can? Even if they stashed a couple thousand in there, and that's a lot for home cash."

"We need to check financials on both vics. Any transfers or withdrawals from any account. People tend to write down their passwords," Eve added before Peabody could speak. "He had plenty of time to dig out the passwords, any codes, dig into their accounts. Cab first. We could get lucky."

Eve started to make the turn to Jerry's listed address when Peabody let out a whoop. "I got him!" She held up a finger, continued to rapid-fire into her 'link. "Got it. Thanks. Rapid Cab pickup," she told Eve, "right in front of the damn building, drop off at The Manor — that's a fancy boutique hotel, West Village."

"Address, Peabody."

As Peabody rattled it off, Eve hit sirens, lights, and took the corner. Peabody grabbed the chicken stick, white-knuckled it, and said a short but heartfelt prayer.

The Manor looked like just that, something found in the English countryside and once owned by a wealthy earl. The gorgeous old brownstone, obviously recently and lovingly rehabbed, boasted a wide portico entrance, fat urns of trailing flowers, and a liveried doorman Eve expected to give her grief when she pulled her dull-looking DLE into the loading zone.

She braced for it as he hotfooted over in his royal blue and gold uniform and shiny knee boots.

"Listen, pal," she began before his expression changed from that of a man about to toss out some stinky garbage to warm yet distinguished welcome.

"Lieutenant Dallas. How can we help you today?"

He threw her off stride. She hated that. But it only took her a moment to understand. The Manor belonged to Roarke, and the doorman had gotten the business-wide memo to cooperate fully with the big boss's wife.

She didn't really hate that, but it kind of irked.

"I need you to leave my car where I put it, and I need the manager, asap."

"Absolutely. Diego!" He signaled to a black-suited bellman just rolling out a loaded cart. "See that Lieutenant Dallas's vehicle remains undisturbed. Let me get the door for you, Lieutenant." He pulled the tall, heavily carved door open, gestured them inside.

The lobby resembled a large parlor, appointed to Old World perfection. Just Roarke's style, Eve thought, all the gleaming wood, glossy tile, the heavy bronze lighting and abundance of artfully arranged flowers. Rather than a team manning a front desk, a woman sat at a long table in a high-backed leather chair, the same color as the doorman's livery. She wore a simple and sleek black suit and her auburn hair in a shining high ponytail.

"Rianna, this is Lieutenant Dallas and . . . I apologize."

"Detective Peabody," Eve said.

"They need to speak with Joleen right away."

"Of course. Give me one moment. Won't you please have a seat?"

"We're fine."

Still smiling, the woman tapped her earpiece. "Joleen, Rianna at the front. Lieutenant Dallas is in the lobby. I — I will, yes."

Another tap, another smile. "She'll be right out. In the meantime, can we offer you any refreshment? We have a lovely menu of teas."

"All good." But Eve pulled out her PPC. "Take a look at this guy. He should be registered under Jerald Reinhold. I need his room number, then I —"

"Oh, but Mr. Reinhold checked out, about two hours ago." Rianna's smile turned to a look of nearly comic distress. "I'm so sorry."

"Damn it. Were you on?" she asked the doorman.

"Yes, I was. I loaded his two suitcases into

our complimentary airport shuttle. He said he had an early flight to Miami."

"Lieutenant." A middle-aged woman in a garnet red suit with a sweep of gilded brown hair clipped across the tiles in sky-high heels, hand extended. "I'm Joleen Mortimer. Welcome to The Manor. How can I help you?"

"I need to see the room Jerald Reinhold was in. I need to know how he paid, what he ordered, if he did so, while in house, who talked to him."

"Of course. Rianna?"

Already swiping madly at a tablet, Rianna nodded. "I'm bringing it up. Mr. Reinhold stayed in The Squire's Suite. He booked Friday evening, via e-mail, reserved with a credit card, but paid in cash on arrival Saturday evening. He also paid cash for room service, ordered at twenty-one-five, yesterday at ten-thirty, last night at seventeen hundred, and again this morning at seven. Additional charges incurred by use of the in-suite minibar."

"What's the damage?" Eve demanded.

"I'm sorry."

"How much did he spend?"

"Oh . . ." Rianna glanced at her manager, got a brisk nod. "Three thousand, six hundred dollars and forty-five cents total on his bill, paid in full. With cash, as I said."

"We'll need a copy of everything you have. And I need to see his room. Now."

"Come with me." Joleen clipped her way across the tiles again to a bronze elevator door. "It's in the process of being turned."

"Make that stop," Eve ordered.

"Yes, I did. I've instructed housekeeping to leave any trash, laundry, dishes in the room."

"Good thinking. I also need copies of your security discs, entrance, his floor, elevators, lobby."

"I'll see to it."

Maybe it didn't irk so much after all.

"May I ask what Mr. Reinhold did?"

"He's the prime suspect in a double homicide."

"Well, my . . . goodness."

Joleen led the way off the elevator, down a wide hall to the left. She swiped her pass key over a pad in front of a snowy white door with a bronze plaque reading THE SQUIRE'S SUITE.

"Peabody."

At Eve's direction, Peabody headed for a tidily tied bag of trash by the door. Eve studied the petite dining table, scattered with plates, cups, glasses.

"He ate a hearty breakfast."

"Eggs Benedict, a split of champagne, fresh orange juice, a pot of hot chocolate, mixed berries with whipped cream, a large apple tart, a rasher of bacon." Joleen glanced up. "I'm checking on the specifics, and can tell you he ordered Shrimp à la Emilie — a house specialty — as an appetizer, a filet mignon — medium rare — with salted roasted potatoes, extra butter requested, candied carrots, a chocolate soufflé, two chocolate chunk cookies, and a bottle of our Jouët Premium champagne on the night of his arrival. He also had eight Cokes, three waters, two jars of cashews, the Chocolate Dandies and the fruit gummies, and assorted liquor from the in-room bar."

"Eating like a king," Eve muttered, "with a massive sweet tooth.

She circled the room. He'd used it, she thought, noting the entertainment discs tossed around, the scatter of glasses.

"Can you check if he used that?" Eve gestured toward the house 'link placed discreetly on a curved-leg desk.

"I did. Only for in house, to order room service, and again to check on the airport shuttle."

"Nothing here, Lieutenant," Peabody announced.

"Miami."

"I've got that going," Peabody told her, tapped her PPC. "It'll take a while to run all the transpos — shuttles, commercial, charter, private."

With a nod, Eve walked into the bedroom. Housekeeping had already stripped the bed, but left the laundry in an orderly pile on the floor. She checked the closet, the dresser, every drawer, the bath while Peabody did the same in the parlor area.

"He's messy," Eve calculated. "Tossing his towels around, playing with all the amenities, spilling a lot, going through the entertainment discs, hitting the in-room bar, ordering heavy meals. Playing hotel, playing big shot, that's what he was doing."

"He figures he can afford it." Peabody frowned at the screen of her PPC as Eve turned to her. "I just got a hit on the financials. The Reinholds had eighty-four thousand and change in joint accounts, another forty and change in a floater, and six thousand in a debit card account. Every bit of it was transferred, via wire, with Carl Reinhold's data, Friday night and Saturday. He did the transfers in pieces, wired them to three different accounts under his name. He got it all."

"Not if we freeze it." Eve grabbed her 'link.

"It's too late, Dallas. He's pulled it out. Cash and cashier's checks, in person. He hit the last bank less than fifteen minutes ago."

"Now he's got a hundred-thirty large after spending some. He's got playing money. And he sure as hell isn't in Miami."

"Lieutenant," Joleen began, "if there's anything we can do?"

"You've done what you can do. It's noted and appreciated. We'll just need copies of the security discs, and his paperwork."

"You'll have it."

Thinking, thinking, Eve moved to the door, and out. "He won't come back, but on the off chance."

"Yes, I'll have his photo and name posted. Should he return to The Manor, I'll contact you personally."

"That works. How long have you worked for Roarke?"

Joleen smiled. "Three years in this position. I was the assistant manager here for the previous owners. When Roarke acquired The Manor, he asked if I would consider taking temporary positions at some of his other hotels for the six months estimated for remodeling. And in addition if I would train staff, specifically for The Manor, then take the manager's position when we opened again."

"Roarke knows how to pick his team. What about the previous manager here?"

Joleen's smile sharpened a little. "Let's say he didn't make the cut."

She walked them across the lobby to where Rianna had a disc bag and a thick envelope waiting.

"I hope you catch him quickly." Joleen offered her hand again to Eve, then Peabody.

"That's the plan."

"That was pleasant," Peabody commented when they were back in the car. "Frustrating, but pleasant. If Roarke owned everything, this part of the job would run smoother."

"He's working on it. I'm going to drop you at the first bank, then check out his last known address, go by the morgue. Get yourself to all three financial places, see what you can find out. Let's put out a BOLO, all transpo centers, rental vehicles."

"No driver's license," Peabody pointed out.

"He could skim on that if he found somebody stupid enough."

"He could buy a car."

"Big chunk of his pie, but let's cover that, and the high-end hotels. He wants the good life now."

After she dropped Peabody off, she circled around, and tried to imagine what Jerry might be doing. He'd either want a way out of the city or a place to settle in it, for a while at least. Hauling two suitcases? Too much work and annoyance.

He had what he wanted from his parents' apartment. Eliminate them, take their money and valuables.

Why risk staying in New York?

But she thought he might. He wasn't stupid, she decided, or not entirely. But he was an idiot. Blowing over three thousand on a hotel room and food — for one night? Smart to hide out until Monday, banking hours, grab the rest of the money; stupid to spend so much of it just so he could gloat.

She pulled up at his last known address, flipped up her On Duty light. Since he liked to gloat, wouldn't he like to brag to friends? Maybe roll out and hit Vegas again, see if his luck improved there, or go sun on some tropical beach?

He'd had a girlfriend, Eve reminded herself, made a note to interview her.

She used her master to gain access to the dumpy three-story walk-up, ignored the rickety elevator, and took the stairs to the top floor.

3

She knocked, expecting she was wasting her time at this hour of the day, but within moments, she heard the slide of locks.

The man who answered was middle-twenties, average height, and gym fit. She could see that easily as he wore snug bike shorts and a skin shirt. His brown hair sported a single red blaze, and was tucked back into a short tail.

He leaned against the doorjamb, one hand on his cocked hip. Posing, she thought, in a way that showed off his bis and tris.

"Well, hi there," he said.

"Hi back."

The flirty smolder blinked away when Eve held up her badge.

"Is there a problem?"

"I don't know yet. Can I come in, speak to you?"

"Ah." He glanced behind, shifted, looked back at her. "Yeah, I guess. I'm working at home today," he said as he opened the door. "I was just taking a break, doing a few miles on my bike."

Eve saw the desk against the short window with its piles of discs, of files, a bag of soy chips, and a tube of some sports drink. A couple feet away sat a gleaming stationary bike facing a massive wall screen.

"Look, I know I got a speeding ticket a couple weeks ago. I'm going to pay it."

"Do I look like a traffic cop?"

"Um . . . I guess not, not so much."

"Lieutenant Dallas, NYPSD. Homicide."

"Homi — Jeez, God!"

"Are you Malachi Golde?"

"Yeah. Mal. People call me Mal. Who got killed? Do I know somebody who got killed?"

And suddenly, he looked very young. "I don't know yet. You know Jerry Reinhold."

"Jerry? *Jerry?*" Now he looked young, and ill. "Oh, Jesus, Jesus. I need to sit down."

Full-weight, he dropped onto a slick-surfaced sofa in shimmering silver. "Jerry's dead?"

"I didn't say that. My information is you know him. How do you know him?"

"From the neighborhood. We grew up together. We lived a half a block from each other growing up, went to school together.

We hang out, have a beer or whatever. I've known Jerry my whole life. What happened?"

"I'll get to that. What kind of work are you doing there, Mal?"

"What? Oh, ah, I'm a programmer. I can work at home most days if I want. I do programming and troubleshooting for Global United."

"Are you good at it?"

"Yeah." He passed a hand over his face, like a man trying to wake up. "It's sweet work, what I wanted to do since I can remember."

"Pays good."

"Yeah, pays good if you're good. I don't understand what this is about."

Just getting a picture, Eve thought. "I'm looking around here, Mal, and you've got some nice stuff — furniture, equipment. The building's kind of a dump."

"Oh." He managed an uneasy smile. "Yeah, but that's just the shell, right? It's what's inside. And I like the location. I can walk or bike to work, to the gym, to my folks' place. I know everybody, you know? I didn't want to move when I started making some shine."

"Got it. Jerry's data lists this as his address."

"It does?" Mal's eyebrows drew together. "We shared the place for a couple years, but that's been awhile, months now. Maybe eight, nine months now."

"Why did he move out?"

"Oh, well, he hooked up with Lori, and —"

"Lori Nuccio?"

"Yeah, Lori. He moved in with her."

"That's not why he moved out."

With a pained look, Mal shifted. "Okay, look, I carried him on the rent for three months, heading into four. It didn't seem right he wasn't holding up his share, or even really trying to. So he moved in with his folks for a couple months, then he moved in with Lori."

"Did the two of you fight about it? The rent?"

"Oh, Jesus, we argued some, sure, you know how it is. He was a little steamed, yeah, but we smoothed it over. We go back, man, a long ways. When I got a solid raise, I rented this place in the freaking Hamptons, man, for a week this summer, and I took Jerry and a couple of other pals along. It all chilled out. What happened to him? How did he die?"

"He didn't."

"But you said —"

56

"No, I didn't. Jerry's not dead, as far as I know. His parents are."

At that Mal sprang up as if he'd been propelled. "What? No. Mr. and Mrs. R? No. Did they have an accident?"

"Homicide, Mal, remember?"

"Man, man." Tears glazed across his eyes, coated his voice. "Were they mugged? They love to go to the vids, and sometimes they'd walk home late."

"No."

He dropped down again, covered his face with his hands. "I can't believe it. Mrs. R, she always has something for me if I drop over. Cookies or pie or a sandwich. Always saying I need a haircut and to settle down with a nice girl. She's like a second mother, you know? Oh, Jesus, when my ma finds out, it's going to knock her flat. They've known each other forever. Poor Jerry. God, poor Jerry. Does he know?"

"Yeah, he knows. He killed them."

His hands lowered slowly. His eyes, glassy with shock and tears, stared into Eve's. "That's not true. That's bogus. That's not possible. No way. No freaking way, lady."

"Lieutenant, and there's absolute way. Where is he, Mal? Where would he go?"

"I don't know. I don't know." Rocking a little, he pressed his fist to his belly. "Where do you go when things are crazy or falling apart? You go the hell home."

"He's finished with that."

"He wouldn't hurt them. You've got it wrong."

"Contact him. Try him on the 'link."

"Look, I'm his friend. You're trying to trap him for something he didn't do. Couldn't do."

Eve leaned forward. "He stabbed his mother in the kitchen. I haven't been to the morgue yet so I can't verify how many times, but he tore her up. Then he waited until his father got home from work and he bashed him to pulp with a baseball bat."

His color faded to a sickly gray. "No, no, he . . . a baseball bat."

"That's right."

Mal swallowed hard. "We played ball. Little League, then a sandlot league my pop put together a few years ago. But he wouldn't do this."

"He did this, then he stole the cash they had in the house, and he found the passcodes and transferred every dime they had into accounts in his name. He spent the last two nights in a fancy hotel, living it up."

"No." He rose, walked to the window in front of his desk. "I don't want what you're telling me. We've known each other since we were *six*."

"Where would he go?"

"I swear, I don't know. My ma's life, I swear it. He didn't come here. He didn't tag me."

"He ditched his 'link. He'll have a clone by now so you won't recognize the ID if he does. And if he does, be chilly, Mal. If he says to meet him somewhere, say you will, then contact me. If he comes here, don't let him in. Don't let him know you're here, and contact me." She set a card on the table as she rose.

"Give me some names. Other friends. And this Lori Nuccio's contact information."

"Okay."

He listed names, and Eve keyed them into her notebook.

"She dumped him, you know. Lori. He lost his job, stopped paying his share of the rent."

"A habit of his."

"Yeah, I guess. He went to Vegas with some friends a couple months back. Joe and Dave from the names I gave you. I couldn't make it. My sister's birthday, and man, did I carp about that. He dropped a pile, I heard, and Lori kicked him. So he was living back home."

Mal rubbed his hands over his face. "I've

59

gotta go see my mother."

"I can drive you."

"No, that's okay. Thanks. I think I need to walk. I think I want to walk. He's practically my brother, you know? They just had him, and I've got a sister, so we were like brothers coming up. He's a screwup, okay? I don't like to say it, but he's a screwup. But to do what you say he did . . . I need to go home."

"Okay, Mal." She picked up her card, handed it to him. "Put those numbers in your 'link. You contact me if you see him, hear from him, or anyone you know does. You got that?"

"Yeah, I got it."

After tagging Peabody, dumping the two other friends Sylvia Guntersen gave them on her partner, she tried for the ex. And wasn't as lucky as she'd been with Mal Golde. When no one responded, Eve tried knocking on neighbors' doors until one creaked open.

"Not buying," the woman said.

"Not selling." Eve held up her badge. "I'm looking for Lori Nuccio."

"You don't tell *me* that sweet girl did a crime."

"No, ma'am. I'd like to talk to her about

60

something, but she's not in trouble."

The door cracked wider, and the woman gave Eve a hard stare over a beak of a nose. "It's her day off. Mine, too. She went out a couple hours ago, I think. Going shopping, maybe she said, having lunch with a girlfriend, maybe getting her hair done. Stuff girls that age do."

"Ms. . . ."

"Crabtree. Sela Crabtree."

Eve took out her PPC, brought up Jerry's picture. "Ms. Crabtree, have you seen him around here?"

The woman snorted, opened the door fully, shoved an absent hand through spikes of brassy blond. "That one? Not since she kicked him out, and good riddance. Now you tell me he done a crime, I'm believing you. Didn't treat that sweet girl right, if you ask me. I told her the same myself, and how she'd find better. I had one like him at that age. Best thing I did was kick him."

No one liked Jerry, Eve thought, but nodded. "If she should come back, would you give her my card, ask her to contact me?"

"I'll do that."

"And if he comes around, Ms. Crabtree? You contact me."

The woman spread her lips in a snarling smile. "You can bet on it, sister."

61

"Don't confront him."

"He hurt somebody, didn't he?"

"Why do you say that?"

"Had it in his eyes. I've tended bar for thirty-three years. I know eyes, and those that got mean in them."

"He hurt somebody," Eve confirmed. "Don't confront him, and tell Lori to contact me as soon as possible."

"I'll look out for her — and for him. But he hasn't come around here in a good month now. Hey!" She shot up a finger. "I've got Lori's pocket 'link number."

"I've got it. I'll try that next. Thanks."

She keyed in the number as she headed out and down, and got dead air. Puzzled, she keyed in the data again, checked the number, tried it again with the same result.

Changed it, didn't you?

Eve hauled herself back, checked with the neighbor, but the number was the same as Eve's data.

"You know, she said something about getting a new 'link," Crabtree remembered. "A new number, the works. Said how she was going for fresh wherever she could get it."

Eve thought, *Crap,* but nodded. "As soon as you see her, tell her to contact me."

She headed down again, decided to start on the list of names she got from Mal via

62

'link on the way to the morgue.

By the time she got there, she'd managed to contact three on the list, and leave word with the manager of the restaurant where Lori Nuccio worked, in case.

Maybe she didn't need this stop — at least she didn't need to confirm cause of death on her vics as the cause had been brutally obvious. But it was part of the process, and part of hers. She wanted to see the victims again, take a hard look. And she wanted Morris's take. The chief medical examiner often gave her another angle, or at least made her think.

She walked into the echoey white tunnel, slowed as she passed Vending. She could really use a nice cold boost, but machines liked to screw with her. She wasn't in the mood to be screwed with by a damn vending machine.

Shoving her hands in her pockets, she marched on, then pushed through Morris's doors.

He had both victims on slabs, their bodies washed clean of blood. The mother's chest was splayed open from Morris's precise Y cut. He bent over her, studying what lay inside.

He wore microgoggles over his clever eyes and a clear gown over a gray suit with hints of steely blue. He'd tied his long stream of black hair into a trio of descending ponytails and bound them with silver cord.

"Their son, I'm told."

"Yeah."

He straightened. "This is considerably sharper than a serpent's tooth."

"What serpent?"

Now he smiled and warmth came into his fascinating face. "Shakespeare's."

"Oh." No wonder he and Roarke hit it off. "Nothing poetic about this."

"He dealt in tragedies, too. And this is one."

"What I'm getting is the son's a fucking asshole who went psycho. Have you got anything cold in your box?"

"We keep everyone cold here." He smiled a little. "But if you mean to drink, yes." He gestured with his sealed, blood-smeared hands. "Help yourself."

"Vending keeps breaking down on me," she said as she crossed to his little Friggie. "I think it's something chemical."

"Do you?"

Grateful, she snagged a tube of Pepsi. She cracked the tube, took a gulp. "Anyway."

"Anyway," he repeated. "Ladies first, as you see. In her case in death as well as life. She'd consumed a slice of wheat bread,

64

about six ounces of soy coffee with artificial sweetener, and a half cup of Greek yogurt with granola about five hours prior to TOD. Not a particularly lovely last meal. She was very slightly underweight, and in very good health. Or she was before she was stabbed fifty-three times."

"Serious overkill."

"The majority of the wounds were inflicted when she was prone — the angle. And several of the blows were forceful enough to nick bone, and in fact broke and lodged the tip in her tibia." He held up a specimen jar. "My opinion is, all wounds were inflicted by one blade, which matches the one you found still in her. There are no defensive wounds."

"She didn't see it coming. Probably didn't believe it when it did."

"I agree. From my reconstruction, it's my conclusion the first blow came here." He held a finger over the body's abdomen. "It did considerable damage, but she would have recovered from that with good and speedy medical treatment. The next, probably this, near the same area."

"They'd be face-to-face."

"Yes, probably very close. After that, they were more random, and more forceful."

"Getting into it," she murmured.

"On the back." He ordered his screen to change views so Eve studied the victim's back. "One or two of them, from the angle again, were probably delivered as she tried to get away, and as she fell. She was dead or at least unconscious before the majority of them. Small mercy. Some bruising where she fell, but she wouldn't have felt it."

"Very small mercy."

"You know who. Do you know why?"

"He's an asshole. A screwup, even according to his oldest friend. He couldn't or wouldn't keep a job, girlfriend gave him the boot. He's back living with Mom and Dad and they're going to give him the 'grow up or get out' routine. I think Mom gave him a heads-up on that."

"Being a parent is full of pitfalls, I imagine. This shouldn't be one of them."

"No." How many times had she stabbed her father? Eve wondered. Had anyone counted? But then, that had been a matter of life and death — her life and death.

"Can you tell me anything about the other vic?"

"Very preliminary." Morris walked over to the second slab. "Your TOD on scene was accurate, and again, the bat you took into evidence matches the injuries. The first blow here? The face, and with considerable force

— meat of the bat."

"Swinging away." Eve nodded. "There's a little jog leading to the kitchen. He stood behind it, that's what he did. Stood behind it, and the husband comes in, starts back. Sees the wife, the blood, the body, starts to run. He steps out, swings for the benches right into his father's face."

"Shattered his nose, left cheekbone, and eye socket. Subsequent blows broke several teeth, the jaw, fractured the skull in three places. Before he moved down to the body. My estimate, which I'll refine, is approximately thirty blows. Some of them straight down — head of the bat into the body. In this case, I believe the first blow would have rendered the victim unconscious."

"I guess he got off easier than his wife."

"She'd have suffered more, yes."

"Did you ever fight with your parents?"

He smiled easily. "I was a teenager once, after all. It was my duty to fight with and exasperate my parents."

"Did you ever fantasize about giving them a couple good shots?"

"Not that I recall, no. I did imagine, regularly, proving them wrong, which I don't believe I ever did. Or running off and becoming a famous blues musician."

"You play a pretty mean sax."

"I do, but . . ." He lifted his hands. "The dead are my work, as they're yours. Now we'll do the best job we can for the mother and father of this asshole."

"Yeah, we will. Thanks for the drink."

"Always stocked for you. And, Dallas, let me thank you in advance for Thanksgiving. It means a great deal to me to be included with your family and friends."

It made her feel a little weird so she shrugged. "Hell, Morris, how many dead have you and I stood over together? If we're not family and friends, what are we?"

Eve drove straight back to Central. She wanted to set up her board and book, write her preliminary report — and if they didn't bag Reinhold by the end of the day, have an appointment set with Mira for a profile and consult. And when a tour group led by an Officer Friendly piled into the elevator, she jumped off, opting for the longer but less crowded route of the snaking glides. As she rode, she pulled out her signaling 'link, noted Peabody on the display.

"Dallas. What have you got?"

"A cheese and veggie pita and soy fries. I'm at the cart, east corner of Central, and on my way in. Do you want me to grab something for you?"

Eve started to refuse, her mind on work, then had a sudden hankering. "Load up a dog. I'm already in house, heading up."

"You got it. Give me ten."

In her bullpen, Jenkinson — still wearing the atomic tie — sat scowling at his screen. Baxter — still wearing his sunshades — spat rapid-fire questions into his 'link. She caught the distinct smell of fried onions over the bad coffee.

She spotted Uniform Carmichael back in his cube, pulling them out of a greasy bag while he worked his keyboard one-handed.

Situation normal, she decided, and moved into her office.

She ignored her blinking message light. It could damn well wait until she'd set up. She ordered printouts of crime scene photos, of her vics, of Reinhold.

She sat at her desk to formulate her time line, printed that, and started on her report.

"Loaded dog," Peabody announced, bringing the scent with her. "I got you fries, too, just in case."

"Thanks."

"Ah . . ." Peabody gestured toward the AutoChef. Knowing her partner, Eve held up two fingers to signal coffee for two.

"What did you get from the interviews?"

"That Joe Klein's pretty much of a dick.

He's not buying his good bro Jerry killed anybody, hit on me in a very slimy way, claims Reinhold's ex is a pushy bitch, and had a good laugh recounting how Reinhold lost over five thousand in Vegas while he himself won eight. A point their friend Dave Hildebran, who isn't so much a dick, claims Klein rubbed all over Reinhold's ass, and still is. Hildebran hit ten on the shocked scale," she added as she brought Eve coffee, "but when he leveled off he told me he wondered if Reinhold was a shaky boomer primed to explode. Pissed at the world, was the phrase he used — considered his parents interfering, demanding, and to blame for whatever came to mind."

Peabody took her first gulp of coffee. "Unless it was a former boss, a coworker, his ex, or some random dude on the street to blame. He said he'd hit a club with Reinhold and Klein the night before the murder, and all Reinhold did was bitch. He, Dave, hasn't been hanging with them as much since Vegas. He's seeing someone, and claims he's a little tired of Reinhold's endless complaints and Klein's general dickishness. He's hung a little more with Mal Golde, who you may have met since he lives at the last known."

"Yeah, we met."

"Neither of my two have seen or heard from Reinhold since Thursday night. Klein tried to tag him Saturday night, but hasn't heard back."

"Reinhold was a busy boy. Golde's not a dick, by the way."

She caught Peabody up with the salient points of that interview while she chowed on the dog. "Banks?" she finished, mouth full.

"I got copies of the security discs, reviewed them while I traveled. He had the 'I'm a smug son of a bitch' vibe going — briefcase, no suitcases. According to the managers, he wanted all cash, but some of the amounts made that tricky, so he settled for the cashier's checks. A couple politely questioned him regarding why the quick deposit and withdrawal. He told them to give him his money or he'd cause a scene. I have a feeling he didn't use such mild terms."

"I'll need to look at them. Did anybody see him leave, what he left in?"

"Outside security caught him, on foot." Trying in vain for comfort, Peabody shifted in Eve's visitor's chair. "He could've had transpo waiting or picked it up once he was out of range."

"Let's send some uniforms around to neighboring businesses, see if they picked

71

anything up. In the meantime, I couldn't connect with the ex. According to her neighbor she's out with a friend today — and buying a new 'link, with a new number. See if you can find anything on that. The neighbor — Sela Crabtree — has my contacts, so I expect to hear from the ex when they connect. Otherwise, we'll round her up in the morning."

"Got it."

"I'm going to set up a meet with Mira, do the notifications. The vics' parents need to be told before the media leaks their names. Get your notes together so I can —" She broke off as her desk 'link signaled. Though she intended to ignore it, she glanced over at the readout.

"Crap. It's the commander." After swiping a hand over her mouth, in case, she flipped it on. "Lieutenant Dallas."

Rather than his admin's, Whitney's face filled her screen. "I'd like to see you in my office, Lieutenant."

"Yes, sir."

"Now."

"On my way."

He clicked off.

"God, I get gut knots just thinking about if it was me he called up like that."

"Shit. I ate most of a loaded dog. I have

loaded dog breath." Rising, Eve yanked open drawers. "I must have something around here."

"Try this." Peabody offered a little box, flipping the lid to the tiny pink balls.

"Why are they pink?"

"Bubble gum flavor. It's good. And they work."

With little choice, Eve popped two. Pink or not, they were pretty good. "If I'm not back in ten, I need you to do the notifications."

"Oh please, be back."

"That's up to Whitney."

Swinging through, she noted Jenkinson and his tie among the missing, and imagined he and his partner, Reineke, caught one. Baxter had shifted to his comp, intensely, she noted. His shades hooked in his front pocket where she assumed he put them, intending to stick them back on the minute the tie walked back in.

It was a joke that would last the entire shift.

She stepped out, spotted Detective Carmichael at Vending.

"Hey, Loo, just getting our current bag of scum a cold one. Sanchez's working him in Interview A."

"What did the bag of scum do?"

"Tossed a junkie down a flight of stairs, then stomped him to death for trying to scam him with play money. I mean actual play money, like from a game. Bag of scum deals mostly to funky-junkies."

And the Funk played hell with eyes. "Play money probably seemed fine to him."

"Yeah, well, he won't be passing Go."

"Go where?"

"You know. Go." Carmichael circled her hands in the air. "Monopoly. The game."

"Dead makes a full stop."

"You got that. Bag of scum's claiming the junkie fell, and he's claiming the reason he ran like a freaking gazelle when we tracked him is how he was late for an appointment. And how all the bags of Funk and zoner we spotted — and managed to even scoop up a few before bystanders swarmed — weren't his. And he's being arrogant about it, which makes you want to bitch-slap him a few times."

"I didn't hear that part."

Carmichael smiled. "Sanchez keeps me in line. He's a peaceful sort."

"Stomped him? How are the bag of scum's shoes?"

The smile widened. "He didn't even bother to change his boots, or get the vic's blood off them. We're getting them analyzed, but he left a goddamn boot print on the vic's chest. Clear as a footprint in wet sand. And we have two wits who were looking out their peeps when he shoved the guy because the bag of scum was yelling his ass off at the junkie."

"Sounds like you've got him. Why are you getting him a cold one?"

"Mostly because Sanchez wanted me to cool off. Asshole said all I needed was a good fuck with a big dick, gave me the crotch grab, and said he had one waiting for me."

"There's more than one way to bitch-slap, Carmichael. Interview A's on my way." She started to walk. "What's his name?"

"Street name's Fang. Real's Alvar Ramondo."

With a nod, Eve gestured to the door. "Just open it, start to go in. Don't close it."

Carmichael obliged.

"So I'll see you after . . . Hey." Eve poked her head in the door, pointed at the bulky man — mid-twenties, mixed-race, leaning Latino, sporting complicated and elaborate tat sleeves. "Hey, you didn't say you had Al in here."

Before Sanchez could speak, Eve sent him the briefest glance. He settled back.

"How's it going, Al? Not so good, I guess,

from the look of it."

"Who's this bitch?" Fang demanded. "You bringing another bitch in? No problem. I can handle both of you." He smiled, proving he didn't spend a lot of his profits on dental hygiene, grabbed his crotch, rocked his hips.

Grunted suggestively.

"Yeah, that's what you said that night after all those tequila shots. I dug the tats," she said to Carmichael, "so I gave him a shot. What the hell. Lemme tell ya."

Rolling her eyes, Eve held up her index finger and thumb, a scant two inches apart, then lifting the index, made a soft whooshing sound as she curled it limply down.

Fang's face went fiery red as he tried to lurch up. "You lying bitch! Lying *puta*! I never seen you before."

"Don't remember me, Al? You said to call you Fang, right? Didn't have much of a bite," she said in an aside to Carmichael, girl to girl.

"Lying bitch! I never seen you."

"Too much tequila." Eve shrugged it off. "That's okay. I remember you. I never forget a . . ." Eve did the falling index finger again. "Anyway," she said brightly to Carmichael, "see you later."

She began to shut the door, considered it

76

a job well done when she heard the shouting stream of curses.

Then she hotfooted it to Whitney's office.

4

The outer office was unmanned, and Whitney's door stood open. Eve stepped to it, waited a moment as he sat at his desk, concentration on his wide dark face while he scrolled down his desk screen.

He fit the desk, she thought, the command of it with the windows at his back full of the city he'd vowed to protect. He'd worked the street once, and had been good at it. Now he rode a desk to run what she considered the best police and security force in the country.

And he was good at that, too.

She knocked lightly on the doorjamb. "Excuse me, sir. Your admin's not at her post."

"She's at lunch." He gave her a come-ahead curl of his fingers. "Shut the door."

"Yes, sir." Since she knew he'd invite her to sit, and she preferred giving oral reports on her feet, she jumped right in.

"Both Peabody and I just returned separately from the field regarding the Reinhold homicides."

He sat back, tented his big hands. "Double murder. Mother and father."

"Yes, sir. Evidence, overwhelming even at this point, supports the fact that Jerald Reinhold stabbed his mother more than fifty times, then lay in wait for his father for over six hours. He beat his father to death with multiple blows using a baseball bat."

She ran it through, top to bottom, side to side, without much interruption. For the most part Whitney simply sat, watching her, giving the occasional nod or asking a brief question for clarification.

"I intend to ask Dr. Mira to profile, and still have to interview the ex-girlfriend, and his former coworkers, supervisors. But the three men he's known to be closest to haven't yet had contact since the murders."

"You believe them?"

"Yes, sir. He has what he wants. He's had his celebration. I expect a report from Officer Cardininni shortly on what's missing from the scene so we can notify pawnshops, secondhand stores. He'll want to get rid of what he took, add to his cash. He was smart enough not to stay in one location, where we could easily track him, but he has to land somewhere."

"Local media will play it up for a news cycle or two. You'll handle that."

Hated that, Eve thought, could and would handle that. "I'll have a more detailed report shortly," Eve began.

"I'm sure you will. I'm satisfied you have this investigation in hand, but I called you up here on another matter." Now he laid his hands on the desk. "You're to be awarded the Medal of Honor."

"Sir?"

"Most specifically for your exemplary work, the personal risks taken, and the countless lives you saved through that work, by those risks in the recent incidents of mass murder by chemical weapons, the apprehension of Lewis Callaway and Gina MacMillon, and the case you built against them."

"Commander, I'm honored. But I didn't investigate, apprehend, or build the case alone. My team —"

"Will be acknowledged, as will Agent Teasdale from the HSO. You headed that team, Lieutenant. You commanded and command those men and women. This is the highest honor bestowed on a police officer by the NYPSD, and isn't given lightly — though some politics may come into play. In this case, and in my considered opinion, they played properly. Do you want to dispute my considered opinion, Lieutenant?"

"No, sir." Neatly cornered, she thought. "Thank you, sir."

"The presentation is scheduled for this coming Wednesday, at fourteen hundred. I've been given the nod to so inform you. I'm proud to do so."

"Thank you, Commander." Actually, the idea left her tight in the chest with a snagged-up combination of pride, gratitude, and outright embarrassment. "I don't want to seem ungrateful. I'm very grateful. But is it possible to keep this . . ."

"Low-key, quiet, small, and relatively private?"

Hope struggled to bloom through the snags. "Any of that?"

His lips curved. "Absolutely not. Suck that up, Dallas."

And quietly died. "Yes, sir."

"And on another matter that also has its tangle of politics, I have a question for you. Do you want a captaincy?"

Eve opened her mouth; couldn't think of a thing. For a moment, she couldn't quite feel her own feet. "Sir?"

"It's a direct question, Lieutenant. I'd like a direct answer." But before she could formulate one, he held up a finger to hold that answer off. "You're young for the rank. Would be the youngest captain under my command. And if it had been my call alone, the bars would've been offered to you long before this. Politics, perception, prejudice have all played a part in the decision not to offer them. Our personal lives are part of who we are, and part of how we're perceived."

"Understood, Commander." And because she did — not only understood him, but the process, and herself, everything in her loosened again.

"I've always understood, and have no regrets on my personal life."

"Nor should you. It's become more difficult, some may say impossible, to use your marriage as a wedge against this promotion. It's particularly difficult now as Roarke will be awarded the Medal of Merit — Civilian."

She actually felt her eyes pop a bit before she let out a half laugh. "I can use that on him for years."

"The two of you have an interesting dynamic," Whitney observed. "Now I'd like your answer."

"Commander . . ." Trying to think clearly, so her answer would be, she raked a hand through her hair. "Three years ago I wouldn't have hesitated. It was more about proving something, to myself. Outside of the job, the ground was pretty shaky for me, and I didn't even know it. Not really. So I wanted that to prove I had the solid under me. And I wanted to earn it."

"You have earned it." As he studied her face, lines dug in between his eyebrows. "But now you hesitate?"

"Sir, I admire your transition from investigator to commander, your skill and your insight. Your work is more difficult than I can imagine, and it's honorable and necessary."

"You've already got the promotion if you want it, Dallas."

That relaxed her, just a little more. "I'm not ready to ride a desk. I'm solid enough on administration, but I'm an investigator. A captain's presence in the field, as an investigator, is the exception rather than the rule. I'm a murder cop; that's my strength. That's my skill and my insight. I wouldn't be offered this promotion otherwise."

She thought of Jenkinson's ridiculous tie, of the rubber chicken above Sanchez's desk when he'd been the new guy. More, she thought how she could trust, without question, anyone in her bullpen to go through the door with her.

"And sir? I don't want to put a buffer between me and my men. I don't want them to feel they have to climb the chain to talk to me, to run a case by me, to ask for my help. I'm not willing to step away from them. They, and the job, are more important than captain's bars. I'm glad to be able to say that, and mean it."

"You've given this considerable thought."

"Actually, Commander, I'd put it away. I haven't given it much of any thought in a long time now." At peace with it, she realized — a not altogether familiar place to be. "I'm grateful to be considered. I believe I best serve the department and the people of New York where I am."

He sat back again, a big man with a big city behind him. "I could have pushed for this harder at several points along the way, and had several debates with myself on doing just that."

"Politics, sir." She shrugged them away.

"Some, yes, but not all. The primary reason I didn't push is I agree with you. Your strengths are your investigative abilities, and your skill handling your department, your insight into the perpetrator and victim. I didn't want to lose that. But now that certain obstacles are cleared, or have been cleared, I felt it was time to ask you directly."

"Frankly, sir?" At his nod, she continued. "It's a weight off knowing the obstacles are cleared, and understanding my own goals and priorities."

"Then I'll relay your answer to those it's relevant to."

"Thank you, sir. Sincerely."

"You're welcome, Lieutenant. Sincerely."

He rose from his desk, came around it, and did something he rarely did. He took Eve's hand, shook it.

"Dismissed."

She walked out a little dazed, but yeah, she realized, okay with it. Like she'd tossed aside a weight she'd forgotten she carried, but knew just where it landed if she ever wanted to pick it up again.

But now? Right now, she felt good staying light on her feet.

The tie was back in the bullpen, busy at his desk. Baxter and Trueheart held a confab at Baxter's desk. Peabody worked morosely at hers, which meant she'd dealt with the notifications.

And every cop in the room, including Jenkinson, wore sunshades.

"It looks like Hollywood PSD in here."

"Dug up a pair for you, boss." Baxter tossed her a pair with black flames and square amber lenses. "Can't have our LT's eyes bleeding all over the floor."

Willing to play, she slipped them on as she walked to Peabody's desk. "Status?"

"I made the notifications. They took it hard. My mother always says no matter how old your kid gets, he's still your kid. I guess she's right. I also contacted local department grief counselors in their areas."

"Good."

"Sweeper's prelim is in, and Cardininni sent the list of missing items the neighbor identified. Copies should be on your unit."

"I'll check it out."

"You were gone awhile." When Eve remained silent, Peabody moved on. "So I sent Dr. Mira an overview, in case you still wanted the consult."

"I do."

"No luck on Nuccio's 'link yet. Either she hasn't activated it, or there's a backlog in the registration and data, which is more likely. When you get a new 'link," Peabody continued, "it's like a toy. You just gotta play with it."

"How long does it usually take to pop on data?"

"Usually? Anywhere from a couple hours to whenever the hell."

"Great. If it doesn't pop, and she doesn't

86

make contact by end of shift, I'll swing by her place again on the way home. If she's making a long day out of it, we'll catch her in the morning. Get the description of missing items out."

"I'm working on it."

"Okay." She started toward her office, glanced back. "Good work, Peabody."

"Thanks."

Eve walked into her office, started to close the door, stopped herself. No, she wasn't going to sit in here thinking about the meeting with Whitney.

She didn't have time to parse through promotions, politics, perceptions. She needed to do her job.

She brought up the list of items first, read it, pondered over it.

A few pieces of jewelry as she'd expected. Small, star-shaped diamond stud earrings, with the note the wit stated had been a twenty-fifth-anniversary gift to Barbara from Carl. An antique ladies' gold watch, set with diamonds and sapphires, circa middle twentieth century, Rolex brand, again with a note stating it had been the vic's great-grandmother's — wit believed maternal. Two gold bangle bracelets, one set of pearls with gold clasp — heirloom from maternal grandmother, and the vic's diamond engagement ring in a plain gold setting.

So the vics had been traditionalists, Eve thought. Engagement ring, a couple of family pieces.

On the husband's side jewelry was limited to a gold wrist unit, again a Rolex (traditionalists) engraved with the vic's initials — a twenty-fifth-anniversary gift from his wife — one pair of brushed gold cuff links, one pair of hammered silver.

More jewelry listed, but the wit believed those pieces were costume, and stated she'd been with the vic when several were purchased.

The wit also listed two e-tablets, two mini-comps, a sterling silver menorah, sterling flatware — heirloom again — service for eight. A cut-glass crystal bowl in the shape of a footed basket, with handle, which the wit stated had been Barbara's only piece from her great-grandmother, and her pride and joy.

Cardininni added to her notes on what struck her that *hadn't* been taken, including a wedding chuppa with the tree of life hand-painted on silk.

Wit states the piece was made for female vic's great-grandmother's wedding, served in grandmother's and in mother's wedding and in vic's. It's in perfect condition, signed by the artist Mirium Greene. Vic confided to wit she'd hoped to pass it to her son, and had it insured for $45k. Photo attached of chuppa and wooden music box wit states male vic's father recently passed to him. It appears old, a cylinder-type mechanism with an inlay of a woman playing a lute on the top. Wit believes the piece was also insured.

Thorough, Eve thought with a nod for Cardininni, and interesting information. Reinhold had limited knowledge, she concluded. The wedding canopy deal meant nothing to him, and he'd been unaware of its market value. The music box didn't look like a big deal in the photo, and he'd probably considered it parental junk.

So he took the shiny, and the electronics, and the cash.

Not stupid, she thought again, just not really smart.

She read over the sweeper's reports, chafed a bit they hadn't yet identified the footwear from the bloody footprints on scene, reviewed the ME's findings, then pulled them together in her own report.

She copied Mira, Peabody, her commander, then added the data to her board and book.

And with her boots on her desk, sat back and studied what she had.

Fairly ordinary people, she concluded. Traditional, long-married, middle-class. Woman keeps the home, man provides the home. Solid family ties, solid friendships, well-settled neighborhood. They'd raised one son. A disappointment? Can't hack college, can't hold on to a job, can't maintain a relationship.

Did they push him some? Yeah, yeah, she thought. Traditional.

Be a man, get a job, think of your future, pay your bills.

Got sick of hearing that, didn't you, she mused, studying Reinhold's face. Sick of them telling you what to do, how to do it, looking at you with that disappointment in their eyes. There's your father, plugging away every day at some stupid job — boring bastard. And your mother, fussing in the kitchen, gossiping with the neighbors, always telling you to pick up your stuff. Nagging bitch.

Holding you back from everything you wanted, both of them.

"That's how you see it," Eve murmured. "You don't have to look at them anymore, listen to them anymore. You're a free man now."

She pushed to her feet. "But not for long."

As she grabbed her coat, Peabody came to the door.

"We've already got a hit on the two watches and the pearls. Upscale shop in the East Village."

"Let's check it out, and Reinhold's last place of employment. Just the watches and the pearls?" she added as they started out.

"That's all he brought in."

"Spreading it out. Doesn't want people asking too many questions, and makes sure he takes them out of his own neighborhood."

"The owner called it in as soon as he saw the alert. He told me Reinhold came in about eleven with the watches and the pearl necklace."

"About two hours after the banks. Lining his nest egg."

In the garage, she got behind the wheel as Peabody keyed the shop address into navigation.

"I'd have wired the money to New Jersey," Peabody commented. "Better, Pittsburgh."

"Pittsburgh?"

"Yeah, maybe Pittsburgh. Then I'd have packed it up on Saturday, walked uptown, caught a bus maybe, transferred, taken another into New Jersey, found a nice quiet hotel. Caught my breath. Sunday, I'd make my way south — after I cut and dyed my hair, picked up an over-the-counter temp eye-color change one place, temp tats another place."

"You have to show ID for the money. Change your look, it's sending up a flag."

"Right. Okay, I wait on that one. I get the stuff, but I wait on it. Maybe I hunt up a shop like we're going to in Jersey, liquidate a few items. By Monday morning, I'm picking up the money, then I use a walk-in flop, pay cash, change my looks, and I'm going to liquidate the rest in Pittsburgh."

"You should wait to change your looks then or we'll have your new one when we track the goods."

"Damn. Right again. I use the flop *after* I liquidate, and I use some of the money to buy new ID."

It amused Eve — and she thought helped train Peabody — for her to poke holes in the master escape plan. "And how is some lazy bastard schmuck from the Lower West Side going to know where to get fake ID in Pittsburgh?"

"Okay, he gets it before he leaves New York."

"Question holds."

"He's got to know somebody who knows somebody. He probably bought fake ID before he hit legal drinking age so he could get into the clubs or buy a brew. Who doesn't?" Peabody slid her glance to the left. "You never?"

"No." She hadn't cared about clubs, Eve remembered.

"Trust me, most kids do. So I'd use that as a springboard, shell out some of the money for new ID."

"Except, back in New York you don't have the new look."

"Shit!" Cornered again, Peabody rapped a fist on her thigh. "Let me think. How would you play it?"

"I'd spend some of the time I'm in the apartment with my dead parents researching how to make my own fake ID. I find a dead guy, get the supplies I need for docs that will satisfy the bored clerk at the ID center. And I liquidate everything on Saturday, well before anybody's issued any alerts. When I leave, I have one easy-to-carry suitcase, backpack, overnight — travel light, travel fast. I don't need or want all my stuff anyway. I'd pack just enough to get me through a couple days. I wire the money to an offshore account, one that doesn't report transactions. It's not that much money; nobody's going to blink. That gives me all day Sunday to travel. I leave looking like myself, hit a flop — that part works, change my looks to match the ID I'm going to make. Take my own picture to go with the docs I've faked. Then I'm going to add some embellishments so I don't look so much like the guy I'm going to become. Layer my clothes to bulk myself up. Take some of the hair I cut — and saved and dyed — and make myself a little goatee maybe, add an earring, a couple temp tats, maybe washable bronzer. Then I take a bus, a train, juggling transpo, but not to Pittsburgh, to someplace like Milwaukee."

"Milwaukee? What's so good about Milwaukee?"

"It just came to me, but it's away — Midwest. That's where I scout out the ID centers until I find one that feels right. I change my looks back, go in with my story about losing my ID while I was on a scuba trip in Cozumel."

Peabody gaped at her. "Seriously?"

"It sounds stupid, and weird, and that's why they'll buy it if you play it right. Then I walk out with my new ID, take a shuttle to the Caymans or wherever I've wired the money, scoop that up, then I'd check into a nice hotel, head to the beach, and have one of those drinks with an umbrella in it."

"You're good at this."

Eve shook her head as she hunted for parking. "Not good enough. It's not enough money to make it all work, or be worth it. And it's still leaving a trail if the cops keep sniffing."

She spotted a second-level spot and another vehicle on the hunt. Ruthlessly, she hit vertical, tipped, veered, and shoehorned her way in.

"We'd follow the money," she continued when she hopped out. "And we'd find it. He'd have been better off to settle for the cash around the apartment, and whatever he could carry and sell. Then run like hell, change his ID, his looks, his name, maybe settle in Milwaukee and get a nice, nondescript job. But most people are too greedy, too impatient. They want it all, and they want it now."

At street level she walked the half a block to Ursa's Fine Jewelry, which hyped their expertise in sales, repair, and acquisition.

She stepped inside to the scent of flowers, the murmur of voices, and the sparkle.

Peabody said, "Ooooh."

"Stomp that down," Eve warned.

"The guy with the flowy silver hair and

cruise ship tan's Ursa."

Spotting him sliding some sparkles on a velvet tray back into a display case, Eve crossed to him. "Mr. Ursa." She palmed her badge, watched him nod as he sighed. "Lieutenant Dallas, and Detective Peabody. We appreciate your cooperation in this matter."

"He looked like such a nice young man."

"I'm sure he did."

"He said he'd recently lost his parents in an accident. He choked up for a moment, so I didn't press there. And he said he couldn't bear to keep the watches or the pearls. He'd tried to wear his father's watch, he said, but it was too upsetting."

"I bet."

"I did suggest he might want to wait a little while longer, perhaps put them in a safety deposit box. That he might regret selling them at some point. But he said no, he was leaving New York, and felt he should try for a fresh start. They're all lovely pieces, the vintage woman's watch particularly. If you'll wait a moment, I put them back in our vault after my daughter noticed the alert on our screen. We've never had this happen before. It's very upsetting."

"I understand."

"Excuse me."

He walked away and through a door. As he did a woman stepped over. She had his dark blue eyes, his nose. "I'm Naomi Ursa. My father's very upset. I saw the media bulletin about the two people — the husband and wife — killed in their apartment on the West Side. I haven't mentioned it to my father. But those watches, those lovely antique pearls . . . they belonged to those poor people, didn't they?"

"I can't verify that. It would help if we could see your security footage."

"Yes, Pop already had a copy made for you, but if you'd like to come around the counter, you can see it on our screen right here."

Eve started around, then had to elbow Peabody, who stood mooning over a necklace that looked like a chain of little pink tears.

"I cued it up when you came in," Naomi told her, and called for play.

Eve watched Reinhold come in. No suitcases, she noted, so he'd found somewhere to stash them, somewhere to hole up. He had what she supposed he thought of as a sad face on, and arrowed straight for the older man.

Interesting, she thought. He'd gone to the father type, the authority type, not the younger female.

She watched the conversation, Ursa's sympathy. He lay a velvet pad on the counter for the watches, a second for the pearl necklace.

Not nervous, Eve thought, her focus on Reinhold rather than Ursa as the man got out his jeweler's loupe, some sort of measuring tool, and began to examine the pieces.

Impatient, she thought again. Excited.

Ursa spoke again, and Reinhold shook his head, looked down, looked away, pressed his lips together. Into the role he'd created for himself.

Ursa laid a hand over Reinhold's, and the sincere sympathy showed, even on screen. Ursa slid the velvet to the side, gestured his daughter over, whispered in her ear.

"He's telling me to put them away, so he doesn't have to see them," Naomi said. "And he offered the man a little more than he should have, but we both felt so sorry for him. And on a practical level, the antique woman's watch would have made up for it."

Ursa stepped out. "I put them in boxes." He set them on the table behind the counter, opened all three boxes. "They're very nice pieces. The man's watch, of course, isn't vintage, but a very good watch, and well cared for. The woman's is quite an

98

exceptional piece, and in excellent condition. The pearls are lovely, and well-kept. I have the paperwork for you as well."

"Thank you, Mr. Ursa. My partner's going to give you everything you need for your insurance on this, and in addition a receipt for all three pieces. You can contact me anytime." She drew out a card. "And please, if Mr. Reinhold comes back, don't confront him. Find a reason to step into the back and contact me."

"You think he'll come back?" Naomi pressed a hand to her throat.

"No, I don't. But I want you to understand, should you see him or hear from him again, he's a dangerous man, and you need to contact the police. Peabody, make sure Ms. Ursa has everything she needs from us."

"Ms. Ursa, why don't we just step over here?"

When she had a little room, Eve spoke quietly. "You were kind to him. Don't let that, or him, make you feel stupid."

The faintest smile moved Ursa's mouth. "It shows?"

"I bet you have a website, and it plays on being in business for a couple generations, how it's family run, gives personal, individual service, and how you specialize in estate jewelry."

"You'd win the bet. We're three generations. It's my mother's and father's day off.
My son and his wife." He gestured to the
other end of the store where a man and a
woman waited on customers.

"It's one of the reasons he picked you,"
Eve told him. "You're solid, you're re-
spected, you're fair. He'd have researched
you, just like he researched the general value
of the watches, and the necklace. And
because as a family business you'd tend to
be sympathetic toward someone who told
you the story he told you."

"His father's name is engraved on the
watch. I asked for his identification."

"You had no reason to doubt his story,
and I'm laying odds you aren't the only one
he's told it to today."

Outside, Eve headed for the second-level
spot. "Secure those until we get back."

"Bet your ass. He walked out of there with
forty-five thousand. I don't know what he'll
pull in for the other stuff, because it looks
like the antique watch was the big-ticket
item, but he's feathering his nest, and fast."

"So we'll find his nest."

Eve pulled open her car door, stood for a
moment scanning the street below. Riding
high, she thought, on a big pile of money
stained with his parents' blood.

5

Fitz Ravinski plated a slice of apple pie à la mode with a paper-thin square of bright yellow cheese. The mode part consisted of a rounded scoop of non-dairy product the color of an atomic kiwi.

"Minty Fresh tofu yogurt," he said with a shake of his head. "Who the hell puts that on a nice piece of pie?"

"Not me," Eve assured him.

"Takes all." He slid the pie and a minicup of black-as-the-soul-of-midnight coffee into a delivery slot, danced his fingers over the keypad, and sent it on its way.

"We're past the lunch rush, but we've had people come in for the pie and the tarts all afternoon."

"So I see." Eve glanced out, beyond the counter to the dining area. It probably sat ninety, in New York sardine mode, during the rush. Right now, it held a solid twenty, including the man busy on his handheld and ear unit taking his first bite of pie with Mint Fresh tofu yogurt.

Even the thought made her stomach turn a little.

"If you could give us five minutes."

"Yeah, yeah. Sal, take over here." Fitz wiped his hands on the front of a white bib apron that had seen a number of wipes already that day. He snagged a big, black drink bottle and with a head jerk gestured Eve and Peabody after him to an empty table. "You oughta try some pie, on the house. Cops don't pay on my shift. Got two cousins on the job."

"Here in New York?"

"Up the Bronx, both of them. Pie's good. My ma and my sisters make 'em."

"So you're a family business."

"Eighteen years, this location." He stubbed a wide finger on the table. "We do okay."

"I appreciate the offer, but we're not going to take up much of your time." Eve all but heard Peabody's happy pie stomach whine. "We'd like to ask you about Jerald Reinhold."

"Fired him a couple months back. Got in late, left early, missed deliveries. Deliveries are a good third of our business. He wasn't dependable, and basically couldn't give a half shit about doing the job."

Ravinski leaned forward, stabbed the counter with his finger again. "He tries to file on me, I got records to back it up."

"How'd he take getting the boot?" Eve asked.

"Told me to fuck myself, and shoved a banana cream pie off the counter on his way out. Moved out fast," Ravinski added with a sharp smile. "Pansy-assed coward put the speed on when the pie hit the floor, in case I came at him."

"Did you?" Eve wondered.

"Nah. Just a pie — damn good pie — but worth it to see him move his lazy ass. He'd put that much energy into the job, he'd still be working here. First time I ever saw him light up, if you know what I mean."

"I do. Did you have any specific complaints about him? From co-workers, customers."

"You want a list?" On that sour note, Ravinski tipped back the drink bottle, Adam's apple bobbing as he drank. "My sister Fran caught him tapping a joint out the back. Shoulda fired him for that, but I gave him another chance, figuring he's young and stupid."

"Were illegals a problem with him?"

"I don't figure. I kept an eye on him after

that, and never caught him at anything. Problem was lazy and shiftless. I got complaints from customers their food was damaged or cold when they got it, and the delivery server — which would be Jerry — was rude."

"Have you seen him since you let him go?"

"Can't say I have. Saw his girlfriend last week — ex, now, which proves she's no dummy."

"Lori Nuccio?"

"Yeah. Lori used to work for me about three years back. Good waitress, personable, fast on her feet. Worked here a couple years before she copped a job in a fancy place for better pay, better tips, and good for her. Anyhow, I hired the fuckhead because she asked me to give him a try. After I fired him, she came in to tell me she was sorry, like it was *her* fault? Lori's a good girl. Looks happier, you ask me, since she kicked him out."

"Did he hang with anyone in particular who works for you?"

"I'd say the opposite. He just didn't get along here. Didn't make friends, didn't especially make enemies. He just put in time — when it suited him. No more than that."

"Okay. We appreciate the time."

"Got me off my feet. Now, are you gonna give me a hint why you're in here asking about Jerry?"

If the media hadn't already lobbed the ball on the vics' names and some of the circumstances, it soon would. "We want to talk to him about his parents' murder."

"The what?" Shock vibrant, Ravinski lowered the big black bottle. "His parents were murdered? *Both* of them. Sweet Jesus, when? How did . . ." He pulled himself in, let out a hard breath. "He killed them. You're saying Jerry killed his own ma and pop?"

"We need to find him. We need to talk to him. I get the sense you don't have any idea where he might be, where he might go?"

"He didn't work here a full three months, and I can't count the times he called in sick or with some bullshit excuse." Ravinski scrubbed a hand over hair buzzed so straight and sharp Eve was surprised his palm didn't go bloody from contact. "He had a couple of friends who came in a few times. Ah, damn it. Mal — one of them's Mal. Seemed like a nice kid. The other was kind of a dick. I can't remember his name."

"We've already got that information. If you think of anything else, get in touch."

"My ma said he'd hurt somebody."

"Excuse me?"

"My ma. She likes to think she's got some

sensitive thing going." He vibrated his hands in the air. "Her great-grandparents were Sicilian. Anyway, she said to me, 'You mark my words, Fitz, that boy's going to hurt somebody. He's got the dark in him.' "

He shook his head. "I don't know if she figured dark enough for this, but I can tell you once she finds out, there'll be no living with her."

Out on the street, Peabody gave Eve a pouty stare. "Some of us like pie."

"Save it for Thanksgiving. We'll make the rounds," Eve decided. "Talk to former employers, coworkers. Maybe we'll hit something."

"He's got to run. It's the only thing that makes sense."

"If he were going for sense, he'd've been running since Friday. We cover the ground. Then you go ahead and swing by the ex-girlfriend's on the way home. I'm going to set up in my home office, look for another angle."

"What about Mira?"

"I'll arrange a consult for the morning. He's gone under somewhere, and he's feeling real flush, real fucking potent right now. So his hole's probably flush, too. He'll have himself a nice dinner tonight. He might even have pie."

"Bastard." Peabody gave one longing glance behind her — toward pie — as they hiked back to the car.

Long day, Peabody thought. And not as much to show for it as she'd figured when it started. Dallas had taught her never to think slam dunk on a case — not even when, as with this one, you knew who, you knew why, you knew how, you knew when, almost from the jump.

"He's having a run of luck," she complained.

EDD star Ian McNab gave her ass a light pat as they turned toward Lori Nuccio's building. "Luck doesn't last. Except ours, She-body."

He made her grin. It was one of his high points, on her scale. That and his own sweet and bony ass, his smart green eyes, his busy brain, and his exceptional energy and creativity between the sheets.

"We have to take the stairs up," she said.

"We do?"

"I can't stop thinking about pie à la mode. Even thinking about it's loading up my ass, and add the fact we're going to stop at the market on the way home so I can buy what I need to make one, then —"

"You're going to make us a pie?"

"My granny's cherry-berry, if I can find what we need, and you split the cost."

"Hey, if you bake that sucker, I'll pay for the stuff." He put on a little strut. "My best girl's baking me a pie."

With a smile on his narrow face, his long tail of blond hair bouncing, the garden of earrings on his left ear gleaming, he climbed the stairs beside her.

He reached over, dancing his fingers against hers. "I like it when we get off shift together."

"Me, too. I'd like it better if we'd caught this jerk-off before end of shift."

"You'll get him. You can walk me through it when we get home, and we'll put our heads together. And maybe some other body parts."

She snorted out a laugh as they stopped on Lori's floor.

"She's over here." Peabody walked to the door, knocked sharply.

"You said she had the day off, spent it with a girl pal? They're probably making a day to night deal. Dinner, hit a club or two."

"Yeah. I just wish —" Peabody turned as the door across the hall opened.

"Ms. Crabtree?"

"That's right."

Dutifully, Peabody held up her badge.

"You spoke with my partner earlier today, Lieutenant Dallas. I'm Detective Peabody, with Detective McNab."

"Lori's not home yet. I'm starting to worry."

"Is it unusual for her to be away this long?"

"No, but it's pretty damn unusual for her ex-boyfriend to murder his parents. I heard the media report when I got home about an hour ago. I wasn't out long, just ran a few errands, and I left a note on Lori's door in case she came home while I was out. It was still there. I'm keeping an eye out now."

"We appreciate that, and we'd appreciate it if Ms. Nuccio would contact us whenever she gets back."

"Hell of a day for her to get a new 'link and number. But if I can't get hold of her, neither can that son of a bitch. I guess I'd just feel better if I knew she was tucked in for the night. I'll keep an eye out for her," Crabtree repeated.

Peabody rolled her shoulders as they started back down. "Now she's got me worried. We don't know who she's out with, so we can't tag her friend and play relay."

"We could probably find that out. Get names from her work, spread from there. Girls are pack animals, so we ID the pack members, play process of elimination. It'd take some time, but it's doable."

"Pack animals."

"Hey, don't blame me. You're the ones who can't even pee solo."

"I'd smack you if that wasn't true, and if it wasn't a good idea. It's probably overkill, but what the hell."

"So we'll start putting a list together and buy pie stuff. You do the pie, I'll run down the list."

She took his hand as they exited the building. "Then we'll put our heads and other body parts together."

"Solid plan."

They missed Lori by twenty minutes.

She dragged herself home as the streetlamps flickered on. She'd planned to shimmy herself into the new dress she'd bought — along with Kasey — then hit the clubs. And just as they'd finished up a well-earned post-shopping/hair/nails eggplant pasta — splitting it to whittle down the calories and the cost — their friend Dru had tagged Kasey.

She didn't believe it. Didn't want to believe it. But Dru had been so adamant, and then she and Kasey had both brought up the report on their new 'links.

Jerry, the man she'd lived with, slept with, had loved at least for a little while, was wanted for questioning by the police. Was a *suspect* in the murder of his parents.

God, Jerry's parents were dead. She'd liked them so much, and now they were just dead. She'd never known anyone who'd been murdered, much less spent time with anyone who had been the way she had with Jerry's mom and dad.

She really believed, down to her heart, it was all a terrible mistake. Yes, Jerry could fly off — and that time he'd hit her had shown her a side of him she couldn't love or live with. But a couple of slaps, as wrong as they'd been, weren't *murder.*

She'd thought about tagging him, but Kasey put the kibosh on that majorly. And had even insisted, when she'd just wanted to go home, they spring for a cab. No walking, no subway. It had taken some serious shoving to convince Kasey she didn't need or want her to stay at her place.

She just wanted to go home, be alone, try to figure it out.

And she needed to cry some. Maybe a lot. For Mr. and Mrs. Reinhold, and for Jerry, too. For what she'd once imagined might be.

She shifted the shopping bags full of

things she no longer wanted, keyed herself in. Because she wanted to get inside quickly, and she'd walked her *ass* off that day already, she took the elevator up. It clunked on her floor, creaked its way open.

And Ms. Crabtree pushed out of her own apartment before Lori reached her own.

"There you are! I was worried."

"I . . . I did a lot of shopping."

Ms. Crabtree narrowed her eyes. "You've heard. About that Jerry."

"Just a little while ago. I think there must be a mistake, because —"

"Honey, the police were here. Twice. Looking for you."

"Me? Why? Why?"

"Just to talk to you, about him. Why don't you come on in here, and I'll fix you some tea. No, hell with that. I'll pour you a big glass of wine. I've got a nice bottle I've been saving since my birthday."

"Thanks, but I just want to go home, and . . . I just want to go home and . . . be quiet, I guess."

"All right. All right now." Crabtree stroked a hand down Lori's glossy, chestnut hair. "You look so pretty."

"We . . . went to the salon."

"I like your hair, the new color. New's good. Here, this is the cop who came first.

She wants you to contact her as soon as you can. I think you might feel better once you do."

She'd never actually talked to any police — not officially — and it made her feel a little sick. "But I don't know anything."

"You never know what you know." Ms. Crabtree tried a bolstering smile. "And this one struck me as smart. So you go ahead in and tag her up. If you change your mind about that wine and company, you just knock on the door. It doesn't matter how late, okay?"

"Okay." Lori looked at the card, read: *Lieutenant Eve Dallas.* "Oh, she's the Icove cop. She's Roarke's cop."

"*That*'s what it is." Crabtree rapped her knuckles to her temple. "I knew I recognized something, but couldn't bring it up. See, you never know what you know."

"I guess you're right. Thanks, Ms. Crabtree."

"I'm right over here," Crabtree reminded her, and stepping back into her own apartment, relaxed again.

Tucked in. Safe and sound.

Lori locked her door, added the deadbolt, the security chain.

She started to just dump the bags — the contents no longer interested her, in fact, made her feel guilty and ashamed. She'd been out, shopping for things she didn't really need, indulging in manicures and facials, laughing, drinking wine at lunch — and all the while Mr. and Mrs. Reinhold were dead.

She wanted to talk to her mother, she realized. She wanted to talk to her mom and dad — and that's what she'd do. But first she'd do what they'd raised her to do.

What came next.

She'd put her things away, then she'd call the police.

She moved through her small, colorful space to the alcove of her bedroom. She'd separated it from the living area with its single bold blue sofa and padded crates she'd painted lipstick red by a curtain formed from stringed beads.

Maybe a convertible sofa would've made more sense, but she just refused to sleep in her living space.

By next year, she could upgrade to a one-bedroom, hopefully in the same building. That was her next goal, anyway, which had taken a hit when Jerry had taken the rent money and her tip savings and blown it in Vegas. She needed to make it up now, and make up the spree she'd just had.

But she'd so needed to just get out, cut

loose for one day. And it *had* made her feel better, and more like herself. Kasey had been right. She'd brooded over her Big Mistake, aka Jerry, for long enough.

Time to jump back in the pool, she thought as she took the pretty turquoise sweater she'd scooped up on sale out of a shopping bag.

She should take Kasey's advice on attitude, too, she decided. She should think about how lucky she was. If Jerry had done what they said — and she still couldn't really believe it — she'd had a lucky escape breaking it off with him. All it had cost her, really, was time, some heartache, a couple of slaps, and money.

It could've been worse.

She didn't hear him step behind her. The dull crack of the bat against her skull pitched her forward so she hit the bed, bounced, then slid bonelessly to the floor.

Standing over her, Jerry smiled, tapped the bat against her leg.

"Batter up."

He hadn't hit her very hard. Not as hard as the old man, that's for sure. He didn't want to kill her — yet. They had some *issues* to discuss first.

But he was well aware of the crap sound-proofing on her dump of an apartment, so the discussion had to be a quiet one.

"Stupid bitch." He gave her a good thwack with the bat on her hip. "Did you think you could just say, 'Get out'? That I wouldn't make copies of the keys? And where the hell have you been all damn day? I've been waiting for you."

He poked at the shopping bags, bared his teeth.

He'd done some shopping of his own the last couple days. Time to put his purchases to good use.

He switched the music on — not too loud, don't want the neighbors to complain — just loud enough.

He retrieved his own shopping bag from the bathroom where he'd hidden when he heard the elevator clunk — and listened to her conversation with the nosy old hag across the hall.

A shame the nosy old hag hadn't come inside with Lori. He could've made it another twofer.

For now, and just for now, he'd settle for Lori.

He hauled her unconscious body onto the bed, and for the first time noticed the new hair color. Bitch probably changed it to try to land some other sucker. That's all he'd been to her, just some guy to fuck and fuck with.

Now she'd be the one getting fucked.

Not sexually, he thought — even the thought of doing her made him sick. But he undressed her. That was to humiliate and intimidate. He'd given this a great deal of thought.

He bound her wrists, her ankles — tight, really tight so the cord bit into flesh. She deserved some pain.

He slapped tape over her mouth, which was too bad as he'd have enjoyed hearing her scream.

Humming along with the music, he propped her up, plumping the pillows behind her before wrapping two more lengths of cord over her torso, around and under the bed. That he secured with a clip lock so it held nice and snug.

"That'll keep you where I want you."

Once again reaching into his bag, he pulled out a capsule of Wake-Up, broke it under her nose.

He watched her eyes flutter, her head turn side to side. A muffled moan sounded against the tape as she struggled to focus.

He straddled her, punched her hard in the belly. "Hi, Lori!"

And he saw it — what he hadn't seen with

his parents. Not just the shock, not just the pain.

Fear.

It filled him with something he'd never fully experienced. It filled him with joy.

He grinned, riding on that joy as she squirmed, as her eyes darted all over the crappy space in her crappy apartment, as choked sounds pushed against the tape.

"Don't worry. I'm not going to rape you. Not that it's rape seeing as how you put out for me plenty. But you just don't do it for me. Look at this, you're naked, helpless, and I don't even have wood. So just put that out of your mind."

He gave her nipple a hard twist, laughing when she bucked under him. "I bet I could make you wet, though — if I were interested. The fact is, fucking you the last few weeks we were together? It was like some chore to cross off my list. Here's a tip. If you want a guy to get you off, don't bitch at him all damn night first, don't turn on the fake tears — yeah, like you're doing now. And *don't,* for fuck's sake, tell him what the hell to *do!* You're not my mother, bitch, and since you heard what happened to her, you should be grateful."

He climbed off, stood studying her, and couldn't think of a single reason she'd ever appealed to him.

"I've got some things to say, and for once you're going to shut the hell up and *listen*. Got that, bitch?"

He didn't just feel happy, he realized. He felt strong. He felt important.

"You thought you could dump me, show me the door because I had a little bad luck? Bitching and whining about yourself when I was the one having some trouble. You think you can humiliate me that way? It's always about you. You selfish bitch. And acting like I'd committed a crime because I gave you a couple taps. You deserved that, and more. Now look at you. This is how they'll find you, naked, helpless, *humiliated*. How does it feel?"

Fat tears rolled down her face, added to his sense of joy.

He kicked at her shopping bags. "You're not the only one who went shopping today. Look what I got." He took a folding knife out of his pocket. "You just push this button, and blam!" A curved, serrated blade, just under the legal limit, whipped out. And he grinned when her eyes bulged, when her body twisted, when the screams muffled to whines against the blocking tape.

"Don't worry, it's not for you. I used a kitchen knife on Ma, and it slid right into

119

her, like into a pillow. Made a hell of a mess though before I was done. I'm not getting your pussy blood all over my new clothes. Nice threads, huh?"

He did a little turn. "I messed up two sets of my old stuff, first with the old woman, and then with the old man. I used my old baseball bat on him, and, man, did blood and brains fly!"

Laughing, he pushed the mechanism on the knife again. "You sent me back to hell. Do you know what it's like to live with those two? Always complaining, always telling me what to do, acting like they were in charge. Who's in charge now?"

Blood stained the cords on her wrists as she struggled against them. A bonus, he thought, and slipped the knife back in his pocket.

"So what did you buy today?" Crouching, he dumped the contents of her shopping bags on the floor, and as an afterthought, took the knife out again, dragged the blade through the scattered clothes. Her sobs choked against the tape.

"Slut shoes, too? Let's have a look." He straightened, shoved them on her feet.

"Yeah, that works."

He climbed back on her. "You messed up big-time by shoving me out, Lori. I've got money now. Lots and lots of money. I can do whatever the hell I want. I can do whatever the hell I want to you, and you can't stop me. You think slapping you was a big deal? Bullshit."

He slapped her now, front hand, backhand, front, back, hard enough her head snapped side to side and her cheeks bloomed red as a rose. "That's no big deal, bitch. I'll show you a big deal."

He balled his hand into a fist, plowed it into her face.

Her eyes jittered, and blood dripped under the tape from her split lip.

"You know, maybe I can get it up after all. Tell me you want it. Tell me you want me to stick it in you. Oh, you can't tell me." He tapped a finger on the tape. "Nod. Nod that you want me to fuck you right now. Nod, or I'll mess you up."

She managed to bob her head, but his fist slammed into her again.

"Not fast enough!" he said as her eye swelled shut. "Nod, bitch. Fast!"

She bobbed her head, sobbing.

"You want it? You want what I got?" He grabbed his crotch, then slapped her again. "You can't have it."

Considering, he took out the knife again. Her good eye wheeled, and her body began to buck. "Hold still or I'll cut you." He sawed off a hank of her hair. "I don't like the new do. I'm going to fix it." He hacked, sawed, sliced until her glossy chestnut hair was a choppy cap of tufts.

"Yeah, that's better. They're going to find you, naked, half bald and ugly. You earned it. You tried to make me your dog. You're the dog. Bark! Bark!"

He held the knife to her throat. "I said fucking bark."

She made sounds, and her eye pleaded with him.

"Good dog! You know who's in charge now."

He pinched her nose shut with his fingers, and she exploded under him.

"You never put that much energy into sex, you stupid bitch. Lousy lay."

When he released his grip, she sucked air in through her nose, her chest shuddering with it. Sobs shook her, a harsh gulping against the tape.

"What's that?" He turned his head, exaggerating the move. "I can't quite hear you? Do you want to say something to me? Do you want to tell me you're a bald, ugly dog, and beg for my forgiveness? You want to state your case now, bitch dog? Well, that seems fair."

He reached down for the corner of the tape, pulled back. "Oh, one more thing?" And laid the knife against her throat. "Scream and I'll slice your throat. Understand me?"

She nodded.

"Good dog." He reached for the tape again, leaned down so their faces were close. "Forgot, there's one more thing."

He reached back, pulled the length of cord from his back pocket. "I don't give a shit what you have to say."

He wrapped it around her neck, pulled, pulled.

And felt the thrill watching her eyes bulge, watching the red crack the white, feeling her body rage and ripple under his, hearing the gurgles.

The tighter he pulled, the more it built, burning inside him. Her bound feet drummed against the bed as she convulsed, her bloodied hands shook like an old woman's. And he yanked harder, groaning with pleasure, hips rocking as the sharp, uncontrollable sensation clawed through him, out of him.

When her eyes went fixed, the orgasm ripped through him. Huge, amazing, like nothing before experienced.

He choked out his own cry, gulped and

gasped for air until his body stopped vibrating.

Then he collapsed beside her, sated, stunned, and for the first time in his life, totally fulfilled.

"Jesus! Where have you been all my life?" He gave her thigh a little pat. "Thanks."

Now he had to shower, and dig out her hoarded tip money, scout out anything in this dump worth taking. But first, he had to see what she had in the kitchen.

Like a fat joint of zoner, killing gave him the serious munchies.

6

Thoughts weighed her down as Eve turned through the gates of home. Often — usually, in fact — after a long day that first sight of the gorgeous, castle-like house Roarke built smoothed things out. The way it rose, spread, jutted against the evening sky at the end of the long curve of road tended to lift weights. Reminded her she had a home. After a lifetime that had begun in nightmares, shifted to the misery of shuffling foster care and state control, and to, at long last, her own place in New York that had been primarily a space to catch some sleep between investigations, she had a real home.

But tonight, there was just too much weight.

It strained against her that a selfish asshole could elude her, even for a day. She needed to start fresh, go back to the beginning, and move through it all step-by-step. And without the distractions of an offer of a captaincy.

She needed to clear her head, look at it all from another angle.

She needed Roarke, she admitted. His ear, his eye, his canny brain.

She'd run it through for him, run it by him, bounce it off him, she determined as she braked at the front entrance. Maybe she'd missed something he'd see, or think of.

He'd help. That wasn't assumption, but fact. And as much home to her as the stone and glass they lived in.

She started to climb out, and Peabody's date night arrowed into her mind. And for Christ's sake, she didn't have time for that.

Didn't make time, she corrected, and slumped back.

He did. Roarke made time, and she couldn't claim he wasn't one of the busiest people on or off planet.

She hardly ever made time for the fussy stuff, and now that added one more weight. Even when she wasn't neck-deep in an investigation she just didn't think of it.

Now thinking of it stacked guilt on her head like boulders.

She couldn't manage a *date* night, just couldn't, but she should be able to put a nice meal together, with a few fancy touches.

And balance out his eye, ear, canny brain.

She shoved out of the car, bolted for the front door, and through.

And saw Summerset, looming in black, with the pudgy cat at his feet.

"I don't have time for witty repartee," she snapped.

"That's unfortunate."

"Is he home?"

"Not as yet."

"I need to put a meal together, on the roof terrace."

Summerset's eyebrows lifted. "There's nothing on the calendar."

"Just . . ." She waved that away as the cat padded over to ripple between her feet. "I can handle the setup, but tell me what he should eat — we should eat. And don't make it something I hate out of spite."

Even scarecrows could be amused, she noted.

"Very well. I'd start with the tomato soup with poached shrimp."

"Wait." She yanked out her PPC to note it down. "Go."

"Then move to a green salad with seasonal pears in a champagne vinaigrette. For the main, I'd suggest Lobster Thermidor."

"What the hell is that?"

"Delicious. You'll enjoy it. I'd serve it with a sauvignon blanc or champagne, and finish with a vanilla bean soufflé, brandy, and coffee."

"Okay. Got it." She raced for the stairs.

"Is that what you're wearing?"

"Shut up!"

She charged into the bedroom. Damn it, damn it, she wasn't wearing some fancy dress. It wasn't date-date. But she strode into the closet, and the cat danced at her heels as if they played a game.

She had enough clothes for a hundred normal people, she should be able to put one decent outfit together.

And she was damned if she'd ask Summerset to consult here.

She grabbed black pants. Black went with everything, didn't it? Then dug out a sweater — really soft — in a color that made her think of fall leaves, and with a sparkly band at the neck and hem. That way she didn't have to deal with more sparkles.

Boots were probably wrong, she imagined, but she would *not* put on skyscraper heels.

It surprised her to find a pair of black shoes with a sparkly wedge-type heel. Shouldn't surprise her, she thought as she veered into the quick change. She never knew what the closet fairy would stick in there next.

Given the circumstances, she slapped on some lip dye, some lash gunk, some face junk.

As good as he was going to get, she decided, and streaked for the elevator.

She leaped out, paused. She supposed she owed Summerset for the fact the sky roof was open to the deep indigo sky, and the internal heaters were spreading a comfortable warmth against the brisk November evening.

Now the rest was up to her.

Still carrying the dregs of the day's irritation, Roarke stepped into the foyer. It surprised him to find it empty — no Summerset, no cat — particularly on a day he'd have appreciated a bit of a welcome home.

He shrugged out of his topcoat, and in a habit he'd picked up from his wife, tossed it over the newel post on his way upstairs. An hour in the gym, he decided, pummeling something, then a quick swim. That should scrape the annoyance away. And if not, a very large drink might do the job.

But when he walked into the bedroom, he saw Eve's weapon, her badge on her dresser.

So the lieutenant was home, he thought. Maybe he could pull her away from her double murder — he followed the crime reports — talk her into a sparring match or that swim, better yet a good shag.

And *that* should take care of the dregs good and well.

In her home office, no doubt, he decided, pacing around her newest murder board or hunched over her computer. He imagined he was in for pizza and a great deal of coffee over the grisly details of her day.

He didn't mind it, not a bit, he thought as he set aside his briefcase, loosened his tie. Her work was nearly as fascinating to him as she was, and the part he played in it made him feel . . . satisfied, he concluded, often involved and excited, but primarily satisfied.

No one would have believed — including himself — that the Dublin street rat, the well-accomplished thief, the man of wealth and power with such dubious and shady beginnings could or would work on the side of the law. Even if his line marking the sides tended to curve and sway a bit.

But she'd changed him — no, more, he corrected. She'd *found* him. And had made all the difference.

So he'd have pizza in her office, listen, think, and lend a hand to his cop as she stood for her newest dead.

And the frustrations of his own day? Well, they paled, didn't they, against all the blood. To save time, steps, and to be sure, he stepped to the in-house board. "Where is Eve?"

Eve is currently on the roof terrace, east sector.

Odd, he thought. It wasn't the last place he'd expect, but it ranked high. Curious, he crossed to the elevator. "Roof terrace, east," he ordered.

He doubted she'd gone up there to take in the view or the fresh air. His wife did little without specific purpose — especially when a case was hot. Just how did all this play into her case? he wondered. Something to do with height perhaps, or the view did play in and she needed that perspective and the scope to find something. Or . . .

He stepped out into the flowers, candle-light, the soft warmth and sparkle of crystal, and his mind went momentarily and un-characteristically blank.

"Hey." She shot him a distracted look. "I've just about got it."

"Do you?" Bemused, and rapidly flipping through his mental calendar, he walked to her. "And what's all this?"

"It's dinner."

She'd surprised him like this once before, he recalled, and had been wearing a red dress meant to be peeled off. A little different, this, he thought if his sense of things was on target. But just as lovely.

"Are we celebrating?"

"No. Well, maybe sort of."

"You closed the case? The double homicide you caught this morning?"

"No. It's . . . there's stuff, but when I was thinking about the stuff, and how I wanted to bounce it all off you, I got this Peabody date night stuck in my brain."

"We're having a date with Peabody? I get two alluring women? Lucky me."

She spared him one quick glance through narrowed eyes. "You got me, and that's it, pal."

"Thank God for it." He cupped her face, leaned in for a soft, sweet kiss. "We're having a date?"

"Not exactly. I can't do the big *D* date thing where you shove all the stuff outside, but I thought I could pay you back a little for all the stuff. Nicer than pizza in my office."

He looked at her for such a long, still moment, she feared she'd screwed something up. Then he pulled her in, wrapped around

132

her, held tight. Tight.

"Thank you."

"It's not that big a thing."

"It is to me, and especially tonight."

"What's tonight?" Shit, did she forget something? She pulled back, focused fully on his face. No, something else. "Did you have a thing mess up in the Universe of Roarke?"

He smiled at her, tapped the dent in her chin. "You could say."

"What?"

"Not important, especially since I see we have champagne."

"No." She shifted before he could walk past her. "You take my stuff. I'll take yours."

He trailed a hand down her arm, over the soft sleeve of her sweater. "Marriage Rules?"

"That's right. What's the thing?"

"I had to fire three people this afternoon. I hate firing people."

"Why did you?"

"Basically for not doing what they're paid to do. I'll give some leeway there for a space. They could be having a rough patch, some personal problems, health problems. So some room, some time, a discussion can settle that down. But when the not doing what they're paid to do comes with carelessness, and worse, arrogance, there's no lee-way."

"So you fired them for being assholes."

He laughed, and felt some of those dregs slide away. "You could say just that."

"I know something about it," she said as he walked to the table she'd set — hope-fully well enough — to uncork the cham-pagne. "The guy responsible for the double homicide's an asshole who can't keep a job — arrogance, carelessness, and I think a warped sense of entitlement."

"It seems our stuff coincides." After the elegant and muffled pop of cork from bottle, he poured champagne into two tall flutes.

"Part of why you hate firing people is because it makes you feel like you made a mistake hiring them."

"And you know me well," he agreed. He handed her a flute, tapped his to hers.

"Did you?"

"Obviously, yes. But at the time they suited the position well, on all the levels. Over time, however, some can become complacent, lazy, and, yes, entitled."

It never paid, he strongly believed, to take a single thing — the good, the bad, the mediocre — for granted.

"And now these three people are out of

work," he added. "They won't have an easy time gaining equal employment as their references won't be stellar."

"And the other part you hate is now their lives are screwed up, and may stay that way at least for a while. It's a tough break, but you wear what you sew — if you know how to sew anyway."

It took him a moment, then he just laughed again — and there went the rest of the dregs. "That's reap what you sow — as in harvest what you plant."

"If you go around sewing something, you're going to have to wear it. So?" She lifted her shoulders.

"So," he repeated. "You're right. They sewed, or sowed, wore or reaped. And now they're out in a damn fallow field wearing something that fits ill. And apparently that settles my stuff, so thanks for that."

"No problem. Hungry?"

"I am now. What's for dinner, darling Eve?"

"We got this soup thing to start it off. Summerset picked the food, so you're safe there."

"I was fully prepared for pizza in your office." He skimmed a hand down her hair, then lightly over her cheek. "We're not ones who need or want to push our stuff outside, or not very often. We do well with it. We do well with it together."

"Good to hear, because I've got a big pile of stuff."

"Let's have some soup, and you can tell me about it."

"I'm doing the deal here." She gestured to a chair.

"What man doesn't like coming home to a hot meal prepared by his adoring wife?"

"Lap it up," she muttered, and pulled the silver warming covers.

"If it's all the same, I'll use a spoon. The reports I heard tell me you're looking for a man — middle twenties — who murdered his parents."

"It's more than that. He stabbed his mother over fifty times with a kitchen knife, beat his father to pieces — hours later — with a baseball bat."

"That's considerable rage." He studied her face carefully. "Were they abusive?"

"No, there's no indication there was anything like that. He's a fuckup. Flunked out of college, can't or won't hold a job longer than a few months, including the one his father arranged for him at the father's office. Decent work. I spoke with the supervisor there, some of the coworkers. The father's been with the company for a couple decades — hardworking, good guy, responsible. The son's none of the above. Same deal with other bosses I talked to."

"So a pattern of irresponsibility and failure."

"Yeah, on a personal level, too. Girlfriend — and from what I've been able to gather so far, the only woman he ever lived with, or had a relationship with for more than a couple weeks — booted him. He took the rent money, and her tip money savings — she's a waitress — and blew it and more in Vegas. He had to move back in with the parents, and again according to what I've learned, hasn't made any move toward finding a job. They'd decided to give him until December to get one, or get out."

He ate soup — warm, comforting with just a little bite — and considered. "He killed them because they wouldn't allow him to continue to feed off the parental tit?"

"That's summing it up. He stabbed the mother around lunchtime," Eve began, and took him through the time line, the financial transfers, the theft, and the selling.

"Cold bastard, and now he has cash. More than he's ever had at one time. It's unlikely he'll be careful with it. Besides being cold and vicious, he's young and stupid. I can put out an alert to all my hotels in the city."

"It's already done, and thanks. And fyi," Eve added, "you sure didn't make a mistake hiring Joleen Mortimer, or anyone else I dealt with at The Manor. She, especially, is a laser."

"I agree. In this case, the previous owners and her former manager were the arrogant ones. Their loss, my gain. I can run searches for accounts your man may open, and will, but it's more likely he'll keep the cash. It's tangible. He can touch it, gloat over it. I don't think you'll track him through deposits and transfers on this one, not with — what is it — about a hundred seventy-five thousand. He'll hoard, then he'll squander."

"It's not going to last him long." Eve rose to clear and set the next course. "The sale of the watches and pearls at Ursa's was a bonus — I doubt he'd expected that kind of a haul. And he'll net a few more hawking the other stuff, but he's living high.

"And by the way, since I know you'll be compelled to buy me shiny things for Christmas, you might try there. Ursa's, in the East Village. They're nice people."

"So noted. Did you see something you liked?"

"The owner. I wasn't focused on shiny things. Nobody likes him," she went on. "My man, Jerry, I mean. He's got three friends, and two of them are reasonably steady types — and both of those aren't as tight with him as they once were. The third's another asshole, so they suit each other."

She decided Summerset had called it well with the salad. If you had to eat green leafy things, this was the way to get them down.

"So he'd be most likely to reach out to the other asshole?"

"If any of them, yeah, maybe." And she'd need to give another good push there.

"I think between me and Peabody we scared them enough so they'll contact us. Wouldn't he want to show off? Especially to friends? Maybe head back to Vegas, try to offset his losses and the humiliation of them?"

"Did you run a probability?"

"Yeah. Seventy-two percent. That's high enough to up the alerts on transpo to Vegas, and to add them in to casinos in New York, Jersey. The thing is, he'd never gambled before that trip, so it's not in his usual pattern."

"Having more than a hundred seventy-five thousand at his disposal isn't pattern," Roarke pointed out.

"Yeah, so the alerts are out. I want to say I know him, and he's gotten this far by sheer luck. But I'm not sure about that. He's got some calculation mixed in there. Getting his hands on the money. That took some thought, some work, even some skill. Just like picking Ursa's for the watches. It was smart."

"What about the girlfriend? Like showing off for his friends, he might want to show off to her, prove to her — or really himself — what she threw away."

"Yeah, and I'm going to nail her down tomorrow. She must still be out." Eve glanced at her wrist unit, unaware Lori Nuccio lay dead while Jerry shoveled in a smorgasbord of food from her kitchen.

"You're worried you missed something," Roarke commented.

"I wonder if I did. There's nothing in this guy's history that so much as whispers about this kind of capacity for violence. He's got a couple a minor knuckle raps, and he may have — not confirmed yet — given the ex a slap or two. He didn't retaliate against the employers who gave him the axe, or the girlfriend who gave him the boot. He mouthed off a little, then walked."

"The sleeping beast?"

"Maybe. I'm going to talk to Mira about it. I think the mother was impulse. He snapped. The knife's right there, and she's complaining or advising or warning —

140

whatever. He picks up the knife, jabs her with it. And . . ."

She trailed off, picked up her champagne. "If you're comparing this to what you did, at eight, I'm going to be very annoyed with you."

He saw inside her, Eve knew. He saw fast and deep.

"I'm not, but I understand the moment, and what it can do. I was being raped, my arm broken, and I was in fear of my life, so when my fingers closed around that knife, I used it to stop the pain, to survive. He used it to strike out at someone who posed no physical threat, who provided him with a home, a family. But I know the moment, and it can go a couple of ways. Most people with a healthy control switch can and do lose it in that moment. The reaction would be, 'Holy shit, what did I do?' "

She took a slow sip, knowing it. Seeing it. "He, and those like him, react with a . . . a jubilant, 'Holy shit, look what I *can* do.' And the thrill, the revelation of that, however twisted, pushes them on."

"We both know those, yes. We've looked in their eyes."

"Too many of them," Eve agreed. "Still, even most of those won't do what he did. But in that moment, you can just lose your

141

mind. You don't stop, can't stop, whether it's the thrill or it's the fear driving you."

This is what she'd needed, she realized as she rose to clear again, and to serve the main. "All that blood, it's powerful, and it's horrible. With me, the shock, the pain, the blood, the reality of what I'd done sent me into a fugue state, right? That's what it was, just wandering around — outside alone for the first time in my life, my arm busted, and the pain from that and the last rape so overwhelming, I blocked it out. The pain, what happened, everything. And I kept blocking it, all that I could, most of my life.

"It was him or me, and I was eight and terrorized. I did what I had to do, but I'm still horrified to know I couldn't stop. *I* was switched off, and couldn't stop. Maybe he couldn't, or when we get him, his lawyer will try that one. But then he didn't run. And nearly everyone would. Just run, or try to cover it up. *Somebody broke in and killed my mother.* He didn't run because he wasn't horrified. He, I think, he embraced what he'd done, and so was able to wait — to plan and gather and work — until his father came home. Then he did it again."

"And still he didn't run."

"No." In her mind she brought back the

image of him on the bank security discs. Smug.

"I don't think there's something broken in him so much as dead. And maybe it was that moment, the moment when he picked up the knife and put it in her, that it died."

"Will that help you catch him?"

"Everything helps. I'll go back to the scene tomorrow, walk it through again. Tonight I'll do another reconstruct. And if you can do that search for accounts, it would cover it. He hasn't used his 'link, so he probably ditched it, bought another. He hasn't been stupid enough to use any debit or credit cards in his name or his parents, but the cash won't last forever. We've got his name and face plastered everywhere."

"You think he'll try to run now?"

"I don't see what else he can do. New York's too hot for him, and he has what he's always wanted. He's got money, and his parents can't bitch at him anymore."

"What about other family?"

"He's got the full complement of grandparents, and they've been notified. He's got an uncle on his father's side, an aunt on his mother's, and five cousins. They've all been notified. I can't guarantee they'd call it in if he contacts any of them, but it's tough to believe they'd help the man who killed their child, their sister, their brother."

"Blood ties run deep," Roarke commented.

"Yeah, maybe. I can't cover them all on what we've got. Some of them live in and around New York, some don't. All we can do there is keep in contact, keep pushing."

His hand brushed hers on the table. "You're worried he'll hurt someone else."

"I think if somebody gets in his way, or doesn't give him what he wants, yeah. If he goes looking for safe haven or more money, and doesn't get it, has the opportunity, he'd kill again. But . . ."

"But?"

"I just don't think he'll hit on family, or not until the money runs dry or the heat's too hot. He doesn't think of family, that's my gut feeling anyway. He thinks of obstacles to his happiness or success. People holding him back or giving him orders. If and when, I think the grandparents first. I think he'd consider them weaker, more apt to help him. The out-of-town set's coming into New York, and he doesn't have any way to know that. So he won't find them at home, not for the next few days."

"My observation's been much of police work is grunt work, drudgery, covering the same ground again and again, countless hours in interviews, writing or generating reports — and terrifying times of extreme risk, furious action, split-second decisions, and finite planning. You've been dealing primarily with the first today."

"They should give me a medal for that," she muttered. When he just smiled, poured more champagne, she shifted. "I'm getting one. A medal."

"That's lovely. Congratulations."

"It's a big one. I don't mean . . ." She held her hands out to indicate big size. "It's a big deal one. Medal of Honor. That's for —"

"I know what it's for, what it means." He reached for her hand, held it and her eyes. "There is no higher honor in your world. It's more than deserved, more than earned."

"They could keep the medal and give me a bigger budget."

He lifted her hand to his lips. "I'm so proud of you, and so amused at your discomfort in being recognized for your dedication and skill."

"Amused? Here's another funny for you. You're getting a medal, too."

He dropped her hand. "What? I'm a civilian, as you continually remind me."

"The Civilian Medal of Merit, and they don't give them out like candy, pal, especially to shady characters."

"I don't think it's appropriate."

She loved it, just loved when he turned all dignified.

"Oh, it is, and now I get to be *amused.* You're the one who started sticking his nose in, then his whole body. Now you're going to have to stand up there on Wednesday afternoon — fourteen hundred, so put that in your book — and take what you get. And I'm pretty damn proud of you, too, so suck it up."

"Aren't we a pair? Christ, the abuse I'll take over this by old mates. A bloody medal."

"The department values you, and it should. So we're having champagne and this really tasty lobster before I get back in gear." She took another drink. "And there's this other thing."

"More? More than double murders, assholes, and medals?"

"Yeah, more than that. Whitney called me in to tell me about the medals, and to ask me if I wanted captain."

"Eve!" This time his hand vised on hers. "That's called burying the lead, and burying it deep. Eve," he said again, and started to rise.

"I said I didn't."

"Sorry?" He sat again. "What?"

"I said I didn't want the bars."

"Are you gone in the head?"

She narrowed her eyes. "Is that Irish for stupid?"

"Crazy's more accurate." Baffled annoyance rode over his face. "Why in bloody hell wouldn't you want it? It's a major promotion, an accomplishment. I understand the discomfort over the medal. You see yourself as doing your job, and you neither need nor want some fancy piece pinned on you for it. But a captaincy? Christ Jesus, Eve, it's your career, it's what you are, more than that. And we both know he'd have offered it to you before this but for me."

"No, not because of you. Because of me. I made my choice. Whatever you think, it was *my* choice. I chose you, and if the brass played politics with that, that was their choice."

"Now they'll give me a medal, and they've opened a door for you. Why aren't you walking through it? Bloody dancing through it."

"No reason for you to be pissed about it."

"I'm not pissed so much as gobsmacked. Why did you turn it down?"

"I can't give up what I have," she said simply. "I'm not ready. Maybe I'll never be. I'm a cop. I have to be a cop."

"How do captain's bars change that?"

"They'd take me out of the field. Right now someone else would be looking for Jerry Reinhold, not me. They'd put distance and space between me and my men because I wouldn't be their direct supervisor. I'd spend more time, most of the time, in meetings, with paperwork, making administrative decisions, and only what I could eke out actually doing the job I'm good at."

She took a long breath when he said nothing. "I need to be a cop, a good cop, more than I need the rank. And I knew that today, without any question at all, when offered the bars."

When he still didn't speak, she shrugged. "I probably broke a Marriage Rule not talking with you about this first, but —"

"It's yours," he interrupted. "It's your work. I don't talk with you about the deals I make, what I buy, sell, develop."

"What you deal and wheel doesn't — usually anyway — put you on the line. I understand it would be easier on you if I took this."

"It would, if you're meaning I'd worry less. But I married you. I made a choice, and like you, I took you for what you are, not what I'd turn you into."

"I wanted it once, a lot. Maybe even too

much. I wanted it when the job wasn't just what I did or who I am, but all I had. That's not true anymore, and I'm a better cop because of that. I need to catch the bad guys, Roarke. And I need to walk into the bullpen every day and see the team I've helped make working to do the same. When I weigh that against the bars, there's no contest."

"All right then."

"And that's it?"

"Lieutenant, I can't argue with truth. I'll say I'm happy, very, they offered it to you. You can say it was your choice, and that's true enough as well. But being with me was a block to this, and now it's not. So I'll take the medal, and suck it up."

"Okay." She let out a long breath. "I love you."

"And I love you."

"But I can't eat the soufflé thing on tap for dessert."

"Soufflé? Quite the five-star meal. Why don't we have a bit of a break from it, and we can enjoy it a little later. In your office while we work."

She grinned at him. "I made a really good choice."

"Oh, that you did." He took her hand, pulled her with him to her feet. "You'd be a good captain."

"Maybe. Down the road. Yeah, okay. I would."

She made him smile. "Whatever your rank, darling Eve, you'll always be my cop."

"That works for me."

"Let's go down then."

"I've got to deal with all this stuff."

"Summerset will see to it."

"Even better. I just want to stop off, get into work clothes."

He smiled to himself. "We'll just detour to the bedroom first then. I wouldn't mind getting out of this suit."

7

Eve toed off her shoes as soon as she stepped into the bedroom. She considered bare feet an indulgence reserved for private areas of home or the beach.

"Maybe just setting up a board here, fresh, will shake something loose."

"Could be."

She pulled off her sweater while Roarke shed his jacket and tie.

"According to the time line, he stowed the two suitcases after he left the shuttle station. The hotel transpo dropped him there — following his cover he was traveling to Miami. Then he doubled back, but I haven't been able to track down his transpo from the station. Maybe he stayed on foot, but it's more likely he caught a cab or bus."

"Might he have secured the suitcases at the station, with the plan to go back after he collected the money, then take a shuttle to some other destination?"

"It doesn't fly for me. He had all the valuables to sell, and we know he started that process after the banking. So he doubled back, had another hole to crawl into, stowed the suitcases there while he hit the banks so he didn't have to drag them around. I'd like his transportation method back to the banks, just to have a clearer picture."

She wriggled out of the pants and, standing in her underwear, started to open a drawer for a T-shirt and jeans.

"Bus is smarter, but —"

He cut her off by spinning her around, yanking her in, and taking her mouth. Hot, lusty, possessive, and lightly edged with humor.

When she managed to grab a breath, she attempted a quick shove. "Hey."

He just took her mouth again, spun her again — twice and toward the bed. She considered putting up a fight, for form's sake, but just wriggled back enough to scowl at him. "I'm working."

"Not yet, and you're mostly naked. Such a fine look on you, one of my favorites."

"Then why is that closet full of clothes?"

"Because being an understanding sort, I appreciate your insistence on being fully dressed in public."

He gripped her hips, boosted her up so he could carry her onto the platform where the bed spread like a blue lagoon. Then he tipped so they fell back on it with her pinned under him.

"Just because we postponed soufflé doesn't mean we can't enjoy a bite of dessert now."

To prove it, he closed his teeth over her jaw.

"And you're what I've a taste for."

"Sex, sex, sex."

"If you insist."

His mouth claimed hers again, muffling the laugh she'd tried to hold back. What the hell, she thought. He was mostly naked, too. She grabbed his exceptional ass, gave it a hard squeeze. "You better make it good."

"I'm always up for a challenge."

"You're always up." And to prove *that,* she slid her hands around, between them, and found him. The next hard squeeze brought on a moan, had him shifting his teeth to her throat.

How quickly he could make her need, each time, every time. No matter how familiar, this sweep of feelings always struck as new. And overwhelming.

The weight of his body, the shape of it, the demands of his clever mouth and skilled hands never failed to make her want and want, and revel in knowing she could have.

She let the hunger, and the greed with it, the whippy storm of sensations — all the sudden heat, the wonderful aches — invade. She let them conquer, and gathering them turned them back to him.

She gave and she took, everything he needed to have, everything he wanted to give in return. Wrapped around him, possessing as he possessed, she met every demand, made her own.

He knew the rhythms of her body, and all the secret places to exploit, to seduce, to inflame. Yet she remained a fascination and glorious surprise to him, a constant gift for body and soul.

The way her hands wound through and gripped his hair when he fed from her breast aroused as much as that firm curve, that silky skin. Subtle as the beat of butterfly wings, her quick, rippling tremors, the catch of her breath at his touch added a keen and lusty edge.

The arch of her body — so lithe, so ready — the pounding drum of her heartbeat under his lips told him she needed, wanted, as urgently now as he.

He pleased himself, riding his hands along skin, smooth and warm over tough and disciplined muscle. Delighted himself with the long, supple length of her, his warrior, his wife.

And when his mouth came back to hers, when hers clung to his, fever-hot, that pleasure, that delight spiked beyond reason.

Wet and hot he found her, and drove her up and up, swallowing her gasps and cries like a man starving. When she broke beneath him, he didn't relent, couldn't, stroking those fires until she thrashed under him.

"Now. Now. Inside me. You."

When she bowed up, quivering, he thrust inside her, hard and deep.

Now, she thought again, her breath sobbing, her hands groping. The quaking shook down to her core, shuddered toward her heart as they rode each other. The mating, fast and furious, ruled them both, carved all else away.

Again she thought, you. You. And when she broke this time, he broke with her.

She lay absorbing the aftershocks of her body, and of his. She remembered she'd thought, before Roarke, sex was a basic — sometimes complicated — method of release.

After Roarke? That didn't start to cover it.

Even now, after fast, crazed sex, his lips brushed lightly over her shoulder. Just a simple and incredible sign of affection.

Those moments, she realized, meant the world to her.

In answer, she trailed her fingers down his back. Then, because they were who they were, pinched his ass, sharply.

"Bloody hell," he muttered.

"Off, pal. You had your bite of dessert. Big, greedy bite."

"You did as well."

"Yeah. Not bad." She grinned at him when he lifted his head, then tugged on his hair, nipped up for a quick kiss. "Not bad at all. Now I've got to go work it off."

"Fair enough." He shifted, then pulled her up to sit, stroked a hand over her hair. "Thank you for a lovely and thoughtful dinner."

"And dessert."

"And dessert."

"How many pizzas do you figure it offsets?"

"Perhaps I can generate a pie chart," he said as they rolled out of bed.

"Ha-ha. Pie chart. You're a funny guy. I want a quick shower after that bout."

"An excellent idea." He only sighed when she narrowed her eyes at him. "Sex, sex, sex. Do you think of nothing else?"

"Yeah, you're a funny guy."

"And a well satisfied one, so you'll have to settle for only the shower." After giving her a light pat on the ass, he strolled into the bath ahead of her.

She was in and out of the jets within five, and tossed on clothes after a quick spin in the drying tube. Every bit as nimble as she, he walked with her to her office.

"Board first, I imagine."

"Yeah, I want the visual."

"While you're at that, I'll start the search for possible accounts. He's no financial genius or comp geek from what you've said, but there's plenty of suggestions and instructions for burying funds right on the Internet." He smiled at her. "And those are child's play to dig out again."

"Go ahead and play."

She set up her board, changing the pattern so she had a different method than the one in her office. She added the time line, the reports, paced around it. Added more.

Then she focused on Jerry Reinhold.

"Who are you, really?" she asked aloud.

Talk to the friends again? she wondered. Give that a harder push? He didn't strike her as someone who'd live in a vacuum. Didn't he need someone to bitch to, to brag to?

More, she thought as she circled the board

again, he'd never accomplished anything real in his life. He might see that differently, and likely considered it everyone else's fault, but from the steps, the stages, the images of him leaving the building, in the bank, in the jewelry shop, he felt very accomplished now.

Wouldn't he want some kudos?

From strangers, she considered. How did you brag to your pals you killed your parents, brutally, and were hiding from the police? Maybe a pickup at a bar, she considered, or maybe hire a fancy licensed companion for the night.

"Couldn't tell them you're a killer," she murmured. "But you could brag about making some killer deal, being some big shot. Hitting some jackpot. That seems your style."

The LC seemed more in line. Sure you had to pay, but that put you in charge. You were already the big deal.

Would he want or need sex? No evidence or indication he'd pursued that area since the breakup, but sex was another kind of celebration, another way for a man to prove his potency.

Maybe she'd consult on that with Charles Monroe, friend, former LC, and current sex therapist.

She checked the time, decided it was still

plenty early enough, and crossed to her desk.

Her 'link signaled even as she reached for it. She noted Peabody on the readout, answered.

"Yeah, what?"

"Hey. I wanted to update you. McNab and I went by Nuccio's place on the way home. I sent you a quick report."

"I haven't gotten to my incomings yet." Not with semi-date dinners and dessert sex.

"Yeah, I saw you hadn't picked it up. She wasn't home yet, and the neighbor — Crabtree — came out. She's keeping an eye out for her, even left a note on Nuccio's door when she went out to run a few errands. Took it off when she came back."

"Okay, we'll hit her tomorrow."

On the 'link screen, Peabody's face mirrored concern. "The thing is, McNab had this idea how we might track down her shopping buddy. Getting the names of her coworkers, mining them, spreading out from them."

"If that's what you want to do."

"Did do," Peabody told her. "It seemed worth a shot, just to nail her down. And we hit. She went out with a Kasey Rider. I just finished talking to her — to Rider. They were going to make a night of it, hit some clubs, but one of their mutual friends tagged Kasey with the news about Reinhold."

"So Nuccio knows." A thread of concern wove its way into Eve.

"Yeah. Major freakout — denial, disbelief, then depression from Nuccio. They cut the night short, and Rider insisted on taking a cab with Nuccio to her apartment, dropped her off at about six-forty, which means Mc-Nab and I didn't miss her by much. I got her new 'link number, but she's not answering. And I figured since you didn't update the file yet, she hasn't contacted you either."

"No, she hasn't." And she'd had over three hours to come through. "Maybe the neighbor didn't hear her come in."

"I don't think so, Dallas. She was a hawkeye."

"Okay. She probably doesn't want to deal with cops tonight." Eve turned back to the board, shifted, evaluated her own gut. "But she's going to. I'm going to go on down there now."

"I'm closer if you want me and McNab to go."

"No, I'll do it. If she's going to be squeezed into dealing with a cop, let's make it rank. I'll let you know. Thanks for the heads-up."

"No problem, but, Dallas, it just doesn't

feel right."

"I don't see her letting him in, or him getting by the hawkeye neighbor if he tried. I'll get back to you."

But, no, she thought as she clicked off. It didn't feel right.

She strode directly to Roarke's office where he manned his desk, his hair tied back in work mode. "I've got to go downtown."

"To Central?"

"No, to the ex-girlfriend's. Word is she's been home for about three hours, and hasn't contacted me or Peabody. She's either avoiding that, or something's wrong. I want to check."

"Well then, I'm with you." He gave his computer the order to continue the search on auto, rose.

"I need to get my weapon and badge."

"And boots," he added, gesturing to her bare feet.

Armed and shod, she let him take the wheel, particularly since he'd called around some sleek, sexy two-seater.

"It's new," he told her. "I haven't really had it out for a good run as yet."

It smelled like leather — a weakness of hers. And the dash held enough gauges to outfit an off-planet shuttle.

"How many of these do you have?"

"One more now," he said, and all but flew to the gates and through.

"I didn't say we were going in hot."

"It's good to take her through her paces." He zipped to vertical, soared over a snake of traffic. "And I've a cop with me should the locals object. You're worried," he added.

"She's probably just playing mole."

"Ostrich, but it comes to the same. Then why are you worried?"

"She dumped him, kicked him out — after he stole from her, and reportedly gave her a couple slaps. But she doesn't take the opportunity to talk to the cops when she finds out he's committed double murder? I got the sense she was pretty sensible, responsible, and her neighbor would've pushed it. So I don't like it."

"Would she have let him in?"

"Don't see it." In her mind, Eve turned it over, around, inside out. "No, I just don't see it. And a friend dropped her off in a cab, watched her go inside. The neighbor would've pounced the minute she got up there, so I'm probably wasting time. I could interview her tomorrow."

"I trust your instincts." He punched it.

"Or you're looking to break the land and

162

air records." She liked speed, but liked it more when she was at the wheel. But she didn't tell him to slow down, and felt some relief when he oiled the car into a tiny street-level space less than half a block from the entrance to the building.

She scanned the street as she stepped onto the sidewalk. Too early for troublemakers, in this kind of neighborhood, she judged. But the shiny red toy on the curb could bring them out.

"That's sitting there saying: Please, steal me."

"It has a sadistic streak, so as it says that, it's aware it's fully shielded and armed."

"Good thing." She walked to the entrance, started to buzz Nuccio's apartment, changed her mind.

"Don't want her to know you're on your way up?" Roarke asked when she used her master for access.

"Not exactly."

"You are worried."

"Bad feeling's sticking. Let's take the stairs." Her fingers danced lightly over her weapon as they climbed. "Are you shielded and armed like your latest toy?"

"Always."

She could hear the throbs from entertainment screens, and someone's bright laughter

163

before a door cut it to a muffle.

She nodded at Nuccio's door, stepped to it, pressed the buzzer.

The locks remained engaged; the peep remained shielded.

She buzzed twice more, then banged on the door with the side of her fist. "Lori Nuccio, this is the NYPSD. We need to speak to you."

The door stayed shut; the one across the hall opened. "You're back."

"Yeah. Ms. Crabtree, do you know if Ms. Nuccio's in?"

"Yeah, she got home about quarter to seven. Thereabouts anyway. I gave her your card."

Her gaze shifted over to Roarke as she spoke, and Eve saw the look in Crabtree's eyes she'd seen in a variety of women's eyes when they got an up-close load of him. She thought of it as a kind of ocular sigh.

"Anyway. I figured you'd come by before this or wait until tomorrow."

"She didn't contact me."

"Damn it." Crabtree's gaze zipped back to Eve. "She said she would. She was pretty upset, wouldn't let me fix her tea or anything. Just wanted to be alone and quiet, she said. I guess she needs to brood some."

"She's not answering."

"I didn't hear her go out. The elevator makes a racket, but she could've taken the stairs. She didn't look like she wanted to do anything but hunker down. Maybe she took a sleeping pill."

"I'm going to access this apartment. I don't have a warrant, but —"

"Wait, wait. I don't think that's right. She wouldn't like that."

Then she should've contacted me, Eve thought.

"I'm concerned for her welfare. I'm accessing it." Eve nodded at Roarke, then shifted to block Crabtree's objections — and view — while he picked the locks.

"She's just hunkered down," Crabtree insisted. "You can't just walk into her place like this. It's not right."

"Then you can file a complaint."

"Done," Roarke murmured.

Eve turned. "Record on." Though her fingers itched for her weapon, she simply opened the door, called out.

"Lori Nuccio, this is the NYPSD. We're entering this apartment."

She barely crossed the threshold when she smelled it — blood and death.

Even as she cleared her weapon, Roarke did the same with his own. "Lights, on full!" she ordered. "You, stay back," she snapped at Crabtree. "Stay back."

She swung left first, then straight ahead. And she could see the death on the bed behind the colorful beaded curtain. "Clear it," she ordered, moving fast through a space small enough to see almost every corner.

And behind her Crabtree let out a choked scream.

"I need you to stay back. I need you to go inside your apartment."

"But — but —"

"Roarke."

"Ms. Crabtree, you need to come with me now."

She was weeping as he drew her out, and leaning against him when he closed the door behind them.

Eve holstered her weapon, moved to the curtain.

More than rage here. This was payback, too, and he had taken some time with it. Rage, revenge, a need to humiliate, to engender fear.

No, not in a vacuum, she thought. Not an LC or a pickup at a bar. He'd found just who he'd wanted to brag to, show off to.

"Victim is Caucasian female, early twenties, reddish hair, blue eyes. She's been bound, ankles and wrists with cord, more cord wound around her torso. She's gagged with tape. Her clothes have been removed except for shoes. They're new — soles are unscuffed. Facial bruises, cuts indicate blows, more bruising on the abdomen, along ribs most likely from more blows. Blood around the cord evidence of struggle. Her hair's been chopped off. A lot of hair scattered on the bed, the floor. Cord around vic's neck evidence of strangulation. He tied it in a nice fucking bow."

She recorded the room, the ruined clothes, waiting, knowing Roarke would bring her field kit. And waiting, contacted Peabody.

"He got to her."

"What? Shit? What?"

"I'm standing in Nuccio's apartment looking at her body. Get here, and call it in."

"On my way. Damn it, Dallas."

"Yeah."

Clicking off, she stepped back, studied the apartment. She saw the debris of food, containers, bottles on a tiny table, more littering the kitchen counter.

No comp again, she noted. Easiest thing in the world to liquidate.

She walked back to the door, studied the locks. No sign of forced entry, as Roarke never left any. And no sign of any recent lock change she could see. They'd check on that.

Did he give back his keys? What kind of idiot didn't demand the return of keys at a breakup. But he might've copied them. Had she been so trusting or naive she hadn't considered that?

Maybe. Maybe.

Roarke came back in, handed her the field kit.

"I don't think she let him in. I don't see her doing that. And if he came banging on the door, or trying to wheedle his way in, Crabtree would have heard it."

"I'll see if the locks have been compromised."

"Probably not. I don't think he's got those skills. But he could've had copies of her keys. He copied them when things got iffy between them — just a backup. He came in when she was out, nice and quiet. Maybe even — probably — when the neighbor was out. Maybe watched the building awhile. But he came in, and he waited for her. He had what he wanted to use. The cord, the tape. Not impulse or crazy rage, not on this."

She opened the kit, took out the Seal-It.

"You couldn't have stopped it."

"You can always stop it. Go left instead of

right, forward instead of back, move ten minutes sooner or later. I didn't stop him. And I didn't see this in him. Not this calculation, not this need. He made her suffer."

She handed him the Seal-It, and took the kit through the colorful curtains.

She stepped to the bed, took out her Identi-pad first.

"Victim is identified as Lori Nuccio of this address. Age twenty-three. Lists her hair as brown. She must've changed it, not corrected the data as yet." She leaned close. "A little dried blood." Carefully, she tipped the head to the side. "Back of the head. He was waiting, and he struck her from behind, knocked her down, out. It gave him time to tie her up, gag her. Fucking coward."

She picked up a broken capsule with tweezers, sniffed.

"To wake her up," she said, and as Roarke offered an evidence bag, dropped it in. "You could go through her bag there, see if he took her wallet, check for her keys, her 'link."

Saying nothing, he picked up the handbag on the floor.

"The cord's tight," Eve said. "It cut into her. He wanted that, wanted to give her pain as well as fear."

"No wallet," he said. "No 'link or note-book, no PPC. Her key's here."

"Took whatever money she had in there, electronics. Her ankles are tied together, no visible bruising on her thighs. I don't think he raped her. He wasn't interested, or he can't get it up. No, wasn't interested," she decided, trying to see inside him.

"If he'd thought about it, he'd have used something to rape her with. It just didn't occur to him. He's not especially sexual or doesn't see rape or sex as a weapon of power. Not yet."

"Why remove her clothing?"

"To humiliate, to terrify. She's completely vulnerable. He whacked her hair for the same reason. It dehumanizes her."

Make her nothing, Eve thought. She knew the type who wanted to make someone nothing. Her father had been the same.

"He punched her, hard, more than once — in the face, in the stomach. It's more personal than his parents. Or maybe he just had more time and space. Experimenting?

"She'd been shopping. So he dumped the new stuff, destroyed it."

With her gauge she measured time of death. "Nineteen-fifty-five. He took just over an hour with her. Risky, but he enjoyed it so much. Little cut here on her throat.

170

Maybe he had a knife. Threatened her, scared her, but he didn't really cut her. Strangulation's more personal, and you get to watch them suffer and die, face-to-face."

"She's very young," Roarke said quietly.

"She's as old as she'll ever be."

A cruel statement, Roarke thought, unless you knew his cop and heard the bitter anger under the words.

"No jewelry," Eve added. "I bet she was wearing some. Out with a girl pal, yeah, she had some on. He took it, whether it's worth anything or not. She doesn't get to keep it. Kick me out, bitch? You're going to pay for that. Tell me to get a job, tell me to get the hell out? Fuck you."

"Why the shoes?"

"Sexy. It's a porn thing, right? Naked woman in high, sexy heels. Kind of slutty?"

"Hmmm."

"She bought them today probably. Pissed him off. She's so goddamn worried about the rent, about money, she whines about him blowing off some steam with his friends in Vegas. But she goes out, spends Christ knows on all this crap. Selfish bitch."

She paused, just for a moment, just one brief moment as that bitter anger Roarke heard wanted to spew. And it couldn't be allowed.

"The shoes make her look cheap, like she's asking for it. He's not going to give it to her. But when we find her, she's going to look cheap and used, and her hair — she had that done today, I think — new color and style from her ID shot. Now it's ruined and hacked. Bruised right nipple. Pinched it probably. Humiliate, humiliate. You humiliated me, now it's your turn."

She examined the hands as she spoke, moved down the body checking for more wounds, anything left behind.

"He tells her what he did to his parents. She's the first one he's been able to talk to about it, brag to. She's safe because he's going to kill her, but he gets to crow about what he's done, how he's got a big pile of money, and she's got nothing. She is nothing."

Eve stepped out to examine the rest of the crime scene.

Roarke stayed where he was a moment longer. You're not nothing, he thought. She's standing for you now, and she won't stop. You're hers now, so you matter.

He wished he could cover her, but knew better.

Instead, he went on to do what he could to help until Peabody arrived.

8

Eve studied the skinny bathroom, the still-damp towels on the floor, the pair of black boxers tossed in the corner.

"He got off on it. Probably while he strangled her. Didn't rape her, but killing her, watching her die, *feeling* all that, popped his fucking cork. Surprised him, I bet. Wasn't expecting the sexual side benefit, so he came in his pants. Doesn't give enough of a shit to take them, just leaves them, leaves the towels after he cleans himself up."

She met Roarke's eyes in the mirror over the sink. "He's a child — throwing stuff on the floor, and I'm betting those boxers are new, something he just bought, but he discards them. More, he doesn't care about the DNA. It's fine that we know he killed her. He wants credit for what he managed to do."

She started to mark the towels and boxers

for the sweepers.

"I'll do that," Roarke told her.

"I misjudged him."

"Why do you say that?"

"I thought he had what he wanted. But killing his parents, taking everything he could from them, it showed him what he could do, what he could have. Now he wants more."

She stepped out, turned when Peabody came in, McNab right behind her.

"Uniforms on the way to secure," Peabody began. She paused, looked through the opening where Roarke had tied the beads up and back. "Jesus, he messed her up."

"I've got this. We need to alert everyone he might have a grudge against. His friends, former employers, coworkers, his grandparents."

"Do you think he'll try for one of them?"

"I didn't think he'd try for the ex-girlfriend," Eve said flatly. "I was wrong; she's dead. Impress he's killed again, but don't ID the vic. I want all of them secured."

"I'm all over it."

"I can check her electronics," McNab offered.

"He took her comp and 'link. No door security or cams, no house 'link, so she must've only used a pocket. I haven't looked for any other electronics yet. I find any, I'll pass them to you."

"I can knock on doors for now."

He wore a long, and she bet billowy, orange coat over cherry red pants and a many-color striped tee. She saw the cop under it, but most wouldn't. "That would save time, thanks, but for Christ's sake show your badge so they don't take you for an escapee from the circus."

He grinned at her, then took it out of one of a multitude of pockets, hooked it on the neck of his shirt before he went out.

"No one tampered with the locks before me," Roarke reminded her.

"So he had keys, or made copies. She kept her tips, saved them. She's had some time to start stockpiling more since he wiped her out. I didn't see anything out in plain sight. Maybe she hides them."

"I'll have a look."

"Appreciate it. I need to —"

"Uniforms heading up," Peabody informed her, sticking her head in the door.

"Have one of them sit on Crabtree, get her statement. I want to know exactly when she left the building, where she went, when she came back. As close as she can nail it."

"Done."

"I want to talk to Mira. Now," Eve said to

Roarke. "I need a better handle on this guy, and I need it before he decides to kill anybody else." She turned to the uniform waiting in the doorway.

"Detective McNab started the knock-on-doors. Coordinate with him. Get the photo of the suspect from Detective Peabody. I want the building covered, then hit the street and cover the block. I want to talk to anybody who saw him."

She pulled out her 'link, moved off to a corner, and tagged Mira.

"Dr. Mira, I'm sorry to disturb you at home."

"It's fine, Eve. Do you need to change our consult time for tomorrow?"

"Yeah, I need it now. He got to the ex-girlfriend."

"I see."

"Indications are he gained access to her apartment while she was out, lay in wait. He brought tools with him — tape, cord, a knife." Eve began to run through the basics.

"I'd like to see the body, the scene."

"I've recorded it. I can send it to you now."

"No, I think it would be better if I came to you."

Weird, Eve thought, and foolish, this initial knee-jerk reluctance to have Mira see, firsthand, the death, the blood, the ugliness of it. Mira hadn't reached her level by being squeamish or needing to be shielded.

"It would help, but —"

"I have the address from your report. I'll be there shortly."

"Thanks. I'll have you cleared through."

She pocketed her 'link as she went to the door and ordered the uniform securing the apartment to clear Dr. Mira. When she turned back, she caught Roarke's glance.

"I'll wager she's seen worse," he said.

"Yeah. There's always worse."

"There's an empty jar here." He held up a pale blue jar with some sort of flower embossed on it. "Just tossed among the rubble I imagine was his doing in the kitchen. I'd say he cleaned her out again, and ate and drank his way through her stock."

She stepped over to the kitchen, programmed the tiny AutoChef for its log. "Yeah. Had some pizza nibs about fifteen minutes after TOD. Swarmed through her cupboards — soy chips, cheesy twists, empty wine bottle, empty Coke tube. Snack food. Got the hungries on after he killed her."

She went back in her head to the first crime scene. "Same deal at his parents' apartment. He grazed through the food. Ate his way through The Manor, too, when he stayed there. Killing sharpens his appetite."

"If he keeps it up, you'll be rolling him into a cell."

That made her smile a little. "He emptied out her tips, took her wallet, her 'link, poked around for whatever else he could find of use, packed up, cleaned himself up, then walked right out with a goddamn spring in his step."

She held up a hand as the first of the sweepers arrived.

"Stay out of the bedroom and away from the body for now." Moving over, she gave them more detailed instructions, let them by.

"I contacted everyone." Peabody edged back in the room. "Golde's heading over to his parents. He freaked, and now he's afraid Reinhold might go after them. I caught Asshole Joe at some club. He did seem moderately surprised, but not especially upset or uneasy."

"He lives up to his name."

"Oh yeah. I also contacted Dave Hildebran, former employers and supervisors from this past year. I tagged Kasey Rider, too. I thought maybe Reinhold knew her, knew she was tight with the vic, and might want to pay her a visit."

178

"That's good thinking."

"She's a wreck, Dallas. I went ahead, called in a grief counselor and a female officer. We'll probably need to talk to her at some point, but she'll feel safer in the meantime."

"Good."

"She's been trying the vic on the new 'link since McNab and I tracked her down, and says it just bounced to v-mail."

"He took it. We haven't found it on scene, haven't heard it signal. Brand-new 'link. He figured he'd get a few extra bucks out of it."

"I'll add it to the alert. McNab's got a wit on the ground floor. He saw the suspect come in. He doesn't know him or the vic, but he's seen them, given them the nod. Being used to seeing him and not knowing he wasn't supposed to be here, the wit just gave him the nod, and went on into his own place."

"Time?"

"He saw Reinhold come in about five, take the stairs. He didn't see him go out again. Crabtree said she'd gone out to run some errands about that time, and was back here by about quarter after."

"No coincidence. He'd been watching the building, working out how to get in and up without anyone who knew about the breakup spotting him. Or maybe he was just watching for the vic, then took the opportunity to slither in when Crabtree left."

"Fifteen-minute window," Peabody commented. "He hit some luck on that."

And we didn't, Eve thought. "I want the uniforms to check out any place across the street or close enough where he could've waited it out. Relay that, talk to the wit again. Mira's coming in, and I need to be here when she gets here."

"Coming in here?" Peabody glanced toward the body, winced.

For whatever reason it made Eve feel less foolish to know Peabody had the same reaction she'd had herself. "She's seen DBs before."

"Yeah. I'll relay to the uniforms and go talk to the wit."

"No 'link on the premises, as you thought." Roarke stepped up beside her. "I ran a quick check on her financials to see where she used her cards today, so you can follow her steps. I sent the list to you."

"I can use that. Did he try any siphoning that you can see?"

"No, not as yet. But he may as he has her comp. EDD can watch for that easily enough."

"Maybe we'll catch a break and he'll be

just that stupid."

"You don't think so."

"No, I don't. I have to go into Central when I'm done here. You should go home, get some sleep."

"I'll see what pieces I can pick at around here, and leave when you do. I've sent for your vehicle so it'll be here for you when you're ready."

"You're pretty handy."

"Just consider it all part of our non-date date night."

She managed a smile that faded when she spotted Mira.

"Thanks for coming down."

"It wasn't a problem. Roarke."

Apparently Mira didn't consider the cheek kiss she and Roarke exchanged before he helped her off with her coat unprofessional behavior at a crime scene.

Mira wasn't in one of her pretty, stylish suits and ankle-breakers. Instead she wore slim dark pants with a steel-blue sweater and short gray boots that looked soft as melting butter.

Her mink brown hair fluffed around her attractive face, and her lovely blue eyes stayed cool and assessing as they scanned the scene.

"I saw Peabody downstairs and she helped

me seal up. Am I cleared to examine the body?"

"Yeah, you're clear."

Eve went with her, rattling off basic information. Age, name, TOD, COD. "I haven't found whatever he used to knock her out. He may have taken it with him, may have brought it with him. He likes a baseball bat, and the injury may indicate that. Morris will know."

"Yes, I'm sure. He brought the tape, the cord, you said."

"Yeah, he prepped for it."

"Planned rather than impulse. More like his father than his mother. But different than that, too. He didn't just want to kill her, destroy her. He wanted to hurt her, terrorize her, humiliate her. And I imagine you've concluded the same."

"Yeah, but it's good to have the opinion. Cutting her hair this way. There's a meanness there, a small-minded one, from one who understands what a woman's hair means to her."

"Yes. I agree."

"I'm pretty sure she'd just gotten it done, changed the color and style."

"Ah, even more so. She isn't allowed to look attractive. I see no overt signs of sexual abuse — but for this bruise on her right nipple."

"He came in his pants, left his boxers in the bathroom after he cleaned up."

Mira nodded. "The killing aroused him, or the torture. Both would have. He left evidence of that, as well as his DNA behind. He wants you to know he's a man — not gender, but a man. You understand me?"

"Okay, yeah."

"He struck her, primarily the face. To hurt her, to mark her, to feel the power of it. Shopping bags. She'd been shopping?"

"Yeah. I figure he dumped the stuff out, tore it up."

"She can't have anything, and he'd have done that before he killed her. Hurting her again. New shoes . . . wearing them so she looks pornographic perhaps."

"That's my take.

"The strangulation, face-to-face. That's intimacy. The bow he's tied there, that's small-minded again, mean again. Eve, I think he took some of her hair."

"Why do you think that?"

"I don't want to touch anything, but you see the length of some of these hanks he cut off? I think there should be more hair. Your sweepers will confirm that if I'm right."

"So he took something of her, a trophy. I

183

didn't see anything like that at the first scene. Maybe I missed it."

"I doubt it. She meant more to him than they did. They were just in the way, an annoyance, and dead a means to an end."

"That's how I saw it," Eve agreed.

"She was more important than that. He slept with her in this bed, had sex with her in this bed. And she denied him, rejected him, sent him, like a little boy, back to his parents. And she shops for new things, gets new hair? No, that would never do.

"So young," Mira said quietly, and moved back to the living room.

"If you're done in there, I want to let the sweepers get started, and bring the morgue team in."

"Yes, I've seen enough there. Did he do this?" She gestured to the little kitchen area.

"Yeah, he ate after. At least some of it after. He used the AutoChef after TOD." Eve signaled the sweepers.

"Junk food. Fun food. Party food. His little celebration, all the more enjoyable as she's dead so close by. Did he take anything else?"

"Her wallet, her tip money, her comp, her new 'link. That's all I'm sure of for now. Probably some jewelry. I think, out shopping with a girl pal, getting new hair and stuff, she'd've had on some earrings, maybe a couple of other pieces."

"I agree. She's a young woman, a waitress, so it's doubtful unless she had a family piece, she had anything particularly valuable."

Watching Mira wander, Eve felt it build up. "I screwed up."

Calm and assessing, Mira looked back. "Why do you think that?"

"I never figured he'd go after anyone else — and not this fast — unless in flight or for survival, or possibly if they refused to help him. But I never saw this."

"I don't know how you could have or why you would have. Coming here, doing this? It's risky and it's calculated. His other killings weren't. They were, first, impulse, then opportunity. Even with that, you tried to reach her, several times. Circumstances prevented it."

"I had the wrong handle on him. He'd never shown particularly violent behavior before, or ambition or calculation. Killing his mother, that was impulse, then blind rage."

"Yes."

"Then his father, hours later. Rage again, but some glee in there, and the cold-blooded ability to stay in that apartment, first waiting for his father, making plans, then with both of them dead by his hand while he completed the plans. He ate, slept, plotted, with their bodies only a few feet away."

"He felt nothing," Mira said. "He's a sociopath, a narcissist. He believes everything revolves around him, and his needs — or that it should. He uses projection bias to shift blame and responsibility to others. He believes this, and feels no guilt or remorse for his behavior, nor any need to change."

"He did change," Eve argued. "When he picked up the knife and put it into his mother."

"Escalated," Mira corrected. "Broke through the restraints. And it was her own fault."

Eve shoved a hand through her hair, nodded. "Okay. And I saw it as they're out of his way, he has a conduit to the money, a way to live like a king for the short term. Just what he wanted. No guilt or remorse, I got that. It was more like glee. But . . . Killing his parents, did it kill something in him, that tiny spark of conscience, humanity, the need to be a part of the whole?"

"I think seeing what he did here, what he enjoyed doing here, no, it didn't kill a part of him, it freed a part of him he'd suppressed. And likely suppressed out of fear of punishment. A part of him he may not have been truly or fully aware of until freed. He's found himself."

"Sorry to interrupt." Peabody walked in, holding a take-out tray. "Roarke sent this in. That's tea for you, Dr. Mira, on the front corner. Coffee for you, Dallas, back corner, and coffee regular for me. Roarke's down with McNab, at this twenty-four/seven café across the street. The waiter recognized the suspect. They're checking out street-level security discs."

"Good. That's good."

"As is this." Mira sipped her tea. "It's my favorite. How does he do that?"

Eve shrugged. "I've stopped asking that question."

"Is it all right to sit a moment?"

"Go ahead," Eve told her. "I can't yet."

"I can, two minutes," Peabody said quickly, and lowered onto one of the padded crates.

"He's validated," Mira went on as she sat. "All those menial jobs he was pushed or forced into? Never meant to be — he always *knew* it, now he's proven it. All the bosses who demanded he work by their rules? Shortsighted, stupid, or out to make him less because they saw he was so much more. He's killed three people, and he's walking

187

free. You know who he is, but you can't stop him — he just proved that with this last kill. He has money now, true freedom now, true self now."

"He'll need to kill again."

"Definitely. His sexual reaction to this kill adds yet another level of that need. Killing rewards him."

"Someone he knows? A stranger won't give him that same rush, at least not this soon."

"Agreed, and knowing his victim, knowing that victim has always underestimated him, considered him less, has even hurt or insulted him in some way is only part of it."

Yes, she could see into him now, into the dark corners of him. "Payback's the other. His parents held him back, shoved him, nagged him, threatened him, and were on the point of booting him. She already had. He's got plenty of others he'd see the same way."

"A long list of slights, opportunities to prove himself, opportunities for the thrill and release, and the gain. The reward."

"We've contacted everyone we know at this point." Eve glanced at Peabody.

"Former employers," Peabody confirmed, "coworkers, family members, friends."

"There'll be more," Eve said. "Some

neighbor who gave him lip or grief, a teacher or instructor, even a fricking waitress, a clerk."

Mira enjoyed her tea. "I absolutely agree. He'll attempt to work his way through anyone who made him feel less of a man, who slighted him or rejected him."

"We've got his name and face plastered everywhere now. He has to know that. He has to change his look."

"He was wearing a suit," Peabody said. "I asked the wit what Reinhold was wearing. At first he said he didn't notice, but I worked on him a little, and he remembered, because he said he'd never seen Reinhold in one before, that he was wearing a suit."

"Interesting," Mira murmured. "He wanted to look professional."

"Spruced himself up for this kill," Eve added. "Slicked up for the ex. Look at me, bitch. I'm high-end now. Salons," she told Peabody. "Anywhere he can get a hair job, a treatment, new eye color. He changes his method. Knife to bat to strangulation. Experimenting?" she asked Mira.

"It could be, yes. Or tailoring."

"Method to fit the kill, and the sin against him. Yeah. More that, I'll bet. That would make him feel . . . skilled and smart. He has to stay somewhere, sleep somewhere, live somewhere. He won't settle for a flop."

"That would be beneath him," Mira concurred.

"Maybe in the very short term if he was on the run, but I don't see it. Not now that he's tasted the big-time."

"A lot of hotels in New York," Peabody commented.

"We cover them."

"He'll spend a lot of time watching and reading the reports on him," Mira added. "It's another validation. People know his name now, respect and fear him now. They know he's a man. A dangerous one."

"The way he's spending the money he has, he'll need more soon."

He'd figured out how to get it, and more. He'd forgotten to get Bald Lori — he'd always think of her that way now — to transfer her savings to an account for him.

He got caught up, Reinhold thought. She had a few thousand tucked away, he knew, and she'd distracted him with all that crying and shaking so he'd killed her stupid ass before he'd taken the money.

Stupid, selfish bitch.

Didn't matter — what did he care? He didn't need her pathetic waitress money.

He thought he'd be tired by now, but

found instead he was revving, like he'd scored really good drugs. Which, he thought, might go on his shopping list.

But for now, he needed a nice place to stay, another infusion of money into his Fuck-You Fund, and a stellar fake ID to go with the new look he had planned.

All of those, and again more, should be available in the tidy brownstone in Tribeca.

No he didn't need Bald Lori's pitiful savings. He'd do a lot better than that.

He just had to wait for the bitch Ms. Farnsworth to take her dog, the little shit-pile, Snuffy, out for his last walk of the night.

Or should we say his last walk ever.

God, this was fun!

He couldn't keep the place in view from a café the way he had for Bald Lori so he had to stay out of sight, in shadows, or pretend to talk on his 'link.

Just after eleven, he saw the door open, and fat-ass Ms. Farnsworth come waddling out with the ugly little mutt on a leash. She talked to the dog in that high, annoying voice of hers, the same voice she'd ragged on him with when she'd screwed him over in Computer Science in high school.

They'd made a big deal of her when she'd retired. He'd even gotten a damn e-vite to her retirement party. Hell of a nerve, after

191

she'd flunked him out of spite.

When she'd made it half a block away, stopped for the dog to take a shit on the square of ground around some tree, he slipped through the gate of her narrow front yard, and back into the shadows near her front door.

Nice house, he thought. He'd be happy here for a couple days. Bitch inherited the place when her real estate daddy died. Lived alone since her stupid husband croaked. No wonder she lived alone, considering she was fat, ugly, and mean as an alley rat.

He slipped the baseball bat out of his bag, enjoyed the feel of it in his hands, knowing what he'd do with it.

He thought how he could've been an assassin. One of those special operatives — licensed to kill — the government ran. Maybe he still could, after he'd finished what he needed to do.

It might be fun to kill people he didn't even know. But he knew so many who really needed to die.

He was going to be really busy for a while. A career opportunity would just have to wait.

He watched her come back, ugly dog prancing. When they clanked through the gate, his heart picked up its beat in anticipation.

The dog stopped, quivered, barked.

Shit! He hadn't thought of that.

"Oh now, Snuffy! Is it that bad cat again? That nasty bad old cat?"

Yeah, Jerry thought, grinning. *I'm a bad cat.*

"Come on now. Don't be such a baby." She scooped up the barking dog, cradling him, hushing him, and walked to the door.

Turned the key. Opening the door.

He was on her like a leech. One swing to send her pitching forward. Slamming the door behind him, breathing fast, fast as he fought the urge to just whale away.

Instead he gave the barking, quivering dog one hard kick that sent Snuffy smashing against the wall, then dropping, just like its mistress.

He had to slow his breath, force himself to slow it down, slow everything down until the tornado roar of blood storming in his head died so he could just think again.

Then with a self-satisfied nod, he propped his trusty bat against the wall. And rubbed his hands together in anticipation of all to come.

In Chelsea, Eve spoke briefly to the waiter

193

who had served Reinhold.

"He came in about four, four-fifteen maybe, ordered a Maxima latte, double-shot caramel and a grande chunky-chunk cookie. He worked his 'link and PPC, but lots of people do."

"Did you hear him talking to anyone?"

The waiter scratched his ear as if it would help him think. "Now that you mention it, I guess not. He was just sitting there, watching out the window, and he'd try his 'link off and on, poke around on his handheld. I figured he was maybe waiting for someone, and they were late, but I asked him if he was, like, expecting someone, and he said no, he was just killing time before an appointment. He paid cash. I mean, after all that hang time, he got up all of a sudden, and fast, left cash on the table, grabbed his bag, and bugged out. Kinda trotting. I went to make sure he covered the tab — he did, not much tip, but covered — and I spotted him cutting across the street, zipping around cars stopped for the light. That's about it."

"What kind of bag?"

"What kind of what?"

"Bag," Eve repeated. "You said he grabbed his bag before he left."

"Oh yeah, right. Pretty nice bag. Looked new, I guess. Black, big. I guess it was like a

194

duffel, but classier. I didn't pay much attention."

"Good enough. If you think of anything else, or see him again, get in touch."

"No sweat on it."

She went outside where McNab and Roarke stood on the sidewalk in geek conversation. She held up a hand to cut that off. "Security visuals?"

"We were just talking about that."

"Not in English."

McNab just grinned at her. "We've got him off a few street cams, and we can put that together. What we were figuring is how we backtrack, see if we can catch him farther back to where he came from."

"Why didn't you just say so?"

"We did, or were," Roarke corrected. "Since the Privacy Laws put paid to use of satellite observation, we're dependent primarily on building cams, where they exist. We were working out the best probabilities to tailing him back to his source or mode of transportation."

"Okay, keep doing that. Let me know when you've got anything we can use. A minute," she said to Roarke and moved a few paces away. "You're not going home, are you?"

"I want to play with my friends awhile. I

may miss curfew."

She glanced back at McNab, currently talking to Peabody and doing what she thought of as the EDD shuffle. His colorfully clad body just couldn't stand still while he was in e-mode.

And here was Roarke, cat-quiet in his perfect black trousers and leather jacket.

Yet they were friends, she thought, with all that entailed.

"Suit yourself."

"My preferred method. So." He grabbed her, kissed her hard before she could evade. "On duty *and* in public. But you did say suit myself, Lieutenant."

She punched him, lightly, in the stomach. "Me, too. Peabody! With me."

She walked across the street to where her car — as promised — waited.

While Eve worked, so did the man she hunted. Here, he could take his time, and enjoy the excitement of wandering through a house without permission. He could do whatever he liked, have whatever appealed to him.

Plenty of electronics here to sell or trade and add to his Fuck-You Fund. An obvious e-geek at heart, Ms. Farnsworth liked her gadgets, including a house droid duded up in a black suit and luckily in sleep mode.

He knew enough about programming from the courses he'd taken — that his dead, tight-wad parents had whined about paying for — to wipe the droid's memory chips. Reprogramming was more of a head-scratcher, but he could handle the basics. And he'd get Fat-Fuck-Farnsworth to walk him through the fancy stuff later if he needed it.

He helped himself to a snack after he'd tied and gagged the old bitch to a chair in her home office. They'd work there, so he'd ordered the rebooted droid to haul her fat ass up the stairs, then shut down again.

Then Reinhold took his tour.

The place smelled like old lady, and of the dog currently quivering and glassy-eyed in the corner. Probably broke something inside the little turdhead with the kick, he decided and stuffed more salt and vinegar chips into his mouth. A treat he washed down with Coke.

Now and again he wiped his salty hands on some of her fussy curtains or the back of a chair.

He poked through her bedroom. Big-ass screen there, the old bitch was loaded. Not the sort of thing he could get down and out by himself. Maybe use the droid for that, he considered. And he could send the droid out to hock some of the e-stuff. Not too close to the house though. Not where the old bitch shopped.

He'd have to think about that one. But for the meantime, he'd enjoy the big screen while he was "in residence."

He cackled over his good luck when he discovered she not only had a jet tub, but a big, fancy shower, multijets.

Now, this was living.

He didn't know dick about art or give a shit, but he thought, maybe, he could take a couple of the paintings to a gallery, spin a tale about his dead aunt Martha, and see if he could get some cash.

But his biggest discovery, and thrill, was the safe.

A good-sized one, built into the wall behind a painting of a dumbass farmhouse and a field of some farming shit.

An old safe, at least it looked old, with its classic combo lock. Probably been in the house for decades. Maybe more. And whatever was inside, now belonged to him.

Back in her bedroom, he dumped all her fat old lady clothes out of the closet and into bags. Maybe he could get something for them, but mostly he wanted them out. He dragged them, the stupid dog bed, the smelly basket of dog toys into another bedroom. Guest room, he imagined with its fussy lacy things and pictures of flowers.

She had an unexpected guest now.

He went back, changed out of his suit into new jeans, a designer T-shirt, and new skids. Work clothes, he thought, checking himself out in the mirror. He set out his things in the bathroom for later. The hair color, the trimmer, the face and body bronzer.

He'd wanted to go to a fancy salon, but he wasn't an *idiot*. Anyway, he'd read instructions on the 'Net on how to do this makeover deal. He could pull it off, and later, he'd try that fancy salon to polish it all up. He just needed to look different, and to have that look for the new ID the old bat would help him create.

He knew just how to convince her.

He took out the pair of metal cutters, the meat cleaver he'd found in her kitchen — handy and full of potential — and a little, battery-operated hand drill.

That should do it for now, he thought, and strolled back into the office.

He smiled brilliantly when he saw her eyes open, terrified, confused. Bumped up the smile when those eyes landed on him, when he watched recognition — and then horror — bloom in them.

"Hi, Ms. Farnsworth! Remember me? You flunked me out of Comp Science — screwed up my life. We're going to have ourselves a teacher-student conference." For effect, he thwacked the meat cleaver into the desk. "Starting now."

9

He pulled a chair over so they faced each other, braced an ankle on his knee. "I had to take your stinking class over because you had it in for me. I got in-home detention for a month, stuck in there with my bitching, carping parents. You fed them lies when they came in for your student crisis meeting. You told them I was lazy and careless, how all I wanted to do was play comp games instead of learning the lame, stupid, worthless science. You cost me my fucking summer, all those weeks taking that class over when my friends were hanging. I couldn't go to the shore."

He lifted the nippers, studied them, smelled her fear sweat. "It was the worst summer of my life. My friends ragged on me every damn day, and I was stuck in class with *losers* just because you wanted to screw with me."

He leaned forward, and though she tried

to curl her fingers, keep them balled in a fist, he pried one out, fit the nippers over it. Smiled at her.

"I'm going to take the tape off so you can explain all this to me. Give me your side of it. If you scream, I'm going to snip this finger off at the knuckle. You got that?"

She nodded, her eyes glued to his as he pulled at one corner of the tape.

"One scream, one finger," he warned and yanked the tape free.

She hissed in a breath at the rip on her skin, let it out in a tremble. "I won't scream, Jerry."

"Nobody's going to hear you anyway, the way you've got this place closed up, but I don't want to hear it." He really wanted to tighten his hold on those nippers, feel the snip, watch her face when he did. But it occurred to him she might need her fingers to make the ID he wanted.

Still, she wouldn't need her toes if it came to that. Slowly, he drew the nippers away, set them down.

"So, what's your side of it, Ms. Farnsworth?" He put on an attentive face, and still couldn't conceal the ugly glee in his eyes. "I'm really interested."

"I wanted to help you. I did," she insisted, when he picked up the nippers again. "I

202

went about it the wrong way. I made a mistake." She had to fight back tears of relief when he took his hand off the nippers, gave herself a moment, just a moment to gather herself. "I shouldn't have been so hard on you."

"You were on my case from day one."

"You had such potential." She wasn't entirely sure that was a lie. She *had* seen potential. And utter laziness. But she'd tried so hard with him, had given him so many chances. For God's sake, she'd worked with him one-on-one, assigned one of her best students as his lab partner.

"I couldn't figure out how to mine that potential, how to reach you." That *was* a lie, she thought. She'd been a good teacher, and she'd tried everything in her arsenal with Jerald Reinhold. He'd been one of her few failures because he hadn't cared, he'd been consistently lazy, obviously ungrateful. "That was my failure. My fault."

"You marked down my work."

Part of her wanted to rise up, to take him down to size with her outraged teacher's voice because she'd done no such thing. If anything she'd given him slightly higher marks initially in hopes to build his confidence, inspire him to try harder.

So she used that. "I sensed great things in

you, Jerry, so I pushed you hard. Too hard. I didn't see that until it was too late. I regret that. I'm sorry for that. I wish I could go back and do it all over."

"Do-over." He snorted the term, but she'd confused him. He'd never expected her to admit all of it. Never expected her to *see* she'd been the one at fault.

Didn't matter, he thought. The plan was the plan.

"Give me the combination to your safe."

He snapped it out so fast, she jolted, and though her stomach clenched, she told him, slowly and clearly.

"If that's not it, you lose a finger."

He slapped the tape back in place, walked out.

Alone, she tried to shift, to turn and twist. She couldn't see the cords around her wrists, her ankles, but she could feel them cutting into her. He'd taped over the cords, taped around and around her and the chair so she was all but glued in it.

But maybe with repetitive motion she could loosen it all, just enough. Or maybe she could find a way to coax him into freeing her hands.

Where was Snuffy? What had he done to the poor little thing? Harmless as a lamb, she thought, and fought tears again.

He'd killed his parents, she'd heard all about it on the media reports. Killed them and stolen their money.

He'd kill her, too, unless she found a way to talk him out of it. Or get away.

When she heard him coming back, she went very still.

Cooperate, she ordered herself. Agree with him. Be contrite.

She'd spent more than half her life teaching, and primarily teens, which could often be a frustrating, thankless job — until they bloomed a bit, turned the corner off that avenue of self-involvement. Watching them bloom had been one of her greatest joys.

With Jerry Reinhold? She'd never seen the first tiny bud.

"You got a hoard in there, don't you, Ms. Farnsworth? Cash, jewelry. Heirloom shit, right? That's worth a lot. Bunch of discs — you're going to explain the ones to me marked 'insurance.' I bet some of the shit you've got sitting around here's worth plenty. You owe me plenty, so we'll get started on that. We may just have to pull an all-nighter."

He shoved her chair to the side a bit, brought himself up to the computer. "First thing? I'm going to need your passcodes. Let's start with your bank accounts."

Because he wanted to, he gave her a hard, careless backhand. "I said, I need your passcodes. Oh, sorry!" He laughed. "I guess you can't talk with your mouth taped up."

He yanked the tape free, watched tears form in the corners of her eyes. "It's payback time, Ms. Farnsworth."

At her desk Eve expanded her notes into a detailed report. She focused on it, setting aside the dregs of the emotional upheaval she'd caused, witnessed when she'd knocked on the door of Lori Nuccio's parents to tell them their daughter was dead.

She couldn't stop their grief, and knew she couldn't take it on.

What she could do, would do, was pursue and catch the man who'd taken their daughter and forever changed their lives.

Lori's face had its spot on her board now. As she'd been, and as Reinhold had left her. The media would have that face by morning — the before — and would run it over and over. But she'd make damn sure they never got their hands on how Lori had looked when she died.

Who else was on his list? Who would he target next?

She got up for more coffee, drank it standing at her window, looking out at New York.

All those lights — windows, sidewalks, the beams from traffic cutting through the dark. All those people going, coming, settling down, partying, having sex, looking for action, looking for quiet.

How many of them had somehow offended or pissed off Reinhold in his twenty-six years? And how many might he get to in his payback spree before she stopped him?

She turned to her board.

Mother, father, ex-lover. Personal, intimate.

Would he stick with that? Grandparents? Did they make the grade? Cousins? Would it be family first — payback for childhood slights, for lack of support, for criticisms?

Friends would come next, wouldn't they, if he followed that sort of pattern. Would it be the one who won big in Vegas while he lost? The one who kicked him out for not paying the rent?

He'd need opportunity, a way to get to them.

She sat again, ran probabilities.

Then sat back, frowning, drumming her fingers over the results.

The computer liked the Brooklyn grandparents. Highest probability. Out-of-town set, very low. Friends got an even split.

She wouldn't chance it. She'd have the

grandparents under protection.

But it didn't fit well in her gut, not yet. Weren't grandparents typically or generally more indulgent than parents? And wouldn't Reinhold see the pattern, too?

Then again, the Brooklyn set had some money, from what she'd dug up. Not roll-in-it and sing-happy-songs money, but a solid foundation. He'd need and want more money.

Offsetting it? Traveling to Brooklyn. Getting out of Manhattan, taking that time, making those plans.

"Not your next stop. I just don't feel it."

The friends didn't have real money. But Asshole Joe, as Peabody dubbed him, had hit it in Vegas. He could get two birds with one stone, couldn't he? Payback, and the money he'd lost and his friend won.

Maybe three birds, she considered, as he'd be happy to brag to Asshole Joe about killing Lori. Someone who'd known her, a *friend* who'd probably agreed after the breakup that she'd been a bitch.

Of friends and family — though she needed to dig deeper into the cousins — Asshole Joe topped her list for targets.

But even he didn't sit quite perfectly.

"Dallas," Peabody began as she started into the office. "McNab —"

"Isn't he going to want to circle back to his friends at some point?"

"What?"

"Reinhold. He's not a loner. Everything we've got on him indicates he likes to hang with his friends, go to bars, clubs. He wants somebody — and somebody familiar — to drink with, to bitch to. He's pumped right now. Adrenaline's flowing. Everything's gone his way. He's having his personal little celebration, but eventually, he's going to need to bump fists with his buds, right?"

"I . . . I don't know. He's killed three people. His friends probably aren't going to want to bump fists."

"You're not thinking like him. He's rich — on his scale. He's famous. He's got power and glory. If you can't rub that in the faces of your friends, then who? Right now, it's fancy hotels and food, new clothes. But he's got to see already that takes more money than he's got to maintain for long."

"Maybe, but . . . We're about the same age. If, say, I had a hundred and seventy-five-odd grand fall into my lap, my initial reaction would be 'Holy shit, I'm rich.' And I'd celebrate, too. I'd buy new stuff, toss some of it around. I couldn't help it."

"Then you'd stop because you're not an asshole."

"Yeah, but he is." Considering, Peabody stepped closer to the board. "He's not going to be thinking of investing for the future or paying his bills off or whatever things mature people do with windfalls."

"I get that. I get it." Eve pointed at Peabody, then because she saw her partner's gaze shift to the AutoChef, pointed at it. "But he's found an ambition," she continued while Peabody scurried over to program coffee. "He's never had one before. That's something I got from Mira. Something broke free inside him, and released this killer from the lazy asshole. Now he's got ambition, and I think, on some level, he *is* thinking about the future."

"Like an investment fund?"

"No, like how he's going to keep doing what he's discovered he really likes doing, and how to make enough money at it to keep up a high-life style. Fucker probably sees himself becoming some sort of big-ticket paid assassin, a hit man. But before that, he has to even the scales, pay back everyone who crossed him, one way or the other. He can't keep moving from hotel to hotel. He needs a base, a hive . . . an HQ."

Though she knew its miseries, Peabody sat in the visitor's chair with her coffee. "Okay. I see where you're going. He needs to score while he evens the score so he can get a place of his own. An iced place. He'd have to score mega to buy one, but —"

"Not as mega to rent. But to rent, he'll need more cash, or better a safe account because cash throws up flags. He'll need that ID, and enough change in his looks so he can move around the city."

"The grandparents in Brooklyn are pretty well set."

"Yeah, the comp likes them for it. Did your grandparents ever piss you off?"

"Not really." As she thought of it — of them — an easy smile bloomed on Peabody's face. "I guess they've kind of spoiled me. Well, all of us."

"That's how it goes, right? Still, considering his meter for offenses, and the fact he's been a major screwup all or most of his life, there's probably enough there. I'm having them covered. It seems he's at least smart enough to figure we would."

"Asshole Joe hit big in Vegas."

Eve nodded, rubbing at the tension in the back of her neck. "Could go for him, especially since that's pretty fresh. But odds are Joe's already burned through a chunk of the big. He needs more than that, another major infusion. In his place I'd start on former employers. Even if they're not well set, wouldn't he see them that way? They own or run a business, they had authority over him — like his parents."

"It's a good angle."

"I think we push that one. And we start taking a look at high-end apartments, condos, townhomes currently for rent."

"Hell of a lot of those, Dallas."

"He only needs one — and so do we."

Hoping to jog her brain, she angled toward the board, propped her boots on the desk in think mode.

"He can't stay deep in his old neighborhood, not if he's got half a brain cell working. Too big a chance even if he alters his looks somebody will make him. Not the ex's neighborhood either," she decided. "But somewhere close. He'd want the familiar, the comfort of it, at least while he's still developing. And it's more satisfying to lord it over everyone. To have a fancy, expensive place close to where his friends have their cheap ones.

"Run some probabilities on that."

"Okay. Meanwhile, McNab let me know they've just about got the street cam angle worked out. They're up in the EDD lab."

"I'll head up. Run the probabilities, send them to me. Then go home and get some sleep, or catch some in the crib. We'll start back on this in the morning."

"What are you going to do?"

Eve dropped her foot to the floor. "That depends on what McNab and Roarke have."

"I'll stick here, in case you get something hot. I've got a change of clothes in my locker. Maybe just tell McNab I'll be in the crib."

Satisfied, Eve headed out and up.

She avoided the EDD bullpen. Even in the middle of the night it jumped and hopped and jiggled with wild colors and constant movement. She steered away, but made a mental note to carve out some one-on-one time with Feeney — her former trainer, partner, and captain of the geek squad.

She spotted Roarke and McNab through the glass walls of the lab, and stepping in almost staggered from the punch of clashing, crashing music.

She recognized Mavis on the vocals, and however much she loved her friend, there were limits.

"How can you think with all that noise?" she demanded.

"Keeps the juices rolling," McNab claimed, but bowed to rank. "Music end," he ordered, and cut Mavis off mid wail. The room descended into blessed quiet.

"What have you got?" Eve asked as she stepped toward a screen where images flew by in a blur.

"A puzzle," Roarke told her. "With the last pieces just in place." He swiveled on his stool to face her. "In plain English?"

"Yeah, let's go with that."

"Starting at the victim's building, we were able to correlate from various security cam footage Reinhold's route to, and to a lesser extent from. It took some time and doing as he made a few detours, and far from all buildings in that sector have cams — or working ones in any case."

"We nailed arrival, Dallas." McNab sucked from a giant go-cup. "But he hit a residential pocket on departure, out of any cam range, and we haven't been able to pick him up. He could've grabbed a cab or a bus, or kept walking. We'd have him if he headed into a subway. We've run all the stations in that sector. But he could've gone down somewhere else. We can keep looking."

"Show me what you have."

"We just put it together." McNab ordered the results on screen. "We'll run it forward, so you can see him arrive, then move into position."

She watched the Rapid Cab swing out of the tangled traffic, brake at the curb. Reinhold, in his new suit and dark sunshades, hopped out, hefted a long duffel.

"Zoom in there, get me the cab number."

McNab paused the run, sticking Reinhold as he'd secured the strap of the duffel on his shoulder.

"He's happy," Eve stated. "Excited. You can see it on his face. He's thinking about what he's going to do to her. How he'll do it."

"We got the number," McNab told her, but ordered the zoom so she could see it herself. "We wanted you to see it before we called it in."

She pulled out her 'link. "Keep it going," she ordered, as she contacted the cab company's central dispatch. "This is Lieutenant Eve Dallas, NYPSD, Homicide. Badge number 43578Q. I need the pickup location of a passenger."

She relayed the information as she watched Reinhold walk, his movements smoothed out by geek-skill as the cams caught him.

She saw his head turn, imagined his gaze shifting, over, up with the movement. Looking at Lori's building, her apartment windows, Eve thought. Taking out his 'link, trying to contact her, see if she's up there. Her day off. He'd know that.

"Outside the Grandline Hotel on Fifth, got it. Thanks. Keep it going," she said to McNab.

She wanted to watch him.

She studied his face when she could see it, his body language as she contacted the hotel. "Show me what you have on departure," she told McNab once Reinhold walked into the café.

She repeated her name and identification data to the hotel clerk. "Do you have a Reinhold, Jerald registered?"

"One moment, Lieutenant . . . We have no one by that name."

"A checkout? Today."

"There's nothing in our records."

"What time did you come on shift?"

"Nine P.M."

Too late, Eve thought, but there would be security cams.

"I'm coming in. I'll need to see your security discs for today, starting at seven-thirty. All of them, all day."

She didn't wait for an agreement, just clicked off.

"You've got him walking south."

"Yeah, then we get to this sector here, we catch him for a nano crossing over west, and that's when we lose him." McNab took another deep suck of whatever overly sweet

216

drink he'd chosen. "Most building cams here have a shorter range. If he'd gone into any of the buildings, the search would've nabbed him."

"Opposite direction from the hotel where he got the cab," she considered. "Unlikely he was going back there."

She paced for a moment. "He knows we're looking for him, knows we'll find Nuccio's body and fairly quickly. Maybe he thinks it'll be tomorrow, but still quick enough. He's not going to grab a cab near her place, so he needs to stay on foot long enough to put some distance between any pickup and the crime scene. Smug smile on his face, just strolling along. World's his clam."

"Oyster," Roarke corrected when Mc-Nab's brows drew together in puzzlement.

"He's too cocky-looking not to have another hole ready to crawl into. The Village maybe, or SoHo, Tribeca. Or maybe he walked south, and then caught an uptown bus. Tucked in by now, wherever the hell he is. I'm going to check out the hotel."

"I'm with you," Roarke said and pushed to his feet.

"Do you want me to keep running the search, Lieutenant?"

She considered it, shook her head. "We've got what we're going to get, and it'll have to be good enough. Peabody's using the crib."

McNab's face brightened. "Oh yeah?"

"And don't even think about doing the deed in there." She strode out, knowing he'd probably do more than think about it.

She decided to risk the elevator, breathed a little easier when she found it empty.

"What kind of a place is the Grandline?"

"I thought you might ask." Roarke tapped his PPC. "Midsized business hotel, twenty-four-hour services to accommodate the business traveler."

"A step down from The Manor."

"Well, most are."

She scowled when the doors opened and a pair of uniforms dragged in a pair of bloody, battered, still spitting street LCs.

"It's *my* corner, you thieving whore-bitch."

"You don't own the sidewalk, Cuntzilla."

"You tried to steal my john, right in my fucking face!"

"I can't help I was walking by and he went for me instead of your fat, dumpy ass."

Noting the fire in fat, dumpy ass's eye, Eve instinctively nudged Roarke back an instant before FDA kicked out with a foot squeezed into a shoe with a toe as sharp and pointed as a stiletto. It connected with bare shin. Thieving whore-bitch let out an ear-splitting yowl, swiped out with inch-long nails as pointed as the shoes.

This time blood flew, and pandemonium reigned as the uniforms fought to drag the women apart.

TWB tore FDA's sparkly pink shirt, exposing one impressive man-made breast.

"And you ask why men enjoy watching women fight," Roarke commented.

"Oh, for the sake of silicone Jesus." Eve grabbed one of them by the hair, she didn't know or care which one. Yanked, dragged, and managed to plant a boot on the other one's neck.

"Knock it off!" Her voice echoed in the confines of the elevator. "Or I'll stun the pair of you. And shut the fuck up," she added when the pair of them screamed out their curses and complaints.

"Secure these two, damn it."

"Come on, Dorie, what the hell?" One of the uniforms crouched to slap restraints on one pair of wrists while her partner did the other.

The elevator doors opened. "Get them off."

"We're actually taking them down to —"

"Now."

"Yes, sir." Hauling them up, the uniforms pulled the now weeping and wailing LCs off the car.

"Well now, that was entertaining." Roarke took out a handkerchief, caught Eve's chin in his hand.

"What?"

"Just a little back-blow from the nail swipe. "There, that's better."

"God" was all she said until they reached the garage level.

"You drive," she told him. "I want to check on some things on the way."

He got behind the wheel. "Such as?"

"I want to make sure Morris is on the third DB. I can put together how and when, I sure as hell know who and why, but it keeps it consistent. And I want to alert Harpo — hair and fiber queen — at the lab. Mira thinks he took some of the vic's hair. That's a personal trophy if so. And I want to check on the probabilities I had Peabody run on his next victim."

"You believe there'll be a next."

"He's got one picked out. If we don't net him soon, we'll have another DB for Morris." She paused long enough to scrub her hands over her face. "If he put half this time, effort, and thought into any one of the jobs he's blown through, he'd be at least middle management by now."

"This is more fun."

"You got that right. He's found himself. They have sites, right? Conduits, avenues, to hype yourself as a kill-for-hire, or to look for one."

He sent her a sidelong glance.

"You'd know . . . people who know people."

"Possibly. That was never my avenue nor did I buy rounds at the pub for those who drove along it."

"But you know people."

"I do."

"It's just a side angle, but he *likes* this, and so far it's working for him. He likes the high life and he likes killing. Right now he's killing people he knows, has some grudge against, but most of them aren't going to keep him in the high life. Why not make your hobby your profession? He might think that."

"It's an interesting side angle. I'll ask around."

"He shouldn't have gotten this far." She let her head rest back. "He hit it lucky with Nuccio. She picks today to be out of reach, get a new 'link and number. Without that, I connect with her, and I'd have asked about the locks. On top of it, he tried her old number, I know he did. We'd have had that, even on a clone, I'd have known he was try-

221

ing to find her. Everything just played in his favor."

"Luck's a potent thing. Skill's better."

He pulled up in front of the Grandline.

The doorman hustled forward. "Lieutenant Dallas? They're waiting for you inside. Mr. Wurtz at the desk."

The place struck her as very clean and entirely too bright. Busy even at this hour, the lobby throbbed with movement. Business people, she judged, coming in from late transpo, going out to same. Others sat slack-jawed with fatigue mumbling into hand or ear 'links.

A striking man with a face too young for the silver mane of hair — and maybe that was the point — stepped around the long black counter at her approach.

"Lieutenant, Michael Wurtz. I'm the night manager. I have the security feed you requested. The clerk informed me you'd inquired about Jerald Reinhold. No one registered under that name. We have the alert in place."

"He got a cab out front at just before sixteen hundred today. So I need to see that feed."

"I have it set up in my office. Just this way. I admit to being unnerved when Rissa told me. I've followed the reports on this man all day."

He opened a door behind the big counter into a small warren of rooms and cubes, then turned into an office.

"People often take advantage of the cab line here," he continued. "In any case, security made copies of the times you requested."

"Take the lobby cams first," Eve told him.

Wurtz used a remote, started the feed on his wall screen.

Eve spotted Reinhold at 8:23.

"That's him. Ball cap, sunshades, the two suitcases."

"Oh dear. One moment." He turned to a comp, operated it manually, and with a very swift touch. "We checked in a guest named Malachi Golde at eight-twenty-eight. He requested a day room. He showed ID, paid cash up front as it says in these notes his credit card had been compromised at the transpo center. Oh dear," he repeated.

"What?"

"I see here the ID card is invalid — it's over a year out of date. The clerk didn't check that or notice."

"What time did he check out?"

"Officially, he hasn't. But we did a room check at six P.M., as he'd only paid for a day room. He wasn't in residence, nor were his things."

"Let me see the feed for thirty minutes before he caught the cab."

Wurtz ordered the time to run.

"Speed it up." She watched, scanned. "Stop it there. In the suit now, no suitcases, just the duffel. He'd been in and out at least once between check-in and this. I'll need a copy of the full day. Is the room he used occupied?"

"No. We have it open."

"I want to see it."

"Right away. It's very disturbing." With nervous fingers, Wurtz tugged at his tie. "I wouldn't like our guests to be made aware he was on premises."

"I'm not going to make an announcement. Let's see the room."

"It's on twelve."

He showed them out, gestured toward the elevators. "I'll take you in, then unless you need me, I'll go arrange for the disc copies."

"That works. I'll also need a list of names. Who checked him in, if anyone helped with his bags, the doorman who got him the cab, anyone else on staff who had direct contact with him."

"I'll see you have it."

He let them into the room on twelve, hurried away.

"Has to cover his ass — or other asses as he wasn't on," Eve commented. "The expired ID should've been questioned, and he doesn't look like Mal Golde. Same age, sure, basically the same height maybe, but that's it. The clerk wasn't paying attention so he got lucky again. He doesn't check out so nobody pays attention. Just a day room for cash, his version of a flop."

She glanced around the streamlined, efficient space. Lots of tile and shiny silver — high-energy colors, its own business center and minikitchen.

She'd have the sweepers go over it, but didn't expect much.

"Just a place to stay for a few hours while he ran errands, made plans, showered, changed into his new suit. We'll see him going out with the suitcases again — who notices that in a hotel lobby, but he's worked out where he'll try to sell what he didn't liquidate on Sunday. Takes it out, or pieces of it. Does some selling, does some buying. The suit, maybe, more clothes, the duffel, the bat. Need the duffel for the bat."

She wandered as she thought it through. "In and out, using this as a temporary home base. Jewelry stores, secondhand stores, pawnshops, selling, trading. Even the suitcases at one point, and probably at least some of his old clothes. Shedding it all now, for profit.

"Then, all done, he just walks out of here, catches a cab, and goes down to kill Lori Nuccio."

She paced circles in the top-flight business-style suite. "Shopping bags. He's bound to have come back with shopping bags, so we'll see where he went at least."

She rubbed fatigue from her eyes. "Look, I'm going to go ahead and review the discs back at Central, catch a couple hours in the crib."

"I have a better idea. I had them hold us a room at The Manor, it's close enough. You can review the discs there and we can both catch a couple of hours in a room that doesn't include Peabody, McNab, and potentially other cops."

It was the room without other cops that decided her. "Sold."

10

The room at The Manor soothed with warm, deep colors, soft fabrics and thick, age-faded rugs over the gleam of hardwood.

Over a small stone fireplace a wide-framed mirror reflected the style and dignity of the parlor. And at the touch of a button inside a wall niche, the mirror wavered away into the dark surface of a screen.

"Well, that's . . . pretty frosty," Eve decided.

"Manor guests prefer the look of Old World, with the convenience of the new. We've blended them wherever we can."

She needed the screen to view the security discs, but there were other priorities. "Does that include an AutoChef with decent coffee?"

"It does, but we've both caffeinated enough at this point. I'll make a deal," he said before she could argue. "If you find something you can move on tonight, I'll load us both up."

It was probably fair. She didn't like it, but it was probably fair.

While she sulked over that, he went through a doorway, came back a few moments later with two tall glasses of water with a slice of lemon in each.

"Really?"

"Yes." He kissed her nose. "Really."

She was thirsty enough to settle for it, and tired enough to sit on the arm of the big, plushy sofa while he set up the disc.

"He didn't want to settle for a business hotel," Eve calculated. "Good enough while he ran around the city, but not where he wanted to bunk. And he was smart enough to use Golde's old ID. He'd need his own to cash the checks, but smart enough, or nervous enough to use a ploy to register at the hotel. Maybe he'll try using it again for his bedtime place."

"Wiser to spend some of that running-around-the-city time getting a new ID, a fake one."

"You need to know how. And yeah, he could've found out how. Run it," she told him.

Roarke sat on the opposite arm of the sofa, watching with her.

Less than twenty minutes after check-in,

they spotted him again. Roarke slowed the feed.

"Same outfit as check-in. Just the briefcase. Bank time, get the cash before the bodies are discovered. He pulled that off," she muttered.

She watched him come back through the lobby, a fat, smug smile on his face — time stamp 9:38.

"He hit the luck again," she said. "Just frigging breezed through the banking, and now the briefcase is full of money and cashier's checks."

He all but strutted into the elevator, and was back again, strolling out — one suitcase — eleven minutes later.

"Just one suitcase. Gotta get rid of everything he can, maybe not the big tickets. He didn't have a suitcase when he went into Ursa's, but the smaller ones. Cash those checks before the bodies are discovered and his face and name hit the media. He's still ahead of the game, by just enough. Speed it up again."

He came back without the suitcase, but wearing a suit, and carrying a garment bag.

"Mission accomplished, and a little shopping, too. Can you —"

"I am," Roarke said and anticipating her zoomed and magnified.

229

"On The Rack, for men," she read on the side of the bag. "Do you know it?"

"No, but give us a moment and I will."

"He's moving fast," Eve noted, "and look at his body language, his expression. He's digging on the suit, likes how he feels in it.

"They have a location a block from the hotel, good location for the business crowd who needs a change quickly. Alterations done on site, and within the hour for an additional fee. They run from suits to casual wear, shoes, accessories, and so on."

"We'll pay them a visit."

She watched, waited for the next appearance. "There. Timing wise, he must be heading out with the watches. Suit and briefcase, and Ursa looks and thinks, 'A nice young man.' Busy, busy. We'll check with the day man on the door. Probably got a cab. Why not? He's pretty damn flush."

She got up to pace, eyes on the screen as Roarke ran it forward. "There again, out nearly three and a half hours this time. Lots to do. What are those bags?"

"Village Paint and Hardware, In Style, Running Man — that's one of mine. Specializes in athletic shoes, clothing, accessories, for men again. The duffel might have come from there."

"It fits. He's a man now, he likes shopping

in male-specific stores. Hardware. He could've bought the cord and tape there. We'll check it out. What's In Style?"

"Trendy clothing and accessories."

"Okay."

She sat again. He went out again, with the second suitcase. On his return, eighteen minutes later, he carried the duffel and wore the stylish new sunshades he had when exiting the cab near Nuccio's.

"Got rid of the other suitcase. And I'm betting the bat's in the new duffel. That and anything else he thought of on this trip. Productive day. And there," she said when Roarke paused a final time. "Leaving with the duffel, done with the place. Catch a cab out front and it's off to kill."

She rose again and paced. "He had an agenda in place, a schedule, a to-do list. Maybe he varied it some — impulse buys, or he might've had to try a couple places before selling off the goods, but he stuck close to it. He had all that time with his dead parents and when he stayed at The Manor to work it out. Day hole, banks, cash checks, sell, shop, sell, shop — grab lunch somewhere maybe, sell, shop, pack up his new stuff. He stays with the suit for the kill. Wants her to see him all duded up. The suit makes him feel important, successful, rich.

All the things he didn't feel when she kicked him out."

She pressed her fingers to her eyes again. "Hung out, had some fancy coffee, saw his chance, and took it. But where did he go after the kill? He had to have another hole dug. Did he buy hair and face crap to try to make himself look more like Golde in the expired ID? Is he going to chance using that again?"

"It would be foolish," Roarke speculated. "He has enough money to make an ID, or, for now, to pay cash for lodging."

"Yeah. Used the Golde idea at the second hotel because, most likely, he blew through the cash he'd dug up at his parents'. But he's got plenty more now. Still . . . we'll add Golde's name to the alert, and EDD will check out the unit in the hotel, see if he used it after Nuccio. You need equipment, specific material to make an ID, and some skill to wiggle fake data into the system so it passes. Unless he got it on that last trip and stuffed it in the duffel, there's no sign he has anything like that."

"He has a schedule, an agenda," Roarke repeated. "And he had the time to plan it. Any plan should include the ID. He could obtain a reasonably good one with the money he has, but a good one would cut into that considerably."

"I'm with you. So we have to figure out where he'd go, and how he'd get one."

"You won't be doing that tonight. You need sleep."

"He's tucked in somewhere."

"Undoubtedly." Roarke rose to eject the disc, and the screen rippled back to mirror glass. "And so should we be."

"I can go straight to Central from here, early. I've got a change in my locker."

"You have one here as well," he told her, as he steered her toward the bedroom. "I had Summerset send down what we'd both need for the night, and tomorrow. And you needn't look quite so appalled. Not only does it save time and trouble, but I told him specifically what to send, so he didn't actually select your wardrobe."

"I guess that's something."

And the big bed with its fluffy duvet and mound of pillows looked a lot better than a cot in the crib at Central. By the time she crawled into it, she was ready to give it up for the night.

Tomorrow? Well, tomorrow Reinhold was going to have her right on his ass.

She curled in as Roarke's arm came around her. And let it go.

In dreams, she sat with Lori Nuccio on

the padded crates in the tiny apartment. Lori's hair swept down to her shoulders, sleek, a glossy reddish brown. Blue eyes reflected sadness out of her unmarred face.

"I didn't want to look like how he left me."

"Yeah, I get that."

"I thought he just needed motivation, and — you know — inspiration. He was cute, and he could be funny. He wasn't stupid, and he wasn't mean. Not at first. He treated me okay, and I wanted to help him. I was the stupid one."

"I don't think so. You cared about him. You thought you could help him grow up some."

"Yeah, I guess. I liked having a steady boyfriend. Having somebody, and he'd had some bad luck. He said he had. A lot of bad luck. People were jealous of him, and screwing with him. But that's not really the way it was. He had such nice parents, and I thought he'd come around."

She knuckled a tear away. "But he just got worse instead of better. He wouldn't work, and he complained all the time, and he never helped clean up the apartment. Then he took the money, *my* money, and when I got mad, he hit me. I had to kick him out. It was what I had to do."

"It was. You didn't do anything wrong."

"But he killed me for it and now I'll never get married or have kids or go shopping with my friends. And he hurt me, really bad. He cut my hair off, and it was so pretty. Now I look like this."

Her hair fell away, hank by hank, her eyes swelled, blackened, her lip split.

"I'm sorry for what he did to you. I should've stopped him."

"I just wanted a fresh start. But he wouldn't let me. I don't want my parents to see me like this. Can you fix it? Can you fix me?"

"I'll do what I can. I'm going to find him, Lori. I'm going to make sure he's held accountable for what he did to you."

"I'd rather not be dead."

"Yeah, it's hard to argue with that."

"He would," Lori said solemnly. "He wants a lot of people dead."

"It's my job to make sure he doesn't get what he wants."

"I hope you do your job, because so far, he's getting it."

Hard to argue with that, too, Eve thought, and slid into the more comforting dark.

While Eve talked to the dead in dreams, Reinhold gloated over his latest luck.

He'd known the old hag had some money,

but he hadn't known she had *money.* By the time he emptied her accounts, he'd have three million, nine hundred and eighty-four thousand in his brand-new name — or the name to come once they generated that new ID.

When he added it to what he'd, *ha-ha,* inherited from his parents, and gotten from his former bitch girlfriend, he'd be rolling in more than four fucking million dollars.

Jesus, he thought the hundred seventy-five thousand he'd had — minus what he'd spent — was a big deal. It was nothing compared to this.

He could have anything he wanted now. Any*one* he wanted now.

He'd never have to work a day in his life to live like a king. Except for the killing, that is. But what was that old bullshit his father always tossed around?

If you love your work you're never working. Something like that.

Who knew the stupid bastard would actually be right about anything?

And now he had a droid — a pretty classy one — reprogrammed to follow his orders, and only his.

He'd really enjoyed that when he'd ordered up a midnight snack.

"Ms. Farnsworth, you sneaky bitch. You've

been sitting on all this money with that fat ass of yours. Why the hell did you waste all that time dragging it around the classroom?"

She only stared at him with dead-tired eyes, rimmed with red from fatigue and tears, and from the occasional backhand he delivered to keep her sharp.

She'd loved teaching, she thought. He'd never understand the satisfaction and fulfillment of honest work. He was rotten down to the core. And she knew now he'd kill her before he was done.

He'd make her suffer first; he'd hurt her in every way he could devise. Then he'd kill her.

"We've still got work to do, but some of it's going to have to wait. I've got to get some shut-eye." He rose, stretched luxuriously. "You oughta get some, too. You look like hell."

He laughed, cracking himself up so much he bent over from the waist. "Tomorrow, we're going to finish routing all that money. And the big new assignment? We're going to work on that ID. I need your best work now, remember that? Remember how you said that a million times? 'I need your best work, Jerry.' Stupid bitch."

He gave her a last backhand, in case she forgot.

"See you in the morning." He gave her chair a good shove so it slammed against the wall, then strolled out, calling for lights off on the way.

She sat quivering in the dark. Then steeling herself began to squirm, rock, twist her aching limbs in the faint hope she could loosen her bonds.

Eve woke to the familiar and the not. The life-affirming scent of coffee hit first, to her eternal gratitude. The *sense* of an empty bed with Roarke close by. Those were every-morning things.

But the bed wasn't her bed, and no sky window above it showed her the filtered roof of the world.

Hotel, she thought. Downtown, near work. And a dead body waiting for her at the morgue.

She sat up, glanced blearily around at the muted gold of the walls, the single white orchid (she thought it was an orchid) arching out of a deep blue pot on a dresser.

And caught the muted mumble from the parlor beyond. Media reports, stock reports, she concluded. Roarke usually kept the sound off as he reviewed all that from the bedroom sitting area.

She rolled out, snagged the robe draped

at the foot of the bed where the cat would often be, and shrugging into it, went out to join him.

Already showered and dressed for business-world domination in a dark suit. Some blonde in hot red sat at a glass counter on screen talking about the market holding its breath in anticipation of the potential acquisition of EuroCom by Roarke Industries.

Eve wandered over to pick up his coffee cup, down the contents.

"You can have your own, you know."

"I'm going to. What's EuroCom, why are you potentially acquiring it, and how come it makes everybody hold their breath?"

"It's been the major player in Europe's joint communication development over the last decade or so. Because I can, and it will slide nicely into other holdings in that region. And because it's been badly mismanaged the last few years, resulting in lost jobs and revenue, and the acquisition should right that ship as well as add to it."

"Okay." She walked to the table where plates already sat under silver warmers, got a cup of her own and came back to pour coffee from the pot on the low table in front of Roarke.

"Why aren't you over there making the deal?"

"Because EuroCom is the one under the gun, and I had them come to me here."

"Your turf, their hand out."

"Close enough. Much of it's been negotiated through 'link and holo-conferences, and my liaison there. As it happens, I just signed off about ten minutes ago while having my coffee — or what had been my coffee. The announcement should hit shortly."

Eve wagged her thumb at the screen. "Blondie thinks it's a big deal."

"Blondie's quite right." He held up his cup so Eve could fill it. "After the transition, which on my terms will be swift and clean and final, there'll be some restructuring."

"Heads rolling."

"Asses booted more like. And some retooling. Within the next quarter we'll generate about a half million new jobs."

He changed lives, she thought, sitting there in his slick suit, coolly drinking coffee. With an eye toward profit, sure; and expansion absolutely, but his go-ahead changed the life of someone sitting in a pub or café across the Atlantic worrying about paying the rent.

The screen flashed like a sunspot before

240

the banner hyping BREAKING NEWS! swept over it. Even with the sound low, Eve heard the excitement in the blonde's voice as she announced the EuroCom/Roarke Industries deal was confirmed.

"Well then." Roarke got to his feet, gave Eve a light good-morning kiss. "Let's have breakfast. They do a fine full Irish here."

Just like that, she thought.

She sat with him, uncovered the plate to reveal the abundance of food. Jesus, what starving Irishman had first come up with the concept of the full deal?

"How much of it goes to Ireland?" she asked him. "The EuroCom thing."

He shot her an amused smile. "Want the figures, do you? Should I have a report sent over?"

She picked up her fork. "Definitely not. I'm just curious if any of this plays in with your family."

"Most of my people are farmers, as you know, but there are some who don't work the land, and they may find their way onto the payroll. You don't look as rested as I'd hoped."

"Weird dream. Dream," she repeated so he understood there'd been no nightmare. "The latest vic and I had this conversation in her apartment. She's pretty bummed out about being dead."

"It's difficult to fault her for that."

"Yeah. She . . . she doesn't want her parents to see her looking the way Reinhold left her. In the dream, I mean. Projecting," Eve said as she began to eat. "And I shouldn't be."

"Why not? You feel for her."

"It's not my job to feel for her. It's my job to find and stop Reinhold."

"You do both, and that's what makes you you."

"My subconscious is putting words in her mouth."

Watching her, Roarke cut into meaty, Irish-style bacon. "Your subconscious, driven by your innate observation skills and your unique sensitivity. I wouldn't discount it."

"None of that tells me where he is now, or what he's planning next."

"You've generated considerable data in a short amount of time."

She had — they had, she knew, but . . . "Time's the problem. He's like . . . like a kid with a brand-new toy and nobody to tell him to put it down. Or an addict who's just discovered a new drug, and thinks there's an unlimited supply. He's not going to pace himself."

"I'd agree with that, exactly. And I'd also say that's his mistake, or one of them. It'll be the rush, the gorging on it, that trips him."

"Gorging, yeah. He's spent his whole life accumulating and hoarding grudges, and now he's figured out what to do with them. Stabbing, bludgeoning, strangulation." She scooped up eggs as she spoke, fueling up. "It's all so much fun he can't decide what to try next. And there's so many ways to kill. And better, so many ways to cause pain and torment first."

Fighting frustration, she stabbed at potatoes. "He's got a target already, and I can't know who."

"If you can't narrow down his next victim, you might narrow down his potential space. As you've said, he has to land somewhere."

"Yeah, he needs a place of his own — and money to get it, to furnish it in the fashion he deserves."

A narcissist, Mira said. So he'd believe he deserved the best.

"Maybe he'll blow a big chunk of what he's got on his headquarters. From the time line, he didn't have much time to scout out places yesterday. He may have done some via 'link or Web, but he'd need to *see*, to walk around in the space, to imagine himself

243

there. Maybe that's today's agenda. But he has to change his looks first, has to alter them enough. He has to know we have his face, and he's not stupid. That's something else Nuccio said."

"You had quite a conversation."

"Well, we both felt pretty crappy."

"Won't most of his potential victims have holiday plans?" At her blank look, he shook his head. "Thanksgiving, Eve. Two days from now."

"Shit. That's right. Family groups, people leaving town or coming in. That's something to look at." It struck her. "Yours. Yours are coming in tomorrow."

"They are, yes, and will perfectly understand if you're busy on an investigation and don't have much time for them."

But the house would be full of people, noise, conversations, questions. She liked them, really she did. But . . .

"Life happens, darling," he reminded her. "However ill the timing."

"I guess it does. Maybe luck will turn our way and away from him, and I'll have him in a cage before the turkey's stuffed."

"Let's hope for that."

"It's going to take more than hope." She pushed away from the table. "I'd better start working on turning that luck because the little bastard's somewhere right now, thinking about his next kill."

He felt *great*! A good night's sleep, a long, hot shower, and a hearty breakfast prepared and served by Asshole, his new droid. He ordered the droid to clean up, to ignore any 'link communications or anyone who might come to the door during the process, then shut down.

The idea of anyone trying to contact Farnsworth made him consider she might have appointments. Armed with her passcodes, he checked both her calendar and her e-mail history on her bedroom 'link.

The fat, ugly blob had a salon appointment at two. As if anyone would look at her twice anyway. He found the salon contact, sent a quick text canceling.

And she was booked to have Thanksgiving dinner with some losers named Shell and Myra, who were probably as ugly and worthless as she was. He considered that, decided to leave it alone for now. If he still needed her and the house on Thursday, he'd make up some excuse at the last minute.

It amazed him to see just how many dates and appointments ran through her calendar. Lunches, dinners, more salons, groomers for the little rat-dog, currently half dead in the hallway.

Maybe he should finish him off, but then again . . .

Helping himself to a post-breakfast cappuccino, Reinhold walked upstairs.

He wrinkled his nose at the smell as he walked into the office and found Ms. Farnsworth slumped in the chair, urine dripping down her legs, blood staining the tape around her wrists and ankles.

"Jesus, you *pissed* yourself. You stink." He held his nose with one hand, waved the other in front of his face, his eyes gleaming bright as her head rolled up.

"Now I have to get Asshole — I renamed the droid — I have to get Asshole in here to clean this up. Oh, by the way, I canceled your salon appointment. Saved you money, because no amount of it could make you less ugly, fat, and disgusting."

He walked back out, called downstairs. "Hey, Asshole! Ms. Farnsworth pissed all over the place, get up here and clean this mess up."

Stepping back in he did what he thought of as a manly pose, one arm cocked up, the other across his body. "So, what do you think of the new look? Frosty, huh?"

He'd spent considerable time with the hair product, lightening his color by degrees, using the tools supplied to streak it through so he now sported a sun-washed, streaky blond. He'd trimmed it, though he thought he needed some pro help there. But it lay slick over his head. He'd mated that with layers of bronzing product. He thought he looked as though he'd spent a month at some fancy tropical resort.

The eyes had been trickier, and he'd go pro there next time, too. But now they were electric blue. Using some of the hair he'd trimmed off, he'd added a soul patch to the center of his chin. and though it had hurt like fucking hell, he'd used the kit he'd bought to pierce his left ear, which now sported a small gold hoop.

"I look successful, right? Young, rocking, rich? I've got an appointment with a realtor to look at a couple apartments today. Gotta look good."

He barely glanced over when the droid came in with cleaning tools.

"He's mine now." He gave the formerly named Richard, dignified in his dark uniform and silver-templed hair, a pat on the back. "Just like everything else that was yours. So don't even think about giving him orders. Oh that's right. Still can't talk. I'll fix that as soon as Asshole's done here. Be right back."

247

When he strolled out, Ms. Farnsworth rolled her eyes toward the droid. She screamed: *Help me!* but all that sounded was a weak moan. It went about its business efficiently, as she'd programmed its domestic duties herself. She tried rocking and bucking in the chair, but her limbs were numb, the only sensation was the burning where she'd rubbed her flesh raw in her attempts to get free.

She'd loosened the tape a little in places, or maybe that was just desperate hope. But she thought if she could regain a little strength, she could loosen it more. If she just had a few sips of water for her burning throat, anything, anything to ease the pain.

Even the humiliation barely touched her now, though when she'd no longer been able to control her bladder, she'd wept.

It didn't matter, didn't matter, didn't matter. Just pee. Just a normal human function. If she peed, she lived. And as long as she lived she had a chance to survive and pay the bastard back.

She'd kill him if she could. She'd never harmed another human being in her life, but she would cheerfully end his by any means possible.

She tried to speak again, slowly, clearly. If she could only get the droid to understand a few words. But the garbled mumbles meant nothing, and he continued his task, then gathered up the cleaning supplies.

Reinhold walked in as the droid walked out, as if he'd been waiting.

"You still stink, but it's a little better, and sometimes we have to work under unpleasant conditions."

He'd brought the nippers with him, waved them at her as he crossed to her. "Scream, lose a finger."

He ripped the tape away. She let out a gasp as much in shock as grabbing air.

"You —" Her voice croaked out, barely audible. "You have the money."

"I sure do, but we're going to hide it, really, really good. You know how, and you're going to show me. And I need a few other things."

"I need water. Please."

"You'll just piss yourself again."

"I'm dehydrated."

Bitch and complain, he thought, his jaw tightening. Just like his mother. Just like Bald Lori.

"Too fucking bad. Now, what we're going to do this morning is make me a nice new ID, and get the data up. I've worked out everything I want. Your job is to walk me through making it happen. Got that?"

"No."

He pressed the nippers against her cheek. "Need me to repeat it?"

"Go ahead, use them." She coughed as the words scored her throat like hot needles. "I'm done helping you."

"Helping me? Is that what you think you're doing? *Helping* me?" He swung back, bashed the back of his fist in her face. "You're following orders, bitch. I don't need your fucking help. You do what you're told."

She made herself look him in the eye, even as she felt blood slide out of her nose. And shook her head.

He turned around, walked out.

She gathered herself, digging for breath, digging for strength. She'd scream, however much it hurt, however much he hurt her for it. She'd scream and someone would hear.

Please, God.

Before she could, he came back, holding her little dog. Snuffy whimpered when he saw her, and she could see from his eyes he was hurt. And still he wagged his tail.

Fear came back, raw as the skin on her wrists. "Don't hurt him. He's just a little dog."

"Too late for that. He's already hurt. Probably needs the vet. Maybe I'll take him to a vet if you do what you're told."

"You won't."

He shrugged. "Maybe yes, maybe no. But if you don't." He turned the nippers, pushed Snuffy's paw out. "I'll just start snipping away."

Tears stung her eyes, ached in her burning throat. "Don't. Please, Jerry."

"Wouldn't take many snips with a rat-dog like this." To motivate her — and because it was fun — he pinched the dog, hard, so it yelped. "But I'd start small. This paw, that paw, maybe his tongue so he can't yap."

"I'll do it. Don't hurt him, and I'll do it."

Smiling, he closed the snips a little more. "Maybe I'll snip just one paw because you said no first."

"Please. Please." The tears rolled now. She couldn't stop them. He was a sweet old dog, he was *family*. He was defenseless. "I'm sorry. I'll make the ID for you, and upload all the data you want. I'll make it perfect. I'll hide the money. I'll bury it so nobody can trace it."

"Damn right you will. And one mistake? Just one? He loses a paw, you lose a finger."

He dumped the dog in her lap where Snuffy whimpered at her.

Reinhold sat at the desk, cracked his knuckles. "Let's get started!"

11

Eve went straight to the morgue. No need that she could see to pull Peabody in, not for this. The investigation was better served with her partner checking out the shops they knew Reinhold had visited, and at her desk, tracking down pawnbrokers who might be slow — or reluctant — to report the purchase of items sold by a murderer.

She traveled the white tunnel as she had the day before, and thought, yeah, it was past time for luck to turn.

She found Morris with Lori Nuccio. As he often did, he'd chosen music to suit either his mood or the victim. This was light, kind of breezy, with a high, clear female voice singing hopefully about what lay behind the bend in the road.

He looked up from his work when Eve entered, ordered the music to low volume. "I'd hoped not to see you again quite so soon."

"Same here," she said as she joined him. "Young. Very pretty."

"Hard to tell now, after he messed her up."

Morris shook his head. "No, not really. Her bone structure, coloring. There's an ugliness to what he did here, but she shows through it."

"She'd like to know that." Eve lifted her shoulders, let them fall at Morris's arched brows. "You know how it is. They get in your head, and you feel like you know."

"Yes."

"She mattered to him, in his own twisted way. He hated her for that. He didn't rape her."

"No," Morris confirmed. "There was no sexual activity, consensual or forced."

"He might go there with another, if he gets the chance. He orgasmed during the kill, so now he has a sexual connection — a bonus round."

"This one's difficult for you."

"I don't know why this one, especially, except we kept missing her. It's like everything was weighted on his side. We're trying to contact her, her neighbor's looking out for her, and still, he gets in, does this, walks away."

Studying the body as he did, Eve hooked her thumbs in her front pockets. "She was living cheap, you know? Padded crates, stringed beads for curtains in this little box apartment. But she kept it nice, kept herself nice, worked hard, had friends, had family. He took it all because she wouldn't let him sponge off her anymore, do nothing anymore. Her parents are wrecked."

She paused, pinched the bridge of her nose as if to release tension. "They told me her older sister and her spouse, their baby were all in from Ohio for Thanksgiving. They were having a big family dinner, and this one here was getting some fancy dish from the restaurant where she works.

"I don't know why they told me all that. Sometimes they tell you things because they don't have anything else."

"Death's cruel. Crueler yet at times when family traditionally gathers."

"Yeah. And about that. They're going to want to come in, see her. I don't know how much you can do, considering, but they shouldn't see her like this."

"Don't worry." He touched a hand briefly to Eve's arm. "We'll take care of her, and them."

"Okay. Good. So." She had to put it away, out of her head, and do her job. "The way it pieces together, he had keys, or he'd made copies. He went in when the neighbor went

254

out. We have him sitting in a café across the street where he had a good view of the building. It was the vic's regular day off, and from statements she usually went out, ran errands, shopped, hooked up with a friend. When he saw the chance he went in. He'd been shopping. We've got him coming and going on his hotel security cams. He bought the tape, the cord. And I'm thinking another baseball bat."

"I'd agree with that. The head injury's consistent with a bat. It would have knocked her unconscious, but it wasn't a killing blow."

"Or meant to be," Eve added.

"He used good quality cord. Strong and pliable. As you see from the ligature marks, he tied it as tightly as possible, much more than necessary to restrain her. She struggled, but it didn't help her. The tape, also good quality. She left teeth marks and blood inside. Some of that would be from the lip, opened from a blow. He struck her with his fist."

Morris balled his own. "In the face, in the abdomen, in the right side. There's slight bruising around her nose, and a deeper bruising on the nipple. From pinching."

"I missed the nose."

"Very slight. You'd need the microgoggles.

This slight cut here, thin, sharp blade with a serrated edge. I can't tell you what sort. It's just a nick."

"A warning. Just showing what he could do."

"Most likely, yes." As if to comfort, he laid a hand on Lori's shoulder. "But the lab may be able to identify the type of knife from the shorn hair."

"I've got Harpo on the hair."

"You couldn't do better. He cut it before killing her."

"Yeah, part of the torture."

Shifting, Morris turned his attention, and Eve's, to the throat wounds. "Considerable force was used in the strangulation. He put his back into that. You can see how deeply the cord cut into her. From the angles, and the crime scene record, he would've straddled her, looped it around her neck, twisting the lines in front." He pulled his fisted hands apart sharply to demonstrate. "Leaving this pattern of bruising here where the lines of cord crossed."

She could see it perfectly, the positioning, the movements, the joy and the terror. "It's what got him off. That connection. Being on top of her, cutting off her air, feeling her body convulse under him. Being able to see her face while she fought for air, while she lost the fight.

"Then he raided her kitchen for snack food."

"He thinks he's outwitting you."

She brought herself back to the moment. "What?"

"He thinks he's smarter than you, than the police. He has no idea how well you already know him, and how deeply you can go."

"I know him," she agreed. "But if I don't find him today, I'll be back in here tomorrow, and we'll have this conversation over another body. He's got a long list, Morris, and he's not going to wait to feel what he felt with her again. This is the biggest rush of his life, and now he's a man who loves his work."

Rather than wait for the report, Eve swung by the lab next. She didn't need to consult with Dickhead — Berenski, the chief lab tech — so wound her way through the maze of glass-walled rooms to Harpo's domain.

Harpo had changed her hair. She'd gone for the short, straight bowl, almost identical to what Peabody used to wear. But Harpo had opted for shimmering ice blue.

For reasons Eve would never be able to articulate or comprehend, it worked.

Harpo had tossed a white lab coat over a purple skin-suit, added a trio of dangling silver earrings to one ear and a series of tiny purple studs to run up the other.

She wore clear knee boots, which Eve assumed was a newly breaking style that showed off toes polished the same color as her hair and a foot tattoo — temp or permanent, who knew — in the shape of a long-legged bird.

Whatever her wardrobe choices, Eve had reason to know when it came to hair and fiber, Harpo ranked genius.

And right now, Harpo sat at her work counter, a sample of auburn hair in her scope, and its microscopic counterpart enhanced on her screen.

"Is that my vic's?"

"Yo, Dallas."

"Yo."

"Recently color treated. I can give you the brand, the color name, and the products used to style if you need them."

"Never hurts, but I don't think it's relevant. Dr. Mira thinks the killer took some."

"Yeah, so you said on the command — request," she amended with a toothy grin. "And props to Mira. Good eye. He took a hank five and a quarter inches in length, one-point-one inches in width. I can give you the exact number of hairs in the trophy, but it's probably not relevant either."

Maybe it was Harpo's sass, or her smarts, but Eve felt her own lips curve. "No, but impressive."

"I so totally am. It's really nice hair. Healthy, clean. She didn't overproduct or heat. Natural color's brown, but she made a nice choice with this new hue."

"She didn't get to wear it very long."

"Too bad, because it's uptown. He didn't snip, by the way. Hacked, sliced, sawed. Not scissors, not a razor."

She did something that had the screen image revolving, and different colors popping out. "Sharp, jagged-edged blade. I'm still analyzing and reconstructing, but it's looking like a one-sided blade about three and a half to three and three-quarters in length, about an inch across, an eighth of an inch deep. I think I can nail it down before I'm finished."

"Just under legal limit for a pocket sticker."

"It's looking," Harpo said with a head bob. "I'm not going to be able to tell you the brand. I can probably give you a list of possibles. Now if he'd stuck it in flesh, Morris could probably get close, or Birdman would punch it. He's the master of sharps around here."

"Good to know."

"Sweepers sent in some fibers from the body, but you said no rush on them."

"We know what he was wearing, and where he bought it. I needed to know if he took the trophy."

"Definitely. My money-back guarantee on it."

"And I could use the list of knives when you have it."

"No prob. I'll have Birdman take a look. He may be able to cut it down some."

"Speaking of birds." Eve glanced down at the one visible through the boot.

"You like? I crush on flamingos, but I'm not sure this is it. It's a temp 'cause you gotta be sure."

Eve couldn't argue with that. "Thanks, Harpo. Good, quick work."

"Our house specialty."

She went back to it as Eve walked out.

Two steps into her bullpen, she stopped dead, pinned to the spot by Sanchez's tie. She looked away from it, fearing, like staring at the sun, she might go blind.

It was the virulent color of an orange repeatedly exposed to excess radiation. On it floated searing yellow dots — unless they just floated in front of her eyes due to the five seconds she'd exposed her corneas.

"For God's sake, Sanchez. What is that thing?"

"Retribution." He glanced behind him, checked Jenkinson's currently empty desk. "Don't worry, boss, I'm not going to wear it out in the field. I mean, come on. I could blind people."

"We're people, too," Baxter said behind the safety of his sunshades.

With a shake of her head she started toward Peabody's desk, then changed her mind, signaled her partner to follow her. Maybe you didn't have to actually look at it to go blind or start bleeding from the ears.

Her office was safer.

Peabody clumped after her. "The crib is a crap place to sleep. I feel like I rolled around on sticks and rocks all night."

"I told McNab you weren't supposed to have sex."

"Ha-ha. As if you can even think about it in there. Plus he may be bony, but he's got more padding than the cots up there. Anyway, I'm going to start calling the stores we ID'd, but in the meantime, I got a couple hits on items from the Reinhold apartment."

"What and where?"

"I could think more clearly if I had real coffee."

"For Christ's sake get some then. What and where?"

"The crystal bowl, a shop just around the corner from the Grandline. The thing with that — oh *mama*!" she added after the first big gulp of caffeine laced with milk and sugar. "The thing with that is he didn't think it was worth all that much. Pawnbroker had a good eye, played him. That's my take from the way the guy danced around things when I pushed him on it."

"Try for coherency or I'm taking that coffee and pouring what's left over your head."

"Right. I started making contacts, and when I hit this place the guy got nervous. I got the 'didn't see the alert until a few minutes ago' bullshit, but he came clean mostly, I think, because he heard enough media reports on the murders to get edgy."

"He hit that shop in the morning, not long after he hit the banks. About ten."

"Yeah, right about ten, with the bowl and the diamond star earrings, the bangles in one of the suitcases. He grabbed the first offer of nine hundred on the bowl, and six hundred fifty on the earrings, three hundred and a quarter on the gold bangles. Turns out the bowl is worth about ten times what

Reinhold took for it."

"Small satisfaction on that. We need that evidence picked up."

"I sent out Uniform Carmichael," Peabody confirmed. "And right after I did, another shop contacted me. I don't know, maybe the word went out or it was just good timing. Reinhold sold the rest of the jewelry there, got another twenty-two hundred for that, then another fifteen for the menorah, and twenty-six hundred for the silver — the flatware."

"Adding to his pile."

"Yeah, not a lot, but decent when you add it up. The second shop is in the same area, about five blocks from the hotel."

"He kept it close in, easy for walking. But he went out of his comfort zone for the big-ticket items. The watches and the pearls."

"I tagged Cardininni," Peabody added. "She got the list from the neighbor. So she's hooking up with Carmichael, and they'll hit both shops to pick up the evidence."

"That works," Eve answered absently, her mind still on the route, the choices of liquidation sites. "He sold the bowl for a fraction of the worth, but he probably got more than he'd figured on."

To confirm, Peabody pulled out her PPC, brought up her notes. "Kevin Quint —

pawnbroker — stated: 'I could see he didn't know what he had, so I lowballed it to get a sense, you know? And he snapped up the first offer like some rube from Kansas or somewhere. I figured him to negotiate some, or whine how it was his dead old granny's, but he just said, *Pay me,* like that. So I did.' "

"Almost a thousand for a stupid bowl — that's what he thought. His lucky day. But when he gets more than he figured for all the rest, it's a pattern even he can see so he picks a classier place for the pieces he knows have real value."

"Trading up," Peabody suggested.

"Exactly. Three generations in business, estate sales a specialty — and the sob story about his dead parents. It dawned on his stupid ass his parents had better stuff than he'd thought. It was all crap to him, just something to sell. He went to a higher-class place because he wanted to make sure he got all he could get."

She took a moment to get herself coffee. "I bet he was pissed he hadn't taken more — the old stuff, the wedding canopy, the music box. Everything he considered junk. The second small satisfaction of the day," she murmured.

"What else have you got?"

"I'm still working on finding the electronics," Peabody told her. "He'd have to stick to the same area. What's the point in running all over hauling comps and 'links? I just finished generating a map and time line of what I've got so far."

"Send it to me. I'll merge it with what I got from his second hotel. Let's get it up on the board."

"Wait." Peabody stooped over Eve's computer, fiddled. "You've got it."

"Keep on the electronics, and the stores we nailed down. Give me a sense if we need to go by those stores for a face-to-face. We'll work on finding a pattern. If Feeney can spare McNab, he might have a better sense of where Reinhold would try to turn the e-stuff, using the map. I'm going to head up to EDD anyway, so I'll check."

She glanced at the board. "I hit the morgue, the lab. Morris's findings confirm ours, and Mira was right about the hair. According to Harpo, he took a good hank of it with him. And with her hair magic, she's working on IDing the knife he used to whack it off. She's got some blade guy on tap to assist."

"Birdman?"

Eve frowned. "Yeah. Who the hell is Birdman?"

"He transferred from Chicago about six months ago. Callendar went out with him a couple times. Didn't gel, but he's okay. And he really knows his sharps."

"Why isn't he called Sharpman or Bladeguy?"

"He has a parrot."

"That explains it. Did you read my morning report?"

"Yeah, and added Mal Golde's name to the hotel alert. He's probably sold everything by now, Dallas. Maybe he'll try to run."

"He's not done yet. Let me talk to Feeney, then we're going to generate a list of everyone he might go for. Relatives, friends, exes, crushes, bosses, coworkers, people who bugged him in school, teachers, doctors, neighbors."

"It's going to be a long list."

"Which is why he's not done."

She took the glide up, entered the three-ring circus of EDD. Sanchez's retribution tie wouldn't cause a single flicked eyelash among the explosive colors, dizzying patterns, and unrelenting motion.

She turned toward the blissful peace and what she thought of as the blandure of Feeney's office, stopped when she saw him talking to one of his geeks.

He made a contrast in his dog-shit brown sport coat and industrial beige shirt. His wiry ginger-and-silver hair made its own mini-explosion around his comfortably saggy face.

He swiped something onto a two-sided screen, and the geek responded with a rapid, incomprehensible spate of e-speak.

After a few grunts, Feeney nodded. "Get it done."

"All over it and back, Captain."

The geek bounced out on platform airboots.

Eve angled toward the open door. "Hey."

Feeney sat back, sipped from a mug with a starburst pattern Eve assumed had been made by his wife.

"Hey."

"I got a couple things. Can I talk to you?"

"You already are."

"Right." She went in, and did something she never did. She shut the door.

Feeney's eyebrows lifted. "Problem, kid?"

"Other than the fuckhole I'm after? Not really. I'd like to borrow McNab if you can spare him. I'm trying to track electronics the fuckhole took from his vics. He's been scattering his loot over lower Manhattan, heavy on the West Side. We're generating a route map. If we pin the electronics, it may give us more."

"The boy's good at juggling. If he can keep his balls in the air, you can have him."

"Appreciate it."

"Did his parents, huh?"

"Slaughtered them, then tortured and strangled his ex. He's a fucking moron, Feeney." She slid her hands in her pockets, jingling loose credits. "But he's cannier than I gave him credit for initially. Right now, he's having the best time of his life. He's not going to want to give that up, to give up his good time."

"Who's next?"

"That's the question."

"You wanna walk me through?"

It was generous of him. He had his own work, but he'd listen, he'd bounce things off her, let her bounce them off him. And it might come to that.

"Actually, I had something else. Unrelated. Or maybe, in a way, it's not altogether unrelated. This is what you want, right? What you worked for. This department, this desk, the bars."

Watching her, Feeney dipped his hand into a bowl and popped a candied almond.

"I wouldn't be sitting here otherwise."

"That's just right." She nodded, pacing, jiggling credits. "You were a hell of a murder cop, Feeney."

"Knew how to train 'em, too."

She smiled a little. "That's just right."

"Medal of Honor," he said, and his basset hound face lit up. "Ain't that a kick in the head."

"Yeah, it is. I guess word's out."

"They don't hand those out like gum-drops, kid. You did real good. And your man's getting something shiny, too. I'm real proud of both of you."

"Thanks." And that meant more than any medal. "It feels weird."

"It's the bullshit around it feels weird," he corrected, with precision accuracy. "But they gotta throw the confetti and blow the horn, Dallas. It's a boost for the depart-ment, and not just the PR blah-de-blah. For morale."

She hadn't wound her way through to that, but could see it now. Feeney saw it from the starting gun, she thought. And that's why he was who he was.

"I could do without the confetti and the blah-de-blah, but you're right. Feeney . . . You could've taken Homicide captain when the bars came to you. But you didn't."

"I'd had enough DBs for a while."

She shook her head. "That's not it, not really, is it?"

269

"It played a part. I needed a break from them," he admitted. "See them in your sleep, don't you?"

She thought of Lori Nuccio — one of many. "God, yes."

"I needed a break from that. Oh, we still get them, but mostly as support, not primary. Mostly, maybe even more, I wanted the e-work."

"You're the best there is."

He popped another nut. "You don't hear me arguing with that. It keeps my juices going. And you're proof I've got a knack for training. I had a choice between EDD and Homicide. I went with my gut, so I'm here. I've got my boys."

He nodded toward his bullpen, where regardless of body shape, his *boys* worked to their own drummer.

"I was a good murder cop. I'm a better e-man."

Not altogether satisfied, she sampled some of the nuts from his bowl. "Do you miss the field? I know you still spend plenty of time out in it, but —"

"I spend a lot with my ass in the chair. I'm good with that. Where's this going?"

"Whitney offered me captain."

First his mouth dropped open, then it rebounded into a wide, wide grin as he

270

slapped a hand on his desk. "About fucking time."

"I turned it down. My gut said no," she continued before he could respond. "It said I'm doing what I'm supposed to be doing now, and how I'm supposed to be doing it. I think I'd be a good captain. I'm a better investigator, so I said no. Am I stupid?"

He had to blow out a long breath, take a moment to evaluate.

"I gotta get over you said no. Okay, hell. From my seat, stupid's not listening to your gut. You'll take it when you're ready, but the point is, you earned it, and you earned it long before this."

"That's how I feel," she told him. "I didn't expect the offer, and I sure as hell didn't expect to say no when it came. But that's how I feel, it's what I know."

"The bars matter, kid, but they're not the day in and out for cops like you and me. It's the job that matters. I didn't have to teach you that. You came in knowing it."

"I think about somebody like Reinhold, and me reading reports on the investigation instead of investigating. Supervising or approving ops instead of running them. I don't want to give it up, Feeney."

"Like Reinhold."

"Yeah, and like you and me — in a twisted

271

way — he found what he really wants. He found it the minute he stuck the knife in his mother's belly. He didn't work for it, train for it, he wouldn't risk his life for it, but he'll learn, Feeney. With every one he kills, he'll learn something new."

"Go back to the beginning."

"Yeah, I'm heading there. Thanks." Feeling more settled, she popped another nut. "All around."

She went, circling around the movement and mayhem to McNab's cube.

"If you don't have anything hot, you belong to me today."

"I've got some warm, no hot. I can multitask."

"Coordinate with Peabody. Find the electronics. When you do, take them apart. I want anything and everything. He had to use the ones in his parents' place to do some of his research, his financial maneuvers. He'd have wiped them."

McNab smiled. "He'd think he wiped them. Nothing's ever all the way clean."

"Find them," she repeated.

She went back down to Homicide, and Peabody got up to follow her into her office.

"Suit store? On The Rack. He went in on Sunday, bought the suit, a couple shirts, some ties, socks. He had the suit altered, arranged to pick it up on Monday morning. Said he had other shopping to do. The clerk described him, once I loosened him up, as a snotty little jerk."

"Sounds like a good judge of character."

"I've got a list of what Reinhold bought there, and at Running Man — they were ready with it."

"It's Roarke's," Eve said simply.

"Yeah, I got that. Report's already sent to your unit."

"Good. McNab's going to coordinate with you on the electronics. Keep at it."

"We're open all day," Peabody said and headed back to her desk.

Eve closed herself in her office. She worked with the maps, expanded her board. Then sat, drinking coffee, studying the route he'd taken, his timing.

Scanning Peabody's reports on his purchases, she cemented her image of him.

Suits, ties, shirts — but beyond that primarily the trendy. Airskids and boots, jeans, a leather jacket, the cargo pockets McNab was so fond of, prime athletic wear, silk boxers.

Clothes, she thought, that reflected his own image of himself. Important, stylish, edgy, and successful.

Rich. He saw himself as a rich man now.

She called up the locations of the stores he'd visited, added them in, calculated the most probable route and timing, added that.

Skirting his old neighborhood. Never going into it, or not deep. Detouring out to the East Side — fresh turf.

He buys things along the route, for his new look, for his new vocations. A suit, shoes, cord, tape, athleticwear, a knife. A new 'link, but a drop 'link at least for now. A tablet? A PPC? Wouldn't he need to continue to research, to keep up with the media reports while on the street?

ID's the sticker, she decided. He has to get a new one. Would he, as Roarke suggested, try to create one on his own?

Curious, she brought up his file, ran through his employment and education history. No stellar comp skills or experience, she noted, despite the short, aborted attempt to work in comp game design.

Crapped out there, barely passed basic Comp Science in high school, and that with an extra semester. Skin of his teeth in his two college e-courses.

No, he didn't have the chops to create a passable ID on his own. He had to pay for one, or find someone to do it for him.

She added every e-instructor he'd had,

grade school to his short college career. Lab partners? she wondered. She'd check on them when she contacted the instructors.

Then there was Golde — he had the chops, Eve imagined — but he wouldn't cooperate with Reinhold. Still, she took the time to contact him, to confirm his safety.

She learned he was still at his parents', and intended to stay there.

Satisfied with that, for now, Eve looked back at her board. Start at the beginning, she reminded herself.

As soon as she generated what would be a very, very long list of possibles, she was going back to the beginning, and the Reinhold apartment.

It was starting to piss him off.

"You're stalling, Ms. Farnsworth. I feel a snip coming on."

Her eyes met his, wearily. "I tried to teach you, Jerry, doing a project right takes time. If you don't do this right, it won't pass. If it doesn't pass, I know you'll hurt me. I don't want you to hurt me anymore, Jerry."

She was stalling, a little. It took time to do a project right, especially when she needed him to carefully insert a beacon that would — she hoped — alert the police if and when the ID was scanned.

Just as she'd needed him to undercode a message into the financial routing she prayed someone with exceptional e-skills would find.

Jerry's skills were good — wasted potential, she thought — but he was lazy, simply too lazy to look deep, to learn more.

The ID was delicate and complicated work, and he was ham-handed and impatient. But they were nearly there.

And she'd wheedled out a little water, for herself and Snuffy, though he'd dripped it into her mouth, then her dog's, a few stingy drops at a time.

"I've got an appointment, goddamn it. If I miss it because you're screwing around, you're losing two fingers, and your ugly dog loses an eye."

He took out his knife, snapped out the blade, and waved it back and forth in front of her face. "I bet I can pop his eye right out with this."

Through sheer force of will, she kept her gaze calm and steady on his. "It's not going to take much longer, Jerry. It's a lot of data to upload if we're going to give you a complete background. Now you need to key in the next code, exactly as I tell you."

"Yeah, yeah, yeah." He checked his wrist unit, one he intended to replace with something mag before he met the realtor. And Asshole was due back any minute with the take from hocking the first round of electronics.

"You've got twenty minutes," he warned her.

"Master Command D, backslash generate . . ."

It had to be right, she thought, just exactly right, or he'd walk away clean. It had to be perfect, or the program itself would alert him to the addition.

He'd make good on his threat then. Though she could no longer feel her fingers, she wanted to keep them. And Snuffy slept in her lap, a warm weight. His little chest rose and fell. As long as it did, she'd do what she could for him, and for herself.

And if the little bastard killed her, at least she'd die knowing she'd handed him the means to his own end.

"Insert code twenty-five backslash B," she continued, her voice soft and slow. Her eyes filled with cold, feral hate.

12

Eve broke the seal on the Reinholds' apartment door and entered. It still smelled of death, with a lacing of the sweeper's chemicals.

"We're going through it again."

"What are we looking for?" Peabody asked her.

Eve scanned the living area, still surprisingly neat and tidy in the wake of murder. "He played Little League, and kept the bat. Or more likely his parents kept it. They'd have kept other stuff, right? Isn't that how it works? Parents hang on to things, to pieces of their kids. Photographs, sure, but mementos."

"Kid drawings, school reports, trophies, and awards, like that, sure. Most would. Mine sure did — do."

"Anything they kept he didn't take we look at. Family photos, too. Vacation and holiday stuff. Anything might connect to someone he's got a grudge against, or somewhere he wants to go again."

She walked into the kitchen. "It started here. When he picked up the knife, turned it on his mother, that's when it all started for him. Reconstruction says she was here. It's lunchtime. He's fixing his lunch or she's fixing it for him. She's fixing it."

Eve put a picture of the mother in her head, as she'd been in her ID shot. "She's fixing it because that's what she does. She fixes the meals, keeps the house. Probably a sandwich so the knife's out. It's right there when he decides to do it. She's nagging at him, that's how he sees it."

And seeing it herself, Eve walked around the table. "You've got to get a job, grow up, get your shit together. Maybe she tells him she and his father are giving him a deadline or he's out. Maybe she didn't wait to confront him together with her husband. So he picks up the knife, jams it into her. And it feels so *good,* the look on her face is so *satisfying* he does it again. Just keeps doing it even when she tries to get away, when she falls, even when she's already dead. And then he eats his lunch."

"What?"

"He ate after Nuccio. Had a big snack. I bet he sat right down here and ate, and started planning how he'd kill his father. Plenty of time, time to start putting what he wanted together, hunting up their passcodes, checking out the bank accounts. Plenty of time.

"He never panicked," Eve continued. "He never tried to clean anything up, hide anything. It's like he . . . came of age here in the kitchen over his mother's bloody corpse."

"Well, God."

"He's got the ambition and the brains to go after the money, after what he recognizes or considers valuables. To take the time for planning that before and after he kills his father. To do that he gets his old bat — that memento. Maybe his old man pitched him a few back in the day, criticized his form. He doesn't take the bat with him. It didn't matter to him. He buys a new one for his tool kit."

"Leaving childish things behind."

"Huh?"

"I just thought . . . you said he came of age. So he left the bat he'd used as a kid and bought a new one. They probably bought him the first bat, the murder weapon. He buys one now for himself."

"That's good." Eve nodded. "That's how he thinks. Still, a little fear of the father. He hides, lies in wait, takes him by surprise. Ambush rather than confront. Then he leaves them both there, where they fell, leaves them swimming in their own blood, and eats and sleeps and plans. It's like a kid again, a teenager maybe, tossing his stuff on the floor, stepping over it rather than picking it up, putting it away. Nobody here to tell him to clean up his space. It's deliberate."

"What part?"

"Staying here until Saturday night. Leaving them on the floor, dishes scattered around the kitchen. She kept a tidy home, raised him to pick up his space, nagged at him about it. Now fuck her, he'll make as much mess as he wants."

"No mess in the living area or their bedroom."

"He's not interested in those spaces. It's all about the little office area, the kitchen, his room, the bathroom. He hates how old it feels in here, all his mother's fancy touches, the old stuff she and his father hang on to, set around, or tuck away. The traditions irritate him. He wants new — like the new bat, the new suit. He wants some shine."

She took a turn around again. "He'll look for a status place. He wants the opposite of this, the opposite of settled, homey, traditional. That's what he's after now."

"A newer building, or something recently rehabbed."

"Modern, I think. Slick and sleek. Everything he's never had because he doesn't see what he had here, he's not grateful for growing up in a home where people cared about making it nice, keeping it nice, where they valued family heirlooms and traditions. He hates all of it. Let's take it apart, then follow his trail."

The silver-and-glass tower rising above the Hudson River boasted its own bank, a two-level state-of-the-art fitness center — with pool, a five-star spa, a select group of high-end boutiques, twenty-four-hour concierge service, two exclusive restaurants, three bars, and for an additional fee, a daily, weekly, or monthly cleaning service.

The apartment on the eighteenth floor was, for him, a wet dream.

Floor-to-ceiling windows comprised the river-facing wall. A touch of a button, or voice command, opened them to the terrace.

The generous living space — humongo, built-in wall screen, floors of cool silver, walls of pale gold — spilled into a dining area already furnished with a floating, free-form chrome table and glossy black chairs. The kitchen beyond, all hard silver, strong gold, rippled glass, held every modern feature he could imagine, and plenty he hadn't.

He listened with half an ear as the realtor buzzed at him about square footage, location, amenities — soundproofing, full voice command, private elevator — blah, blah, blah.

He nodded, trying for knowledgeable and sophisticated as he circled around to the master suite.

He all but felt tears rush to his eyes.

Like the dining room, like the living area with its gel platform sofa, chrome tables, gold scoop chairs, it was already furnished.

She fussed with a remote that had the black headboard glowing, the privacy screens on that wall of glass sliding up, then down, the glass opening to the terrace.

He struggled to maintain his composure, glancing at the bathroom — big, sunken jet tub, clear glass multijet shower. Drying tube, flash-tan tube, another screen, a small gas fireplace, an attached dressing area complete with wardrobe comp.

The second bedroom, described by the yammering realtor as the perfect home office for a bachelor, also had its own bath — smaller than the master's but no less swank.

He poked around, opening closets, wandering out to the terrace, giving her short answers or no comments.

It was, in his mind, already his. Everything he wanted, everything he deserved.

He wanted her out of it so he could flop down on the couch and kick his feet, wave his fists in the air in triumph.

"It's prime real estate," she continued — talk, talk, talk. "The complex has only been open for six months, and is already at ninety-three percent. The previous tenant hadn't fully moved in, was still furnishing as you can see, when business required him to move to Paris. This unit has only just become available, and I expect it to be snapped up by next week. And only that long due to the holiday."

"It might do." Reinhold tried for weariness. "I really don't have much time to spend on hunting."

She gave him an easy, professional smile — a short, solid woman in a purple suit and sensible shoes. "You said you'd just come back to New York from Europe yourself."

"Hmmm." He merely nodded. He wandered back, frowned at the kitchen, opened a few doors, drawers. "It's a bit small for

284

the entertaining I do, but it's here."

"The caterer on site is one of the best in the city. Of course, you'd hardly expect less from a Roarke property."

He glanced at her. "Roarke?" He felt the thrill spear through him, couldn't suppress the smile. "Roarke owns the property?"

"Yes, so you can be assured the security, the staffing, all the amenities are top of the scale."

"I'm sure. His wife is a police officer, isn't she?"

"That's right. Have you seen *The Icove Agenda*? It's based on one of her cases. Fabulous vid. Just fabulous."

"I've heard of it. I don't have much time for vids." He dismissed it as if such things were too frivolous for his notice. Inside he reveled. The cop trying to find him was married to the man who'd built his new headquarters.

It couldn't be more perfect.

"What about the furnishings?"

"As I said, the previous tenant had to leave for Europe, and quickly. He'll make arrangements to have the furniture taken out, or is willing to sell any and all."

"I see. It would save time, and time is money." He glanced at his spiffy new wrist unit as if verifying. "I'll take it, and the furniture."

"You . . . You don't want to see the other properties?"

"Time, money, and this suits well enough. What does he want for the furniture?"

"All of it?"

"As I said." He gave her a hurry-it-up finger wiggle. "I don't waste time."

"Just give me a moment to check. Building management will need first and last month's rent, as well as the security deposit, on signing."

"Understood. I'll have my girl wire it today. I'll move in this evening."

"This —"

"I prefer not to spend another night in a hotel," he said, rolling right over her. "I don't have much with me. I'll make arrangements to have the rest of my things sent once I'm settled. Make it happen."

So saying, he wandered off again, leaving her scrambling.

Eve followed Reinhold's footprints. To banks, hotel, shops, pawnbrokers. She talked to clerks, reviewed security discs. Studying him, watching him revel in his newfound life, his murderous freedom.

She'd found more photos — tucked away. And, as Peabody had suggested, school

286

reports. Average at best. They'd unearthed an old vid of him from childhood — labeled *Jerry, Talent Show, Grade Five.* He'd competed with a song, and had carried it fairly well.

Well enough to place third. The vid had clearly shown his anger, his sulkiness when accepting his little trophy. Another vid memorialized his Little League team's bid for the championship. They lost, and Reinhold struck out on his last at bat.

Other vids showed family vacations — Reinhold belly-flopping into a pool, swimming choppily. Not the athletic type, Eve judged. Holidays, birthdays, high school graduation.

On foot now, Eve and Peabody walked between pawnshops. And Eve stopped outside of a fancy salon.

"He needs a new look."

"He didn't change it. We've got him on the feed from the hotel."

"That doesn't mean he hasn't changed it since."

She pushed her way in, badged the first tech she saw and flashed Reinhold's photo.

Tapping out there, they hit the next pawnshop, the next salon.

And Peabody stopped, pointed. "There. He could've stopped there for hair and face

287

stuff. He'd have passed it."

"True Essence? What is it?"

"A chain, but a pretty high-class one. Mostly above my pay grade unless they're having a good sale. Enhancements, hair stuff, body stuff, bath stuff," Peabody elaborated. "The works. The uptown one — on Madison — has a frosty little day spa attached. You can go in for a makeover, but then, well, if I do that I feel like I've gotta buy something. But the staff's really helpful. It's part of their rep. Solid and personal customer service."

"Let's see if they gave any of that to Reinhold."

Eve didn't understand places like this. The walls — all artily lit — the kiosks, the lower-level area — were all loaded with products created to enhance you, change you, transform you, or improve you. Skin, hair, face, eyes, lips, ass — there was even a whole section dedicated to throats and boobs, though they called it décolletage.

But she had to admit, the trim, stylish, and perfectly groomed staff didn't swarm as they did in some places.

They were approached by one woman in classic New York black. The tall blonde with killer looks looked pretty normal to Eve's eye. No spikes, visible piercings or tats, no explosion of odd-colored hair.

"Welcome to True Essence. Can I help you with anything this afternoon?"

"Yeah. Have you seen this man?"

Eve took out the photo, and since the blonde didn't seem to be an asshole, palmed her badge discreetly.

"Oh, that's the man who killed his parents." Instantly her voice went to stage whisper. "I saw him on the media reports. You're looking for him?"

"That's right."

"I haven't seen him, but I had the last two days off. Would you like to talk to the manager? I can call her out."

"Appreciate it."

"Sure. Give me a minute."

"Oooh, look at this lip dye."

"No," Eve said flatly when Peabody snagged a sampler.

"Popping Pink. Who doesn't want to pop?" Peabody squeezed some on an applicator, tapped it on her lips.

"Cut that out. You're not a girl in here. You're a cop."

"I'm a girl cop." And Peabody did a quick, agile turn toward eye crap.

Apparently, Eve noted, the managerial position required less normal. She watched the woman with plum-colored hair and silver brow studs clip her way over on high zebra-striped boots.

"I'm the manager. And you're —"

"Lieutenant Dallas, Detective Peabody. We're looking for this man."

"So I saw on screen last night. Why do you think he came in here?"

"He was in this area, and he shopped in this area. We're checking other venues."

"I see. Do you know what he might have wanted, what sort of products he might have come in for? Frankly, I hardly see why a suspected murderer would shop for enhancements or body products. We're hardly a den of iniquity."

"You recognized his face."

"I told you I saw it on the media bulletin last night."

Put it together, sister, Eve thought, but spelled it out.

"I bet a lot of other people did, too. A lot of people who might recognize him if, say, he walked into a deli for a freaking bowl of soup. So being the suspicious type I figure he might have enough brains to change his hair color."

"Oh." The manager took a deep breath that projected both annoyance and concern. "We should move into hair then. Perhaps one of our stylists can help you. That's a lovely shade on you," she said to Peabody, with a much warmer smile. "You shouldn't be without it. Should I have it held for you?"

"Oh, I . . . it does look mag."

"No." Eve cut them both off. "I think, I don't know, just spit-balling, but we should spend our time here trying to track down a murderer. Hair?"

"Of course." The smile faded, the eyes chilled. "This way."

She wound through the kiosks, the shelves, the customers who, like Peabody, played with samples or loaded up silver baskets with products they figured would make them sexier, prettier, softer, smoother, younger.

Feeling Peabody's attention wander, Eve bared her teeth. Peabody quickened her pace.

"Marsella? I'd like you to help these women."

"I'd love to." Marsella, her short, sharp cap of raven black edged with candy pink, beamed a welcoming smile. "What a stellar and interesting cut," she said to Eve. "So few could pull that off. I have a wonderful product that would punch out your highlights. And I love the casual day-do," she said to Peabody. I bet you'd look *mag* in hot curls for an evening bounce. The home-care kit is incredibly easy to do. And you could —"

"Fascinating," Eve interrupted in a tone that said otherwise. "But we're more interested in him."

She flashed the photo of Reinhold, and her badge.

"Oh. Oh." Marsella shot a wide-eyed — smoked lids, heavily kohled — glance at her manager. "I don't understand."

"Do you recognize him?" Eve demanded.

"Well, yeah. I don't understand," she repeated.

"How do you recognize him?"

"From yesterday, when I served him. I don't —"

"Understand," Eve finished. "What time did you serve him?"

"Um, um. He came in maybe around one-thirty. I'm not sure, but it was right after I got back from lunch."

"I need your surveillance discs from yesterday. Open till close." After ordering the manager, Eve turned back to Marsella. "Do you remember what you . . . served him?"

"Tropical Blond Hair Color, with a caramel lowlights add-on kit, Drenched shampoo and conditioner — color bond — the Master of Your Own deluxe styling kit."

She rattled them off as if itemized in her head.

"He wanted other products from other sections, so I stuck with him, recommended the Sun Blast Bronzer — face and body in number four. Um . . . the Solie Quench, again face and body, and the Lightning Blue Eye kit by Francesco. He wanted the top of the line. I suggested he apply for the store credit service, which would give him ten percent off on his purchases, but he wanted to pay cash."

She bit her lip. "I offered him the free consult, and recommended Aly do his eye change here on site for a very reasonable fee, but he blew that off. If done incorrectly, it can cause swelling or redness, but he insisted on pay and go. He signed the waiver, so if he had a problem, I don't understand why he called the police."

"Don't watch much screen, Marsella? Don't keep up with current events?"

"I've been pretty busy. My sister and her fam's coming in for Thanksgiving, and I'm helping my mother . . . Why?"

"If you had I think you'd recognize him from media reports. His name is Jerald Reinhold, and he killed three people in the last couple days."

"He — I — *God!*" Taking a quick step

293

back, she slapped a hand to her heart. "Oh my God! He was right here, and I worked with him for at least a half hour. Am I in trouble?"

"Why would you be?"

"I don't know. I sold him all those products. It was a really nice commission. I even did the comp morph to show him how he could look after using everything."

Now Eve smiled. "Can you still call that up?"

"I — Yes! I can. I think. I just feel so . . . Can I get some water? I feel a little shaky. He seemed so *normal.* Kind of clueless and trying to act like he knew all about it. Oh, oh, he bought a piercing kit, too. I forgot."

Pausing just a moment, she fanned a hand in front of her face. "He bought the A Hole in One kit, and a gold hoop from accessories. I forgot."

Sympathetic — and impressed with her memory — Eve tried to calm her. "No, you didn't, and this helps us a lot. Get your water, Marsella, take a breath, then show us the morph."

"Thanks. I feel kind of sick. Who did he kill?"

"His parents and his ex-girlfriend."

Her exotic eyes filled. "Come on! Not really."

"Really. Let's move it, Marsella."

"Okay. Okay." She scrambled away, wobbling some on her towering heels.

"Good call on this place, Peabody."

"Jackpot."

"I can't figure out why he didn't spread his purchases out, other venues, the way he did for the clothes, the tools, the selling his loot."

"Because you don't get the lure." On a lusty sigh, Peabody turned a little circle, scanning with eyes full of reverence and desire. "If I could afford it, I'd spend *hours* in here. I wouldn't be able to walk out without loading up — especially if one of the servers started priming me. I couldn't resist."

"Huh."

"The music's all pumping, the lighting's bold. Sexy energy. Lots of it. All these products just saying how mag you'd look if you bought them. All these totally iced servers — male and female — telling you the same. Drop a couple thousand, and walk out a whole new you, a better you."

"And people buy that?"

"I'm buying it right now, and arguing with myself. I could get the lip dye. I'm not spending anything on travel for Thanksgiving. I have enough lip dye. But I don't have *this* fabo, uptown, new lip dye. It costs too much. It's a personal appearance investment. I —"

"Got it. Shut up. Go push the manager on those discs," she ordered as Marsella came trotting back with a tablet.

"Malachi Golde! That's his name. I remembered after I got some water, calmed down."

"No, it's not his name, but that's the name he gave you?"

"Yes. I asked him, for the morph, and that's what he said. We keep them for a week, in case the customer comes back, wants something else, or says something didn't work." She tapped her way through. "See! See! Here he is. We have to take an as-is shot, and this is as is."

"Yeah." Eve looked into Reinhold's smug, smiling eyes. "That's as is. Show me the morph."

Marsella tapped again, turned the tablet. "If used properly and to full potential, he'd come out about like this. They're not a hundred percent, but it gives a good representation."

"I bet." Eve studied the newly blond, blue-eyed, bronzed and pierced Reinhold.

"He bought the styling kit, but he was really vague on how he'd style the do. So I just had to go with the as-is do, new color and lights."

"This is good, this is excellent. I need you to send it to me at this code, and I need a hard copy now."

"Oh, sure. I can send right from the tab, but I have to look for the print. It'll take a minute."

"Make it happen. You did good, Marsella."

"Thanks." She smiled wanly. "It's my first murderer."

"Let's keep it that way. And get me that — what was it — Pink Pop, Popped-Up Pink — that lip dye."

"Popping Pink, by La Femme? It's mag, totally, but I have to be honest. It's not really your color. Now the Blooming Poppy or the —"

"Not for me." Eve dug for credits. "How much?"

"Sixty-two dollars."

"You're shitting me."

Marsella's face fell into apology. "No. It's a really excellent product, honestly, and lasts all day. It's waterproof, smudge-proof, has conditioners, and —"

"Fine, fine." Considering the cost, Eve dug out a credit card. "Put it on this."

"Of course. It really does well with the Rose Petal liner."

"Don't push it, Marsella. Just the lip crap and the hard copy. And make it quick."

Marsella swiped the card on the tablet, turned it so Eve could sign. "I'll have the picture and the product right back to you. Two minutes," she promised, and dashed — no wobbling now — away.

Taking a moment, Eve glanced around, thumbs in front pockets. No, she didn't see the lure. What she saw were countless products that given half a chance the Terrifying Trina would smear, brush, paint, rub, and coat all over her face, hair, and body.

That alone was enough to make her want to get the hell out.

"Got the discs." Peabody held them up and she strode back to Eve. "The manager got really cooperative when it turned out he got his stuff in here. Anything we need, want, anything she can do. Total CYA."

"Works for me. I've seen the morph, and Marsella's sending it to my PPC, making a hard copy."

"We can have it out to the media, on screen inside ten minutes."

"No." Eve shook her head. "He sees it, he changes again — and he'll be a lot more careful about it next time. Now we know what he looks like *now* — potentially anyway. We keep it in house, away from the

298

media, until circumstances call for the spread."

"I have everything." Marsella came back with a pink and black leopard print bag, offered it to Eve. "The morph's in the white envelope, the product's in the small bag. I threw in some samples, you really should at least try the Blooming Poppy."

"Thanks. If you remember anything else, contact me."

"I will. And believe me, I'm going to watch the screen. This is scary. Like I said, I never served a murderer before."

That you know of, Eve thought as they headed out.

"You bought something." Peabody's voice was an accusatory whisper. "I turn my back for a *second*, and you buy something after dissing the whole idea of the store." She huffed. "What did you buy?"

"Some crap called Popping Pink lip dye." She slipped the envelope out, shoved the bag at a speechless Peabody.

"You — you — you bought it for me?" The *me* ended dangerously close to a squeal. "Dallas!"

"If you hug me I'm shoving that lip dye up your ass."

Peabody did a little dance in her pink cowboy boots. "I wanna. I really, really wanna. But I won't because I won't have pretty pink lips if it's up my ass."

"Keep that in mind."

"That was really nice."

"It was the best way to get you to stop whining."

"Really nice," Peabody repeated. "Thanks."

Eve consulted the route map. "You called the store, and we hit. We hit big. You get a prize."

"A totally mag prize." She riffled through the bag. "Oooh, samples!"

"Peabody."

Peabody stopped riffling, but kept grinning. "Okay, he went blond and blue right? Rich man's tan, pierced ear — most likely ear with the hoop. He'd need at least a couple hours to do all that. More like, I'd say, four to do it right."

"And a place to do it. A hotel again? Go in looking as is, leave looking new. Not a smallish hotel then. Someone might notice, *should* notice. Maybe another business hotel, a big, busy hotel. Or . . ."

"Or?"

"He spent the night with his murdered parents, several hours with his dead ex. Maybe he picked his next victim, and did his makeover there."

300

"Creepy."

"He hits that note. Not a family place for this. He wouldn't want to take on a spouse, kids. Look through for singles, and we'll start there. Start contacting them via 'link. Anyone who doesn't answer or seems off, we pay personal visits to. And I want to talk to Golde again, in person. How did Reinhold get his old ID?"

"And the fact he's using it? I think it ups Golde on the hit list."

"Agreed. Start looking," Eve said when they reached the car. "Start contacting. Start with Golde — he's at his parents' — and tell him we're coming."

"All over that."

13

While Eve drove, she used the in-dash 'link to send Reinhold's morph to Baxter, and instruct him to distribute copies to the rest of the department. She added a media lock. As she updated the commander, checked her own incomings for anything relevant, Peabody worked her own 'link.

And when her partner fell silent, Eve glanced over. "What?"

"The Brooklyn grandparents. I talked to the grandmother. She says Reinhold hasn't contacted them, and it rings true."

"I don't see him going that route, not yet. So what's the problem."

"It's not a problem," Peabody began, but sighed. "The out-of-town grandparents are coming in later today, and they're going to stay with the Brooklyn ones. Together. There are sibs and family members for both sides coming in, or opening their homes to those who're coming. The ME's releasing the bodies tomorrow, but they're planning to wait until Saturday for a double memorial. They're all getting together for Thanksgiving. Family needs family. That's what she said."

Peabody stared down at her 'link. "It's sad, really sad, but it's kind of great, too."

"Great?"

"They're all pulling together, coming together, staying together. I think Reinhold has a really good family, on both sides. He never appreciated what he had, what they gave him. But now, when they're facing one of the hardest things that can happen, they appreciate each other. And it made me realize I'm going to miss seeing my family this time around. Made me wonder if I appreciate them enough."

"I hear it every time you mention any one of them. Don't slap yourself over that." But since she could see Peabody was doing just that, Eve pushed the theme. "You and your family are a big, sloppy pile of Free-Agey appreciation. It's a little embarrassing."

On a half laugh, Peabody's broody look shifted to sentimental smile. "Yeah, I guess it is, a little."

Satisfied with the response, Eve considered as she drove. "He's not going for any family then. Not yet anyway. Too many of them together. He wouldn't know that, but he'd see it pretty damn fast if he decided to target any of them. Friends, employment, childhood grievances, teachers, exes. That's where we look first. And eliminate anyone with kids at home for now. I don't see him dealing with kids."

"Too messy, too complicated, too much trouble."

"Exactly. He's gone one at a time so far, all with him having the initial advantage. We follow that pattern."

"He's probably not going for Golde, or not top of his list, since Golde's staying at his mother's, working from there, too, primarily. He's freaked about leaving her during the day while his father's at work."

"He'd be on the list, but no, not top of it," Eve agreed. "I want to talk to him anyway."

"He's expecting us. And he said he was going to tag Dave Hildebran. He's been staying at his parents', too."

"What about the other friend. Asshole Joe?"

"I connected. He's at work, not worried. He thinks we're way off base. And even if Reinhold went crazy, he won't believe he might be a target. They're buds, man. Tight buds. And being tight buds he's positive

304

Reinhold will tag him, and soon. Swears he'll tell us so we can straighten this all out."

"Rat out his tight bud."

"Didn't sound like he had a problem with that at all. It's why we call him Asshole Joe."

"We should get him a name tag," Eve said and started hunting for parking on Golde's block.

A proud and happy new tenant of the elaborate New York West, Reinhold let himself back into Ms. Farnsworth's brownstone. He'd imagined himself living there for a few days, maybe even a week, but he'd hit the freaking jackpot.

He'd spend the night in his frosty new apartment. Once he tied up a few loose ends.

It had all taken longer than he'd expected, so he reactivated the droid, ordered it to fix him a snack. All that paperwork, he thought. Miles of it. And he could admit he'd sweated it some when they'd gone over his data with goddamn microgoggles. But he'd passed. Points for Fat-Ass Farnsworth.

Lucky for her, he thought, while he chowed down on a Reuben and a couple kosher pickles. Now he wouldn't snip off her fingers and toes.

Probably.

The thing to do first was go through the place again, finish piling up what looked like it was worth taking. He'd have the droid pack it up, transport it to his new place. He'd enjoy having the droid to do his grunt work.

And a man in his position needed a house droid. The New York West would expect it of him.

Ms. Farnsworth sure didn't — or wouldn't — need it.

He'd already emptied the safe, packed that up in one of the fat old hag's red suitcases.

He wasn't sure about the color or the brand, if they really suited his new persona. But he didn't have time to worry about it.

Time is money, he thought, and cracked himself up.

He'd gone through her jewelry. He didn't have much of an eye there, but figured anything in cases had to be worth something, even if it was ugly.

He ordered the droid to wipe the drives on the remaining electronics, then unhook the rest of the comps and equipment and haul them downstairs.

A lot of e-stuff, he mused. Good thing he'd thought ahead, had the droid start liquidating.

He chose what he wanted for his new

home office, separated them.

"Take that bunch there." Reinhold picked up one of the memo cubes he'd separated into his take pile. "Follow these instructions."

He recited a shop name, an address.

"Get what you can for them. You should be able to handle it in one trip this time. Get cash. Just cash," he repeated. "Whose property are you, Asshole?"

"I am the property of Anton Trevor, president and CEO of Trevor Dynamics."

"Don't you forget it. Get the cash, come back. No detours. We've got work to do."

While the droid took care of business, Reinhold took another tour of the house. Maybe that picture frame was real silver. Maybe that fancy bowl was worth something. She had so much crap in the house, who knew if it was junk or sell-worthy?

He could probably take the bags of her clothes and get something for them, but he didn't want to touch all those old-lady clothes again. Besides, he was rolling in it now, why bother with the small shit?

He had the equipment he wanted. The droid could box it up, transport it, set it up in the new place. Same with his clothes, and the suitcase full of stuff he'd have the droid sell over the next couple days.

Maybe he could scrape out more if he stayed a little longer, but all he could think about was getting into his new place, having the droid fix him a drink. Maybe he'd try a martini or something fancy like that. Drink it on the terrace.

He'd watch screen, have the droid fix him a big-ass dinner.

Now he had somebody to wait on him that wouldn't nag and bitch and try to make him feel worthless. Now he had somebody else on shit detail, and nobody to tell him to get a job, grow up, be responsible, do his work.

Fuck all of that. Fuck all of them.

Starting, he thought, with Ms. Farnsworth.

He'd considered how to do it. He liked the knife. He really enjoyed the way it felt when the blade went in, came out. But it was so damn messy, and he had nice clothes on.

He should buy some protective gear for down the road.

Same went for the bat. Blood and brains everywhere, and that was a rush. But he'd fuck up his clothes.

Definitely buying protective gear.

He could strangle her, but he kind of wanted to try something new. To expand his horizons. Wasn't that one of her favorite things to say? Expand your horizons.

Yeah, he'd expand them on her. See how *she* liked it.

He got what he wanted, sauntered into the office.

She didn't look so good. Or smell so good.

She'd pissed herself again, which surprised him. He hadn't given her more than a couple sips of water all day, and no food.

He thought she maybe looked like she'd lost a couple pounds.

The Jerry Reinhold Diet, he thought with a cackle that had her head snapping up.

No, make that the Anton Trevor Diet. New look, new digs, new name. New man.

"Hey, there!"

He didn't see the dog; didn't give Snuffy a thought. Out of sight, out of mind.

But he did see she'd been trying to get free. The tape around her right hand was looser, and she'd managed to drag her hand out about halfway up. The wrist that showed beyond the cord and tape looked like raw meat.

"Ouch!" He clucked his tongue, ticked his index finger back and forth. "But that's what you get when you don't listen to the rules. Where'd you think you were going to go if you got loose? What'd you think you were going to do? I mean, clue up, Ms.

Farnsworth. I'm a lot smarter than you gave me credit for."

He posed, tapping thumbs to his chest. "I've got all your money. I've got all your shit that's worth taking. I look iced, and you look like crap."

Smiling, smiling, he stepped closer to her. "And you did everything I told you to do. You're the useless one. The stupid one. And I'm the one who's going to live in a totally mag apartment. I'll probably get one in London or Paris, too, once I finish my . . . personal business and hire out. People pay a lot of money for an experienced hit man — governments, too."

His eyes narrowed at the derision in hers. "You don't think I can make the big bucks, bitch? I already did, and most of it used to be yours. With my rep I can name my own price. I'm rich, and I'm famous, and you're sitting in your own piss. Who's the winner now? Who's the winner now?"

He ripped the tape off her mouth, taking dried flesh with it.

She looked him hard in the eye. Her voice was little more than a croak, as dry as her skin. But she'd have her say. "You're nothing. Nothing but a vicious little turd."

He punched her. He hadn't intended to because, *fuck,* it hurt his hand. But nobody was going to talk to him like that. Nobody.

"You think you're better than me. You think I'm nothing? I'll show you nothing."

She knew she was dead before he put the plastic bag over her head. She'd come to accept it. Still she fought. Not to survive, not any longer. But to cause him pain. To give him something back.

She rocked in the chair, even as he twisted the opening of the bag tight, even as he tried to wrap the tape around and around. She shoved back with what strength she had left, hoarded the small satisfaction when she felt the chair slam into him, heard him yelp and curse over the roar of blood in her head.

The chair overbalanced, her weight carrying it back. Though she gulped like a fish, her body screaming for air, somewhere inside she smiled when he screamed in pain.

He kicked her. Her belly exploded with agony, her chest burned, and everything began to shake.

Then it quieted, and all slid away.

She died with the smile deep in her heart.

He kept kicking her long after she went still. He couldn't stop.

She'd called him nothing. She'd hurt him.

It wasn't fair, it wasn't right. So he kicked her, and he wept and raged until he'd exhausted himself.

Dropping into a chair he struggled to get his breath back. His foot throbbed like a rotted tooth where the chair, with her fat ass in it, had dropped like a boulder. And his midsection hurt, felt bruised and tender where she'd slammed the chair back against him.

He should've sliced her up. Fuck the mess, he should have sliced her to pieces like he'd done with his old lady.

Now he was sweaty, shaky, and he thought maybe something in his foot might be broken.

He ought to burn her house down and her with it. That's what he ought to do.

But he wasn't stupid, he thought as he swiped tears away. He *wasn't* nothing. The longer it took them to find her fat, dead ass the better.

Besides, they'd never tie him to it. Who'd tie him to the old bitch? Some bitch who taught high school Comp Science?

All he had to do now was walk away. And he could soak himself, and his aching foot, in his new jet tub.

He rose, let out a whining whimper, and was forced to limp out of the room. Blinking back tears of self-pity, he hobbled downstairs where the droid stood awaiting further instructions.

"Take the rest of this, on foot." He made another memo cube, with the address, instructions. "Straight there, straight to the concierge. Give her that memo, and get things set up. Where's the money?"

"Here, sir." The droid handed him an envelope.

After a moment's consideration, Reinhold pulled out a few bills. "Walk to West Broadway, that's far enough. Take a cab from there. No leave those," he said when the droid reached for the duffel and one of the suitcases. "I'll take those. I want everything set up before I get there. Then you go out, buy what you need to make me a big steak dinner, and a martini."

"Yes, sir. Gin or vodka?"

Reinhold went blank. He hadn't known martinis came in more than one variety. "What do you think, Asshole? Vodka — and don't get cheap shit. Now get moving."

Reinhold hobbled into the kitchen. He'd seen blockers in there. Hunting them up, he took two. Then out of pique, he yanked dishes, glassware out of cabinets, hurled them against the wall, used a kitchen knife to gouge at the refrigerator, the front of the dishwasher, across the counter, the cabinets.

And felt better.

Satisfied, he went out, retrieved his duffel,

the last red suitcase, and walked out of the house. But even with the blockers and the release of breaking and destroying, the foot troubled him. After two blocks, he ran a search for the closest clinic on his latest victim's handheld, limped another block before he managed to catch a cab.

He should've snipped off her toes, he decided. He should've made her scream. Being dead wasn't enough, not when she'd hurt him first.

He slumped in the corner of the cab and dreamed of his new place, a jet tub, a manly drink, and money to burn.

Eve rang the bell by the door of the Golde apartment. Within seconds she heard locks clicking, snicking, sliding. The woman who answered was still on the shy side of fifty, and wore lip dye Eve assumed Peabody would claim popped. She boasted impressive breasts and broad shoulders, and gave Eve a dead-on measuring stare.

"You're taller than I thought."

"Okay" was the best Eve could offer.

"Could use some meat on you. Skinny girls," she said to Peabody with a quick, crooked smile. "Hard to understand them."

"Yes, ma'am."

"Come on in. Mal's back in the den putting in a new screen. I don't allow the screen in the living room. Living rooms are for living, and living means having conversations."

There was plenty of seating for just that — chairs, sofa, cushioned squares. Where most might've put that wall screen, she'd opted for shelves loaded with photos, fussy pieces, and several books.

"I like books," she said, noting Eve's gaze. "Pricier than discs or downloads, but I like holding them, looking at them."

"My husband does, too."

"Well, he can afford it. My kids give them to me for special occasions. You go ahead and sit down. I'll get Mal, and he's got Davey with him back there. I'm going to fix you a snack."

"There's no need to bother with that, Mrs. Golde."

Mrs. Golde merely gave Eve that dead-on stare again. "I'm fixing you a snack." She walked off in navy skids.

"We're getting a snack." Peabody grinned.

Eve shook her head. Mrs. Golde struck her as a woman who ran her home and her family, and had enough punch left over to run most of the neighborhood. It was mildly intimidating.

Mal came out with a shorter, beefier guy

with a lot of brown hair. Eve recognized Dave Hildebran from his ID shot, and saw in both of them barely contained nerves.

"Um, Lieutenant." Mal started to extend his hand, obviously wondered if he should, started to pull it back. Eve solved his dilemma by taking it for a brisk shake. "Mal. Mr. Hildebran?"

"Dave. Nice to meetcha." Immediately, he flushed. "I mean . . ."

"I got it."

"I asked Dave to come over when you said you wanted to come by. We're both just . . . God, this is just fucking awful."

"You watch your language in this house!" The booming order came from the back of the apartment, and had both men wincing.

"Sorry, Ma! Like I said, I'm going to stay here until . . ." He trailed off again. "And Dave's staying with his folks, too. It just feels like we should."

"The neighborhood can't talk about any-thing else," Dave put in. "People really liked Mr. and Mrs. R. And even if they didn't, well, Jes . . . jeez," he corrected with a quick glance toward the kitchen.

"They were good people." Mrs. Golde came back in carrying an enormous tray.

"Lemme get that, Ma." Mal muscled it from her, set it on the table in front of the sofa. In addition to little plates, glasses, a big clear pitcher of some sort of deep amber liquid, the tray held tiny sandwiches — basically a bite — cookies sparkling under a dusting of what must've been sugar, and a ring of carrot sticks circling some chunky white dip with green flecks.

"We could've come on back to the kitchen, Ma."

"Living room's for company." In what Eve now saw as her no-bullshit way, Mrs. Golde hefted the pitcher, poured out glasses. "This is sassafras tea, and it's good for you. It's my grandma's recipe."

"My granny makes that." Delighted, Peabody accepted a glass.

"Does she now?"

"Yes, ma'am." After a sip, Peabody grinned like a child. "It's got to be the same recipe, or close to it. It really takes me back."

"What's your name, girl?"

"Detective Peabody. My granny's a Norwicki."

"Polish." On a wide, beaming smile, Mrs. Golde pointed an approving finger. "My grandma was, too. A Wazniac. She died just last year. A hundred and eighteen. Went skydiving two weeks before she slipped off in her sleep. Can't say better than that."

"No, ma'am."

Eve supposed this was living room conversation, but they didn't have time for it. "We have a few follow-up questions," she began. "We believe Jerald Reinhold will target someone else."

"I kept thinking, I don't know, he just had some sort of breakdown. But after I heard about Lori, what he did to her." Mal stared down at his hands. They held steady, but his voice shook. "I don't know how he could do that. I don't know how he could do what he's done."

"He's a spoiled, good-for-nothing whiner, and always has been."

Mal rolled his eyes toward his mother. "Ma."

"Actually, I'd like to hear your opinion, Mrs. Golde."

After sending her son a smug look, Mrs. Golde nodded at Eve. "You show some sense. I watched him grow up, didn't I? His ma and I, and Davey's ma, too, we spent a lot of time together, or handling each other's boys. My Mal's a good boy, and it's not bragging to say so. He had his times, sure, and he got slapped down for them when he needed to be."

"Still happens," Mal muttered but with a smile.

"Always will. I'm your ma, birth to earth.

Davey here, he's a good boy. Not that his ma and my own self didn't slap him down a time or two — and still will," she added, jabbing a finger at him. "Barb and Carl, they were good people, and they did the best they could with that boy. But he was born a whiner, and he never did grow out of it."

She plucked up a carrot stick, waved it. "Somebody else's fault always with him. Never appreciated anything they did for him, and always found fault. Maybe I could say they indulged him more than they should, but he was their only chick, and they did their best by him. Worked with him on schoolwork, even hired on tutors when he didn't do so well. Boy wanted to play ball, so Carl — and the man, bless him, wasn't much of an athlete — he spent hours throwing the ball or chasing it with Jerry. I remember when these two, Jerry and that Joe Klein, swiped candy and comic discs from down at Schumaker's, we all — Barb, Davey's ma, and Joe's and me — we all dragged these boys in there to make it right."

"Worse day of my life," Mal mumbled.

Mrs. Golde's expression clearly transmitted she was fine with that. "Davey and Mal here, they were shamed and sorry, and rightfully. That Joe, he was mostly shamed and sorry he got caught, but Jerry? He was mad."

"He was," Dave confirmed, and took a cookie. "He went off on me. He said I'd screwed the whole thing up. He punched my guts out before Mal pulled him off."

Mrs. Golde's finger ticked between the two men. "You never told me that."

"Ma, I can't tell you everything."

"Hah." Her sniff was her opinion on that. "Jerry apologized to the Schumakers, sure, had no choice with his mother holding him by the ear and seeing he did. And when a rock went through Schumaker's store window one night a couple weeks later, I know Jerry's the one who threw it."

"You don't know that, Ma. And we weren't there. I swore to you then, and I swear to you now, we didn't do it."

"I'm not saying you did. If I thought different, you still wouldn't be sitting down easy. Barb knew it. She didn't tell Carl, but she told me. Sitting back in the kitchen, and shedding some tears over it, too. Couldn't make him say he did it, but she knew."

"Is Schumaker's still there?"

"Fifty-one years, same location. Frank and Maisy."

Eve noted it down. "What I want from

you is the names of anyone you can think of he has something against, he had trouble with, who he complained about. Going back. I don't mean just recent problems."

"I hope you've got a lot of time," Mrs. Golde said, and helped herself to a sandwich bite. "Because that boy stacked up grudges like a kid with building blocks. I'd be one of them."

"He's not going to hurt you, Ma. I'd kill him first." Mal's face went fierce as he turned to Eve. "I mean it."

"You're a good boy." Mrs. Golde patted his arm. "But I think this skinny police-woman and her friend with the Polish granny can take care of Jerry."

"That's just what we're going to do," Eve said. "We have his former employers, his coworkers, you and your families, and Joe Klein and his. Who else comes to mind? How about other ex-girlfriends?"

"Lori was the first one he lived with, was really in a serious deal with," Mal began.

"There was Cindy McMahon," Dave put in. "They dated pretty regular for a few months a couple years ago."

"Is she in the neighborhood?" Eve asked.

"She was. She moved to East Washington just, I don't know, like in June maybe?"

"She got a good job," Mrs. Golde added.

"A media job, writing news and such. She's coming home for Christmas though. I talked to her ma."

"I think he'll stay local, for now."

"There was Marlene Wizlet."

"He never dated her," Dave objected.

"He *wanted* to. She shut him down. That's the kind of thing you mean, right?" Mal asked Eve.

"Yeah, it is. Do you have contact info?"

"I can get it. She lives Upper East, with some guy. She's modeling. She's really frosty, and Jerry had a thing for her. She wouldn't give him the first look, and told him to screw off."

They ran through a few others, right back to the sweaty days of puberty, with Mrs. Golde adding in the occasional parent, shopkeeper, older brother, younger sister.

She'd been right, Eve thought. A long list.

"How about teachers, instructors, coaches?"

"He was really piss — upset," Mal corrected quickly, "with Coach Boyd. He was our Little League coach for three years. Jerry got picked off twice trying to steal bases after Coach told him not to, so Coach benched him for three games. Then we were in the championship game, and Coach told him to take the pitch — their guy threw a bunch outside, and he wanted him to try to take for a walk, but Jerry swung away, and struck out. We lost, and he blamed Coach. Wouldn't play after that. Shit. Sorry, Ma. I just started realizing how many people he had a hard-on for. How many people didn't do anything for it."

"You've got a good streak of loyalty, Mal." She handed him a cookie. "That's nothing to apologize for."

By the time they got to high school, the list of names hit unwieldy. Considering how to refine it, Eve took a cookie without thinking. "These are . . . amazing."

Mrs. Golde preened. "Family recipe, and you have to be willing to spring for real sugar, and plenty. I'll give you some to take."

"Mr. Garber caught him cheating in Global Studies. He got suspended and grounded for it."

Mal shrugged at Dave. "Yeah, but he didn't really care. He said it was like hooky with permission."

"Nobody likes getting caught cheating," Eve put in, and noted the name down.

"Well, he was a lot more pissed, seriously pissed. Damn it, Ma, sorry."

"You're excused, considering the circumstances."

"It was Ms. Farnsworth, Computer Science."

"Oh yeah." Dave nodded. "That burned his . . . chaps. He flunked. Truth is, though I said I was on his side back then, she gave him like six chances, even worked with him after school, but he didn't care. He hated her. And when he flunked, he got grounded again, and worse, he had to go to summer school."

"We ragged on him," Mal added. "We really rubbed his face in it. Especially Joe. I know there were some instructors when he was in college, before he crapped out. But I don't know who. I went to NYU, so we didn't see each other much during the semester."

"Let's add an element. He needs money, or things he can liquidate into money. Anyone you've mentioned have money, to speak of? Or any sort of valuable collection you know of?"

"Marlene's making some bucks now. She's raking it in with the modeling, and I heard the guy she's with has a pile." Mal's face screwed up with thought. "We always figured the Schumakers had the scratch. And if he's got it against any of us, Joe likes to buy big-deal stuff. He doesn't keep a lot of money because he blows it on things."

"He's a showoff, always was. And he's got a mean streak." Mrs. Golde pointed at her son before he could protest.

"He does," Dave confirmed. "He's tough to be friends with, when you think about it. Farnsworth," Dave added, with a grin. "Everybody said she was rolling."

"That's right." Mrs. Golde lifted a finger. "Mostly her dad's money, if I remember. He died pretty young. And her husband had some, too, and he died in a car wreck about six, seven years back. I remember I sent her a sympathy card. She has money, or had it anyway. She always had nice shoes. Not flashy, but quality. And she donated comp equipment to the school."

"I didn't know that," Mal said.

"She didn't want to be flashy about it, like the shoes. But I hear things."

"You got ears like a cat, Ma."

"Ma ears," she countered and winked at him. "Goes with the territory."

"I forgot one. My brother. My big brother, Jim." Dave scrubbed his hands over his face. "He can't stand Jerry, never could. Used to call him Fuckweed. Sorry, Mrs. G., but that's verbatim, you know? Jim's not rich or anything, but he does okay. He lives in Brooklyn, him and his lady. They're getting married next year. Jim tuned him up once.

325

Jerry said something ugly about the girl Jim was seeing then. You remember Natalie Sissel, Mal. So, Jim punched his lights out. Just *pow, pow,* and walked away. It was pretty humiliating because Jim let Jerry throw the first punch, then just rocked him out. Right outside Vinnie's Pizzeria, so everybody saw it. I've gotta talk to Jim."

Dave sprang up, dragging out his 'link as he hurried into another room.

Looking ill, Mal watched Dave run out. "You really think he'll try to hurt somebody else, try to do what he did to his parents, to Lori?"

"I think it's good you're staying here, looking after your mother. You need to contact me, immediately, if he contacts you, if you see him."

She pulled out the morph. "He's changed his looks. This is more what he'll look like now."

"God. He looks . . . different."

"That's the idea." Eve got to her feet. "If you think of anyone else, anything else, contact me. Anytime. Something strikes in the middle of the night? Pick up your 'link and tag me. Don't mess with this, Mal."

"I'll get you those cookies."

Eve started to refuse the offer, but realized she wanted them — and that Mrs. Golde was giving her the eye. "Thanks. I'll come back and get them."

She followed Mal's mother into a spotless, working kitchen.

"He's not going to want to tell you if Jerry gets in touch." Mrs. Golde kept her voice low as she laid cookies in a clear, disposable tub. "He's loyal, and there's a part of him still that can't believe it. He's a good boy, a good friend. But he won't leave me alone, and he'd tell me. So I can promise you, if that fuckweed — and I can swear in my own house — tags him or comes by, you'll know, and know quick. And if he thinks I'm afraid, he won't hesitate to tell you himself. I'll make sure he thinks I'm afraid."

"But you're not."

"I can take care of myself, and that mean little brat. Believe me, he's not getting anywhere near my boy."

"He's lucky to have you, and you're lucky to have him."

"You're right, both times. You eat these cookies." She passed the tub to Eve. "You can use the calories."

14

Out on the sidewalk, Eve took a moment to think it through. "Brother Jim kicked his ass. He'd want payback there, but that's dealing with a guy who's likely stronger. He'd need to get in close with a weapon. But maybe snatching the fiancée. We'll check on that. Little League coach, maybe something there since one of his weapons of choice is a baseball bat."

"The model," Peabody put in. "Dented ego, like with the ex-girlfriend. And she may have some money."

"Yeah, a more likely on the scale. The schoolteacher. She cost him his summer, embarrassed him, and she's got money. Lives alone. And she's got e-skills, maybe the kind that can create good fake ID."

Too many of them, she thought. He could pick any one of them out of his murderous hat.

"We check on them all."

"All?"

"Reach out to Brooklyn, get a couple of cops to check on Dave's brother and the fiancée — and you take the Schumakers. They're practically around the corner. Head that way while you tag Brooklyn. I'll get people on the rest."

Pulling out her 'link, she hit on Jenkinson. "Re the Reinhold investigation. I need alive and well and stay that way checks. Take down these names and addresses."

"Ready when you are, boss."

"Marlene Wizlet," Eve began, and ran down the list. "I want a two-man team on each, and I want a face-to-face, in-person checks. Jerald Reinhold is looking for his next target, or he's picked one. I need these people taking precautions. Better, convince them to agree to protection."

"All of them?"

"All of them. If they've heard from Reinhold, I need to know. If anything, I mean anything, in their demeanor seems off, push it. I want everyone with eyes peeled for Reinhold."

"We're on it, LT."

"Report back when it's done."

She clicked off as Peabody came huffing back. "They're clear — the Schumakers. They were calling in their grandson when I left. He's retired Army. And Brooklyn's sending a unit to check on Brother Jim and lady."

"Good enough. We'll take the teacher — the computer teacher. She's close, and Jenkinson's sending out teams on the rest."

"Got her address here. Want to tag her first?"

"Yeah, go ahead," Eve said as they got into the car. "Let her know we're coming."

Older woman, Eve thought as she drove. Living alone. Easier pickings than the men, or that would be the assumption. Family money. Can't live the good life without money.

E-instructor.

"She's not answering." Peabody shifted. "Straight to v-mail."

Eve went with her gut and punched the speed. "Tag the coach and the model," she ordered. "I want them on alert. Offer protection if they want it. And I want a probability on the names Mal and Dave gave us. We'll work down the scale after Farnsworth."

Still following her gut, she double-parked rather than looking for a space near the brownstone.

"Nice house. Neighbors close, but still private. It's a good target, damn it. A really good target."

She pushed through the little gate and hurried to the door with Peabody behind her still talking on her 'link.

She rang, she knocked. And the feeling in her gut sharpened.

"The security's not engaged. If she went out, why isn't the security engaged? Take the place on the left, see if they've seen Farnsworth. I'll take the right."

Eve jogged to the neighboring house, rang that bell. Moments later a female voice spoke briskly through the intercom.

"Can I help you?"

"Ma'am, I'm the police." Eve held her badge up for the scan. "Lieutenant Dallas, NYPSD. I'm looking for your neighbor. Ms. Farnsworth?"

The door opened. The woman sported a messy brown ponytail and bold red sweats with thick striped socks on her feet. As she studied Eve out of sleepy eyes, she shifted a bundle wrapped in a blue blanket from one arm to the other.

It took Eve a moment after hearing the mewling sounds to identify a baby.

"Why are you looking for her?"

"I need to speak with her on a matter. She doesn't answer her door or her 'link. Can you tell me when you last saw her?"

"I guess it was last night. I got up to feed Colin, and she was out walking Snuffy."

"Snuffy?"

"Her dog. She got a sweet little dog. I noticed her leaving the house with Snuffy, about eleven last night."

"You haven't seen her today?"

"Now that you mention it, I guess not. But Brad took the morning feeding — when she'd have walked the dog again. Wait a minute." She stepped back, turned her head. "Brad!"

Eve heard a thud, a distinct *"OW!"* The woman laughed. "He fell off the couch," she told Eve. "Colin's almost three weeks old. And it's been almost three weeks since either of us got any real sleep. We're on parental leave."

The man came out to join the woman. He looked rumpled, glassy-eyed, and rubbed his elbow. "What is it?"

"It's the police. They're looking for Ms. Farnsworth."

"Why?"

"I need to speak with her," Eve put in. "Have you seen her today?"

"I'm lucky to see period." He rubbed at his eyes. "No, I guess not. Wasn't she supposed to come by with that soup?"

"Was that today?" The woman swayed side

to side as what was in the blue blanket made piping sounds. "I guess it was, they blur. She was going to bring us soup, her grandmother's recipe. She's been sweet about checking on us and Colin, even picking up things at the market, or having her droid check in to see if we need anything."

"I think I saw her droid."

Eve shifted attention to the new father. "Her droid?"

"Yeah, I was out a little while ago, just a walk, some fresh air. I think I saw her droid up the block, carrying some of the electronics. She's got a load of them, used to teach Comp Science."

"Is something wrong?" the woman asked.

"Stay inside."

Eve bolted back just as Peabody stepped away from the neighbor on the other side.

"They haven't seen her all day," Peabody began. "She's got a dog, and walks it regularly, but today . . . shit," Peabody finished when Eve whipped out her master.

"She's got a droid. Neighbor spotted it carting electronics away. Record on."

"Shit," Peabody said again, drew her weapon.

They went through the door, Peabody right, Eve left.

"Ms. Farnsworth," Eve called out as she

moved through the first floor, clearing. "This is the police."

She saw spaces on shelves and tables where the lack of balance told her something might have stood. She saw the destruction in the kitchen. And not a single comp or 'link on the first floor.

She knew, head and gut, before they started upstairs, she knew they were too late.

She smelled the urine, and the death, motioned Peabody to take the right again as they topped the stairs. She went left and into the home office.

Barely cold, she thought as she checked the body. Another mean, ugly death, with her swimming in its wake.

Then she put it aside, straightened.

"We got a body," she called out, and pulled out her comm to call it in.

"Second floor's clear, except for . . ." Peabody walked in, carrying a whimpering bundle. For a stunned instant Eve thought it was another baby.

"What the hell?"

"He was under the bed. I heard him crying when I went in to clear. And there was this little blanket, so I wrapped him up. He's hurt, Dallas. I don't know how bad."

"However bad, she's worse."

"It's her little dog. The neighbor said she

walked Snuffy several times a day, but not today."

"No, she won't be walking Snuffy anymore. We need field kits. I called it in."

"I'll get them, but we have to do something for Snuffy."

Eve dragged a hand through her hair. She saw the dog clearly enough now, and pain in its soft brown eyes. "What?"

"I'll see if I can tag a vet while I'm getting the kits. He's really hurt. Okay, Snuffy," Peabody crooned as she walked away. "We're going to take care of you. It's okay."

On a sigh, Eve turned back to the body. "I guess that leaves you and me. Victim is Caucasian female," she began for the record.

She glanced over when Peabody came back with the kits. "What did you do with the dog?"

"The father next door — the house you took — he came out when he saw me. He knows the vet. It's only a couple blocks away, so he took Snuffy and he's running him there right now."

They sealed up.

"Take this floor first," Eve told her. "Nobody saw her today, so it's likely he got in last night after she walked the dog. He probably put a lot of hours in here. He slept somewhere. Let's see if he left anything behind. And see if you can find the droid. I didn't see one when we cleared."

Eve confirmed ID for the record, took out her gauges for time of death. Forty-three minutes, she noted. She'd been less than an hour behind him.

"He had you all night, most of the day," she murmured. "Bashed you first, didn't he?" She checked the back of the head through the plastic, studied the wound, the dried blood. "That's his way. Walking your dog. Just taking your dog out before bed. He was waiting for you — like his father, like his ex. You come back, open the door, and he attacks from behind. Then he's inside in seconds, and can take his time. What did he do, kick the dog, heave it, use it for a little batting practice?"

She examined the body as she spoke. "Hauled you upstairs. There's a reason for that. You're a big woman, and why cart you all the way up here? Office equipment. This is your office — desk, chair, small couch. Computer Science teacher. You probably had good equipment."

She examined the blood, the skin tears on the wrists and arms, the ankles. "You tried. Looks like you tried pretty damn hard. Kept you alive all that time, so he had a use for you."

"Dallas? It looks like he used her bedroom. I checked the recycler in the bath, and I can see some of the packaging, the stuff he bought. Hair product, skin product. Some hair, too. He cut his hair."

"Okay."

"Uniforms are here."

"Give them a copy of the morph for the canvass. I want them to show his ID shot and the morph."

Peabody nodded. "Do you think he pushed her over like that? Maybe she fell over, struggling."

"Hard to say, but she sure as hell didn't just sit and take it. She ripped skin off trying to get out of the tape."

"The neighbors I talked to like her. You could tell." Peabody drew in a breath. "There's no droid up here. I still have to go over the main floor, but I didn't see one down there either."

"He kept it. Handy to have a droid. Clean up after him, run errands. He'd like that. Let's find out what she had, get a BOLO out there, too."

"On it. He could come back, Dallas. It's a nice place, a big house. It'd make a good base."

"Neighbors. They'd have started asking questions in another day or two. About her, the dog. Or she'd have an appointment. He got what he wanted here."

Face grim, Peabody looked down at the body. "Because she flunked him in Computer Science. In high school."

"Because she pissed him off. It's all he needs now. And money. Get the uniforms started."

Eve pulled out her 'link.

Feeney said, "Yo."

"I got another DB. Computer Science teacher, retired."

"What? He get a D?"

"She flunked him, so he paid her back by smothering her with a plastic bag after keeping her tied and taped to a chair for about eighteen hours. And bashing up her little dog."

"Fucker."

"Yeah, he is. She's supposed to have a lot of nice equipment, but he cleaned her out."

Feeney's already droopy face drooped further. "Can't help you if I don't have the toys."

"I'm going to do a search to find out what she had, but, meanwhile, she's supposed to have some nice scratch. He'd want it."

"You want me to look for the money? No problem."

"He knows we'll find her sooner or later,

knows we know who he is. She'd know some tricks, right? Bouncing money around, tucking it away."

"If she was any good at her job, she'd know the ins, the outs."

"She was good at her job. If he got her to pull out the money, transfer it, he'd make her cover the tracks." She looked down at the torn skin, the raw bruising. "But she wasn't a pushover. Maybe there are tricks in the tricks. So, it takes an e-man."

"I happen to be one. Give me the data you've got."

"Farnsworth," Eve began, "Edie Barrett."

When she finished with the body, she started on the room.

She believed he'd spent considerable time in there, forcing Farnsworth to drain her accounts. And wouldn't she be the perfect source for a new ID? A veteran e-teacher.

Eve closed her eyes a moment. He'd changed his appearance here — hair, skin tone, eyes. He'd waited until he'd come here.

"He'd already planned this next move." She turned as Peabody stepped up to the door again. "He probably came here straight from the ex's. The timing works well enough with the last sighting of his vic. He had what he needed in the duffel. Tape, rope, knife, bat, clothes, the products. Kill the ex, come here, use Farnsworth not only for the next kill, but as his vehicle for a new ID, more money."

"This place is worth a nice bundle," Peabody commented. "How much did she have?"

Eve's 'link signaled, and she read Feeney on her display. "Tell you in a minute. Dallas."

"Your vic had nearly four mil not including real property, jewelry, art, and like that."

"Damn it. He's rolling now."

"Every account she had I found on a quick search was emptied as of today."

"You're not going to make my day and tell me by a simple transfer."

"No can do. Some fancy fingerwork, but we'll find it. Just giving you a heads-up."

"Appreciate it. He hit the jackpot," she said to Peabody when she clicked off. "And he was smart enough to make it complicated. We're going to stick with she was smarter, and we're smarter. But right now, he's feeling rich."

"He could rabbit with that much money."

"I don't think so." Enjoying it too much, she thought. Batting a thousand so far. "More scores to settle. He's still going to want money. Why quit when you're ahead? But that won't be as urgent. He may do the next without that as a particular factor."

"It's a long list, Dallas."

"We're going to contact every name on it, and we're going to ask everyone we contact if they know of anyone else we should add on. If any of them wants protection, we'll put a cop on them. I'll find it in the budget."

"He had a tantrum down in the kitchen, at least it looks like one."

"Yeah, I saw."

"It's mean when you really look at it. Broken dishes, gouged counters and appliances, glassware shattered, food tossed around. Something pissed him off."

She took one last look at the body. "I hope it was her. He wanted her to suffer. He learned the perks of that with the ex. That's part of the fun, the power, the payback. He kept her alive the longest. He'd want to keep the next one alive so he can enjoy himself."

She started out just as a uniform started up the stairs. "Lieutenant? We've got a wit outside says he saw a man fitting the morph description."

"I'll take him."

"Yes, sir. And the sweepers just pulled up."

"We're ready for them."

She stepped outside where between her

vehicle, the black-and-white, and the sweeper's van they'd screwed traffic to hell and back.

Eve ignored the blasting horns, the enthusiastic cursing, and homed in on a boy of about sixteen in a fake leather jacket, high-step airboots, and a mop of brown hair shaved high on one side to show off the cluster of silver studs along his ear canal.

Didn't it hurt, she wondered, to get holes punched there?

"Lieutenant Dallas. Your name?"

"X."

"Your name's X."

"It's like Xavier. Xavier Paque. I'm X."

"Okay, X. You saw this man?"

The kid glanced at the morph again, bopped his shoulders up and down twice. "Yeah, hey. So I live, like, over there." He gestured across the street. "Just riding my board back up from the mart. Went for a fizz and a pop, and I saw the dude over here, gimping along with a couple of rollies."

"He limped?"

"Yeah, hey, you know." The boy demonstrated, hobbling some. "Looked peeved, got it? But nice, tight threads."

"Describe said threads."

"Good jacket, looked like real cow. Mostly that's what I noticed, and the gimping.

Maybe nice boots." He screwed up his face in thought. "Yeah, nice boots. Cow, too, I bet, so he had some. The one rolly was mag — duffel style, sharp. But the other? Been around. Pretty dumpy, and man, it was *red*. Bogus for a dude. Wrap shades. Had some, busted them. Bummed."

"Limping, tight threads, and pulling a rolling duffel and a red suitcase."

"Yeah, big red rolly."

"How about his hair? Long, short, color?"

Now the boy scratched his head. "Short. Not you short, but not me long. Blondie, I think. Maybe he had a patch." The thoughtful face again. "Maybe a patch," he said, tapping his chin. "I only took the good look because his jacket was fine, and he's gimping along with the rollies like he's hurting bad."

"Heading west?"

"Yeah, that way." X's eyes shifted to the Farnsworth house. "Something wrong with Ms. F?"

"Yeah."

"Like what?"

Word would spread, and quickly. No point, she decided, in evading. "She's dead. We suspect the man you saw is responsible."

In a fingersnap he went from frosty teen to stunned boy. His eyes filled, the sheen of tears, the gleam of shock. "Come on, no, man. Fuck that. No way."

"I'm sorry. You knew her?"

"Ms. F? This is sick bad. Ms. F? She's up, you know? She helps me with my e-shit for school. It's not my thing, but she helps me out. That gimp bastard did her? I'da stopped him. I'da done something."

"You have. Talking to me, telling me what you saw, it's going to help us find him."

"Where's her dog? Where's the Snuffman?"

"He's at the vet," Peabody told him.

"Is he hurt? Man, more sick bad. She freaking loves that dog."

"They're taking care of him."

"I want to go talk to my mom. I want to go home."

"Go ahead." Eve dug out a card. "If you think of anything else, you contact me."

"She never hurt anybody. It's not right. She never hurt anybody." He stuffed Eve's card in his pocket before running across the street.

"Maybe she did," Eve said. "Maybe she managed to hurt him. Cabs, Peabody."

"I'm already there." Working her 'link, Peabody started back to the car with Eve.

"Officer!"

Eve stopped, waiting as the new father

rushed up. "Lieutenant," she corrected.

"Oh, sorry. They're keeping Snuffy over-night at least. I thought you might need the name of the vet, so I had them give me a card."

"Thanks."

"Is . . . is Ms. Farnsworth really . . ."

"Yes, I'm sorry. I didn't get your name."

"Brad Peters. Was it a burglary?"

"Not exactly."

"She . . . she was really good to us. We moved in right after Margot got pregnant. Margot's family lives in St. Paul, so it was nice for her to have a, well, motherly type right next door. I didn't hear anything, or see . . . We're so wrapped up in the baby."

"There was nothing you could do."

"Can we keep the dog?"

"Ah . . ."

"She really loved that dog." And like the boy, his eyes filmed with tears. "I don't want Snuffy to end up in the shelter because there's nobody to take him. We'll pay the vet bills. He knows us. He likes us. They were like a unit. He's going to miss her something fierce."

"I'll see what I can do. She may have rela-tives or an heir who'd need to sign off on that."

"Okay. But we'll take care of him until . . .

He shouldn't have to go to a shelter with strangers. He *was* her family."

Eve thought of Galahad. "I'll clear it so he can go from the vet to you, unless family claims him."

"Thanks. I'd better go tell Margot. I don't know how this could happen. Right next door."

It happens everywhere, Eve thought as he walked away. Because there's always someone like Jerry Reinhold.

"Cab," she repeated to Peabody.

"They're checking. A lot of pickups, so —"

"Have them cross-check with a drop-off at a clinic or health center, urgent care, ER — a medical. Closest one going west from here. Limping, hurting. Maybe he dropped something on his foot. Or maybe the vic managed to drop herself and the chair on him. I like that image."

"Hard not to." Peabody retagged the cab company, gave her contact the drop-off element. "Score! Pickup Varick and Laight, drop-off Church Street Urgent Care. Single passenger, two bags."

"Let's move."

Maybe he'd still be there, stuck in a waiting room, cooling heels in exam. She resisted the urge to go in hot, but not the one to leapfrog through traffic until Peabody's color dropped away.

"I might need this place," Peabody managed as Eve, once again, double-parked.

Eve simply strode across the sidewalk, shoved inside the spacious, and unfortunately uncrowded waiting area. A crowd might have kept him hanging until treatment.

She headed straight to the receptionist on duty, held up her badge, signaled Peabody for the morph. "Is he here?"

The receptionist frowned at Eve, at the badge, at the morph. "No, but he was."

Frustration wanted to choke her. "When did he leave?"

"Maybe an hour ago. About an hour."

"Do you know where he was going, his mode of transportation?"

"No, he walked out the door. Why?"

"What was wrong with him?"

Now she pokered up. "I'm not allowed to share any patient's information."

"Name. What name?"

The receptionist checked her computer. "He signed in as John. That's all that's required if no insurance is involved. He paid cash."

"I want to see his doctor. Now."

"If you'd have a seat in chairs, I'll see if —"

"I said now." Eve leaned over the counter. "I just left a retired schoolteacher who's on her way to the morgue. You treated the man who sent her there. I'm about an hour behind him, according to you. I'm not going to waste time arguing. Get the medical who treated him out here, or I go back there and make a hell of a mess."

"Wait. Just wait." The receptionist all but flew back, vanished around a corner. In under a minute she was back in the wake of a tall, lean Asian man with a flapping white lab coat.

"What's all this?"

"All this is murder. This man has killed four people. I need to know why he came in, what you did, what he said. Everything."

Without a word, he gestured her back around the same corner and into a small office with a lush potted palm near a fake window.

"The patient is a murder suspect?"

"Multiple. I need to know what name he used, his injuries, his treatment, and if he scheduled any sort of follow-up."

"You don't have a warrant."

"I have four dead bodies. But we can play that way. Peabody?"

348

The doctor just lifted a hand, waved it. "He elected not to use his full name. Just John, and neglected to check the privacy form. So. The patient had two broken metatarsals on his right foot, along with a hairline fracture of the first cuneiform."

He picked up a tablet, tapped, swiped. And showed Eve a diagram of a foot.

"So . . . A couple of broken toes, and a hairline deal on this part here, before the arch?"

"Basically, yes. There's little you can do, other than wand, wrap, and treat for discomfort, advise the patient to rest the foot. All of which I did. He also had some minor bruising along his diaphragm. There were no internal injuries. He left — perfectly ambulatory, and with the medication in no particular discomfort."

"No follow-up, no referral."

"Offered and declined. He said he was traveling — and he had a couple of suitcases with him. He claimed someone had dropped a heavy case on his foot at the transpo center, then he'd tripped over it, jamming it into his diaphragm. He'd assumed the foot was just bruised, but soon decided it might be more, so came in for exam and treatment. He paid for the exam, the treatment, the meds, the wrap, and the soft cast in cash."

"How long before it heals?"

"It depends. With daily wand treatments, rest, he could be fine in a matter of days. Without the follow-ups, a couple of weeks. The first treatment is the most intense."

"Yeah, been there. If he comes back, decides to do another treatment, contact me. Don't let him know, just keep him waiting, or draw the treatment out. He's violent, he's dangerous, and he won't hesitate to kill."

"Then I'll hope he doesn't. We often have children in here."

"Just give him a seat, tell him to wait his turn, and tag me. I'll take care of the rest."

The minute she walked outside, Eve strode over, kicked her own tire. "Crap! He just *has* to luck into a fast, efficient medical. He couldn't get bogged down with hackers and bleeders and pukers for an hour."

She kicked the tire again, then walked around to the driver's door, sliding behind the wheel to a cacophony of horns.

"Cab," she said yet again to Peabody.

"Already on it."

15

After bombing with the cab angle, Eve swung back into Homicide, arrowed straight to her office. She'd update the board and book while Peabody contacted every potential target on the list.

Once she had, had reviewed her notes, written an updated report, she sat, coffee in hand, and studied her board.

Parents to ex to teacher.

He wasn't killing chronologically. Not by a measure of intimacy. Not by financial gain as he'd known or had certainly believed Farnsworth had more there than Lori.

Was it, in his mind, by level of offense? By what or who insulted or angered him most? Ease of access?

Circle back, she ordered herself.

First killing, mother. Impulse. Fit of rage, convenience of weapon.

Second killing, premeditated, lying in wait, choice of weapon.

Third, planned, lying in wait, purchase of weapons, elements of torture.

Fourth, planned, possible lying in wait — probable, she decided — uncertain if he found the murder weapon or brought it with him. More extensive torture, additional use of vic for financial gain and very likely for false ID.

Different weapon for each, but the use of the bat on three out of four, use of tape and cord on the last two.

And all four killed in their own homes.

He'd probably stick with that, she decided, but ran a probability to back up her own conclusion. Would he sully his own nest, wherever he built it? And he liked, didn't he, killing them where they felt safest. Pawing through their things, eating their food.

Didn't that add another level of humiliation to murder?

"The place matters," she said aloud.

She heard the thwack of Peabody's cowboy boots coming fast, pushed away from her desk.

"What do you have?" she demanded.

"We might have something on the electronics. There's a woman out here who came in. She works at Fast Cash Pawnbroker, five blocks from the Farnsworth crime scene. I've got her waiting at my desk. She says she checked in three comps that match the numbers on Farnsworth's equipment. I checked, and they do."

"I'll talk to her. Get McNab or whoever Feeney can spare over there to pick them up."

The girl — as she barely hit legal age to Eve's gauge — fidgeted in her chair. She was bone-thin, black, with hair in ruler-straight cornrow braids. She wore a red jacket over coat-of-paint jeans, and bit her nails.

"Juana Printz," Peabody told Eve. "Juana, this is Lieutenant Dallas."

"Okay. Hi. I have to report it. It's the law, right?"

"Why don't you tell me what you have to report?"

"I work for Mr. Rinskit at Fast Cash? And this droid, you know how you can tell it's a droid, even mostly the really good ones?"

"Yeah, I know."

"He came in hand carrying three comps — full, high-end D&Cs. It was a load, right? Maybe I thought it was a little tilted, but hey, you get all kinds. But then I'm supposed to check them in after the transaction, and I saw the alert. I told Mr. Rinskit, and said how I'd report it, and he said to mind my business. And I said, 'But, Mr. Rinskit, there's the alert, and they're stolen and part of a police investigation thing,' and he said to just shut up, check them in, and forget it if I wanted to keep my job."

She stopped biting her nails long enough to bite her bottom lip. "I did — I mean I shut up and checked them in, but I didn't forget it. So I took the bus here as soon as I got off work. Because it's the law."

"You did the right thing. Have you seen the droid before?"

"No, ma'am, no. But I think, maybe, Mr. Rinskit doesn't report like he's supposed to. And maybe I shut up about it, but this was *three* high-end, and I just couldn't keep shutting up. Does he have to know I told?"

She started on her nails again, her dark eyes full of worry. "If he knows I reported it after he said not to, he'll fire me for sure. I'm going to lose my job."

"You like your job?"

"It blows." Juana smiled a little. "It blows wide, but I gotta work."

"Hang on a minute."

"McNab and two uniforms are on their way to pick up the evidence," Peabody reported.

"Good. Arrange a voucher for Juana. A hundred for the report."

"I'll take care of it."

Eve held up a finger, signaling Juana to wait another minute as she pulled out her 'link.

She'd expected Roarke's admin to pick up, but got the man himself. "Hey."

"And a hey to you. I'm just leaving the office."

"Oh. I'm not. I've got another DB, three stolen comps coming in that may help me find the route to money transferred from the DB's account to the killer's, and a little thing."

"E-work, is it? I could use some recreation. Why don't I come to you?"

"You could do that, but it would be to Feeney at this point."

"I prefer you, but I'll settle. What's the little thing?"

"It's actually why I tagged you. I want to give someone a job."

"Doing what?"

"That's the thing. I don't know. And actually, I want you to give someone a job."

His eyebrows rose. "You want me to give someone a job doing . . . you don't know what?"

"What's the point of having somebody who employs half the planet anyway if you can't say, 'Give this girl a job'?"

"A girl."

"Well, early twenties. Honest, straightforward. She's going to lose her job in a pawnshop for reporting those comps, but she came in anyway. She's neat, clean, polite — and honest," she repeated. "You must have something — Lower West would work best."

He said, "Eve," on a sigh. "Have her contact Kyle Pruett," he began and rattled off information.

"Who is that?"

"One of the assistants in Human Resources, downtown. She'll have to pass a background check, come in for an interview, but I imagine Kyle can find something. Give me her information, and I'll pass it on."

"Great. I'll send it to you, and I'll owe you."

"You certainly will." But he smiled at her. "I'm on my way to you, via Feeney."

Satisfied, she turned back to Juana. "Peabody, did you get all Juana's information?"

"Yes, sir."

"Send it to Roarke." The look she sent Peabody cut off any questions. "Juana, I need you to note something down."

"Oh, yes, ma'am."

"Lieutenant," Eve said as Juana pulled out an old, battered 'link.

"Yes, ma'am, Lieutenant."

Close enough. "Kyle Pruett," Eve said, giving Juana the information to key in. "Contact him. He'll be expecting it. He's going to help you find a job."

Juana looked up from her 'link, blinked twice. "A job?"

"We're going to shut your boss down for seventy-two hours, more if we find other stolen merchandise. He's going to be fined, and he may face criminal charges. Unless he's an absolute moron, he's going to know you reported him. Don't go back there. Use the contact I gave you. Be honest with him the way you were with me. If there's anything off in your background, tell him up front. Have you ever been arrested, Juana?"

Those dark eyes went huge. "No, ma'am! Sir! Lieutenant! My mama would skin my butt."

"Make the contact. And thank you for coming in."

"Detective Peabody gave me this voucher. I didn't know you got paid to report. I didn't come in for the money, but we can use it. And I can sure use a chance for the work." She got to her feet, held out a hand to shake. "Thank you for the chance. Mama says doing the right thing's its own reward, but she'll sure be happy I got this. We'll be saying a special thank-you before Thanks-giving dinner. Thank you, both of you. I'm going straight home to tell her."

"That was a nice thing to do," Peabody commented when Juana hurried out.

"This could be a solid break, and she gave it to us." She shifted to block Baxter before he could pass. "Where are you going?"

Wiggling his eyebrows, he smoothed the knot of his tie. "I'm off shift and onto a hot date."

"You're back on, and your hot date will have to cool down some."

"Man." He cast his eyes to the ceiling. "I was *this* close."

"Peabody, split the list of potential targets up geographically."

"Is this the Reinhold murders, Lieuten-ant?" Trueheart, looking eager, stepped beside Baxter.

"That's right. We've got a list of people who've pissed Reinhold off in the past, and any one of them might be next. They've all been notified, offered protection."

"You want us to babysit?" Baxter asked.

"No. His tally's four, and all were killed in their own homes. I want face-to-face inter-views, in those homes, and a full report on the locations, the accesses, the security, the basic rhythm of the households. Also take note of easily portable valuables, keen eye on electronics. If said potentials know of other potentials not currently on the list, I want to know. Show them all the morph. If they have cohabs or family members living with them, show them, talk to them. If he doesn't already have his next kill picked, he's picking one now."

"How long's the list?" Baxter wondered.

"Your date's going to cool off some," Eve repeated. "If you can't heat her back up, it's on you."

He flashed a grin. "Heating up's my specialty."

"Give them above SoHo," Eve decided. "You and I will take SoHo and down. You get a model, reputedly frosty, as a reward," she told Baxter.

"Hot dog."

"Got it, sending to your PPCs," Peabody announced.

"Full reports," Eve repeated before turning back to Peabody. "Split up ours. I want to talk to Morris before I work the list. You can take a uniform if you want any help."

"I've got it. Sending your share."

"Saddle up then. I'm checking in with EDD, then heading out. Anything pops, tag me."

Eve detoured into her office, grabbed her

coat, a file bag, and avoiding even the thought of the elevator took the glides to EDD.

Apparently half of Central had the same idea.

Even braced for the blast of color and movement that was EDD, it rocked her senses before she made it to Feeney's sane office.

"I'm heading into the field, wanted to touch base first."

"Juggled you in."

Since it looked as if he had at least six programs going on his screens, she assumed he was doing considerable juggling.

"You said this asshole flunked Comp Science?"

"Yeah."

"Well, he learned enough to keep her making the transfers without an easy trail. We're bouncing, vanishing, popping, then sinking. I'm saying offshore and off-planet, at least for the bulk, but we're not there yet. I'm saying, too, he'll go numbered and/or sheltered. We're going to find the money, sooner or later, but we may not get an ID out of it any time this decade."

He sent her a look out of basset hound eyes. "Not shooting straight anyway."

She jammed her hands in her pockets. "I

don't want to give him so much as a rat hole for his lawyers to shove him through once we've got his sorry ass."

"Some are good enough shooting angles not to make a rat hole. Not that I'm saying that's the way." He lifted his shoulders. "Roarke's heading in."

And he knew every angle. Had probably invented some. "He likes to play with his nerds."

Feeney only smiled. "We can use him. I'm going to move into the lab once McNab gets back with the comps. I can run some of this on auto, for now. We may have quicker luck with the equipment."

"Let me know when . . . That was quick," she said when Roarke strolled in.

"Some luck with traffic." His elegant dark suit and topcoat stood in contrast to the frenzy of color through the doorway behind him. He glanced at the screens, a quick scan with those wild blue eyes. "Ah, multishifts, cross-funnels, lateral dips."

"Yeah," Feeney confirmed. "And then some."

"Won't this be fun?"

"Have at it. I'm hitting the morgue, then I have some interviews with potential targets."

And where, Roarke wondered, would any sort of food be in the mix? She looked, to his eye, tight and tired. "I'll go with you."

She frowned at him. "What about the fun?"

"I'll work by remote, and have the best of both. You can send what you'd like me to do to my PPC," Roarke said to Feeney.

"Can do. If you hang until McNab gets back —"

"He's back," Roarke interrupted. "I ran into him briefly. He was logging in evidence then bringing it up to the lab."

"We'll log out one of the comps. See what you can do with it."

"Delighted. Should I meet you in the garage?" he asked Eve.

"I can wait." She stepped to the side, pulled out her 'link, and took the time to notify those on her list to expect a visit.

She finished up with the last one walking with Roarke as he carried a sealed comp to the garage.

"You're supposed to have a minion haul stuff when you dress like that."

"Am I now? Are you volunteering?"

She ignored that, keyed in her code to unlock the car doors. "How are you supposed to work on that while we're driving all over lower Manhattan?"

"Easily enough as you'll be behind the wheel."

He unsealed the comp then took some sort of minidrive out of his pocket, attached it to one port, attached his PPC to another. Glanced at her as she pulled out of the garage and into perfectly miserable traffic.

"You're tired," he said.

"No, I'm not."

"You are, and you show it very likely because you haven't had any real food since breakfast."

"I had a cookie. And I have a little box of them — which, damn it, I left in my office. Say good-bye to those."

"Real food," he repeated.

Had she? She couldn't remember. "I'll eat when we get home. Mommy."

He drilled a finger into her side in retaliation, then tapped and swiped on the in-dash 'link. "AC mode," he commanded, "twelve-ounce protein shake, chocolate."

Received . . . Selecting . . .

"AC mode? What AC mode?"

"The one programmed into the system because my wife starves herself most days."

Delivering . . .

He had to take off his seat belt, shift, reach

through the seats to the back. She heard the quiet slide, little click, and frowned into the rearview, but couldn't quite get the angle.

"Where is it? How is it?"

"It's in the backseat console. Just a mini," he said as he handed her the shake. "It'll only hold a few basics. A couple of shakes, coffee —"

"Coffee?"

He gave her a long look, dry as dust. "It must be love."

"Coffee," she said again.

"A few protein bars as well. You told me you'd read the manual."

"I did. Most of it. Some of it. A little of it," she admitted. And because it must have been love, drank the shake. It didn't suck.

"Why aren't you tired? Why don't you have to have a protein shake?"

"Because I had a decent lunch and a little tea with biscuits a couple hours ago."

"I was chasing a killer a couple hours ago."

"Maybe if you'd eaten something you'd have caught him."

"Would not. Lucky bastard. Who gets in and out of a health clinic inside thirty minutes? Nobody. But he does. It's been breaking his way, but with this" — she jerked her chin toward the comp — "maybe it'll start breaking mine."

She pulled up at the morgue.

"If you don't need me to come in, I'll start working on that break."

"Yeah." She started to get out, hesitated, then put her seat back. Reaching under, she tugged, then pulled out a candy bar with sticky tape crossed over the wrapper.

"Clever girl."

"That damn candy thief can't get into a shielded vehicle, so I keep emergency candy." She broke it in half, handed him a share. "It is love," she confirmed, then climbed out.

Amused, and since he knew her feelings about candy, touched, he unwrapped it while he began the work.

Interesting, he thought after his initial scan. And challenging, he added after a second, deeper one.

He lost track of time with that interest and challenge, pausing only to make or take 'link tags if they were relevant or important enough.

He came out of his work zone when Eve opened the car door again.

She sat, put her head back, shut her eyes.

So he set the work aside altogether, laid a hand over hers, said nothing.

"Morris figures he had her for about eighteen hours. Taped and tied to a chair in her home office. He'd bashed her good, back of the head first. A bat again. She had a mild concussion, probably a blinding headache. She was severely dehydrated so it's unlikely he gave her any food or water. Several blows to the face — hand, fist. Some of the blood and urine in her lap was canine. She had a little dog. He'd busted it up some, it's at the vet. She'd torn her wrists, back of her hands, her ankles."

Ah, God, he thought, but said nothing.

"She tore the skin off trying to get the tape loose. Dislocated shoulder. We think she did that right before or when he was killing her, smothering her with a plastic bag over her head. We think she managed to tip the chair over so it fell on his foot. He has a couple of broken toes and a hairline fracture in his foot. I think she did that. She didn't let him stroll away. She made him pay a little. At least a little."

"Who was she?" Roarke asked quietly.

"A good teacher, a good neighbor. A woman who loved her damn dog. I think he used that. Everyone said she loved the dog, the dog was her family. I don't see her just doing whatever he wanted, but if he threatened to hurt what she loved, threatened her family, she probably would. At least try to stall him. And then hurt him when she knew

366

she wouldn't live through it."

"You'll find him."

She glanced at the comp. "Will I?"

"You will, yes. This part may not be quick, but it'll be done. This unit wasn't wiped by an amateur. It's thorough and professional."

"He must've forced her to do it."

"When did she die? The time, I mean."

"Right about sixteen hundred."

"Then no. It was done shortly after."

"No way he could do it if you say it's thorough and professional. He doesn't have the chops. It's . . . the droid," she realized. "She had a droid, and she would've programmed it herself. He had the droid wipe the comps. There's nothing there?"

"There's always something. It's the bringing it back, the finding it that's the trick. I'll do better with this in my own lab. I'll work the financial data Feeney's sent me until we get home."

She nodded, straightened, then called up the list Peabody had sent her, and followed the computer's suggestion for route.

She was tired, Eve realized when she came to the last address. At this point she just wanted home, just to get inside her own space, work this thing through.

"I'll go in with you this time," Roarke said.

"I've done most of what I can this way."

"Okay. This is Reinhold's former Little League coach. He benched Reinhold for not listening, so Reinhold basically picked up his bat and went home."

"And you think he'd kill this man for something that happened when he was a child?"

"I know he would," Eve corrected. She lifted her badge to the security scanner of the squat, six-unit building. Waited for verification and clearance.

"They're on two," she told Roarke when they went inside. "Wayne Boyd, his wife Marianna. Two offspring, one in grad school, one in college."

She chose the whistle-clean stairway, then knocked on 2-B, held her badge up to the security peep.

"Lieutenant Dallas?" came through the speaker.

"That's right. I spoke with you earlier."

"There's someone with you?"

"My civilian consultant."

It took another moment, but locks cleared, the door opened. Boyd stood cautiously studying both her and Roarke, a fit man in his late fifties who'd let a little gray sprinkle through his deep brown hair. He had a strong face, clear blue eyes, and beside him stood a burly, ugly dog whose study was anything but cautious.

"All right, Bruno, rest."

The dog immediately leaned against Boyd's side, and his tongue rolled out in a strange and goofy grin.

"We're a little edgy since we heard about Ms. Farnsworth."

"Understood. Can we come in?"

"Yeah, sorry. It's okay, Marianna! It's the police. I told her to go upstairs, in case. Our kids are here, for the holiday."

He closed the door, stepped back into a large, high-ceilinged living space ringed by a railing along the second level.

The dog padded over to a square of dog-haired red rug and immediately began gnawing on some sort of bone.

Three people appeared on the second level — a slim blonde, a broad-shouldered man, early twenties, and a willow-slim brunette, a couple years younger than the man.

"They're old enough to argue," the blonde told Boyd, "and I'm outnumbered."

"We're all in this, Dad." The young man led the way down.

"Okay. Okay, Flynn, you're right. We're all in it."

"I should make coffee. Can I get you coffee?" Marianna asked.

Eve decided she could kill for coffee, even fake coffee. "That'd be great. Mr. Boyd, is there anyone else staying here at this time?"

"No, just us. Flynn and Sari will be here until Sunday when they go back to campus. We all have until Monday before routine starts again."

"You've seen the morph of Reinhold. All of you?"

"Yes. None of us have seen him."

"I hope I do," Flynn muttered.

"Stop." Boyd leveled a warning glare. "Flynn had Ms. Farnsworth in high school. We're all shaken by what happened to her. Lieutenant, I benched the kid for a few games more than a decade ago. Maybe fifteen years ago. Not that he learned anything from it. When he didn't listen at his at-bat, championship game and struck out, I didn't come down on him. It's Little League. They're kids. You don't dump on them."

"He was a little bastard then, now he's a bigger one."

"Flynn," his mother said wearily as she brought out coffee.

"It's true." Sari spoke up. "Maybe I didn't really know him, but I remember he was mean and spiteful. And maybe I didn't have

Ms. Farnsworth, but I have friends who did, and they liked her."

"I'm not making excuses for him. He's sick," Boyd continued. "And he needs to be caught, stopped. We're going to be careful, just the way we talked about, but he's got no reason to want to hurt any of us. He probably doesn't even remember me."

"Believe me when I say he does," Eve corrected. "Believe me when I say he's vindictive and he's violent, and he's looking to pay back every perceived slight. You're one of them, Mr. Boyd. He used a baseball bat on three of his victims."

"Oh my God, Wayne."

Eve waited while Boyd took his wife's hand, tried to keep her calm. The coffee, she decided, hit somewhere between the horrors of cop coffee and the joys of Roarke coffee. She couldn't complain.

"Listen, I haven't seen or spoken or had any contact with Jerry since he was about eleven."

"Give me your assessment of him, at eleven. No filters, Mr. Boyd. Honest take, you worked with a lot of kids. You have a take."

"Okay." He shoved a hand back through his hair. "Lazy, arrogant, sneaky. Not wild, not right-in-your-face, but he had an edge, and under the edge, he — God, he was a kid."

"Honest," Eve repeated.

"Soft. Look at him crosswise, he took offense. A backbiter. He was pretty good at the game, and he'd have gotten better with some discipline, some practice. He'd miss or come late for practice all the time, always had an excuse."

He still had his wife's hand, and looked at her briefly before he turned his gaze back to Eve. "I didn't like him, that's honest. I was glad when he quit, and I felt bad about it. But he was a problem, and I wasn't sorry to lose him."

Eve nodded, glanced at Flynn. "He was a little bastard, now he's a bigger one. And he's a killer. You've got a good place here, pretty good security, but it wouldn't take much to get past it. Not with some planning, and he's learning how to plan. He slips in behind somebody, poses as maintenance, delivery. You've got a nice family, Mr. Boyd."

"All right. All right. We'll take protection."

"That's good. When any of you go out, don't go alone. If you see him — and this goes for you, Flynn — don't engage, get to a safe place, back home or a public place, and contact the police."

"For how long?" Boyd asked.

"I wish I could tell you. Finding him, stopping him, is my priority."

"She won't stop," Roarke added. "Until he's in a cage, she won't stop. I can promise you that."

"You'll have an officer here within the hour," Eve said as she rose. "And around the clock until this is done."

"Thank you. I'll walk you out."

"I'll do it, Mom." Sari got to her feet, walked to the door. "I know who you are," she said quietly. "I recognize you both. I'll tell them after you go. They're too upset to recognize you, I think." She managed a smile. "They'll feel safer when they know who you are."

"Stay together," Eve advised. "That's safer, too."

16

The lights of home glimmered against the dark. As she drove through the gates the wind began to whip, lashing denuded trees, sending out a whistling groan.

It's going to be a rough night, she thought, *in more ways than one.*

As she got out of the car, that fierce wind clawed at her coat, sent it billowing.

"What?" she demanded when Roarke grinned at her.

"The wind, the gloom, the halos of light. You look like some other-worldly warrior queen about to battle."

"I don't know about that, but the battle sounds about right."

She pushed her way in, assumed the first stage of battle started in the foyer as Summerset gave her a cool stare.

"Ah, you did remember where you live."

"I keep hoping you'll forget."

He merely shifted his attention to Roarke

as Eve shrugged out of her coat, and the cat hurried over to rub against her legs.

"Your aunt contacted me to let you know your family will arrive tomorrow as planned. I estimate their ETA here at two P.M. our time."

"Good. I'll do what I can to be here for their arrival."

"I should hope. Richard DeBlass also confirmed. They arrived in New York this evening. The children are very excited." His eyes pinned Eve now. "Nixie is particularly excited to see you, be here with you."

"I'll be here," Eve snapped back. Sometime. Somehow. God.

And because she could see Nixie as she first had — cowering, covered with her parents' blood, shaking in the shower where she'd hidden, Eve went straight up the stairs and into her home office with a new weight on her shoulders.

"What am I supposed to do?" she demanded when Roarke came in behind her.

"Exactly what you need to do." He set the comp down. "And right now? It's eat dinner."

"Jesus, lay off, will you? I have work. I need to update my board, check in with Peabody, Baxter, and Trueheart, and the cops I put on various protection details. I need to cross with Feeney and start pushing on hotels because the son of a bitch is *somewhere*. Add in rental units, property purchases because he's got a pile of money now and you can bet your ass a spanking new ID. And, oh, while I'm doing that, I'm supposed to stuff food in my face, and worry about a freaking houseful of people and a holiday dinner. I can't *think* with everybody crowding me."

"It must be difficult," he said in a voice deceptively, dangerously calm, "to be the only one in the city, possibly on the planet who can catch this particular son of a bitch. Or, in fact, so many murdering sons of bitches. Harder yet when so many around you are inconsiderate enough to expect you to eat and sleep and have the occasional conversation. What a burden we are in your world."

"That's not what I mean. You know damn well —"

"I know I don't have to stand here taking slaps because I have friends and family coming to our home. Or because you're overstressed and jittery. So do as you please."

He picked the comp up again, walked out.

"Jittery?" Appalled, deeply insulted, she balled her fists, stared down at the cat who

stared back at her. "Where does he come off with that crap?"

Galahad turned around, stuck his tail in the air — adding further insult — and strolled out after Roarke.

"Right back at you," she muttered. She stalked to her desk, kicked it, then ordered her computer to read out her incomings while she updated the board.

She made it nearly two minutes before she swore bitterly. "Computer, stop and save. Goddamn it."

She started to ask the house system where he'd gone, then knew. He'd taken the evidence comp, so he'd gone to his lab.

Well, he didn't get to walk away during a fight, and he especially didn't get to walk away to spend time doing work for her so she'd feel shittier than she already did.

She tracked him down, shoved into his computer lab where he sat, jacket off, sleeves rolled up, hair tied back, a glass of wine in his hand, and his focus on the wiped comp.

"I am not jittery, and that's a dumbass word."

"As you like."

"And you don't get to do that." She jabbed a finger at him. "You don't get to respond in that reasonable voice that's completely fake so I come off looking unreasonable. It's fighting dirty."

He spared her one cool look. "I fight as *I* like."

"I don't have time to fight. I'm trying to do my job because if I don't somebody else is going to end up on a slab. Morris is going to start charging me rent."

"Then go do your job, by all means, Lieutenant. I'm not standing in your way."

"You are, too." She snatched up his wine, took a gulp. "You're screwing up my head, making me feel stupid and selfish and —"

"Jittery?" he suggested, and earned a burning, narrowed-eye stare.

"Call me that again, and I swear I'll punch you."

He stood. Nose to nose, eye to eye. "Try it. A bloody good brawl might do us both some good."

She slapped the wineglass down again. "Oh, don't tempt me."

"I'd call it more a dare." He smiled, very deliberately. "Unless you're too jittery to follow through."

She didn't punch him; he'd be expecting that. Instead, she hooked her foot behind his, angled for a takedown. Which he countered, so momentum took them both down.

He tried to turn, take the brunt of the

impact, but they both crashed, hard enough to jar bones on the floor of the lab. She scissored her legs, tried a roll that would've landed an elbow in his gut, but he'd always been slippery, and blocked it.

He used his superior weight, almost had her pinned. But she was slippery herself, slid clear. And nearly, very nearly, had her knee in his balls.

And she called his tone fighting dirty.

They grappled, rolling and bumping into stools, cabinets, each willing to take or give a few bruises, until he did manage to pin her — and she managed to press her knee, none too gently — against his balls.

His hair had come loose, and fell to curtain his face and hers. Breath came fast over the hum and click of equipment. His eyes, fiercely, furiously blue met her seething brown.

His heart, her heart, beat like war drums.

Then, in the flick of a switch his mouth was on hers, her legs wrapped around him. All the fury, the frustration, the insult, channeled into violent and primal need.

She nipped at his tongue, he tore at her shirt, all while that need, that violence, built and burned. Now they rolled, they grappled, to take in an urgent, almost vicious quest for release.

He filled his hands with her, filled his mouth with her, while his blood raged, while her body arched, quaked. She coiled under him, surrounded him, inflamed him beyond any thought of control.

He yanked her trousers down her hips, ripped away the thin, simple barrier and drove her to gasping, shuddering peak with his hands.

And more and more, from him, from her, in a wild whirlwind of mindless, reckless, impossible lust.

Soaked in the flood of dark pleasure, blind with greed for more, for all, she dragged him to her. Bridging up, she demanded that first savage thrust, then the next, the next. With her legs locked hard around him, she drove him, brutally as spurs to flanks, until he'd filled her. Until he'd emptied her. Until he'd emptied himself.

He collapsed on her, his breath gone, his mind gone. She'd destroyed him, he thought. She'd stripped him to the bone, then shattered him. Now she lay under him, limp, and he could feel the tremors, those aftershocks of crazed sex shake her.

Or him. Or both of them.

His. Every maddening, infuriating, fascinating, courageous inch of her. His.

And he'd change not one thing.

"It seems you had time for that." His throat felt as if he'd swallowed fire — and he'd have given a million for the wine on his workstation — or the strength to stand and get it.

He barely managed to lift his head to look down at her. All flushed, all soft, all long, glinted whiskey-colored eyes.

"It was pretty quick."

He smiled at that, and at the touch of her hand on his cheek after she spoke. He pressed his lips to her cheek in turn.

Now, with the anger and lust washed away, the love beneath stood solid and strong.

"I'm not jittery. Think of another word. I like your family, you know I do. It's just . . . right now, with everything, all of them, it's . . ."

"A bit overwhelming."

She thought about it. "That's okay. Overwhelming's okay. When we went there last summer, it was mostly — well, except for the brief pause for the dead body that was *not* my case — hanging out, drinking some beer."

"I understand that perfectly well."

"I guess, maybe. And add on Nixie. It's not fair, it's not right, but every time I see or talk to the kid I get twisted inside. It eases off, but it always starts out that way. I just see her the way she was when I found her, after she'd crawled through her parents' blood and hidden. I can't get why she wants to see me, talk to me. I must remind her of that, what she went through, what she lost. It messes with my head, and I can't afford that right now."

"If you brought her pain, Richard and Elizabeth wouldn't allow her to see or talk to you."

"I guess not."

"Take this friends and family business as it comes for the next couple days. You give what you can, when you can. And as they are friends and family, every one of them understands what you are, what you do, and what it means."

"Summerset." She sneered it.

"And Summerset as well." Roarke flicked a finger down the dent in her chin. "He enjoys drilling you, just as you do him."

"Maybe."

She closed her eyes a minute. "I was too late. And I see them in my head, see what he did to them because I was just too late."

"Eve." He pressed his lips to her brow. "You know better than to blame yourself."

"Knowing better doesn't always stop it. Everything I turn up says his parents were good people, did their best to be good parents, and because he didn't get his way, he slaughtered them. He annihilated them. Lori Nuccio, just an ordinary girl, a good waitress, responsible, who went out of her way twice to help him get work. He debases her, ends her because she wouldn't let him live with her after he stole from her, after he hit her."

She curled to him when he wrapped around her, and found such comfort.

"And Farnsworth — a good teacher, the kind students remember, a woman who loved her ugly little dog and offered to make soup for her neighbors. He tormented her for hours, and he killed her because he was too lazy to do his goddamn schoolwork."

"You know him. You'll stop him."

"I have to find the worthless bastard first."

"And you will," he repeated.

She let out a long breath. "I will." Let it go, she ordered herself. Just let it go. "Anyway, sorry. Sort of."

He smiled down at her. "Considering where we ended up, it's hard to say the same."

And she found she could smile back. "*Now* I'm hungry."

"Is that so?"

"Yeah, it's so."

He levered off, sat back on his heels. Then just grinned at her.

Following the direction of his gaze, she looked down at herself. She wore one tattered sleeve of what had been her shirt, most of her support tank, and her weapon harness — with her pants bunched around the ankles of her boots — and her clutch piece.

"That was probably a nice shirt," she thought aloud.

"It's good you have more. As do I."

He tugged off the rags of his own.

"We need to get the torn stuff into a recycler. I'm not having Summerset getting a load of it."

"I keep reminding you he's aware we have sex."

"There's sex, then there's sex."

He considered the torn clothes as she hiked up her pants again. "There is, yes. We'll gather them up." He offered a hand, pulled her to her feet. "Then what do you say we change, eat, then get to work."

"I say it's a plan."

"And what do you say to spaghetti and meatballs?"

"I say it's a genius plan." She let herself lean on him a moment. "I've been pissed under it all, all day. It's nothing to do with anything but the case, and it doesn't do any good to get pissed about a case. I guess I needed to blow off some steam."

"Happy to assist."

She poked his bare chest. "You got your steam off, too, pal."

"We both have something to be thankful for."

Together, they picked up torn shirts.

The food helped, as did the routine of updating her board, reading the reports from her people in the field, touching base with Feeney.

She couldn't say what Roarke did in the lab, but knew without question if anyone could find something to help on the wiped machine, he could. He would.

She ran probabilities, but didn't feel confident in the results. Indeed, when she factored out the Boyds' two college-age children, the percentage increased for targeting. And how could Reinhold know the kids were home for Thanksgiving?

Would he even think of family and holidays?

He'd want Boyd, she thought, drinking yet more coffee as she worked. To prove he could hit one out of the park, that would be his thinking.

But Boyd was no slightly out-of-shape salesman, ambushed by his own son — a son who lived in the same apartment. Boyd was fit, tough, had good security. Reinhold would need to plan carefully there. More, Eve thought, he'd need to build up his courage.

More likely to try for women first, for older targets, less secure targets.

Marlene Wizlet and the Schumakers topped her list, along with his friend Asshole Joe, followed by Garber, his former Global Studies teacher.

If he stuck to pattern, it would be one of them. If, she thought, as she highlighted each.

Maybe he'd take a little vacation on his latest victim's money.

No, she decided as she rose to pace and circle. He'd need that euphoria again, that power again, that payback again. But he was hurt, so that might buy a little time.

"Where are you, you bastard?"

Once again, she put the map on screen, highlighted each crime scene, each sighting. With the aid of the computer, she calculated more routes, more probabilities until her head throbbed.

When Roarke came in, she stood studying results, rocking back and forth on her heels more from frustration than fatigue.

"Too many damn possibles. Hotels, apartments, condos, duplexes, single-family residences. Even when you calculate high-end and focus on sectors near his old neighborhood, there's too many. And hell, he could decide to live uptown. Freaking New Jersey. Brooklyn, Queens. No, no." Annoyed with herself, she rubbed at the tightness in the back of her neck. "It's going to be Manhattan, and near what he knows. He won't want to feel superior from a distance. But . . ."

"You're working in circles, Lieutenant."

"I know it. It's pissing me off."

"You need sleep. Clear your mind," he continued, and cupped her face in his hand. "Come at it fresh in the morning."

"I hate this guy, and that's stupid. I don't even know why especially, as I've dealt with worse. But he's stuck in my throat."

"When you have him in Interview, you'll be stuck in his." He pressed his lips to her forehead. "Let's go to bed."

Might as well, she thought, as working in circles wasn't going to find her mark.

"Did you get anything?" she asked as they walked to the bedroom.

"It's slow, and bloody frustrating. I've got some bytes, and enough to see she'd interfaced her units. When we pull out more, we may be able to follow the money trail more precisely. Feeney's banging his head against that wall. We've connected on it a few times tonight. He'll bang it again tomorrow. And before you ask, yes, McNab's been at work as I have, and they pulled in Callendar as well. We'll get there, but it's going to continue to be slow and frustrating for all of us."

In the bedroom, she stripped down. "If we find the money trail, the accounts — and they're out of our reach, legally — you could hack them with the unregistered."

He glanced over as she dragged on a nightshirt. Her skin had that faint, translucent glow it developed when she'd exhausted herself. "I could, yes, and enjoy it as well."

"I need to think about it. Well, we need to get there first, and I need to think about it. If I can't find him my way, I may have to find him yours. Because he's got his next target in mind, and he's figuring it out now. He's working it out, and feeling smug about it."

He slipped into bed with her, pulled her against him. "One way or the other you'll have him. He won't be so bloody smug then, will he?"

"Not when I'm done with him." She closed her eyes, tried to will herself to sleep.

In his new penthouse, in his swanky new bed, Reinhold swallowed another dose of pain meds, chased it with the last of the complementary bottles of champagne from building management.

His foot fucking *hurt*!

It hadn't been bad when he'd left the clinic, in fact he'd felt damn good cruising on the drugs. Then he'd felt like a million — or four — when he'd walked into his new place, found the big-ass gift basket from management. Champagne, fancy cheeses, and candy and fruit and cookies, and all kinds of rich-man snack food.

He'd felt so damn good, he'd ordered the droid to unpack, then go out and buy some imported brew, and fix up that steak dinner.

He was going to like getting used to steak dinners.

He'd walked all over the apartment, all over the building checking out the shops, the fitness center, the restaurants and bars.

He'd thought about hanging out at the bar — for longer than the one drink he'd had — maybe hooking up with a woman.

But he wanted to get the lay of the land first.

He'd walked around the neighborhood some, too, just getting that feel and feeling fine.

It wasn't until the foot started throbbing some he remembered being told to stay off it, keep it elevated.

The idiot doctor should've made it more clear, he told himself, teeth gritted as he waited for the meds to kick in. He should've given him stronger drugs, more specific instructions, better care.

Maybe he'd give the asshole doctor a taste of his own. See how he liked a broken foot.

"You're on my Shit List," Reinhold mumbled.

He could go back for a "follow-up," teach the asshole a lesson, grab some good drugs.

He liked the idea, rode on it through the pain until the miracle of chemistry clicked in, and eased that pain away.

Not smart, he thought, to go back to the asshole doctor. Smarter to do a little research, find out where said Asshole, M.D., lived, and take care of it. He probably had money, too.

Fucking doctors rolled in dough.

Yeah, he'd start working on that, maybe catch him some night when he left the clinic, or when he was in his own fancy apartment.

Something to think about, but he had other business first.

He ordered the bedroom screen on, had to think through to remember how to call his computer up on it. Then decided he wanted pizza.

Steak dinner had been hours ago.

"Hey, Asshole!" He enjoyed programming the droid to answer to the insult. It made him laugh, every single time.

"Yes, sir." The droid came to the bedroom doorway.

"Get me a pizza — pepperoni, mushrooms, peppers, onions. A large. Get it at Vinnie's, that's my place."

"Yes, sir. Should I go out and get one or arrange for delivery."

"Go get it, for Christ's sake. You think I want to wait for some fuckwad to deliver it? And make it snappy, you shithead."

"Yes, sir."

He liked the "sir." About damn time somebody called him sir. In fact, from now on, he'd make anybody he planned to kill call him sir before he did them.

He called up what he termed his Shit List, studied the names, the addresses he'd found, the workplaces he either knew or had been able to find.

Beside each were their offenses, and his current — subject to change — method of making them pay.

He'd have been surprised to see just how closely Eve's list aligned with his. But he didn't think about the police. He'd begun to consider himself a professional. After all, each kill had generated pay — payback and cash.

Jerry Reinhold — and he had another program with possible code names — was a Hit Man with a (S)Hit List. It cracked him up. After he'd worked his way through his own list, he'd use the code name and hire himself out.

His current favorite was Cobra. Fast and deadly. Except he really liked Reaper. As in Grim.

As he studied his list, he relived each insult, embarrassment, rejection.

He thought of how it would feel to burn Marlene Wizlet's pretty face with acid until she looked like a monster. Then he'd force her to look at herself — before he slit her throat.

Teach her to flip him off, teach her to think she was better than he was. And she'd made some good money, he was sure, whoring her face, the one he'd ruin, her body.

And the Schumakers. God, he hated them. He'd get plenty from them. He figured on beating the old man to death, drowning the old hag in her own bathtub.

Coach Boyd, good old Coach Boyd. That would be the best time ever. Wanna see me swing away? He'd figure out how to get inside Boyd's place — just figure it out. Then he'd rape the wife right in front of him. Then he'd get busy with the snips. He really wanted to use those snips. And when that was done, he'd beat the bastard's brains out with his trusty bat.

Pure satisfaction.

Even if he didn't get much profit out of Boyd, that would be — what was it? Yeah, yeah, a labor of love.

He cracked himself up again, kept going down his list.

He changed a few methods. He had enough money now to get his hands on a stunner. You could do a lot with a stunner. And he figured he'd pick up a hammer, maybe a saw.

A guy wanted to be well-rounded.

He thought of Mal. The way to Mal — what kind of friend boots you just because you were short on the rent — was through his mother. That pushy bitch. He liked the idea of the hammer there. First mother, then son.

But not quite yet.

He smiled as he studied his next pick. Oh yeah, that would be good. That would be fun — and he knew just how to pick up the bucks for his profit on that one.

"Asshole, where's my pizza! And bring me a damn beer."

He took a few more minutes to go over his plan. Jesus, it was really so simple. Why hadn't he ever thought of doing all this before?

The droid brought pizza and beer on a tray, with a napkin.

Not bad.

"Go on out there, active rest. I want you around if I need you."

"Yes, sir. Enjoy your pizza."

"Bet your ass."

He switched the screen to entertainment, scrolled through his choices, settled on porn.

He amused himself with pizza, beer, and violent sex until he dropped contentedly off to sleep.

17

She woke early and alone. In the murky light before dawn she *felt* the alone even before her eyes adjusted.

Roarke was up and . . . somewhere already, she thought. She'd have wondered how he managed to rise, even shine so damn early, but even as she lay there she knew she'd finished with sleep herself.

Her mind had already circled to Reinhold.

Even as she sat up she cued into the snoring, a sound even kindness and affection couldn't term a purr. She made out the heap of fur and limbs that was Galahad at the foot of the bed.

At least somebody knew how to sleep until actual morning, she thought, and shoved out of bed.

She'd grab a workout and a quick swim, she decided. Tune everything up since she had the time. She hunted up ancient sweat shorts, a support tank, tossed an NYPSD

T-shirt over it.

The cat never stirred, the snoring never ceased while she pulled on shoes, then slipped into the elevator.

A hard thirty-minute run, she calculated, maybe fifteen on weights, ending with fifty laps in the pool.

She stepped out in the pool area with its lush plants, exotic flowers, deep blue water. Of all the luxuries, the indulgences spread through the home that Roarke built, she considered the pool her biggest personal perk.

Tempting, she mused, to just strip off and dive in, but more satisfying to work up a sweat first.

And circling around toward the gym, she saw the light glowing.

She paused before she entered, and heard Roarke's voice, then someone else's.

Easing around the corner, she saw him — in workout gear nearly as ragged as hers — steadily bench-pressing while he carried on a conversation. He had the comm on speaker, she realized as the voice — male, high-toned Brit — rattled off a lot of equations and buzzwords she didn't completely, hell, didn't remotely, understand.

While Roarke lifted, tossed out questions and comments about fire codes, something to do with egress, some sort of three-dimensional blueprint flashed on a wall screen, shifted, revolved, zoomed in, went from side to bird's-eye views.

It looked, even to her untrained eye, big and important.

She slipped in, got an easy smile from Roarke, and angled over to program one of the machines for her morning run.

The beach, she decided, programming manually while Roarke's conversation continued. Tropical sunrise.

She liked the feel of sand under her feet, and the rosy light blooming on the eastern horizon, the sight and sound of waves kissing the shore then rolling coyly away again.

Okay, maybe the cutting-edge gym, so far removed from the crowded space and iffy equipment she'd once had to settle for at Central, equaled another really big personal perk.

She took a couple minutes at a light jog to warm up, then steadily increased her pace until she ran full out.

While she ran, she heard the clink and thunk as Roarke set his weights on the safety, then, a switch in tone as he started a new conversation. Italian? she wondered before the opening greetings switched to English — and talk about engines (she thought) and aerodynamics.

He'd switched to free weights, she noted, doing biceps curls as he studied the screen and schematics on some sort of muscular air transport.

Shortly, he moved onto a lab in France — she thought maybe they discussed perfume. But it could've been serums. By the time she'd finished her thirty, he stepped onto a machine himself for his own run.

She lifted, curled, pressed while he ran and did whatever he did with Europe. When she stopped, grabbed water, he turned off the speaker and the screen.

"A happy morning meeting of the minds," he commented.

"Is that what that was?"

"I meant you and I, but the rest went well enough."

He'd worked up a healthy sweat, she noted, had talked business with three or four countries, and looked alert and revved.

And it was barely dawn.

"Does it make you dizzy jumping from country to country that way?"

"It's all a matter of maintaining your rhythm."

She eyed him as he ran. Slick, limber, strong. "Meaning you establish yours, and they have to match the pace."

"That's about it, yes. You're up early. Dreams?"

"No. At least none I remember. I'm just up. And it gave me a chance to squeeze this in — and a swim."

"I'll join you there. I've tied off most of what I wanted to tie off this morning before the holiday."

"That's tomorrow." She'd done her best to etch it into her brain.

"Family's in today. So . . ." He slowed for his cool down, smiled over at her. "And it clears some time for me to work with you, Lieutenant."

"Find the money, find him," she said. "Failing that, he's going for another, probably tonight. Unless he's crying over his broken toes."

Roarke stepped off the machine, took a water as she had. "You're not considering he may take a holiday himself? On the simple factor his targets are probably expected somewhere tomorrow?"

"He can't wait." Her conclusions mixed with Mira's equaled immediacy to her. He wanted, felt he deserved, instant gratification.

"It's too exciting. And if he's thinking about the Thanksgiving deal at all, he'd want to screw with that. Devastate someone's family on a day they're all supposed to be stuffing pie in their faces and saying how grateful they are. It just makes it more satisfying that way."

"You've a point. It's going to take some time through legal means," he said as they started out to the pool. "I can cut that considerably with the unregistered."

"I'm thinking about it." Torn, she stripped off. "There's some time, one way or the other. He's not the broad daylight sort, doesn't have the balls for it, not yet. He likes sneaking around at night. There's some time," she repeated, reassuring herself.

She dived in. Cool water on her skin, that slight shock to the system, a quick rev to smooth laps. And Roarke, his body slicing down through the water, then matching her stroke for stroke so they hit the far wall together, turned, powered back.

She lost track of the laps — five, ten — but her body and mind hit that line between energized and relaxed. The burn of muscles created the perfect contrast to the coolness of the water.

When her heart labored, when those muscles began to tremble, she pushed for one more lap, then let herself sink before surfacing.

"God. Why don't they make another hour

in the day, then we could start every morning this way?"

He slid over to her, ran a hand down her slicked-back hair. "Would you?"

"Probably not, but it's a really nice thought." She angled toward him, tipped her head back, found his lips with hers.

Glided skin to skin.

"And an even better one," Roarke murmured.

Twin beeps sounded from the 'links they'd both set on the table near the pool.

"What the hell? That's not my signal."

"It's the notification signal, on both," he told her.

"I didn't set any notification."

"I did — on both. Bugger it." He shoved back his hair, climbed out of the pool, grabbed a towel. "For the bloody medal business this afternoon."

"What? Today? It's today?" And how had she managed to completely erase it from her mind. "What's worse than bugger it? I want something worse."

He only sighed, tossed her a towel. "We'll get through it, then it'll be done."

"I've got a homicidal crazy as lucky as he is stupid to find, and you've got a horde of Irish relatives coming in. You should tell Whitney we need to pass — postpone," she amended.

On the faintest smile, he angled his head. "*I* should?"

"He's my superior. I can't tell him we're too busy." She hissed at Roarke's steady stare. "And neither can you. I mean, you could, but you won't — and I get it. Damn it. It's an honor. It really is," she continued as she dried off. "But why does it have to be a public one? It's your fault."

"Mine?" Amusement growing, he hooked the towel around his waist. "And why is that, exactly?"

"Because you're really rich and famous, so that plays into the politics."

"Well, that's an interesting conclusion. I thought that played into the difficult politics of it all, and why they've held you back from captain until recently."

"It's all stupid politics. Who knows which way they roll?"

"But my fault, whichever direction?"

"Yeah. Yours."

"And it wouldn't have anything to do with you being so fucking brilliant at your work?" He arched his eyebrows over eyes dancing with humor.

"I ought to be able to be fucking brilliant at my work without them making me stand in front of crowds of people and cameras and Christ knows. How come I get punished for being good?"

"It's an honor, remember? And, yes, a punishment from your view. And bloody sticky from mine. It's what I get for marrying a cop."

She jabbed a finger at him. "Warned you."

Laughing now, he grabbed her, spun her around. "I wouldn't have it otherwise, even with the bleeding medal. So we'll suck it up, Lieutenant."

"Maybe we'll get lucky, and I'll be putting restraints on Reinhold this afternoon. Even the mayor can't argue that one."

"Let's hope. And let's eat. I'm starving."

She ate, even though he pushed stupid oatmeal on her. And since she'd gotten a jumpstart on her day, started the next round in her home office. Galahad joined her, sitting in her sleep chair giving himself a casual morning wash.

"The computer likes the model for his next target," she told him. "I don't know about that." While Galahad continued to wash, she rose to study the board. "Female, probably physically weaker, so that's a plus. But she has a male cohab. She lives uptown — out of his current comfort zone. Even without the police protection he shouldn't know about, her building has top-notch security. He's going to want her," Eve mused. "And yeah, he probably wants her now, but he doesn't have the chops to get past her security and her cohab."

Baxter's report had confirmed Marlene Wizlet rated Extra Frosty with a Side of *Yow*. More important, he assessed her security — electronic and human — as solid, the cohab as smart, and protective enough to have already hired a bodyguard.

Reinhold would want her, Eve thought again, but had to know she wouldn't be an easy get.

She'd take more study, wouldn't she? More of a plan. Lure her out, take her off the street. Possible. Possible he'd try. But wouldn't he need somewhere to take her?

"Is he going to start soiling his own nest, wherever the hell that is? More control in your own place. Would that offset the thrill of messing around in someone else's safe zone?"

Also possible, she thought.

But he was hurt. The foot had to be giving him some trouble, should make him reconsider any sort of physical altercation.

He liked taking his victims from behind, by surprise.

The shopkeepers were a better bet to her

thinking. Older couple, right in his neighborhood. If he could get to one of them, he could use that to entrap the other.

He had money now — a nice pile of it, and more than enough to invest in a black-market stunner, a fake badge, a uniform. With the holes in the Schumakers' building security, and again not knowing about the police protection, he could access their apartment easily enough. Just slide in behind another resident, or pose as a delivery or maintenance guy. Or a cop.

"I'd wait. Bide my time, watch the building, the routine. Go in at night. Cop uniform's the most direct."

She glanced over at the cat, but apparently the washing had exhausted him so he lay on his back, all four legs splayed in utter relaxation.

"You'd think you'd had sex instead of kibble. Anyway, then you just knock, ID yourself as NYPSD. Law-abiding citizens are going to open the door. Use the stunner, keep it quiet.

"Soundproofing's not good on those older buildings. Lock it up, gag and restrain, then you can do what you want to them. Hours of doing what you want to them."

"Lucky for the populace you're also law-abiding."

She frowned over her shoulder at Roarke. "I thought you were busy with empire stuff."

"I was, now I'm not. And as I'm about to shift my efforts into find-the-stolen-money stuff, I wanted to see you before you left for Central."

"Going in a few minutes. This is the best way in, right?" She gestured to the building on screen. "A minor investment in costuming, hit them late, stun, lock up, restrain."

"These two as targets?" he asked, stepping closer to look at the photos of the Schumakers.

"Yeah. They live over their market. See, the building has security cams on the main entrance, card swipes for residents, and buzzers for lock release — visitors, deliveries."

"And potential thieves and murderers. What floor are they?"

"Third. Northwest corner unit."

"Fire escape?"

"Yeah."

"I wouldn't bother with the costume. I'd invest in a good jammer, a good scanner. He grew up in the neighborhood, and has probably accessed fire escapes before. I'd go that way, scan the windows for alarms, jam if any. If they've locked the windows, which a great many people comfortable in their third-floor unit don't, a simple glass cutter can be used to lift a window lock. A child could do it."

"Which you did."

"Oh, as often as possible. Then he's in, and unless he's drawn any attention getting in, he doesn't have building security picking him up."

"He's got a bum foot."

"That's what blockers are for."

"Yeah." She jammed her hands in her pockets. "The comp likes the model." Eve tapped the photo.

"She's lovely."

"And she's got a male cohab. He's lovely, too — and bigger and fitter than Reinhold. Plus her security's out of his reach. This would be his first break-in, if he goes that route. He was already in his parents' apartment, had the key for the ex's, and bashed the teacher as she came back in with her dog. He's never had to deal with locks, security, or an actual break-in. Logically, he should aim for the target with the easiest access."

"And you see this couple."

"No, I see Asshole Joe — this guy. He's the only one of Reinhold's friends who's shrugging off what he's done. I think Reinhold could talk his way into Joe's place, or lure him out, depending on what he wants. He may even know a way in since he's probably hung there often enough. He's the easiest hit, but probably not the most satisfying."

"Ah." Roarke scanned the board, the photos, the notes applied. "And not covered, I see, as the others are."

"No, he shrugged off protection, too. Crowding him, cramping his style with the ladies or some such shit according to the reports. I'm going to have a face-to-face with Asshole Joe today."

"Who'd be the most satisfying?"

"On my scale, Wayne Boyd. Reinhold's carried that grudge close, and I'd bet every time he bashes someone with a baseball bat, he thinks of Coach Boyd, getting benched, being the goat instead of the hero in the championship game."

"Boyd said he hadn't come down on the boy about the strike out, but kids being kids . . ."

"Yeah, some of them would've had some choice words for him. And reaching that conclusion, I've done what I can to find and reach all the members of Reinhold's team, the opposing team."

"Do you honestly think he'd go that deep, that far?"

"I think it's a damn good thing he wasn't involved in Red Horse," she said, referring to a major case she'd closed. "If he had a chance to use the Menzini virus? He'd take out everyone who's ever sent him a cross-eyed look, and all the bystanders he could while he was at it.

"He's not that different from Lewis Callaway — the same whining, entitled, pay-you-all-back mentality. The difference is he likes being there, he likes the power of killing face-to-face, having his hand in it."

"He lacks Callaway's control, if control's the word for it. And needs that connection, we'll say, with his victims."

"That's close enough," Eve agreed. "Still, with the Boyds, you've again got pretty good security on their building, and a whole family to take on. He'd never get in the door, or a window without excellent equipment and honed B and E skills. His best move there would be to grab the wife or one of the kids, use that to bait Boyd into coming to him or giving him access. But that's risky. Really risky."

She paced away, paced back. "He's pissed off. The injury has to have him pissed off. At the same time, he walked out of Farnsworth's with millions, so he's smug. He's won every round, so that's made him cocky.

And still he's a coward. He thinks he's brave, he thinks he's found his strength, his purpose, his life's work, but everything he's done is with the mind-set of a scared, spoiled, ungrateful child inside a man's body."

"Well now, it couldn't be said by any definition I was spoiled as a child, but ungrateful I surely was. It's hard to be thankful for the boot or the fist. And scared, that, too, most of the time. I'd've gone for the shiniest prize, I'm thinking."

"You were never a coward."

He met her eyes, thought of his father. "He terrified me, every day, even when I learned defiance could be a shield of sorts. And the last beating he gave me, one that nearly put me in the ground? I wonder still if I'd've been scared enough to go back to him, as he was all I knew. But Summerset found me, took me in. Gave me a choice. Not that I was altogether grateful for it, at the start of it."

Eve took his hand. Sometimes she forgot he'd been a child, as frightened, lost and beaten down as she.

"He'd have been my shiniest prize," Roarke murmured. "Somewhere down the line, if someone hadn't beaten me to it. I couldn't have lived in the world, or felt a man if he'd been breathing in it."

She wondered what he would think or feel if he knew the person who'd beaten him to it had been Summerset. And that, she thought, wasn't hers to tell.

"His parents never hurt him, never abused him. There's not only no evidence of that, but plenty to the contrary."

"But, as you say, it's a mind-set."

"Yeah." She looked back at the board. "Boyd or the model. They're the shiniest. The other teacher, Garber — not as hard to get to, but he's just done a teacher. I think another, back-to-back would . . . bore him. There's former employers, supervisors, even coworkers, so they're on the watch list."

"And you've dozens on that list," Roarke said.

"Yeah. I'm going to hope you're right about the shine. They're both well covered. If he tries for either Boyd or Wizlet, we'll take him down. The trouble with that? There's bound to be more who aren't among those dozens. People no one thought of or knew about."

Impossible to know, he thought, and hardly a wonder she continued to circle the same ground. "So finding him before he settles or moves on a target is the only way to be sure."

"New ID, new place. If he had the smarts, he'd hole up for a few days, heal up, put a real plan together."

"But he's not smart."

Eve shook her head. "Not smart enough."

"Then I'll go back to finding the money. I'll work here for now," he added as he turned her to him. "And likely go in at some point to mesh up with Feeney. But I'm damned if I'll set foot in Central today if I don't have your word you'll not be leaving me hanging on the damn medal business."

"If I'm in the field —"

"Ah." His eyes glinted a warning that had her rolling her own.

"I'll stay in contact. And if I hit something hot enough to get out of the ceremony, I'll let you know. You're slick enough to slither out of it."

"That's a deal then." He kissed her, surprised and touched by her quick, hard embrace.

"I'll see you when I do," she told him. "One way or the other."

"If we go through with this thing today, you'll be wearing your uniform, won't you?"

"Yeah. That's how it goes."

His smile lit up. "At least that's something. Mind my cop till I see her next."

When he walked away she told herself being grateful for Summerset, right down to her core, was a secret she could take to the grave.

She sent Peabody an alert to meet her at Joe's apartment. She'd just get that out of the way first, she decided as she headed downstairs.

She found her coat over the newel post. She knew Summerset hung it up at night, then laid it back out in the morning. She'd never understand why he didn't just leave it there. Same with her vehicle, she thought as she walked out, swinging on the coat.

She left it in front of the house, he remoted it to the garage, then remoted it back in the morning.

Routine, she thought. Everybody had one.

She glanced up at the sky as she crossed to her car, and felt a little bubble of hope. If those heavily overcast skies opened up — and timed it right — they'd at least be spared the medal ceremony on the very, very public steps of Cop Central.

Something else to — maybe — be grateful for.

She drove away and through the gates. In less than two minutes she found herself caught in a thick knot of traffic, punctuated with a wild orchestra of clashing horns.

Since the car came outfitted, she used the camera to see how bad it was, and zoomed in on a broken-down maxibus effectively blocking two lanes.

Though she suspected Traffic had already been notified, she called it in before punching vertical. She skimmed over roofs, cut east. A longer route, she thought, but at least she wouldn't be sitting, stewing.

Besides, a different, even longer route equaled a break in routine. Different buildings, different patterns, different glide-carts and street vendors — and who did they sell NYC souvenirs, scarves, hats, gray-market handbags to this early in the morning?

Holiday time, she reminded herself, the start of the insane Christmas shopping season. Tourists, slap-happy with a vacation or trip to New York, swarmed what they considered bargains like ants on sugar.

Early setup, she supposed, to take advantage of that change of usual patterns, that break in routines.

Routines, she thought, straightening in her seat. Reinhold was breaking them — reaching for more upscale with food, clothes, accommodations. But routines were routines for a reason.

Wouldn't he have a favorite arcade? He liked games. A favorite club, pizza joint?

414

Sports? Baseball was out given the season, but did he have a favorite Arena Ball team — football, basketball, hockey?

He could afford tickets now. He could afford courtside, fifty-yard line. Box seats.

Vids, music, hot clubs — what was trending right now?

Struck, she tagged Mal Golde on her in-dash 'link.

"Ah, hey, Lieutenant."

She saw from the droopy eyes, the tousled hair, she'd either woken him or he'd put in a rough night. Maybe both.

"Questions. Neighborhood pizza joint, the one Reinhold favors."

"Vinnie's, sure. It's always Vinnie's."

"What's he get — routinely."

"Ah . . . Sorry," he said as he scrubbed his hands over his face. "Didn't get much sleep. Um . . . pepperoni, onions, mushrooms, green peppers."

"Okay. Favorite sports teams."

"Yankees, all the way. We used to go around 'cause I'm a Mets fan, and —"

"Not baseball. Arena Ball, football, basketball. Something in season."

"Football — Giants. Dug-in Giants fan. He's not big on Arena or roundball."

"Okay. Hangouts. Arcades, clubs, delis, whatever."

"We'd mostly hit Jangles, in Times Square. It's worth the ride, then maybe grab a brew if we were flush enough at Tap It — it's right on Broadway between Forty-fifth and Forty-sixth. Jangles has tourneys. Jerry always scraped up the scratch to enter. He nearly won once, too, but Bruno nipped him out. Pissed Jerry off big."

"Bruno who?"

"Oh." Mal's eyes widened, his face paled. "God, I didn't think of him before. I don't know his name. Bruno's his game tag. Big guy, just a kid though. Maybe eighteen. Freaking game wizard."

"Anything else you can think of? Routines, favorites, usuals."

"Pistachio float from Gregman's — a neighborhood place. He's been hooked on them since we were kids. Oh, and um, Lucille." He glanced around, lowered his voice. "I didn't think of her before either. If I so much as think of an LC with Ma in the room, she'll know it. She's got that power."

Having met his mother, Eve didn't doubt it.

"He frequents an LC named Lucille?"

"Well, see, all of us did. She'd — This is embarrassing."

"Murder trumps embarrassment."

"Yeah. Yeah, it does. See, she used to give

us a group rate on bjs — me, Jerry, Joe, Dave. Back when we were sixteen, seventeen, like that. Jerry, and look I didn't know about this until after, but you don't rat out your friends anyway. He stole some money from his mother, and paid Lucille for a full ride. I think, I'm pretty sure, it was his first. Like when he was around eighteen. I know Joe ragged on him some about being a virgin, and Jerry said how Lucille had done him, all the way."

"You all still hire her?"

"No. Man." His ears went a little pink, and he took another wary glance behind him. "I don't. And Dave doesn't, not that I know of. But I'm pretty sure Joe and Jerry still see her sometimes."

"Where's Lucille?"

"She used to hang around Avenue A, back when she had a street license. But she got her own place, and upped her license. I'm not real sure, but maybe she's still in Alphabet City. I haven't seen her, you know, since I was about eighteen. It was just too weird getting — having the same LC do all of us."

"Okay. Just give me a basic idea on her. How old? Race?"

"Ah, I think she's not much more than me — like maybe twenty-seven, twenty-eight. Like that. Mixed. I think Black and Asian. She's really nice looking, or was."

"Okay, thanks. Anything or anyone else comes to mind, contact me."

"Sure. Um, Lieutenant? Dave and I — and Jim, Dave's brother — we did a sweep of the neighborhood last night. We didn't see him, or talk to anybody who has."

"Trying to do my job, Mal?"

"No, really, no. Dave and I, we just had to get out of the house for a while. And we stuck together. We're all sticking together."

"Keep doing that," Eve advised.

The conversation nearly took her to Klein's building. As she navigated the rest of the route, she contacted Charles Monroe.

Instead of the slickly handsome sex expert, the pretty blond doctor he married came on the 'link. "Hi, Dallas."

"Hey, Louise. I thought I tagged Charles."

"You did. His 'link was here on the counter and he's making me breakfast."

"Sorry to interrupt."

"No problem. And his hands are free again. We're looking forward to seeing you tomorrow, seeing everyone. Here's Charles."

"Morning, Lieutenant Sugar."

"Charles. Just a quick question. Do you know or can you find out about an LC who started street level maybe ten years ago, and young when she did. Probably just legal. Goes by Lucille."

"Seriously?"

"I've got a little more. Mixed race, probably Black/Asian, Avenue A turf back at the start, then moved up, but likely stayed in the same area. And before you ask, no I don't know how many LCs work Alphabet City, but I figure it's a lot. I'm just looking for one. She's not in trouble, but I'd like to keep it that way."

"I never worked that area, but I know some who did or do. I'll see what I can find out."

"Appreciate it. What're you making?"

"Honeymoon pancakes."

"How long's the honeymoon?" she wondered as they'd been married for months.

"I'm looking at forever."

"Nice thought, and thanks in advance for the help. See you," she added, clicking off as she zipped to the curb a block from Asshole Joe's.

She climbed out, calculating. Pizza joint wouldn't be open yet, and neither would the arcade. She might be able to try Gregman's sooner, and she'd get a line on any recent purchases for high-dollar tickets to Giants games.

Or better yet, she thought, when she spotted her partner in her puffy purple coat and pink cowboy boots flooding out of the subway stairs with a million others.

Eve fell into step beside her. "Good timing."

"It was like being held hostage in an airless box with a bunch of refugees. They really need more trains on this line."

"Routines," Eve said. "They're comfort, habit, patterns. Everybody's got some. Routines, favorite things. I've got a list of Reinhold's. I need you to check on tickets, premium tickets for Giants games. That's football."

"I know it's football. I like football. Everybody wears those tight pants and has big shoulders."

"They're shoulder pads, so that's false vision."

"I like it fine."

"Gregman's," Eve continued. "In Reinhold's old neighborhood. Sells pistachio floats."

"Yuck. I draw the line at green floats. But I got it."

"I've got Charles doing a reach-out for an LC named Lucille. She reputedly broke Reinhold's cherry, as well as giving him and his pals discount rates on bjs. Reinhold and Asshole Joe here may still use her from time

420

to time. Then there's Jangles, an arcade in Times Square — and some gamer named Bruno who beat Reinhold in a tournament. A beer joint nearby called Tap It."

"How'd we miss all that?"

"We didn't," Eve said as she pulled out her badge for Joe's building's security plate. "It's called follow-up. Mal remembered a little more when I tried the routine angle. Meanwhile, Roarke's working the money angle."

"So's McNab, that and the ID. It's slow going, Dallas."

"We'll be pushing it. And we'll be pushing the location. He's here somewhere — in someplace plush, you bet your ass."

She held her badge for a scan. "Lieutenant Dallas, Detective Peabody. We're here to talk to Joe Klein."

ID verified. Mr. Klein has not cleared you for entry. Authorization is required.

Eve rolled her shoulders, smiled fiercely. A workout, a swim, a new angle — and now busting electronic chops.

Not a bad start to the morning.

"Listen, you worthless piece of e-crap," she began.

18

After her satisfying smackdown of an electronic moron, Eve rode the elevator up to seven with Peabody.

"Nicer, tighter building than, say, his friend Mal's," she observed. "He sells insurance, right?"

"Uncle's firm," Peabody confirmed. "Insurance Sales Producer. It's a midsized operation, pretty solid. From my scan of his financials, he's good at it. And he likes to spend those bonuses and commissions. Nest egg isn't a term he considers."

"Where do terms like that come from? If you leave an egg in a nest it either hatches or it doesn't. If it hatches, it flies or crawls away, right? If it doesn't you've got some stupid egg, and what good is that?"

"Um . . ."

"Exactly." Eve strode off the elevator, aimed for 707.

Interesting, she noted, that Joe had installed a palm plate and a cam — not standard as the other apartments on the floor didn't have them.

Which either made him more security conscious than his neighbors, or more into status. Maybe both.

She pressed the buzzer, unsurprised with the electronic greeting. Status primarily, she decided, and overkill in a building like this one.

Mr. Klein is currently on Do Not Disturb. You're welcome to leave your name and a message.

"It's Lieutenant Dallas, NYPSD." She held up her badge for the routine scan. "And my message is you're going to disturb him. We're here on police business. And don't even think about giving me the runaround, or I will assume that Mr. Klein is either harboring a murder suspect or being held by same against his will. That assumption will lead me to circumvent the security of this apartment and enter."

One moment.

"Good one," Peabody commended. "Though technically we'd need probable cause rather than assumptions."

"I don't get technical with technology."

Mr. Klein will be with you directly, Lieutenant Dallas, NYPSD.

"Fine."

Directly took a couple minutes. Eve saw the reason for the short delay when Asshole Joe opened the door. They'd obviously disturbed his beauty sleep.

His eyes, an eerie and likely enhanced green — still looked slumberous, and there was a slight sleep crease denting his right cheek. He wore loose black pants and a biceps-baring tee. His feet were bare.

"Hey, Detective." He shot a wide, sales-man's smile at Peabody. "Sorry for the wait. I had a late night."

He shifted his gaze, gave Eve what she as-sumed he thought was a flattering sure-I'd-do-you study.

"My partner, Lieutenant Dallas. We'd like to come in and talk with you."

"Sure, but right now?" Smile still in place, he lifted his hands, his shoulders. "It's not a good time. I've got . . . company, if you know what I mean." He actually winked.

Eve just stared him down until he shrugged.

"I guess it's fine. She's out for the count.

Like I said, *long* night."

He stepped back into an obsessively trendy living area that screamed Single Guy Looking For Action!

Lots of glass, metal, black fake leather, enormous entertainment screen with an open-front cabinet below loaded with discs. A small bar, black and silver, outfitted with various glassware ruled a corner. Photos and pencil sketches of nude females decorated the walls.

Scattered over the floor were a pair of high, hot pink heels, a black skirt the width of a place mat, and what looked to be an animal-print thong.

"Wasn't expecting company." With an easy laugh, he scooped up the female debris, tossed it all on a chair. "So, I need coffee. You want?"

"No, thanks."

"I gotta jump-start the brain cells." After tapping his temple, he walked behind the bar.

Eve heard the faint beep, deduced he had a mini-AutoChef built into it.

"So what can I do for you ladies?"

Eve swallowed the "ladies." He just wasn't worth it. "You're aware by now that Jerry Reinhold has killed four people."

Joe's eyebrows drew together in a frown

as he shook his head. "I'm no lawyer, but I think you need some serious proof to make that stick."

"His fingerprints and DNA all over the murder weapons and the crime scenes are a pretty good start. Seeing him on the security discs of the banks where he transferred his parents' funds pick up on that. And having him identified by several eyewitnesses selling valuables from his parents' apartment kick in, too."

"Okay, I know it looks bad." He took a sip of coffee from an oversized black-and-white-striped cup. "God, that's good! Are you sure you don't want a hit?"

"Positive."

"Okay. The thing is," he continued as he skirted the bar, gestured to the long, low sofa, "I've known Jerry for years." He took a seat in the chair without women's clothing, slid down, kicked out his legs. A man at his ease. "It's really hard to process he might have tripped out and killed somebody."

"His parents, his ex-girlfriend, and his former Computer Science teacher would disagree with you, if they weren't dead."

"Harsh." He drank more coffee, crossed his ankles. "I'm just holding out that there's been a mistake."

"Have you had contact with Jerry since last Thursday night?"

He shifted in his chair. "No. And — full disclosure — I did try to tag him, just to hear his side of things, you know? Maybe he's just freaked — who wouldn't be — and keeping it real down-low."

"Are you just that stupid?" Eve wondered.

"Come on, no call for that." Irritation flicked briefly over his face. Here then gone. "Maybe somebody framed him. Maybe tried to kill him, too, so he's hiding out. He could be dead himself. Or, okay, maybe he went totally whack and did all this. There's nothing I can do about it."

"He's working his way down a list, Joe. You could be next."

He laughed, shooting his legs out again, tossing his head back. "Please. NPW — no possible way. Lady —"

"Lieutenant," Eve corrected with a whip-lash in her voice. "The homicide lieutenant who waded through Jerry Reinhold's parents' blood two days ago, who stood over the body of Lori Nuccio that same night, and over the tortured body of Edie Farnsworth the day after."

"Well, sure, I'm really sorry about all that, but —"

"There's nothing to laugh at here. He

427

beat, stabbed, bludgeoned, strangled, smothered human beings. You should start wondering what he's got in store for you."

The smile had vanished, but he waved a casually dismissive hand. "He's got no reason to hurt me. We're bros."

"You won in Vegas; he lost. And you rubbed his face in it. That's more than enough for him."

"Hell, Jerry's not like that, he knows I was just yanking. Plus I bought everybody a round of drinks."

"Joe." Peabody tried a voice of reason. "Why don't you let us put you under protection, just for a few days."

"No can do. How am I supposed to score with cops looking over my shoulder? It's one thing for Mal and Dave to weenie out on it, they don't see the kind of action I do. And hell." He made a dismissive *pfft* sound. "I can handle Jerry. Been doing it for years."

"Not this Jerry," Eve said, but saw they hadn't made a dent.

Joe just waved a hand again. "Listen, I'm going to tap my latest, then we're going to have some breakfast. I'm putting in a couple hours' work later, then I've got another frosty lady to entertain tonight, and that's before I put in some time at the old homestead tomorrow for T-Day. Schedule's tight, and I'm covered. But hey, if I hear from Jerry, I'll let you know."

Done, Eve pushed to her feet. "Your choice. Does he now or has he ever had the code and keys for this apartment?"

"No way. Nobody but me has them. I like my privacy."

"Watch your back today, Joe. That comes from the person who'll be standing over your corpse if you don't."

Eve caught his smirk just as she turned to walk out, and just kept going.

"Do you think he'll contact us if he hears from Reinhold?" Peabody wondered.

"Fifty-fifty. I'd say it depends on his mood at the time. He really is Asshole Joe."

"Yeah." As they rode down in the elevator, Peabody considered. "Reinhold wouldn't be able to access the apartment unless Joe lets him in. Even getting into the building's a little tougher than what he's done before. He could do that, but the apartment's secure. If Joe goes into work, he'll be in an office, with other people, then he'll be with some woman stupid enough to give him the time of day. He's about as safe as we can make him without forcing protection on him."

"I've stretched it to put officers on people who want it. I can't stretch it for someone who doesn't."

She stepped outside, took a breath of cool, damp air. No rain yet, damn it.

"We're going into Central. You work the angles I gave you. I'm working the map and real estate. He'd want better than this." She turned to study Joe's building. "If for no more reason than his bro can afford this. He's got that shitpile of money now, and he's looking for the shine."

"He'd need to snag a shiny place, and furnish it," Peabody pointed out.

"Yeah." Eve mulled it over as they walked back to the car. "High-end there, too. He'd go for the trend, like Asshole Joe. Nothing classic, nothing antique. Shine, shine. We'll check that out. He'd need a few key pieces fast. Swank hotel suite's still possible, so we keep hitting that. But the fucker's nearby."

When Eve walked into the bullpen, she saw the tie gag hadn't gotten old. Now Detective Carmichael wore one. She'd gone for a herd of purple, prancing horses over a field of virulent green.

Everyone, including uniforms, who sat at desks, in cubes, or milled around, wore sunshades.

Peabody pulled her own rainbow lenses out of a pocket, jabbed them on as she went to her desk. She shot Eve a toothy smile, then got down to work.

No harm in letting it play out, Eve decided, then headed to her office.

She hit the AutoChef for coffee, then brought up the map she'd generated. Somewhere inside the area she'd triangulated, or no more than . . . a six-block perimeter, she decided, outside. That would be her starting point.

She adjusted the map, highlighted her target area.

"Computer, search and list all luxury hotels, all luxury apartment buildings, condos, or rental homes within highlighted area."

Acknowledged. Working . . .

"Secondary task. Search and list all high-end furniture stores, specialize in contemporary, trendy. Just the borough of Manhattan for now."

She paced as the computer acknowledged.

"Next task. Search and list any and all gourmet markets that deliver within highlighted area."

He had the droid, she thought, and he could send it out to shop, but it was worth a shot.

Initial task complete. Results on screen . . .

Eve looked at the list, dragged her hands through her hair at the number to wade through.

"Okay, there has to be a way to refine that."

She'd spread herself thin with assigning men to protective details. And it would take a squad of cops hours if not days to check with every single location.

His own place, she thought. Privacy, status, less chance of being nailed by security or a nosy desk clerk, even with the change in looks.

"Computer, save hotel list, but separate."

She'd scrape up a uniform, put him on a 'link, have him contact the hotels — again. But her gut said he'd rent his own space now.

Secondary task complete. Result on screen, split with residential locations . . .

Eve scowled at the list. "I said Manhattan only."

Affirmative. Results listed are for Manhattan only . . .

"Shit." This time she pulled at her hair.

Some results are specialty outlets, the computer continued. *Some deal only or primarily with one type of item. Lamps, tables, chairs —*

"Okay, okay, I get it. Would he do that?" she wondered. "Would a guy take that kind of time, going to a lamp store, a table store? I don't think so, but . . ."

She stepped out into the bullpen briefly. "Baxter! My office."

She circled back, paced. Foot hurts. Probably wouldn't walk around the city. Use websites, the 'link. Order that way, pay electronically. If he —

"Yeah, boss?" Baxter flipped off his shades, hooked them in his breast pocket.

"You've got pretty swank digs, right?"

His grin spread. "I do what I can."

"I've seen your ride. Shiny penis metaphor."

"Hey."

"It is what it is." Eyeing him, she eased down a hip on her desk. "You got the slick wardrobe, the slick ride, so you've got slick digs and sexy furnishings, right?"

"I like looking good, living good. What's the deal, LT?"

"Reinhold. I figure he's got to be getting or already has a place of his own. Something swank, and I'm working on it. But when you get a swank space, you need to furnish it. He'd go for trendy, high-end. He'd like paying a premium. It'll make him feel superior. My list here has all these specialty shops."

Taking a look at the screen himself, Baxter nodded. "Yeah, City Lights — I got my bedroom lamps there. And . . . Urban Spaces. I got my couch, a couple of chairs, and a floor cabinet there."

So shit, guys did spend all that time and effort. "How long did it take you to furnish your digs?"

"Who says I'm done?" He smiled again. "To get it where I want it — for now anyway — six, seven months."

Thinking back, she remembered furnishing her apartment in about a day and a half. "He's not that patient." Or, she calculated, as fussy or discerning as Baxter. "He wants it now. All of it."

"Then he needs to go to more full-service, at least for the bulk."

"He's got a bum foot, so I figure he's going to check out his options online."

"Well, that opens the world, but if he really wants it now, he'd stick local." Baxter scanned the screen again. "He'd look for a place with same-day delivery maybe, or delivery within twenty-four. Like that."

"I'm thinking yeah. Okay, cut out the specialty shops, for now, go full-service, stick local, quick delivery. Thanks."

"Anytime." He slipped his shades back on, strolled out.

She started making contacts herself, switching from full-service furnishings — a much smaller list — to gourmet markets when the computer spat that out. Then back again.

She juggled in conversations with building security and/or management. And had batted zero when Peabody poked in.

"I hit on the pizza."

Her gradually-going-pissy mood jumped high. "Jesus, for a pie? Where is he?"

"Not that big a hit. But Vinnie's sold a droid — matching the description of ours — the pie last night. It's a different guy on the counter now, but the manager checked the discs for me."

"I want a copy."

"Already sent and copied." Peabody handed it over.

"Did he call in the order?"

"No, the droid came in and ordered."

"What time did the droid get the pizza?"

"Time stamp's twenty-three-twenty-one on the order."

"Nighttime hungries," Eve mused. "Check on cabs — dropoffs, pickups at the pizzeria."

"Already got that in."

Eve ordered the pizzeria onto the map.

"I'm betting no cab, but if I'm wrong, we got really lucky." Frowning at the map, she picked up the closest subway stations. "Mass transit's possible, but still probably not. Not that he'd have a problem sending the droid on a mile hike to get a pizza, but I'm going with reasonable walking distance. You want pizza after eleven at night, you don't want to wait a damn hour or more.

"Routines," she thought aloud again. "Habits, favorites. He's got a place close by what he knows. No other way." It justified the time she'd spent on the damn map, and real estate, furniture.

"Okay, I'm going to generate another map, using the pizza joint as the bull's-eye. Try a ten-block perimeter around it. It's going to cut the options down more. And I want pictures of the morph, and of the stolen droid at every shop in this sector, every diner, market, restaurant, glide-cart, street vendor. I want them in the hands of every beat cop, street LC, sidewalk sleeper, and illegals dealer."

"That'll be a trick."

"I'll squeeze a couple thousand out of the budget for a reward — information leading to capture. And yeah, look pained because we're going to get a few million bogus sightings, but Reinhold's here, and even saying he's got the plushest of plush new digs, he's going to want to get out and about. He has to live, right, and he's damn well going to go after his next target sooner rather than later. Local clinics, too, in case he hits one for more pain meds. Get it done."

"Getting it done."

Eve turned back to the screen. "Okay, you bastard, let's figure this out."

An hour into it, she got up for more coffee. As she lifted the mug, she glanced toward her skinny window.

It was pouring outside.

"All right!" She pumped a fist in the air. "Let's go rain!"

She executed a quick, happy boogie, did a spin, and spotted Roarke in her doorway.

"I had no idea you were so fond of inclement weather."

"Rain, think about it. Big, pounding rain. No outside ceremony. They'll have to move it inside."

"And that matters?"

"To me. It's" — she wiggled her shoulders, winced — "weird doing it out there, in front of the whole damn city. Inside it's cops, and some politicians."

"And media."

"Yeah, you can't get around that, but it's more, I don't know, contained. Are you here to work with Feeney?"

"I have been, a bit. There's something . . ."

She leaped like a panther. "What? What something?"

"I don't have it yet. We don't," he corrected. "But there's something in the data we've been able to regenerate on one of the wiped drives. I think your Ms. Farnsworth wound some sort of code within the codes. I think she tried to leave us some clues, as best she could. If the drive hadn't been wiped, we'd have an easier time deciphering, but we're still working piecemeal."

"But it's something."

"It is, yes. Definitely something. We'll get back to it."

"Get back?"

"Despite the heroic rain, you've just about got time to change before we're due — wherever we're due to be."

"Shit." She checked her wrist unit. "Shit."

"As you're not currently slapping Reinhold in restraints, we're stuck with this. So be a good girl, and get into that oddly alluring uniform."

"Shit," she said again. "Give me —"

She snagged her signaling 'link. "Dallas."

"Lieutenant." Kyung, media liaison, gave her his excellent smile. "I wanted to inform you, due to the unfortunate weather, we're moving the medal ceremony indoors to Auditorium A, West Wing, Sector Six, Level Two."

"Okay. Roarke's with me now. I'll pass it on."

"Excellent. I'll see you shortly, Lieutenant, and many congratulations."

"Yeah, thanks." She clicked off. "Give me fifteen," she said to Roarke, "and meet me at the down glide."

"That's about all you have." He made himself comfortable at her desk with his PPC as she dashed out.

She cut through the bullpen, shook her head at Peabody, and bolted straight into the locker room.

Changed, she fit her uniform hat on her head, gave herself a critical study. Okay, squared away. And when this was done, she'd change back, and get the hell to work again.

Deliberately avoiding the bullpen, and any possible questions, comments, ragging, she left by the side door.

She beat Roarke to the glide by about

thirty seconds. And watched him walk toward her, the glint in his eye.

"Don't get any ideas, ace."

"Too late. You look sexily official." He took her hand, and when she realized he intended to lift it, kiss it, she snatched it back.

"Come on!"

"We'll save it all for later then." He stepped on the glide with her.

"They'll make speeches, especially the mayor," she warned him.

"I'm aware."

"After that it's a little more blah-blah, presentation, photo op, done."

"Hmmm."

"You could've sent a rep. Nobody would've blinked if you'd done that, considering you're managing most of the universe. It's good you didn't. It matters you didn't."

"That would've been ungrateful, and I'm not ungrateful. And when this gets out, there are countless cops in the universe you're so fond of gifting to me who are going to be well buggered. And that's a bit of a plus for me, isn't it?"

"Hadn't thought of that."

"Oh well, I have. Still, I'll need to duck out quickly as I'd like to be home to greet the family. And don't worry, Lieutenant," he added, "I'll get back to work on this business as soon as I've settled them in."

"If we can nail him today, he won't have time, not that I can see, to kill anyone else. And, hell, easier to shove in the cranberry sauce when I'm not thinking about the bastard."

"Agreed, altogether."

He was right about being grateful for the acknowledgment from the department, she thought. And she wasn't ungrateful for the family coming over from Ireland.

Thinking that, she told him, "Either way, I'll carve out as much time as I can to, you know, be home."

He trailed his fingers down her arm. "Something else to be thankful for."

"A lot of that going around."

After hopping off on Level Two, she aimed toward Sector Six. "This should take about thirty, maybe a little more because the mayor can't shut up. I'm heading right up to change after."

"That's a pity."

"I'm working on location, using a pizza joint as the hinge. He had the droid pick up a pie last night."

"Interesting."

"And I'm figuring he's got to have furniture, so I'm checking outlets there. High-end, trendy — that's my sense. And I'm on condos, apartments, townhouses. Something's going to hit."

Circling, Roarke thought again, but it seemed her circling was getting smaller and tighter. "You'll bag him, Lieutenant. I have every faith."

"Sooner's better."

Two uniforms flanked the double doors of Auditorium A, and they snapped to attention. Kyung, tall and lean in his meticulous charcoal suit, stepped forward to intercept her.

"Lieutenant, Roarke. I'll escort you around to the back staging area."

"Fine."

"A pity about the rain," he said as they walked. "The steps of Central provide such a fine and dignified visual."

"Yeah, too bad."

He smiled down at her, humor lively in his eyes. "I'm sure it's a disappointment to you both. The mayor will speak first. Chief Tibble will follow with his remarks, then your commander will say a few words. Roarke will be presented first. A few remarks after the presentation and the photos are appreciated."

"Certainly."

"Then you'll be presented, Lieutenant."

"Got it."

"The presentations will be followed by a short reception."

She stopped dead. "What?"

"At the mayor's . . . request," he told her. "More photo ops, some quick interviews."

"Is the mayor aware I'm neck-deep in tracking a killer already responsible for four bodies?"

"He is, as I am. Ten minutes," Kyung promised, "less if I can manage it. I *will* get you out and away. My word on it."

She scowled, then reminded herself Kyung wasn't an asshole. "Ten. Tops."

"Done." Kyung pulled open the door to the staging area at the back of the auditorium.

Already too many people, she thought, tripping straight over to cranky. The mayor, the entourage, Tibble, a couple of uniforms, Whitney — and a couple of Trina types bustling around dabbing crap on faces or fiddling with hair.

When one aimed for her, Eve just bared her teeth. "Touch me with any of that, you'll be eating it."

Tibble stepped over, shook hands with Eve, then Roarke. "This is very well deserved, on both counts. I'll speak to this in my remarks, but I want to say to you personally the NYPSD and the City of New York are fortunate to have you as one of their own, Lieutenant."

"Thank you, sir."

"And you," he said to Roarke. "We're grateful for the time, effort, and expertise you contribute."

"You're more than welcome for it."

"And I think it's safe to say that the time spent on acknowledgments such as this, however well earned, is something you'd both rather devote to work. But it's important for the department and the city to make the acknowledgment."

"Understood, sir, and appreciated."

"Appreciated more, I expect, if we can keep it brief." He gave them a nod, stepped off, had a word with Kyung.

Even as the mayor spotted them, which Eve knew could mean an endless blather, Kyung gently tapped his shoulder, gestured toward the door leading to the auditorium stage.

"Here we go," Eve murmured.

They filed out. When she faced the auditorium, Eve had to order herself not to gape.

Not only was every seat filled, but people stood in the back, along the side walls.

She'd expected to see Nadine, no crime beat reporter would miss the moment. She hadn't expected Mavis, Leonardo, even the baby. Who the hell told them? She spotted her entire division, Mira, Feeney, McNab. Jesus, she thought, who was chasing bad guys?

And there, Charles, Morris, Caro, Reo.

She watched Jamie Lingstrom slide in the doors. Feeney's godson, an e-ace who wanted to be a cop, had longer hair than the last time she'd seen him.

"It's the family," Roarke said quietly.

"What?"

"The family. They're here."

She followed his gaze, found his aunt Sinead, his uncles, grandmother, cousins, and God knew. And Summerset. He'd arranged it, Eve realized. Letting Roarke think they were coming in later, but bringing them for this.

For pride, for family. Hell, it *did* matter, she thought when she saw Sinead beaming. All of it mattered.

She started to say something to Roarke as the mayor approached the podium, then spotted another face in the crowd.

Nixie Swisher. Face sober, eyes steady. She didn't smile, just continued to give Eve the serious, even stare. In the stare Eve read something she hadn't considered.

This was for her, too — for Nixie. For all

445

the victims, all the survivors. For every one of the dead she'd ever stood for, or would stand for.

So it mattered. All of it mattered.

19

It took too long, had too many words, far too many cameras. She could tune some of that out. The speeches, the media, the politics didn't count, not in the long run.

But she allowed herself to touch her fingertips — just the slightest brush — to Roarke's as Whitney called him up. What mattered was the sheen of pride in Sinead's eyes, and yeah, even the glint of it in Summerset's. The unmistakable satisfaction on Feeney's face, the unified acknowledgment from her division.

The acceptance by the people in her world for the man who meant everything.

"It's my privilege to present to you the New York City Police and Security Department's highest civilian honor with gratitude for your invaluable assistance, your contribution, and your valor. You hold no badge, you have no sworn duty, and yet you have given your time, resources, and skills, you have risked and incurred physical harm in the pursuit of justice for the people of New York. Today, we thank you and we honor you for that contribution."

Did it surprise him that they stood for him? Eve wondered. The uniforms, the detectives, the brass, the rank and file and the bosses of NYPSD? He was so accustomed to power, to position, to holding a room of people in the palm of his hand. But yes, she thought, it surprised him when they all rose to their feet.

And she had no doubt he considered the irony of it all.

The Dublin street rat, the slick and slippery thief who'd spent most of his life outwitting and evading cops now had them standing for him.

"I thank you, all, for this honor. But it's been my privilege to work with New York's very finest, to come to know the men and women who serve. And more, to come to understand their dedication, their courage, and their sacrifice. You call it duty, but from what I've seen it's more than that. It's who and what you are. I'm grateful to have any part of that."

When he stepped back Eve broke her dignified cop face long enough to grin at him as he stood with the brass for the quick photos.

"Nice," she murmured when he stepped back beside her.

"So it was. The room would enjoy it if you kissed me now."

"No." She might have laughed, but she understood he was perfectly serious. "Firm on that."

She put the dignified face back in place as Whitney began to speak again.

"We take an oath to protect and serve," Whitney began. "Every cop takes that oath, accepts that duty. A good cop does more than accept duty, but lives it. Lieutenant Eve Dallas is a good cop. Today she receives the NYPSD's Medal of Honor, the highest honor given. It is never given lightly.

"The certification specifically addresses the Red Horse investigation, where under the lieutenant's lead, through her dogged pursuit, her clear-eyed leadership, and her keen skill, Lewis Callaway and Gina Mac-Millon were identified, apprehended, and will face trial for mass murder and domestic terrorism."

Applause rippled through the auditorium at that. Eve was tempted to join in — to applaud justice — but knew better.

"This successful investigation saved countless lives," Whitney continued. "But it doesn't tell the whole story. Throughout her career, from her very beginnings in uniform, Lieutenant Dallas has displayed the skill, the dedication, and the valor that merit this honor. For that, for the dozen years, for all the cases, all the risks, the sacrifices, for justice served, it's my professional and personal pleasure to award the Medal of Honor to Lieutenant Eve Dallas. A good cop."

It was those three words that got her. *A good cop.* For her that was the highest accolade, the most important tribute she could earn. She had to fight back the emotion that flooded through her — good cops didn't choke up — as she stepped forward.

"Thank you, sir."

"Not this time." He pinned the medal on her, shook her hand. "Thank you, Lieutenant, for your exemplary service."

He nearly did her in by stepping back, saluting.

She could take a minute, while the crowd stood and applauded, take a minute to pull herself together. And remember what she'd planned to say. Except she couldn't remember a damn thing.

"Okay," she managed, hoping that would settle everyone down, including herself. But they just kept going. She glanced toward Kyung for help. And he only gave her a smile, an elegant shrug.

"Okay," she said again, and as she took another breath, spotted Nixie again.

The young girl stood on her chair so she could see, smiling now. Kevin, the boy she'd be raised with, stood on the chair beside her. Richard and Elizabeth flanked them.

And they were all a part of this, she thought. Richard and Elizabeth, who'd lost their daughter; Kevin, whose junkie mother had deserted him; Nixie, whose entire family had been slaughtered.

And Jamie in the back of the room, once a grieving and defiant kid determined to avenge his sister's murder.

All of them, and so many more.

"Okay," she said a third time. "Okay, thanks. I'm . . . honored and grateful to be awarded this distinction. I'm honored to be part of the NYPSD, and to work with so many good cops. To be commanded by one, to have been trained by one, to partner with one, to head a department with many really good cops. And to have the brain and the canniness, I guess, of a civilian who'd make a pretty good cop himself if he wasn't so opposed to it."

That got enough of a laugh to settle her

down. "This distinction is theirs as much as mine. Probably more. You don't close cases without someone having your back, or trusting the cop — or the civilian — going through the door with you.

"This is for all of us. And it's for every victim we've stood for or will stand for, every survivor we work to find answers for. They're what count. They're why we're here. That's it."

Thank God, she thought, even as she was angled for photos, as applause rang out. Thank God that was over.

They wanted more photos of her with Roarke, and despite her instinct to shake him off, he took her hand and held it. "Well said, Lieutenant."

"I was supposed to say something else, but I forgot what it was."

He laughed, squeezed her hand. "And I'm not permitted to kiss you, even after that?"

"Forget it."

She got through more blah-blah with the mayor, more handshakes, a few more photos. Then Kyung, in his delicate way, extracted them. "I realize you have very little time, Lieutenant, but there are a couple of people who'd very much like a moment."

He led her offstage, gestured to where Nixie waited.

"Hey, kid."

"You look different wearing that."

"I feel different wearing this. A little weird."

"We're coming to your house tomorrow, after the parade."

"That's what I hear."

"There'll be lots of kids. We saw Summerset, and he said."

"Yeah." Eve glanced over, saw Roarke embrace his aunt while a herd of kids — various ages — flocked around. "He's right."

"I'm supposed to talk to you mostly tomorrow when you're not so busy, but . . ."

"Go ahead."

That laser look came back, straight into Eve's eyes. "You said it was for all of us. My mom and my dad and my brother, and my friend. And everyone."

"That's right."

"Then can I touch it?"

"Sure." Eve crouched down, watched Nixie's face — serious blue eyes, soft cheeks, stubborn little mouth — as the girl handled the medal.

Then Nixie looked up. "It's important."

"It's important."

She smiled then, and that too-adult seriousness flicked away from her face. "I have a surprise for you."

"What is it?"

Nixie rolled her eyes. "A *surprise.* You can see it tomorrow when we come for Thanksgiving. I'm going to say congratulations to Roarke, then we have to go. Are you looking for a bad guy now?"

"Yeah, I am."

"Did he kill somebody?"

"Yeah, he did."

"Then you have to catch him."

Simple as that, Eve thought. And maybe, on some level, it was. "That's the plan. I'll see you tomorrow."

"And there's our Eve."

Sinead enfolded her in a hard, swaying hug. Soft skin, Eve thought, soft hair, strong arms. It was weird, this hard, loving embrace, Eve decided, like wearing the uniform was weird. Not bad, just different.

"Oh, it's good to see you!" Hands on Eve's shoulders, Sinead drew back, her green eyes damp, her smile brilliant. "And so stalwart you are in your uniform. We won't be keeping you. Summerset told us you were very busy on an investigation, but we so wanted to come and see you and our Roarke honored. It meant so much to us, Eve. So much to all of us."

"It meant a lot to him when he saw you."

"His mother would be so proud, so I've

her pride and my own to give to both of you. And I'll be after getting a copy of one of those photos of the two of you. Oh, this was such a thrill for all of us. I have to let you go, as if I don't the whole family will swarm you. We'll wait till you're home to do that then."

With a laugh, Sinead kissed Eve's cheek.

She got caught a couple more times before Kyung touched her arm. "Excuse me, Lieutenant, you're needed over here for a moment. I'm extracting you," he murmured near her ear as he steered her away.

"Great. Good."

"Roarke assures me he can handle his own extraction, and I imagine he does so often."

"Yeah, he's slippery."

"You did very, very well," he said, maneuvering her back into the staging area, then through.

"You, too. You got me out in under ten. I can take it from here."

"Then I'll go back and have some cake."

That hitched her exit stride. "There was cake?"

"You wanted out in ten."

"Yeah." She sighed. "Talk about sacrifices." But she hopped a glide and headed back to the locker room to change.

She hung up her uniform, put the medal

in its case. Then wondered what she should do with it. Her office for now, she decided. She should probably take it home, put it away there.

She tucked it under her arm, stepped back out through the bullpen.

Her men rose, which would have put her right back to choked if they hadn't all been wearing sunshades. Carmichael had put the crazy horse tie back on.

So the ovation made her laugh, and put her right back where she wanted to be.

"Get back to work, you idiots."

"We saved you some cake," Peabody told her.

"Seriously?" The idea of so much as a crumb getting past her men was as shocking as a stunner blast.

"In your office."

"I take the 'idiots' back. Get to work anyway."

She walked into her office, touched and still surprised to see the neat piece of cake on a small disposable plate on her desk. She stowed the medal in a drawer, programmed coffee.

And sitting at her desk, broke off a corner of the cake, and got back to work herself.

Fifty-five minutes, she thought. Longer than she'd hoped, but still the whole thing had taken under an hour. And what, she wondered, had Reinhold been up to for the last fifty-five minutes?

He had a plan. No reason he could see why it wouldn't work — and he'd have some fun with it. Plus, changing things up would save him some legwork. His foot still hurt like a *bitch*!

He sent the droid out with a shopping list, and instructions to buy each item at a different shop.

And while he had the apartment to himself, he blasted music as he limped through, speculating on where to set the stage.

The living area. Sure, the second bedroom was big enough, but he liked having the easy access to the kitchen, and the dining room. It made more sense, he thought, since he was having company for Thanksgiving dinner.

It would be his most daring kill, and he'd do it all in his own space. Good practice for when he started selling his services, he decided. Body disposal could be an option he needed to offer clients, after all.

Sometimes people like the Mafia or the CIA or whatever didn't want bodies found. He'd read shit about that.

The cops didn't have a clue where he was

— how could they — or now *who* he was. In his own place, undisturbed, he could take all the time he wanted with his . . . selection.

No, prey. He liked that term. They, all of them, were prey, and he was, code name: Reaper. He really liked it.

Reaper. Death for sale. Anytime, anywhere. Terms to be negotiated.

Something like that, he decided.

When the droid got back, they'd set the place up, just the way he wanted it. Then, contact, lure, trap. Snap, snap.

He'd have all night, through the next day to do his work, while people were sitting around pretending friends and family meant a single happy shit.

He could stretch it out another night, if he wanted. If he got bored, he'd end it.

Then between him and the droid, they'd take care of body disposal.

"I have the best job in the world!" he shouted over the music, then dancing — wincing a little — out to the terrace.

For the hell of it, he yanked down his pants and mooned New York.

It seriously cracked him up.

He went back in, popped another pain pill, got a beer. It was great to be able to drink when he wanted, eat when he wanted, do whatever he wanted.

All of his life people had held him down, held him back, fucked with him.

Now he was the one doing the fucking.

And he was never going to stop.

"Found myself, Ma!" He cackled it. "And today, oh yeah, I am a man."

He turned as the door opened, and the droid carted in a big box. He saw the droid's mouth move, but couldn't make out the words.

"What? Jesus. Music off. What?"

"Sir, I was unable to purchase and carry all the items in one trip. I —"

"Well, fuck." Idiot. Maybe he'd spring for another droid. Female, he considered. One with sex options. "Go back and get the rest. I want to get started."

"Yes, sir. Where do you want these items?"

"Just put the whole box down there." Reinhold pointed to the center of the living area. "And go get the rest. Make it fast, Asshole."

"Yes, sir. I'll return shortly."

"You'd better." Excited, Reinhold sat on the floor and pulled things out of the box.

More rope, more tape, a carving set. He smiled at the shining blade, at the long prongs of the fork. Perfect for a turkey — or whatever you wanted to slice up.

"Now that's what I'm talking about!" He pulled out the portable saw, flicked the switch. And grinned as the twin, toothy blades whirred.

"Oh yeah. We're going to have the best Thanksgiving ever."

He set the saw down, laid flat on his back, and laughed like a loon.

He honestly, sincerely, had never been happier in his life.

Eve circled, bisected, intersected, detoured, expanded, contracted. She spent more time on the 'link in an afternoon than she normally did in a month.

And couldn't find him.

Peabody poked her head in the door, correctly gauged her lieutenant's mood. She might have preferred just slinking off again, but ordered herself to woman-up.

"Dallas."

"Do you know how many supervisors, managers, landlords, owners, and clerks start their stupid holiday a day early?"

"Not exactly."

"All of them, or damn near. Everybody's head's up a turkey's ass."

"Well . . . lots of people have to travel to —"

"He's not traveling," Eve snapped out.

"He's dug in. And he's got a target. Whoever it is isn't going to get a nice piece of pumpkin pie tomorrow."

"We've got protection on —"

"We've got protection on most of the people we know or have reason to believe may be a target. Most gives him room, and that doesn't begin to cover ones we've missed."

She shoved at her hair, pulled at it in frustration. "He's a frigging amateur, Peabody. He shouldn't have gotten through the first day, and instead, he's had almost a week free and clear since his first kill."

"Dallas, we didn't even know about the first two DBs until Monday. There was no way we could know."

"That's the whole thing, isn't it? He just keeps catching the breaks. We know who he is, we know how he killed every one of them, when he did it, we even know why. We have a reasonable list of possible targets. We believe we know his general area. And we can't find the son of a bitch."

"He has a lot of places to hide. Add the money, and it gives him more yet."

Impatient, Eve shook her head. "I've narrowed it down — strongest probability — to this radius."

Peabody eased in, turned to the screen,

blinked in surprise. "You made a graph."

"Whatever. Highest probability area in red, secondary in blue, and so on raying out from that core. Most likely locations within each area are highlighted on the second map, same color code."

"That's a lot of comp work."

"So?"

"Don't kick me, it's not your strength. You'd never say it was."

Eve hissed because truer words were never spoken. "I had to break down and take a damn blocker because generating this gave me a *pisser* of a headache."

"I could've helped you with it."

"I gave you assignments. Speaking of which?"

"No hit on any sports tickets yet. The sales rep I talked to said a lot of the venues offer sales on tickets, including the big ones, on Black Friday. That's the day after Thanksgiving, and the biggest shopping day of the year."

"Because people are so juiced up on too much food they feel like they have to go out and spend more money than they've got. Friday." She blew out a breath. "Hit it again on Friday."

"Nothing on the arcade or the bar, not yet," Peabody continued. "But I talked to security in both places, and they're on the lookout. I had uniforms start distributing the images — his, the morph, the droid, throughout the target area. Markets, shops, restaurants. They're pushing them on building supers, managers. It's going to take time to hit every location, but the word's out, Dallas. We've got literally hundreds of eyes looking for him now. More like thousands. Someone's going to spot him and call it in."

"And the tip line?"

"Not as much as I figured, but that's probably because people are heading out of town, or dealing with out-of-towners, or shopping for what they forgot to get for tomorrow. Like that."

Disgusted, Eve slumped in her chair. "I hate holidays."

"Well . . . It's kind of unavoidable, and again, don't kick me, but you really ought to think about going home and dealing with your own out-of-towners."

"What?"

"Dallas, it's already nearly an hour past end of shift."

"What?" she repeated and looked at the time. "Damn it, damn it, damn it!"

"I'm just the messenger," Peabody reminded her as she took a cautious step out of range. "But Feeney had to take off. He's going to try to get some work in at home. So am I, and McNab. And Callendar. Roarke's already home, and I know he's connected with Feeney a few times."

Eve dragged her hands through her hair then shoved them in her pockets. "Go home. I'm going to copy this graph thing, send it to you, to everyone. Take a look at it, more carefully. If something pops for you, let me know."

"You haven't managed to contact all the managers in all the hotels, apartments, condos yet."

"No."

"I'll take a share of them."

"I'll earmark yours."

Peabody smiled. "How about I do you a favor? I'll earmark yours. Traffic's going to be a coldhearted bitch. I'll get home before you anyway."

"Something else to look forward to. Go home. I want you and McNab to get to my home office tomorrow. We're going to put in some time on this. Two hours before whenever you were supposed to come."

"We'll be there. We're going to get him, Dallas."

"Oh yeah, we'll get him. It's just a matter of how many more he can rack up before we do, but we'll get him."

She took the time to copy and send her work to Peabody, to Feeney and Roarke, to McNab, to the commander, to Callendar. Every one of them had better comp skills than she did, she admitted. Maybe they could refine, or maybe they'd see something she'd overlooked.

But the simple fact was, she should already be home, dealing with the other part of her life.

She put together a file bag, grabbed her coat, and headed out before she talked herself into locking her office door and pretending she didn't have another part of her life.

Peabody's traffic prediction hit the bull's-eye. While the bitter hell of it didn't improve her mood, it did give her time to think, to make more contacts — and hit more answering services, message loops, and skeleton staffs.

Out of stubbornness as much as concern, she tried Asshole Joe one more time. Maybe, just maybe, she'd wear him down and convince him to accept protection.

Then she let it go when her tag went directly to v-mail.

She drove through the gates already calculating how long she'd have to socialize before she could sneak off and get back to the job.

The lights exploded out of the gloom. And despite the dribbling rain, there appeared to be some sort of ball game going on over the wet, lush green grass.

Men, women, kids ran around like maniacs. Most of them had stripped off jackets to play in sweaters or sweatshirts or shirtsleeves — and all were thoroughly wet and filthy.

She saw the round and rugged leather ball sail, watched someone pass it across with a leaping head strike, then someone else in a blur of bodies execute a lateral kick. She slowed to a crawl in case one of the crazed players ran across the drive. Then winced a little at the ensuing ugly collision and pileup of bodies.

Obviously, the game was vicious.

She parked, got out, and had her ears assailed by shouting, hoots, insults — delivered with oddly musical accents in two languages.

"There's herself!"

Despite the dirt on his face, Eve recognized the boy Sean. Sinead's grandson had, for some reason, developed an unshakable attachment to Eve. And that even before he'd discovered a body in the woods outside his quiet village the summer before.

"We're losing terrible," he told her, as if they'd just spoken an hour before. "Uncle Paddy cheats something fierce and Aunt Maureen's no better come to that."

"Okay."

"You'll come onto our side. You can take the place of my cousin Fiona. She's useless as teats on a billy goat, and does nothing but squeal when the ball comes within a bleeding kilometer of her."

She found herself flattered on some strange level that he'd assume she could save the game for his side. But.

"Can't do it, kid. I don't even know how it's played."

He laughed, then goggled. "Is that the truth then? How can you not know how to football?"

"Over here it's soccer — sort of." But meaner, she decided, which was a point in its favor. "And it's not my game."

"Sean!" From the doorway, Sinead shouted. "Leave your cousin alone, pity sakes. She hasn't so much as gotten in the door yet, and you won't let her come in out of the rain."

"She's saying she doesn't know how to play football!" Absolute shock vibrated in his voice. "And she's heart-stopping seri-

467

ous! That's all right then," he said kindly to Eve. "I'll teach you."

Damn, the kid had a way about him. If she hadn't had a killer to find, she'd have taken him up on it. And enjoyed it.

"Appreciate it, but . . ." She trailed off, her shock as vibrant as Sean's at her lack of essential knowledge as she saw Roarke break from the pack and walk her way.

He was every bit as wet and filthy as his young cousin. Grass stains smeared the elbows of his shirt, with some bloodstains mixed on the left. Light but distinct bruising colored the side of his jaw.

He gave Eve a cheeky grin, then slapped a hand on Sean's shoulder. "You're needed, mate. It's near do or die now."

"I'm off!"

"What the fuck?" Eve said the minute the boy ran off bellowing a war cry.

"Don't ask. We're all but done for in any case, taking that Fiona couldn't hit a cow's arse with a banjo, and Paddy and Maureen both cheat like tinkers at a fair."

"What are you talking about? Why would anybody hit a cow with a banjo?"

He only smiled. "The point is, Fiona couldn't, so we'll be done soon enough. I've a report for you, and it's already on your unit. And I've got some programs running,

468

but the sad truth of it is, it's taking all the time I said it would. Little bits, but not enough, not yet. It's there, that's certain. The clever Ms. Farnsworth slipped some sort of code by him. But we don't have it yet."

"Okay, any progress is good progress at this point. I've been working on something, and I've copied it to you. We'll get to it."

They were shouting for him, she thought. The family he'd lived his life without. "Go hit some cow in the ass with a banjo or whatever. And try not to bleed too much."

He laughed, grabbed her, spun her, kissed her hard to the cheers of the players before she could struggle free and swipe at the wet and dirt he'd just transferred.

"God," she muttered as she strode to the house. "Irishmen are crazy."

She'd barely stepped in, shrugged out of her coat, when Sinead was there taking it from her and handing her a glass of wine.

"Welcome home and to considerable bedlam. It's been a long day for you from what I'm told. Can you take a minute to sit, catch your breath? Those of us who aren't outside or off adventuring in the city or scattered somewhere else are in the parlor."

She could escape, Eve thought. Sinead would make excuses for her. She heard laughter from the parlor, murmuring voices, the fretful cry of an infant — they were always popping out more infants, Eve thought. And she could escape all of it, and close herself in with murder.

And she thought of Roarke's quick grin and filthy shirt.

Life, she remembered, had to be lived, even — and maybe particularly — in the middle of death.

"Yeah, I could sit for a while."

20

When Joe pulled out his 'link, saw Dallas, Lieutenant Eve, on the readout, he was walking the last couple blocks to his last appointment of the day. Of the week, he thought, and looked at it as a bonus.

He smirked at the readout, hit Ignore.

Stupid cop, he thought, trying to scare him. More, trying to shove Jerry's problems on him. Maybe Jerry'd gone wig, maybe he had, but it had nothing to do with him.

Anyway, no chance, at all, shriveled-balls Reinhold worked up the guts to actually kill anybody. Or dug up the smarts.

The way Joe looked at it — and the cop would, too, if she wasn't an idiot — somebody busted into the Reinhold place to rob them, ended up killing them. Probably did Jerry, too, or took him hostage.

They got his ID, scared him into telling them about the bank accounts. And who knew the old Reinholds had that much scratch? If he'd known he'd have worked them into buying some nice, fat insurance policies.

Too late now. Opportunity missed.

As for Nice-Tits Nuccio? She'd probably had a new boyfriend who'd gone whack on her. If she nagged the new one the way she had Jerry, it was just a given. Nagging, whining, complaining was what she'd done best — and *always* looked for a chance to spoil a good time.

And Farnsworth? Please. The rich old bitch had been prime to be taken out. People got killed in New York every day, for God's sake. It was just part of the urban experience.

You had to be smart, take care of yourself, and watch your ass.

Simple as that.

Better yet, get yourself enough scratch — which he was working on — to get yourself into a frosty penthouse with doormen, cams, and all kinds of mag-ass security shit. Maybe a driver and a bodyguard, the kind who watched your back when you took some fine piece of ass to the slickest club in the city.

Yeah, he was working on that.

And when his great-grandmother finally croaked — which couldn't be soon enough

— he stood to inherit a decent little pile. The old hag hoarded money like a starving man hoarded bread or whatever.

He'd take the little pile and head back to Vegas. He'd hit for eight big the last time, close to ten when you added in the smaller wins.

He'd hit for more next trip out.

Then he'd get himself a fine and frosty place.

Like this one, he decided when he reached the address. It took up a freaking block — maybe more. And it shone in the lowering gloom of the rainy fall evening.

The droid's instructions had been very specific, and Joe figured a man who used a droid as an assistant was picky and paranoid.

Fine with him.

He'd done a quick check on Anton Trevor, and the picky, paranoid future client was rolling in it. The guy wanted to discuss business on his own turf? No problem. The client was always right, even the fuckheads. He wanted to revamp his insurance, and possibly discuss a position with his firm.

I'm all over that, Joe thought. About damn time he started rubbing elbows with the real movers, the real shakers.

If this went as well as he planned, he'd

buy himself and his date a bottle of champagne, toss a little of his Vegas winnings around to celebrate.

Today, he thought, might just be the first day of his *real* life.

As instructed, he coded in the number the droid had given him. And the droid answered immediately.

"Answering for Mr. Trevor."

"Yeah, hey. Joe Klein here. I'm outside the building, main entrance."

"Very good, Mr. Klein. Please remain there, and I will come down to escort you."

"No problem." While he waited he texted his date for the evening.

Might be a little late, baby. Got a big fish on the line.

He checked the time before he pushed his 'link back in his pocket. Maybe more than a little late, figuring an hour for the meeting, more if it went really well. Then he'd need to go home, shower, change, get buffed for the night.

She'd wait, he thought with a smirk. People were going to get used to waiting for Joe Klein.

He spotted the droid, moved forward.

"Mr. Klein."

"Yeah."

"Please put these on." The droid handed

him a hat and a pair of dark sunshades.

"What for, man?"

"Mr. Trevor prefers to keep his business and his visitors private, even from building security."

"Whatever." Amused, Joe put on the hat, the shades, and went inside with the droid.

The place had everything — totally up-scale, moving maps, fancy to the ult shops, women with fuckable bodies, men who looked important without trying.

The droid led the way through, stopped at a short bank of silver-fronted elevators, then stood for a scan before using a swipe card, then a manual code.

"That's a lot of lockdown for an elevator."

"Private elevator, limited access."

Joe stepped in — silver walls, even a black leather bench, and a pot of white flowers. In a frigging elevator.

Yeah, this was his life — a preview.

Once again the droid swiped, keyed in, submitted to a scan. "So, what's the boss like?" Joe asked as the elevator rose without a sound.

"Mr. Trevor is very particular and very private. He looks forward to your arrival."

"Excellent." Joe patted his briefcase. "I've got a lot to show him."

They stepped off into a wide, private

foyer. More flowers, a mural of the city painted on the walls.

And for a third time, the droid was scanned, used the swipe, the code, then stepped back to allow Joe to enter.

He saw the view first — the wall of glass with the skyline, the lights, the scope of wealth behind it.

He began to smile as the door clicked shut, the lock snicked behind him.

Then he frowned, noting the clear plastic covering the glossy floor of the spacious living area.

"What? He's just moving in."

"You could say that," Reinhold commented, and choking up some on the bat, swung it hard.

Eve sat with the relatives, as she collectively thought of them. Mostly female here, and kids apparently considered too young to join in the war being raged outside.

She liked them. How could she help it? Even if she didn't know exactly what to do with them, from the woman she couldn't quite get used to calling Granny (I mean, really, how weird was that) to the fat-cheeked baby girl (assuming the pink band around her bald head meant girl) who stared at her endlessly while she sucked on one of those plug deals.

Some of them did handwork — crocheting or knitting or whatever people did with balls of yarn and long needles. Or had tea, or wine as she did, or beer.

Most chattered happily. Sinead did, not even missing a beat when one of the younger women passed her the infant who made mewling noises like a starving cat.

"This is the newest of us," Sinead told Eve. "Keela. Seven weeks in the world."

Keela wore a pink and white knit cap with a pom-pom over what was probably another bald head. She let out a distinct belch when Sinead rubbed her back.

"There now, that's better now, isn't it? She's fed and dry and happy if you'd like to hold her."

Rather hold a ticking homemade boomer, Eve thought, and managed an "Um . . ." before — thanks be to God — the front door burst open and the ragged and motley football crew charged, limped, all but crawled inside.

"Look at the lot of you!" That came from Granny holding court by the fire. "Dirty and wet and soiling the floor, you are! Outside and hose off, or up to bathe the lot of you. Not a one of you are welcome in here until you do. You as well," she added, pointing a sharp finger at Roarke.

"Granny!" Sean sent up a protest. "We left our boots at the door, and we could eat a cow right from the field we're that starved."

"Not until you're washed."

Eve saw her own escape as everyone who'd come in began to slink off again.

"I'll, ah, be a minute."

She dashed for it, and managed to make it to the bedroom as Roarke stripped off his sodden, ruined clothes.

"It was a sad and pitiful rout," he announced. "I'm shamed to have been a part of it."

"Buck up. I'm just going to sneak into my office for a few minutes, read your report, check a couple things."

"It'll be dinner within the hour. If you can't make it down, I'll send your regrets."

"It shouldn't take longer than an hour."

"I'll come along myself, see what you've got, before I go down."

"Good."

She made her escape, went straight for Roarke's report.

She could tell he'd dumbed it down to layman's terms, but it still took her time to decipher.

Since they'd been able to regenerate some

of the wiped data, they had the beginnings of routing on the accounts, and she took some satisfaction there.

If they had some, they'd get more.

He'd included what he and the e-team agreed was part of a subcode, shadowed in with the other data.

It looked like every other computer code she'd ever studied. Which meant it looked incomprehensible.

She brought up her map on the wall screen to keep it settled in her head while she read through other reports, and went through incomings to be certain every one of the details assigned had clocked in with an A-OK.

"Protection details, where we have them, are five-by-five," she said when she heard Roarke come in. "I've read your report, but I don't speak geek, so some of it's lost on me. You can walk me through it, and I'll walk you through the map I've got going on —"

She looked over.

Not Roarke, damn it. Sinead. Who stood, pale as glass, staring at Eve's murder board.

"Hey, listen." Eve shoved up fast, moved over to block Sinead's view. "You don't need to see that. I'm coming right down."

Sinead merely laid a hand on Eve's arm,

shifted to the side. "This boy here — for he's hardly more, is he? This is the one who did this?"

"Sinead —"

"I know violence and cruelty. It was my own sister, wasn't it, who was murdered? My twin. And not a day goes by, not a day, I promise you, I don't think of my Siobhan, and the loss of her. He killed his own parents, they say. His own ma and da."

"That's right."

"And he did that to this young girl." She touched a finger to Lori Nuccio's photos — before and after. "And this to a woman who was his teacher. I know of this, as I follow what you do. And it was only one of the reasons why I was so proud today to see you and our Roarke honored. And now . . ."

"You don't need to explain."

Again Sinead touched her arm. "Do you wonder, ever, what makes a person capable of taking a life when there's no threat to his own or another? What makes them end life, and so often, so very often, with real cruelty, even with pleasure."

"Every day. Sometimes finding out why matters. Sometimes it doesn't mean a thing."

"Oh no, I'm thinking it matters always." Voice and gaze steady, Sinead angled to look at Eve. "And matters to you. How could you face this day after day, year after year unless it mattered? I was so proud today, and thought I could never be prouder of the pair of you. But I am now. Seeing this, I am prouder yet."

She took a long breath. "You'd have found him, Patrick Roarke, for taking the life of our Siobhan. You'd have found him, and seen him pay for it."

"I'd have tried."

"No one ever did, you see, and that was hard and bitter. We needed someone to try."

On another long, slow breath, she pushed back her gilded red hair. "I can tell you from one who never found that justice, it's needed. When someone did for him, left him dead in an alley, I was glad of it. But it didn't close that awful hole inside. Time did some of it, much time, and family. And then Roarke came to my door, and that gave me what I needed after all those years. I thank God for that, and him. But I'm telling you, and hope you already know, what you do, beyond the law of it, is needed."

"Sinead." Roarke stepped up, pressed a handkerchief in her hand.

"Ah well." Sighing now, she dabbed at tears. "The world can be so dark. It's foolish to deny it, and the Irish know the dark better than some in any case. It reminds us to hold on to the light, every minute we can, and to prize it. You're a light to me." She kissed Roarke's cheeks. "Don't ever forget it."

He murmured to her in Irish, made her smile, turn to Eve. "He said I showed him light when he'd expected the dark, but the fact is, we did that for each other. And I'm keeping you from where you're both needed. Don't worry about the family. We'll be fine, even grand, as Summerset's promised enough food for the army we are. We'll send up some for you, all right with that?"

"There's nothing more, really, to do tonight," Roarke told her, glanced at Eve.

"No, there's not. Wherever he is, whatever he's doing, we're not going to find him and stop him tonight."

"Then you will tomorrow, unless you're after telling me the entire New York City Police and Security Department is wrong about the pair of you."

"Let's hope not."

"Then come down for a bit. I find when I've a problem I can't fix or solve, doing something entirely else can help me find the way through. God knows, the family is something entirely else."

She took them both by the hand.

"And we've gifts from Ireland we're all but dying to give you."

"All right." Nothing more to do now, Eve reminded herself, though it stuck in her throat, burned in her gut.

And still, she closed the door to the office and the murder board as she went out.

Joe didn't come around as soon as Reinhold had anticipated. He'd given his old pal a good hard hit — maybe harder than he should have, considering — but all that power and fury just came boiling out.

Besides, he'd wanted Joe with X's in his eyes while the droid dumped him in the sleep chair.

He'd already had the droid cover the chair with plastic from one of the big rolls. It was a damn fine chair, mag leather — the real deal — and in a rich man's chocolate color.

He didn't want to mess it up.

He figured the sleep chair was just another inspiration. He could work on Joe as he sat, reclined, or laid full out. The multipositions offered so many choices.

He'd dubbed it his Kill Seat, and had already decided anybody he did here in home sweet home would get to try it out.

He'd been anxious to get started once he had Joe secured with rope and tape, but he hadn't thought to get any more of those wake-the-hell-up-asshole capsules.

He considered sending the droid out for some, then opted to have it fix him dinner, then shut down. That way he could eat, then work in private.

He chowed down on a double cow burger and fries — the real deal — and thought he'd never tasted anything as absolutely ultra. He watched a slasher vid while he ate, considering it research, and was about to top things off with a bowl of chocolate cookie ice cream when his guest moaned.

He could wait on dessert. Time to start the main feature.

He hadn't taped Joe's mouth. Reinhold had tested the soundproofing himself by strolling out into the communal hall with his own music up to blast. And hadn't heard a thing.

He switched the entertainment unit to thrasher rock, but not too loud. He and Joe needed to have a conversation.

Joe continued to moan. His eyes were about halfway open, and glassy. A thin trail of blood out of his left ear had dried, and more matted in his hair, smeared on the plastic covering the chair.

"Wake up, dickwad." Reinhold punctuated the order with two hard slaps — each cracking the air and throwing Joe's head right, then left.

His eyes rolled around a little, then focused on Reinhold's face.

"Jerry. What's going on, Jerry? God, my head. My head hurts."

"Aw, want a blocker?"

"I don't — I can't move my arms. I can't —" Comprehension dawned slowly, and behind it came the terror. "Jerry. What're you doing? Where am I?"

"We're hanging, man. In my new place. What do you think? Frosted extreme, right? Check the view." Roughly, he spun the chair, slamming it to a halt when it faced the wall of glass.

"Jerry, you gotta let me go. Come on, Jer, stop fucking around. I'm hurt, man."

"You think you're hurt?" Thrilled, somehow more thrilled than with any of the others, Jerry leaped in front of the chair, slapped his hands on the armrests, and soaked up the wild fear on his friend's face. "We haven't even started yet."

"Jerry, come on, man, it's *Joe.* We're buds."

"Buds?" Bending down, Reinhold snatched up a length of hose he'd had the droid cut from a reel. He lashed it across Joe's chest like a whip, got a shocked, high-pitched

yelp. "You think we're buds?"

He lashed again, hardening at Joe's scream of pain. "Were we buds when you dared me to steal that candy from Schumaker's? You made me do it, you fuck."

"I'm sorry! I'm sorry! We were kids!"

"How about when you gave me the wrong answers on that history test so I flunked it? Or when you screwed April Gardner when you knew I was going to ask her out?"

He kept lashing as he raged, kept lashing as Joe screamed. As he cried, blubbered out pleas and apologies.

He stopped to catch his breath while Joe's heaved and hitched, while tears ran down Joe's face. He'd already wet his pants, and that was its own satisfaction.

"Please, please, please."

"Fuck you. Fuck you, Joe. You made fun of me that whole summer I had to take Comp Science over, rubbed my face in it every day. Just like you rubbed my face in it in Vegas, and over Lori when she kicked me out."

"I didn't mean it!" He sobbed it out, all but choking on his own tears. "I was just fooling around."

"Hey, me, too," Reinhold claimed and slashed the hose against Joe's crotch.

The sound Joe made was like music.

Reinhold tossed the hose aside, went to get a beer. And a sap.

His face a pale, sickly green, his lip bleeding where he'd bitten it in pain, Joe wheeled glazed eyes toward the sap. His harsh breathing jerked his chest.

"Don't. Please, please. I've been sticking up for you, Jerry. The cops, the cops are all over you, and I'm the only one taking your side. Mal and Dave, they're blabbing to that cop bitch, and hunkered down with their mothers. But I've been on your side. You can ask anybody. Please."

"Is that so?" Reinhold slapped the sap against his open palm.

"I swear to God. Look, look, you can check my 'link. She's been trying to tag me — that cop, that Dallas. I don't even talk to her. Because I'm on your side."

As if interested, Reinhold took Joe's 'link from the counter where he'd put it, scrolled through. "You've been busy. Talking to Mal, to Dave, getting tagged by the cops, and who's this one — Marjorie Mansfield? A new whore?"

"No, a reporter. She's looking to do a story on you, on what's . . . what's been happening. She tracked me down."

"Is that right?" Reinhold smiled broadly. "What did you tell her?"

"Nothing! I wouldn't rat you, man. Never." His chest trembled in pain and fear as he struggled to speak. "I told her you were innocent, you'd never have killed anybody. You were framed, that's what I said. Somebody —"

Reinhold swung the sap, and delight spilled through him at the snap and crunch of teeth and bone. "Wrong answer," he said, and swung again.

In a direct about-face from her usual position on it, Eve blessed the time difference that had most of the Irish contingent heading off to bed at a reasonable, if not early, hour. Babies and kids were hauled off first, many of them limp in sleep as a parent tossed them over a shoulder or scooped them into arms.

Others followed, bit by bit — though she suspected some of the older kids — age or attitude — were all but camped out in the game room.

But the minute it seemed reasonable, she snuck off and up to her office.

Not that she hadn't enjoyed the long, noisy dinner, and the people. Roarke's family was so damn likable, so funny, and so full of the bullshit they liked to call blarney it just wasn't possible to resent the time.

Very much.

She went straight to her comp to check on any further incomings and reports. She found plenty of both, but not much in them to add any real weight or introduce new angles.

Still, she studied Peabody's refinement of the map, and found some good work there.

She looked up from it when Roarke stepped in.

"I owe you a very big solid for the evening," he began.

"No, you don't. Not only because visiting relatives are in the Marriage Rules, but because I just like them. And maybe it gave me some rest-the-brain-cells time. We'll see."

"I'll thank you anyway." He walked over to kiss the top of her head. "I'll be putting some time in the lab yet tonight, see if something shakes loose."

"Even if it's a crumb, tell me."

"I'll do that very thing. And give it as much time as I can possibly spare tomor-row. Meanwhile" — as he turned to go, he stopped to study the map on screen — "you've made some changes."

"Peabody. I need to go through it all, but my sense is they're good changes. Hopefully the right changes."

"Taken down like this . . ." With his head angled, he stepped a bit closer to the screen. "I believe I own some of those properties."

"You — of course you do," she said on a frustrated sigh. "Stupid brain cells. You can probably get through to the managers, the supervisors, whoever has a tenant list."

"I could, yes, but even that would take some time. Holiday, darling. Offices are closed at this hour, and will be tomorrow. Some of those managers will be out of town, and accessing the data will take time. I can do it myself, but unless you have a name, I wouldn't know who I'm to look for."

"New tenant. The first kill wasn't planned. He wouldn't have starting looking for a place, this kind of place, sooner than last Friday, probably later than that, but we can work it from last Friday. New, single male tenant, that cuts it down."

"It would. I'll start something, but first I'll need a copy of the revised map — in the lab," he added, "so I can work the other program as well. I don't know how many I have in a sector that large, but it's easy enough to find out. And in a sector that large, they won't all be mine. I could, with a bit of finesse, access other tenant lists with the same criteria."

She bumped against her own line, slid a

toe across. "Go ahead. I'll push for a warrant. Start with your own, okay? I'll push hard and get it. I'll damn well get the warrant."

"All right then. I'll see what I can do. With or without the warrant, it'll take time. I'll wager there's easily a hundred properties highlighted there."

"A hundred and twenty-four buildings," she confirmed. "Whatever you can do to cut that down's a plus. And it's time we had luck swing our way. Maybe you'll hit."

"That would be something to be thankful for. I'll let you know, when I know."

Renewed, she pushed through the reports again, and started adding to her notes.

21

Somewhere around eleven, Reinhold's craving for Onion Doodles refused to be denied. Torture was hungry work. He swiped the sweat off his face — it was heavy work, too — checked the AutoChef, then cupboards.

Cursed.

He'd forgotten to tell the idiot droid to buy Onion Doodles.

The AC, the pantry, the refrigerator, the chiller, were all well-stocked. But not a single bag of Onion Doodles lived among the rest.

And he *had* to have some.

He thought about rebooting the droid, having it go down to the store. The fancy food shops would be closed, but he knew there was a 24/7 market on the mezzanine level. Then he decided he could use the longer break, maybe a short stroll around, even a drink at the all-night club, also on the mezzanine.

Joe was out for the count anyway, and it wasn't much fun to pound on an unconscious guy. Big effort, low reward.

He'd used the hose, the sap, a miniburner, toothpicks — talk about inspiration! — and the razor knife the droid had used to cut the plastic.

No wonder he was hungry.

He left the bloodied, burned, bleeding man unconscious and went to wash up.

He sang in the shower, masturbated, sang again.

He changed into fresh clothes — the new black jeans with a touch of silver stud work, a collarless shirt in strong blue, the leather jacket and boots. And he looked completely iced.

He reminded himself to put crap stuff back on before he got to work again. He didn't want to mess up tight new threads.

He made sure he had his swipe, his code, his spanking new ID and credit cards, and some cash in case he wanted to flash it around.

He checked himself out in the mirror a final time, saw himself as dangerous, sexy, successful — and gave the fake soul patch an extra press. He'd grow one of his own soon enough, he thought, and whistling, left the apartment.

He checked out the bar first. Smoky blue lights rolled over the walls, and a holoband crashed onstage. He'd expected more of a crowd, people sexy and dangerous and successful much like himself, but plenty of the tables and stools sat empty.

Dead zone, he thought in annoyance, but since he was there, he swaggered over to the bar. He ordered a whiskey, neat, like he'd seen men do in vids.

"House brand or you want to call?" The broad-shouldered bartender gave him a bored look that immediately put Reinhold's back up.

He tapped an imperious finger to the bar in front of him. "Best you've got."

"You got it."

He didn't take a stool, but posed against the bar. He expected people to notice him as he gave the club a cool-eyed stare. Two couples shared a table near the stage, and the women were prime.

He imagined strolling over, giving them both a come-with-me jerk of the head. They would, too, he thought. They'd leave those limp dicks without a thought, and scamper after him like good bitches.

Do whatever he told them to do, let him do whatever he wanted to do.

And maybe he'd kill them after, just to

see how it felt to do some strange.

The bartender set the glass of whiskey in front of him.

"You want to run a tab or pay as you go?"

"I pay as I go."

With a nod, the bartender slid a small black folder across the bar.

"Where's the action around here?" Reinhold demanded.

"Not much tonight. Holiday. A lot of people are out of town or heading that way. Friday, you'll see some action — and the band's live."

"Maybe I'll be back." He flipped the folder open, fought not to goggle at the tab. He could buy fifty goddamn brews for the one glass of whiskey.

He interpreted the bartender's impassive look as a pitying smirk, and wished he had his sap. Instead, he tossed down the new credit card, lifted the glass.

He took a deep gulp. Nearly choked. Because he felt his eyes water, he turned quickly away as if taking a longer look around.

He'd never tasted whiskey before, but he was damn well sure the asshole of a bartender had cheated him, charged him for high-grade and served him crap.

Oh, he'd pay for that, Reinhold promised

himself. He'd make a point of seeing the asshole paid for it.

He forced more of the whiskey down, just to prove he had the balls, then dashed off the signature he'd practiced off and on the last couple days.

Pocketing the card, he walked out.

Fucking prick, he thought. He'd meet Reaper some night very soon. And he'd see how he liked having acid poured down his throat.

Desperate for anything to kill the taste of the whiskey, he pushed into the market, picked up a bag of cheese and bacon–flavored Onion Doodles — a favorite — a family box of Spongy Creams, two Chunky Chews, and a Grape Fizzy.

He charged all of it, sucking on the fizzy as the droid clerk bagged the rest.

Starving, he broke open the bag of Onion Doodles on his way back to the elevator. Munching and slurping, he headed back up.

He'd take a real look around the next day, he thought. Before his own Thanksgiving feast. Maybe see if the same bartender was working, get his name.

Do a little research on a future target.

He found Joe still unconscious, so out even slaps didn't bring him around.

No fun playing with a sleeping asshole,

Reinhold decided.

He took his snacks up to the bedroom. He'd watch some vids, catch some sleep. And get a good start on Joe in the morning.

He had plenty left to try out on his old pal before Turkey Time.

Roarke gave it until half-one, coordinating with Feeney, McNab, and Callendar until after midnight. Like them, he'd meant to leave the work on auto and walk away, but he'd been too caught up.

He'd seen progress — real progress — when they'd untangled the initial routing, found the shadow beneath it. But then, there'd been a shadow under that.

He had considerable respect for the late Ms. Farnsworth, and had she lived, would have hired her in a finger snap in any number of positions.

He'd managed to crack the initial code, and felt pure satisfaction. Until he'd understood she'd switched codes for the next section.

Smart, he had to admit, making certain her killer didn't, likely couldn't, catch on to the pattern. And all this while she'd certainly been in terror, likely in pain.

The trouble was, she was so bloody good, it was taking him a great deal of time. Put-

ting back the wiped material, byte by bitter byte, and then going under it all for the message he now knew she'd left wound in it.

Tomorrow, he promised himself, and gulped down a half bottle of water. By Jesus, he'd have the rest tomorrow.

He set up the auto, scrubbed at his face, then went off to fetch his wife. He had little doubt she'd crashed by this time.

And he wasn't wrong.

She'd laid her head on her desk, with the cat curled around the point of her elbow.

He saw by the subtle jerks of her body she dreamed. Fearing a nightmare, he walked to her, spoke gently as he eased her back, then up.

"It's all right now. I've got you."

"I said I would," she muttered.

"Then you will," he said, shifting her into his arms.

"What?" Her eyes opened, dark and bleary. "Oh. Hell. I fell out."

"You're entitled. You started before dawn, and if we're at it much longer we'll go round the clock with it."

"I was talking to Ms. Farnsworth."

He smiled a little as the cat padded quickly ahead to reach the bedroom first. "Were you now? As it happens, I was myself,

in a way. What did she have to say?"

"She's just really pissed off."

"And who could blame her? She put his name in it, coded through the routing."

"What?" Her eyes went instantly alert even as he dumped her on the bed. "What?"

"Jerald Reinhold. His name, and a short statement we've untangled so far. Jerald Reinhold did this."

"But where's the money? What name's he using? Where —"

"If we knew, I believe I'd have led with it."

He pulled her boots off for her, heard her involuntary groan of relief.

"We've got a start on the routine, which is miraculous, and more so this much of her encoded message. She didn't make it easy — over and above the whole lot being wiped, and well wiped at that. I'm supposing she knew he wasn't a complete idiot when it comes to Comp Science, and had to be careful about it.

"It's good progress, Eve," he assured her. "Better than any of us who know the business expected at this point."

"Okay, all right. She coded in his name, pointed a finger at him. It adds weight. Though we won't need any, weight never hurts."

She switched gears. "What about tenants?"

"Moving through them. A lot of buildings, Lieutenant, and not all the data is current because of the —"

"Goddamn, stinking, stupid holiday."

Her biting tone nearly made him smile. "True enough. But I was able to order a rush on my own places, and all the new tenants and/or applications from new tenants will be current tomorrow, holiday or no."

"Thanks."

"I've thrown a spanner into some holidays, but it shouldn't take long, and then they can get back to their stuffing."

"A lot of uniforms are cursing my name. The ones on the twenty-four/seven tip line for sure. But it only takes one person to see him, to call it in."

"And we'll see to all of it tomorrow."

They'd both undressed as they spoke, and now crawled into bed.

"I don't want to go to the morgue tomorrow, Roarke."

"You're doing everything you can to prevent that."

"Yeah." She curled against him in the dark, and hoped it would be enough.

When her 'link woke her just after five A.M.,

she groped for it. "Block video," she ordered even as Roarke ordered lights on to twenty percent. "Dallas."

"Lieutenant, man, I'm really sorry for the early tag."

"Mal." Instantly awake, she shoved up to sit. "What is it?"

"It's just — we can't find Joe. It's probably nothing, but I'm a little freaked, and Ma said you should know."

"Okay." She flipped through the notes in her head. "He had a date last night, right?"

"Yeah, that's the thing. He was a no-show, and Priss tracked me down at like midnight, bitching me out because she figured Joe'd ditched her to hang with me or Dave. But I hadn't seen him or talked to him. Dave either. And she said how he'd texted her he might be a little late; he was working on some deal. But he never showed, and didn't answer her texts and tags. Me and Dave, we even went over there, to Joe's place. He doesn't answer the door."

"Okay, Mal." She didn't need a gut-check to assess a bad feeling. It shoved straight through her. "Give me the name and contact of the woman he was supposed to go out with."

"Sure, sure." He reeled it off. "The thing is, well, it wouldn't be a stretch to say he maybe hooked up with somebody else, maybe got lucky, and he's at her place, wherever. And maybe he's not answering his texts and tags because he doesn't want any shit, you know. But, it's scary."

"It's good you let me know. Any idea, if he hooked up otherwise, with who?"

"Not so much. I tried some girls I know he's hooked with, but hit zero there. But he's not above taking a spin with strange if he had the chance. So . . ."

"Got it. Let me see what I can do. I'll get back to you."

She clicked off, shoved at her hair, in pure frustration. "Asshole Joe."

"I got that." Knowing her, and understanding, Roarke handed her coffee he'd programmed while she'd talked to Mal.

"Maybe he is with some strange, but that's not what it feels like. Going to be late, working on a deal. Money and status and sex — those are his pulls. And Reinhold knows his pulls. Lure him with a business opportunity maybe. I need to go check out Joe's place."

"I know it. I'll go with you."

"I can use you better right here. If I find him, or if I don't — either way, whatever you pull out of those computers is going to help the most."

He'd have argued if he hadn't agreed with

her. "I'll concede to that if you agree not to go alone."

And she'd have argued if she hadn't seen the solid sense in the deal. No time for bullshit, she reminded herself.

"I'll take a couple uniforms along, and I'm going to wake up our APA, have Reo get me a warrant. I need to be able to go in. If he's not there, I'll be back inside an hour. If he's there and humping some strange, less. If he's there and dead, I'll be longer."

"And if Reinhold's with him?"

"I'll be grateful."

It took under an hour because traffic was nonexistent and she went in hot. And, what the hell, came back the same way.

She managed to avoid the relatives when she dashed into the house and up, but she heard them — hushed adult voices, babies crying, kids chattering.

And found Roarke already at work in his comp lab.

"He's not there," she announced. "And there's no sign of duress or violence. I had a quick conversation with the woman he stood up. She's worried now instead of pissed. And I woke McNab, had him run a trace on Asshole Joe's 'link. Can't trace it, because it's turned off. If and when it's turned back on, we'll see. And why are your relatives up and swarming around at barely six in the morning?"

"Middle of the morning in Ireland," he reminded her. "And that doesn't address the fact many of them are farmers who'd be up at six in any case. I'm getting somewhere here, and might have better luck if you stopped talking."

She narrowed her eyes at him, but stopped talking long enough to program more coffee.

"Reinhold's got him."

Roarke turned away from his work. Impatience simmered inside him — he *knew* he was close to something. But he could see, clearly, the stress on her face.

"Men will grab strange, darling, with the smallest provocation."

"Yeah, pigs. But, he had reservations at a hot spot, which he never canceled or used. I woke up the manager at the restaurant for that one. She was not pleased. He left work bragging about a potential new client — a rich one — I woke up his boss for that — he was okay with it. And I've got McNab going in to check Asshole's work comp and 'link, in case there's something on there about the new client. But —"

"You think Reinhold — the new client —

tagged Asshole Joe on his personal 'link, so no record there. And if Asshole Joe did any checking, he also did that on his personal PPC."

"That's just what I think, but McNab — who damn well better be okay with it — will make sure.

"He's not dead yet."

It wasn't a question, Roarke noted, not even a supposition. She said it with absolute certainty.

"Because he'd want to prolong the power and excitement."

"And the pain. He's added time with each kill." Thinking it through, sticking with logic, with pattern, she paced off the tension. "From the time line, Asshole Joe probably got to the location after eighteen hundred. About then anyway. Reinhold would want time. A day, maybe two. And he'd know, unless he's cut himself off, and I don't buy that, that today's a big holiday. That Joe would be expected somewhere. Given the notifications, the media, the investigation, when he doesn't show up today, we'd start looking."

She paced around, gulping coffee. "He'd enjoy that. Having Joe tucked away, hurting him and watching reports on a search. We've got some time. Some hours, maybe, maybe a day. Then that's it. He won't have enough control to stretch it longer."

She looked at Roarke then. "I'm going to screw up your big family holiday."

"Ours," he corrected. "And there's not a single person who'll be here today who doesn't value a life more than your presence at a turkey carving. Not a single person who doesn't understand what's at stake."

"Okay. Okay." The sheer casualness of the support lowered her guilt threshold. "I'm going to go into my office. I have to keep the doors shut. I don't want some kid wandering through and getting traumatized for life by my murder board. I've got Peabody coming in within an hour, and McNab will be in as soon as he clears Asshole Joe's office equipment. I told him to come straight to you."

"I'll be happy to have him."

"Roarke, as soon as you have anything I can use on new tenants, anything on that damn code —"

"You'll be the first to know it. I'm close," he told her again. "If I'm reading this right it won't take more than an hour or two. If that. Give me some space now, and some precious quiet."

"Yeah." She took the rest of her coffee with her.

She dug in for a while, trying to retrace Joe's steps — hitting holiday disinterest from cab companies until fear of her wrath won out.

If he'd taken a cab, he hadn't caught one in front of his workplace, or within a block either way.

She put the Transit Authorities on it, requesting they search their recordings on the chance he'd taken a subway. Spotting him could narrow the area.

Then she tagged Mira. Rather than her usual stylish do, Mira wore her hair in a short little ponytail. The style, or lack of it, made her look younger to Eve's eye.

"I'm sorry. I know it's early."

"It's fine. I've been up nearly an hour. I have a lot of cooking to do."

"You're cooking?"

"Dennis and I are cooking, and my daughters threatened — that is, promised," she amended with a smile, "to be here by eight to pitch in. What can I do for you?"

"He's got another. Joe Klein. I'm trying to pare down the possible locations. I think he's got his own place by now, in or very near his old neighborhood. He'd go for swank. We're working on getting lists of new tenants, but there are a lot of possibilities."

"An apartment or condo," Mira said immediately. "Not a detached or semi-attached home."

"Why?"

"He's sociable, and wants to show off. He's not a loner. Under it all, he wants a hive. He just wants to be important in that hive."

"Okay."

"Look first at newer buildings — shinier, if you understand me. His parents valued tradition, the old, the histories. He'll want the opposite. And the most exclusive first."

"I leaned that way for the same reasons, but factoring in the cost —"

"He won't concern himself," Mira interrupted, and firmly. "He has more money than he'd ever imagined, and he's certain he'll continue to bring in more. A place near clubs, arcades, bars, good shops, or that provides them. Status. He's always wanted it, but lacked the ambition or the ethics to attain it. He believes he's found it now."

"Okay, yeah, I see that. It helps. Appreciate it."

"I hope you find him, Eve. I'm going to say Happy Thanksgiving, because I believe you will."

"Thanks. Same to you."

She jumped on the map, shadowed out the detached and semis, any building more than a decade old unless it had been completely rehabbed in modern style.

"That's better," she murmured, studying the results.

She started to cross-reference with the tenant lists Roarke trickled to her.

Cursed when her desk 'link signaled. "Dallas," she snapped just as Peabody hustled in.

"Lieutenant Dallas, this is Officer Stanski outta Fraud and Financial Crimes?"

"What do you want, Stanski?" she demanded, and seeing Peabody's puppy dog plea, jabbed a thumb toward the kitchen and the AutoChef.

"We got an auto-alert came in about midnight, and it just got passed through. Not a lot of people working due to the holidays and all."

"Move it along, Stanski, for God's sake."

"Well, sure. What I'm saying is we just got the notification, and it don't make much sense altogether. It's on an Anton Trevor, with this code we don't get — not one of the standards — and it says to notify you asap. So I'm notifying you asap."

"I'm Homicide, Stanski, not Fraud."

"I got that, LT, sure." Stanski's round face transmitted utter earnestness just as her voice transmitted Queens.

"But it says you, Lieutenant Eve Dallas, Homicide, clear on it. You want us to go ahead and shut down this Anton Trevor's card, go through the process, or what?"

"I don't . . . Hold on." Something tingled at the base of her neck as she did a quick run.

"Computer, search and display ID for Anton Trevor, New York, New York. Age between twenty-three and twenty-eight." That should cover it.

Acknowledged. Working . . . Results displayed on screen one.

"Holy shit. Holy fucking shit."

"LT?" Stanski said, doubtfully.

"Don't shut it down. Where was the card used?"

"Got that right here for you. Place called Bar on M, and another, few minutes later — Handy Mart. Both in the New York West, condo center. That's at —"

"I've got the address." It was one of her buildings. It was one of *Roarke's* buildings. "You hold, Stanski. Don't notify, don't shut down. Don't do a damn thing until you hear back from me."

"No problem here."

"Send me everything you've got, and

hold," she said, and clicking off jumped up just as Roarke pushed open her office doors.

"I've got him," they said together. Both frowned. "What?"

Then Roarke held up a hand. "Go."

"She — Farnsworth — must've tagged a fraud alert onto his new ID. It flagged for me when he used it. She saw the media reports, knew I was primary. He's going by Anton —"

"Trevor," Roarke finished. "I pieced that name from the codes she embedded in the transfers. He's the newest tenant in —"

"New York West," she finished in turn.

"And there we are."

"We've got him!" Eve announced as Peabody came out with coffee and a bagel.

Peabody said, "What?"

"Reinhold's using the aka Anton Trevor. Notify McNab. I want to move fast, but we're going to do this smooth. Get him, Baxter, Trueheart —"

"Baxter left for his sister's in Toledo last night," Peabody interrupted.

"Shit. Make it Carmichael and Sanchez." She paused a beat in case one of them was having breakfast in goddamn Toledo. "We'll do a 'link briefing," she continued. "I want six uniforms, seasoned, Peabody. Roarke, I need you to —"

"Notify building security," he said. "I know this drill very well. I'll take care of what you need. And to start." He ordered the computer to display new data.

"That's his level, and the blueprint of his apartment. I have all the building specs, so you'll have the points of egress."

"Makes it easy." And rolling her shoulders moved to operation strategy. "Okay, private elevator — we'll shut that down. Two other exits. We'll close them off. He'll be armed, and God knows with what, so we go in protective gear. I want eyes and ears in there asap. And I don't want him looking over that terrace and seeing a bunch of cops moving in on the street. Let me see the big picture," she asked Roarke, "so I can put this op together."

As he did, she pulled out her 'link to update her commander.

McNab made it there just as she began the 'link briefing.

Straightforward was how Eve saw it. By the book. Tight and right.

She paced as she ran it through, wanting to move, to move, knowing she had to cover every contingency. She had her weapon strapped over the soft sweater — the same vivid blue as Roarke's eyes — Sinead had knitted for her. She wore rough trousers and old boots, all the first to come to hand before dawn. And the flat, dangerous glint of cop-on-the-hunt in her eyes.

"That's how it's going to work," she finished. "McNab, eyes and ears, Roarke security, and between you you'll shut down all electronics and power to that unit on my go. Team A — me, Peabody, Officers Carmichael and Prince, main-level door. Team B — Detectives Carmichael and Sanchez, Officers Rhodes and Murray, second-level door — enter on my go. Officers Kenson and Ferris will hold position here, block and disperse any and all civilians from entering the hot zone. Are we clear?"

"Yes, sir."

"No lights, no sirens, and no black-and-whites within a block of the target building. Protective gear is worn. This is not optional. Again, if the subject is seen exiting the building before this op is in place, take him down. If he's seen inside the building, track but do not engage. We're moving," she added. "Go in soft, wait for my orders. All weapons, medium stun."

She turned, snagged the coat Roarke had brought in, then her stride forward hitched when she noticed Sinead standing in the doorway someone had neglected to secure.

She had a baby on her hip, a hand on a gleefully fascinated Sean's shoulder.

"Ah, we have to go out. Sorry. We're in a hurry."

She left it at that, double-timed it out and down the stairs. Roarke paused, just for a moment. "We'll be back before too long, and I'll let you know."

Then he was gone, too, rushing out with the rest.

"Nan!" Sean sent Sinead a look of awe and joy. "They're after the bad guy."

"They are, yes. Well then, let's go down, have a little tea."

Reinhold slept the sleep of the satisfied, and woke to Joe's harsh, sobbing screams.

"Jesus." Reinhold rolled, stretched, yawned. "What a pussy."

He hit the bedroom AC for hot chocolate — extra whipped cream — and stood at his window wall, looking out at New York, at the city he knew feared him, while he drank.

When Joe didn't show up at his mother's by about noon, Reinhold calculated, to hang out with his stepfather, his brother, and his brother's ugly wife and uglier kids, his fat cousin, Stu, who'd have his piss-faced grandmother in tow, they and the city would fear him more.

All around the Thanksgiving tables he'd be the talk. Jerry Reinhold, a killer who did what he wanted, who he wanted, when he wanted.

Taking his time, he dressed — crap clothes again because holiday or not he was *working* — then went into the spare room to activate the droid.

"Good morning, sir. Someone appears to be in distress."

"Don't worry about him. Don't talk to him or listen to him. Got it, Asshole?"

"Yes, sir."

"Go down and fix me, what is it, yeah, eggs Benedict, a couple slices of toast with strawberry jelly, and whatever ought to go with it. Then come up here and clean up my bedroom, take care of my clothes. I'll let you know when to come down again."

"Yes, sir."

Before he went down himself, Reinhold checked himself out in the mirror. He thought he might dress up later, catch some football — which reminded him to tell the droid to get him some prime Giants tickets. Maybe he'd have some fancy drink out on the terrace, too.

He'd planned on keeping Joe around another night, having some fun there. But if the fucker was going to keep screaming . . .

He strolled down.

Joe looked worse for wear, that's for sure. His face — and he'd always been a conceited fuck — all bloody and bruised. A lot busted in there. The shallow cuts had stopped bleeding, something he'd fix after breakfast. And the burns looked like circles and streaks of charcoal.

Reinhold picked up the sap, gave Joe an absent smack. "Shut the fuck up, or I'll slit your throat and be done with it."

"Please, God, please." The words came garbled through broken teeth. "I think I'm dying. I'm hurt bad. Don't hurt me anymore, please, man, please. I'll do whatever you want. I'll give you anything you want."

"Oh yeah? That's something maybe. You've got some money, Joe. The Vegas money, and more. Maybe if you give me your passcodes so I can take it, I'll let you go."

"Anything. You can have it. I — I've got my uncle Stan's passcodes, too."

"Is that so?" With a smile, Reinhold gestured to a nearby chair. "Set me up there," he ordered the droid.

"I found them when I was helping him out with some stuff. He's got some real scratch, Jerry. I'll get it for you. Just let me go. Promise to let me go, and I'll get you all of it."

"I'll think about it."

"Please. I need water. Can I have some water, please?"

Easing into his seat, Reinhold took his knife and fork from the tray the droid gave him.

"Can't you see I'm having breakfast? Shut up before you piss me off. You," he said to the droid. "Turn on the screen. It's got to be about time for the parade." He smiled, cut into his eggs. "I'd hate for us to miss the parade, Joe. Just lie back and enjoy."

22

Eve coordinated with her team en route. She couldn't afford the time or the exposure for a final briefing on site. Too many people with too many ways to get the word out that cops were gathering at New York West. A leak to the media, on the Internet, might alert Reinhold.

She believed, strongly, Asshole Joe was still alive. She believed they had time. But the very fact Joe was an asshole might tip Reinhold over the edge.

She'd be damned if they'd be minutes too late this time.

When she said as much to Roarke, he touched a hand to hers. "We'll have him locked down minutes after we arrive. And we'll have your eyes and ears up minutes after that."

Minutes, she thought. They had to be on her side this round.

"Luck's turned," she stated. "Luck's

turned our way. You've got to see it that way. We hit on him, both of us, almost at the same time. It all fell together."

"It fell together because you haven't let up on it for three days and nights."

"That, and Ms. Farnsworth. She pulled off a hell of a thing."

"I admit, I wish I could have met her."

"You wish you could've hired her," Eve added, and he laughed.

"You know me very well."

"Sanchez's on site, Dallas," Peabody told her from the back. "Detective Carmichael's less than a minute out. Uniforms are checking in."

"Talking to your security head now, Roarke," McNab announced. "They've cleared the parking space you directed. Have eyes trained on the hallways on Reinhold's two floors."

"Good enough, and here we are."

"It's really pretty." Peabody craned her head to take in the tower. "Shiny, and all that glass just sparkles."

"Head in the game, Peabody," Eve ordered, and jumped out the minute Roarke pulled to the curb. "Record on. All records on. All teams move into position. I want all elevators but his blocked from his floor the minute Team B reaches his second level."

"Sir." A tall curvy brunette clipped over to Roarke. "We're in place, awaiting any further instructions."

"Lieutenant, this is head of building security, Veronica Benston."

"Lieutenant." Benston nodded at Eve. "There's been no activity outside of the target area. Two units on the subject's main level, and one on his secondary level are not occupied today as the tenants are out of town. In-residence tenants, as you instructed, have not been notified, as yet, of any police activity."

"Give me the rundown as we go. We're moving."

"We've kept this elevator clear for you." Benston led the way, explained any and all occupants and activities on the target level.

"You're backup, Benston, and thanks for the assist and the speed of it." Eve stepped out on Reinhold's level. She sent Team B a thumbs-up, moved on as they rode to the next level.

"Shut down his private elevator, block all access and egress to this level. Roarke, I want him blind. I want his alarms and backups shut down."

"Benston, would you mind?"

"It's done, sir." She tapped her earbud. "Blind him," she ordered. "Kill alarms, both levels of target unit."

"At hallway door," Eve said into her own comm, accessing.

Since Benston offered it, she used Security's master, then drawing her weapon, went through the door.

"Get me eyes and ears, McNab."

"All over that deal." He squatted, went to work on a portable. "Good filters," he said absently. "Excellent shielding. This would take longer without the specs." He shot Roarke a grin. "Saves me work. You got two human heat sources, LT, and one robotic charge, all main level. Nothing human or e on second level."

Eve crouched, studied the screen. "Right in the main living area." Seconds later, she heard sobbing, pleading.

"Got your ears," McNab murmured.

Please, God, please, I think I'm dying.

"Team B, in position," Sanchez said in Eve's ear.

"Hold there. Subject and victim are both on main living area. Single droid also on main level."

I've got my uncle Stan's passcodes, too.

Eve held up a fist, signaling, "Wait," watched as the heat source she identified as Reinhold moved a little farther away from Joe.

"He's sitting down — got the droid by him. Put some space between him and the vic. Open it," she asked Roarke. "Nice and quiet. Move in, Team B. Slow, quiet."

Just lie back and enjoy.

Eve held up three fingers. "On three," she murmured.

She went through the door, fast and low, with Peabody fast and high beside her.

Reinhold squealed. There was no other word to describe it, Eve thought in disgust. He squealed like a little girl, threw his tray of food in the air, and ran for the stairs.

"Stop! Freeze! Hands in the air!"

Instead, as Team B charged down, he veered away, grabbed a vase, threw it. It missed by a mile, shattered on the floor.

Eve considered stunning him as he ran, basically in circles, throwing whatever came to hand while Joe screamed. God, she wanted to stun him. And because she did, she tackled him instead.

He went down in a skid, kicking, flailing, adding screams to Joe's, until Eve pressed her weapon to his cheek.

"Oh, give me a reason, you fuck."

"Get off me, get away from me. Kill her!" he ordered the droid, who just stood looking as distressed as a droid was capable of looking.

Eve dragged Reinhold's arms behind his back, cuffed him. "Jerald Reinhold, you're under arrest for murder, multiple counts, for kidnapping, for identity fraud, breaking and entering and all sorts of additional charges. You have the right to remain silent," she began, and with Peabody's help managed to get him to his feet.

He kept letting his legs buckle, so by the time she'd finished reading him the Revised Miranda, she'd had enough. "Officer Carmichael. Take this asshole into custody. Put him in top-level holding at Central until I say different."

"You've got it, Lieutenant."

"And somebody call the medics and a bus for that poor bastard."

"Already done." Detective Carmichael tapped her comm. "On their way."

Harnessing her weapon, Eve walked over to Joe, shook her head. "You're a real goddamn mess, Joe, but you'll live."

"He hurt me. He hurt me."

"Yeah, he did." Eve watched as Roarke and another uniform worked on cutting through rope and tape. "I'm sorry about that. Maybe the next time you start to smirk at a cop, you'll remember."

"Water." He sobbed, twisted some pity out

of her. "Please. He wouldn't even give me water."

"Here you go." Peabody held a cup to his lips. "Slow now. We've got you now, Joe. We've got you now."

"I'm sorry. I'm sorry. I didn't listen."

"It's okay. It'll be okay."

Maybe it would, Eve thought, but he'd paid a hell of a price for being an asshole.

She didn't rush it; let Reinhold stew and sweat awhile. With her team, she went through every inch of the apartment, passed the electronics, including the droid, to Mc-Nab — and Feeney, who'd showed up as the MTs wheeled Joe out, a little steamed they hadn't waited for him.

She found it interesting, and a little sad, to discover Reinhold had stocked the full, traditional Thanksgiving feast. And wondered if he'd planned on tucking into it before or after he killed one of his oldest friends.

She held up the minisaw as Roarke approached. "A new tool for him. I'd say he'd have tested it out on fingers, maybe hands, feet. Then he'd have used it to cut Joe into more easily disposable pieces — using the industrial waste bags we found to get the pieces out."

"A lovely thought. And likely accurate. I took the droid," he added. "Its memory loop is fully intact, going back to when Reinhold reprogrammed it — prior to murdering Farnsworth. It will be very solid evidence for the prosecution."

"We've got nothing but solid evidence — and a live witness."

"So you'll be visiting the hospital at some point, and not the morgue."

"Happy Thanksgiving."

"For most of us. I also spoke with the realtor who arranged the rental. Easy enough now to track it."

Idly, Roarke glanced around the main level, and even under the circumstances found satisfaction in the flow of the layout, the use of materials.

"Reinhold snapped the place up just yesterday, and made arrangements to purchase the furniture already in place."

"Trendy and expensive. It suited him, and it saved him time and trouble."

"Mmm. So you were right on his style, but he lucked — again — into finding a place where he didn't have to shop for his furnishings."

Eve's lips turned up in a sharp, grim smile. "Luck changes, and I'm about to finish his run for good. I'm sending the electronics with McNab — and Feeney since his ass is burned I didn't call him in away from his wife, family, and day off. Anyway. They'll just log and secure, then they're sprung. Sanchez and Carmichael are going to work with Crime Scene to seal and secure, then they're sprung, too. Peabody's stuck with me. I have to deal with Reinhold today. Now. If it goes smooth enough, I'll be home for dinner."

"We," he corrected. "I'm with you."

"Your family —"

"You're my family first. I'll let them know, and if we're not going to be back at a reasonable time, they'll start without us."

"Fine." If it took too long, she thought, she'd push him out. But she needed to get started. "Peabody! Let's go have a nice little chat with Jerry."

"Can't wait."

She worked on strategy as Roarke drove to Central. She had Reinhold's number now. With Mira's profile, her own observations, interviews with friends, coworkers, supervisors — she knew what he was, and believed she knew how he thought.

"You're good cop, Peabody."

"Aw, damn it."

"He's going to respond to bad cop — me — make excuses, try to hold a line, be a big shot as long as he can hold on to his guts there. And he's going to respond to good cop, see someone who's willing to give him leeway on the excuses. He's not smart enough to understand the dynamics, the rhythm, or how that push-pull undermines."

Roarke flicked a glance at Peabody's sulky face in the rearview. "It's a classic for a reason," he reminded her. "And you always know when to slip in with the softer touch. It's masterful."

As Peabody perked up, Eve slid a glance toward Roarke. Talk about masterful.

In the garage, she reached for the box of props she'd brought from the crime scene. Roarke nudged her aside, hefted it himself.

"I'm going to know pretty quick how this is going to go," she told him. "If I think it's going to drag out, go into hours, I'm going to signal you, or step out and tell you. Let's make a deal."

"I do love a deal."

"If it's going to bog down, you go home, do the turkey thing. Then you can come back. I'll even get word to you when I think I'm close to wrapping it up. Your aunt shouldn't have to feel she's in charge when she's supposed to be a guest," Eve added.

"That was a good one." He shifted the box as they rode the elevator up. "All right then, that's a deal."

Satisfied with that, Eve got off the elevator. "Peabody takes the box. He'll look at me as in charge. He's going to be afraid of me, and I'll make sure of it. He's a coward, and fear's going to break him. He'll try to push me at first, then he'll appeal to you," she told Peabody. "You're close to his age, you're not the primary authority figure, and you'll be sympathetic, to a point. Call him by his first name. That's connection from you, lack of respect from me."

"I get it. He's in Interview A."

"Then I'll be in Observation," Roarke said. "Good luck, both of you."

"That's just what we've got now." Eve led the way.

As she'd instructed on the way in, he'd been put in Interview, but not in restraints — restraints indicated he was something to fear. The uniforms who'd pulled him out of holding and brought him up hadn't spoken a word. Asked no questions, answered none.

So now he sat alone in the box, lights on full — sweating, she noted when she stepped in. Beads of sweat on his upper lip, his brow.

"Dallas, Lieutenant Eve, and Peabody, Detective Delia, entering Interview with Reinhold, Jerald." She read off a series of case files as she took a seat. "Reinhold, Jerald, you have been informed of your rights, on record. Do you understand your rights and obligations in these matters?"

"I don't want to talk to you."

"That's one of your rights. Do you understand that right, and the rights and obligations as given to you in the Revised Miranda?"

He turned his head away, stared at the side wall like a petulant child.

"Okay, fine. Peabody, arrange for him to be taken back to a cage."

"I'm not going back down there!"

Eve just stood, started for the door.

"All right, all right! Jesus, yes, I understand the stupid rights and shit."

"Good." She came back, sat again. "We can make this quick and easy, Jerry. I mean, for God's sake, we walked in on you with Joe. You'd done a number on him."

"You came onto my private property. That's a violation of my rights. You can't use anything you found when you violated my rights."

"Seriously?" She eased back and laughed. "That's your defense? If you're going to watch fictional crime shows, you should at least pay attention. Ever hear of probable cause, Jerry? Or duly exercised warrants? You abducted and were holding an individual against his will, causing him severe bodily harm. You assaulted said individual, you committed battery, battery with intent, assault with a deadly, and so forth on this individual, and you planned to murder this individual, then saw him to pieces and dispose of him."

"You can't prove any of that!"

"I can prove all of it. Let's start with the first part. You abducted Joseph Klein."

"Did not!" His voice cracked a little as he jabbed a finger at her, twice. "He came to see me. He walked right into my place on his own. And I was just fooling around, just messing with him."

"That's what you call it? Bashing him in the head with a baseball bat, breaking his teeth, his cheekbones, his jaw, burning him with a torch, cutting him. That's just mess-ing with him?"

"He screwed with me; I screwed with him. That's self-defense. He . . ." His eyes actu-ally shifted, left and right. "He came to my place and he *threatened* me. I protected myself."

"He gave you a bad time, so beating the shit out of him while you've bound him to a chair is self-defense? You're an idiot, Jerry."

"I'm not an idiot!" Harsh red color stained his face, ran down to his neck as if his fury needed to pump through his pores. "I'm smarter than you, smarter than most people. I proved it."

"How?"

"I did what I had to do. I got what I needed to get."

"Starting with stabbing your own mother over fifty times."

"I don't know what you're talking about." He looked away again. "I wasn't even there. I came in, and I found them. It was awful."

He covered his face with his hands.

"You're saying you came home and found your parents dead, Jerry?" Peabody did her masterful slide, a touch of sympathetic horror in her voice. "God."

"It was . . ." He dropped his hands, and for the first time looked at Peabody. "I can't even tell you. I'd warned them not to just open the door for anybody, but they never listened. And I came in, and they were . . . all the blood."

"Give me a break," Eve muttered, but Peabody shook her head.

"Come on, Lieutenant. We wondered about that. What did you do, Jerry?"

"I don't know exactly. It's all kind of crazy in my head. I just freaked. I think maybe I blacked out or had a kind of, I don't know, seizure or something."

"So you don't really remember what you did after. When did you find them, exactly?"

"Ah, I guess late Friday night. I came in and —"

"Where had you been?"

"Just around. Anyway, nothing made any sense, you know?"

"Did you come out of your seizure long enough to steal the watch you sold? To transfer your parents' life savings to accounts you opened?"

Eve's question snapped him back. "It was mine since they were dead. I didn't know what else to do. I was scared — and, and not thinking straight. *You* try coming home and finding your parents dead, see how you act."

"It had to be awful, but . . . You should've called the police, Jerry," Peabody said, gently.

"I know. I know that now, but then, I just wasn't thinking straight."

"Straight enough to take what cash and valuables they had in the apartment. Straight enough to withdraw the funds you'd transferred Monday morning," Eve pointed out. "To book a high-flyer hotel suite and eat hearty Saturday and Sunday nights."

"That's not a crime." But he swiped at

the sweat on his lip. "I needed some money to get by, didn't I? I needed time to think, then I saw how you cops were after *me,* and I needed time to figure it out, so —"

"So you went to Lori Nuccio's apartment, used the key you hadn't given back to her after she dumped your sorry ass, and you tortured and killed her."

"I did not! And she didn't dump *me,* I dumped her. It wasn't working for me, so I dumped her — and she begged me to stay with her, give her another chance. Then, I figured it out when I heard about how she was dead. The same person who killed my parents killed Lori."

"Now, that I agree with."

"But Ms. Farnsworth," Peabody began, gave Reinhold a worried look.

"Her, too!" Excitement lived on his face as he grabbed his theme, ran with it. "The same person did it, trying to screw with me. See, it was all about screwing with me, so you cops would come after me — maybe *kill* me before I could prove my innocence. Joe."

Eve all but saw the metaphoric lightbulb flash on over his head.

"I knew it had to be Joe who did it. He's crazy, anybody'll tell you, and he was really jealous of me. That's why I got him to come to my new place, why I was messing with him. I needed to get him to confess so I could turn him over to you."

"Wow." Peabody hoped she looked shocked and impressed instead of showing the absolute disgust she felt. "So Joe killed your parents, and Lori, and Ms. Farnsworth because he was mad at you, jealous of you?"

"Yeah. He hit on Lori a few times — she told me — and she blew him off. So he was pissed about that, too. And he ragged and ragged on me about Vegas, kept buying me drinks so I got a little, you know, impaired, then pushed me into betting all that money. He made me lose all that money. And, oh! He knew I didn't really hold anything against Ms. Farnsworth — she taught me a lot. But he *ragged* on me, so I made like she was a bitch. Just saving face like. Then he goes and kills her so he can pin it on me."

"This is very serious, Jerry."

"I know, right?" Trying for sincerity, he bobbed his head up and down. "He's crazy, I guess. But he was ready to admit it. He told me some of it, but I didn't have the recorder on yet. He said how my ma let him in, was going to fix him a sandwich — she did things like that — and he picked up the knife and stabbed her and stabbed her."

He covered his face with his hands again.

"My ma."

"Golly. Where was your father? Did Joe say?"

"He said how he got the bat from my room, and he hid and waited till my dad got home. Then he bashed him, and bashed him. And he just left them there."

"It's funny," Eve said, "how he walked in and out of the building without ever once showing up on security."

Oops, she thought as Reinhold's eyes shifted again. "Ah, sometimes those things don't work right. The super's supposed to get it fixed, but he doesn't. He's lazy."

"So the security on the door magically shows you going in Thursday night — late, and not leaving again until Saturday night — suitcases in tow. And also magically never showed Joe entering or exiting the building."

"It can happen."

"Well, at least we can check with the super," Peabody said doubtfully.

"He'll just lie."

"You know all about liars," Eve said. "Just let me ask you one question. Just one that's bugging me some. How'd you get the fake ID and the money to rent that swanky apartment?"

"I . . . won some money in Vegas I didn't

tell the guys about. And I paid this guy I met at a bar for the ID."

"What guy, what bar, how much?"

Eve rapped the questions out.

"Some guy, I don't know. Just a bar. Um, maybe a thousand dollars. About, um, five hundred dollars, I guess."

"Bullshit, bullshit, bullshit." Eve pushed forward, into his space, so he jerked back.

"You lost your ass in Vegas. You didn't just happen on an expert on fake IDs at some bar, and you sure as hell didn't get one, with the accompanying database, for five hundred. You lying piece of shit. We've got the comps you stole from Ms. Farnsworth after you tortured her, after you killed her. The ones you had her droid take to a swap store. The data's right on them."

"They were wiped. Wiped clean!" Wound up, he leaned toward her, shoved his face toward hers. "You're the liar."

"How do you know they were wiped, Jerry?"

"I . . ." Jerking back, he ran his tongue around his lips. "Just figured. Joe's not stupid. He'd've wiped them first."

"You should've paid more attention to Ms. Farnsworth in Computer Science, Jerry. With the right techs, the right equipment — and believe me the NYPSD has both —

you can retrieve damn near anything. Your ID was made on her comps."

"Okay, okay. I didn't want to get her in trouble."

"She's dead, Jerry."

"Her . . . reputation. She made the ID and stuff for me. I went to her, explained things, and she helped me out. That's why Joe killed her. After I left."

"But she was dead when you left, Jerry, when you left carting your new duffel and *her* suitcase, and caught a cab to the clinic because she'd managed to break your foot."

"That wasn't me. That was Joe. It was all Joe." He began to cry, tears of terror and self-pity. "I didn't do anything. Get off my back. I didn't do anything."

"We've got witnesses. We tracked you, you stupid fuck. We know where you bought the hair color, the eye color, the bronzer." She shoved to her feet again. "And these." She began dropping sealed evidence on the table. "The tape, the rope, the knife. This saw you intended to use to cut Joe to pieces, these bags for disposal of body parts."

"I did not! I did not! The droid bought that stuff."

"Some of it, on your orders. Ms. Farnsworth's droid. Then there's this."

Eve lifted out the evidence bag holding

537

the hank of Lori Nuccio's hair. "How'd you get Lori's hair, Jerry?"

"She gave it to me. Like a love token thing."

"Really? How did she manage to do that when the person who hacked it off her before killing her took it? Had her hair colored just that afternoon, Jerry. This color."

"That's . . . I got mixed up. You're mixing me up. Joe had that with him. He brought it with him. He showed it to me to prove he killed Lori."

"You killed Lori, and got off doing it. You left the boxers you had on in her bathroom, you fuckhead."

"Joe planted those. He told me."

Eve sat back. "Not going to fly, Jerry. Not even going to get off the ground. On top of everything else, Ms. Farnsworth left a deathbed statement, too, right on her computer. Coded it in right under your idiot nose while you had her terrorized. Your name, Jerry, and everything we need to wrap you up."

"That's a lie! She did not."

"She really did, Jerry." Peabody spoke quietly, pushing what sympathy she could into her tone. "It's all right there."

"She did that to get back at me, that's all.

She always had it in for me."

"Then why did she make you the ID? Why did she help you out?"

"I . . . you're confusing me. You're mixing me up on purpose. I want a lawyer. I want a lawyer, and I'm not talking to you."

"That's your right." Eve began to box up the evidence again. "Peabody, have him taken back to holding."

"I am *not* going back there." Shouting, he gripped the edge of the table as if to secure himself in place. "I want a lawyer now. I've got plenty of money. I can hire the best lawyer there is, and he'll make you sorry."

"You don't have any money, Jerry," Eve corrected.

"I have millions!"

She sighed. "Jerry, Jerry, you moron. The money was stolen in the commission of various crimes. None of it's yours."

"Everything my parents had is mine. That's the law."

"Not if you killed them."

"She's right about that, Jerry. You can't use any of that money." Peabody rose, too. "I'll notify the Public Defender's office. With the holiday, though, it could be Monday before they assign anyone."

"I'm not waiting until Monday."

"If you want a lawyer." Eve shrugged. "It

could take a while to get you a PD."

"I want one *now!*" His eyes went wild, spittle flew. "I want to use *my* money to hire a lawyer, you bitch."

"Tough shit, Jerry. We'll work on getting you a public defender, as is your right."

"Don't you walk out of here! You come back here, you stupid bitch. You come back here right now."

"You've exercised your right, requested a lawyer. This interview is done until you are represented. Get the door, will you, Peabody?"

"Fuck a bunch of lawyers. I don't want a lawyer. I want you to get back here. I want to go home."

Calm as a lake on the outside, Eve turned back to him. "You're waiving your right to representation at this time?"

"Fuck you, yes. I'm telling you, Joe killed all of them, and you're trying to pin it on me. You're just pissed because I was smarter than you."

"Oh yeah, I can promise if you were smarter than me, I'd be pissed." Eve set down the box, sat again. "Here's another little" — what had Roarke called it? — "spanner in the works. Joe's alibied for the time of your mother's death, the time of your father's death, your ex's death, and

Ms. Farnsworth's death. Do you think we don't check these things, Jerry?"

"He's lying. You're lying. I want another cop."

"That's not one of your rights. You killed them, Jerry, every one of them. You liked it. You found what you were missing in life, didn't you? And you got rich doing it, you got everything you ever wanted, everything you deserved. All those assholes screwing with you? You got them back for it. And you were good at it. You fucking excelled."

"You're damn right!"

"It came to you when you were sticking that knife in your mother, didn't it?"

Eve kept her eyes trained on his, kept her tone quiet and smooth. Praise and threaten, she thought. Juggle both the praise, the threats, and toss in the facts.

"She's bugging the shit out of you. Get a job, get out, get off your ass. Nagging bitch, you'd had enough. Who wouldn't? So you picked up the knife, right there in the kitchen where she was making you a sandwich, and you carved her up. And you knew, right then, you'd found your calling."

"She wouldn't get off my back. They were going to kick me out. Just kick me out. What was I supposed to do?"

Get a job, Eve thought. "So you killed

them. Your mother with the knife. And you waited until your father came home from work and you beat him to death with your old baseball bat."

"It was self-defense. I had to protect myself, didn't I? They made me crazy. It's their fault. I did what I had to do to protect myself."

"What you had to do," Eve said with a nod. "Then you took their money, their valuables. You stayed in the apartment with their bodies from Friday night until Saturday night."

"I couldn't stay there forever, could I?"

"Right. Of course. But you needed some time to do the whole transfer with the accounts, find all the money they had, open your own accounts, wire the money out and over using their passcodes."

"My money," he reminded her. "My parents, my inheritance. They owed me."

"It was pretty smart," Peabody said, and worked some admiration into her tone. "I mean, the way you transferred the money, then withdrew it so fast on Monday, spent some time in that nice hotel figuring out your next move."

"People underestimate me. That's their problem. I figured it out, and I did everything right. You had my name and face all over the screen, but you couldn't find me. I've got skills."

"And you used those skills on Lori Monday night."

"That bitch didn't respect me. Another nag, nag, nag. She humiliated me, so I humiliated her right back. She deserved it."

"Stripped her, cut her hair," Eve said. "Tore up her new stuff. You got off when you strangled her, didn't you, Jerry? They're powerful, those skills of yours. You found your power."

"Best I ever had, and I did it myself. She deserved what she got. It was self-defense," he repeated, jabbing a finger on the table. "All of it. I had to look out for myself. It's my right."

"How was Ms. Farnsworth self-defense?" Eve wondered.

"She ruined my life. Screwed with my grades so it looked like I flunked, and I had to lose a whole summer making it up. My own friends made fun of me. I made her give me my life back, that's all. Made her give me a new life. That's fair."

"You assaulted her, bound her with rope and tape, forced her to generate your new data and identification, credit cards, to transfer her funds, her property into accounts for you."

"She *owed* me. They all owed me. They all thought I was nothing. I made them nothing. It's fair," he repeated. "I've got a right to look out for myself."

Eve glanced at Peabody.

"Let me just make sure we get this all straight, Jerry," Peabody said. "You killed your mother, your father, Lori Nuccio, and Ms. Edie Farnsworth, you abducted, assaulted, tortured, and planned to kill Joe Klein because they owed you — having played parts in ruining your life. So taking their lives was fair. Taking their money and their property was fair."

"That's right. That's exactly right." Pleased with the summation, he gave Peabody a sharp nod. "They all screwed with me, so I screwed with them bigger. Did you see my apartment? That's who I am now. And I know damn well it's going to turn out you're wrong about the money. It's mine. It's in my name, my accounts. Possession's more than half of something. I heard that somewhere. The money's in my possession, so you'd better get me a damn good lawyer in here, now, or I'm going to sue your asses. It was self-defense, and I'm not going back in that cell. You can't make me."

He actually folded his arms over his chest, jutted out his chin. Like a kid making a dare.

544

"Oh, Jerry, Jerry, I can't begin to tell you how happy I am to disabuse you." Eve allowed herself a single happy sigh, and a big, wide smile. "How my heart actually sings with gratitude for this moment. You're going down for murder, you asshole. One count second degree, three first degree, one of assault with intent, plus all the related charges. You're not just going back in that cell, Jerry. You're going to live the rest of your small, stupid, miserable life in a cage."

"I will not! I'm not going to jail."

She let him spring up, let him run for the door — and just shot her foot out to trip him. And yeah, there was a little heart singing when he did a sliding face plant.

"No, you're not going to jail," she agreed, stirring herself to slap restraints on him as he cried big, self-pitying tears and sobbed for his money. "It's called prison. And I'm betting it's going to be a nasty, bust-your-ass prison, off-planet, where they eat weaseling little cowards like you for lunch."

"I'll take him down to Booking," Peabody said as she helped Eve haul Reinhold to his feet.

"Nah. We're passing him off to a couple unlucky uniforms. We're going to go have ourselves a nice turkey dinner."

"Yay!"

Together, they dragged the limp, sobbing Reinhold out of the box, and into the rest of his life.

There was some paperwork to deal with, some contacts to make — procedure was procedure — but Eve figured they pulled up at the house at a reasonable time.

She hadn't screwed up Thanksgiving.

"Champagne," Roarke decreed. "For both of you. Exceptional teamwork in Interview."

"Champagne?" Peabody did a seat dance before climbing out. "Oh boy, oh boy!"

"It's a good day," Eve decided. And she could wait for the next to talk to Asshole Joe in the hospital.

She stepped into the house, into a wall of voices, music, into the scents of applewood burning, candles flickering, flowers, and food.

Into, she supposed, family.

They'd spread around the living room, and had broken out musical instruments. Some of them danced — including, she saw with considerable shock, the huge Crack, the sex club owner — with his tattoos and feathers. The Irish white skin of the little girl he had on his hip glowed against his ebony.

Mavis's little Bella clung to McNab's hands and stomped her feet in a mimic of the step-dancing going on.

They called it a *ceili,* she remembered from her visit to the family farm in Clare. And she supposed they'd brought a little Irish to an American holiday.

It fit just fine.

Before she could evade — or even think to — one of them (uncle — no cousin) whizzed by, snatching her, swinging her into the whirl of it.

She managed a "No, uh-uh," but he just plucked her off her feet, spun her in circles.

She laughed, then staggered a bit when he dropped her back down, and the music ended with riotous applause.

The noise didn't end. A million questions and comments burst out, and made her think of a media conference.

"Easy now," Sinead ordered. "You're all smothering the lot of them. Ian tells us you got your man," she added. "And all's well with the world."

"For now."

"Now is good and fine enough. We've

been entertaining ourselves as you see, until you were home again."

"Don't let that stop you." She took the glass of champagne Roarke handed her. "That was quick."

"It was already out and open."

Nadine walked over, gave Eve a hard, completely unexpected hug. "I love them," she murmured in Eve's ear. "I love them all, and want to marry them."

"How much have you had to drink?"

"Just the right amount. God, they're so much fun! You're a lucky woman, Dallas."

"I'm feeling pretty lucky."

"I'm having the best time." Easing back, Nadine plucked up her glass of champagne, lifted it in toast. "And I'm getting an exclusive with you and Roarke together, on *Now.*"

"No, you're not."

"Oh, but I am." Fun and affection danced in Nadine's crafty green eyes. "I'm going to get you drunk enough to agree before we have the pie."

"Good luck with that."

"I'm feeling pretty lucky, too. Oh, Morris is going to play the sax. I want to marry him when he plays the sax."

One of the uncles sang with the wrenching melody, and half the room shed tears.

Eve thought they liked it.

Mavis bounced up to give her a squeeze, then Charles. Everybody seemed to need to hug.

"I got that name and contact for you," Charles told her. "It turns out you didn't need it."

"I'm glad I didn't."

She started to step back. She really needed to take her weapon harness off, secure it upstairs. But she glanced down to see Sean and Nixie staring up at her.

"What?"

"You got the bad guy," Sean stated.

"Yeah, we got him."

"Did you zap him a good one first?"

Violent little bugger, she thought. She liked that about him. "No. I just knocked him down. Twice."

"That's something then."

"He killed people," Nixie said.

"That's right."

"Now he won't anymore."

"No, he won't."

She nodded, smiled. "I have your surprise."

"Yeah? Hand it over."

She ran to Elizabeth, got a slim rectangle wrapped in gold paper.

Gifts were always weird to her, so Eve

ripped the paper off — like a bandage from a wound — to get it done fast. And looked down at a framed drawing of herself.

She stood, eyes hard, weapon drawn, coat billowing. A little reminiscent, she thought, of an illustration in one of Roarke's classic graphic novels — and just as frosty.

"I drew it, but Richard helped."

"A little," he confirmed.

"A lot," Nixie whispered.

"It's great. It's really great. I look kick-ass."

Nixie giggled, slid her gaze toward her adoptive parents. "It's an assignment. My therapist said for me to make a picture of the person I'm most thankful for this Thanksgiving. I thought about it a lot. Because I'm really thankful for Elizabeth and Richard and Kevin, but I wouldn't have them to be thankful for except for you. I wrote an essay on the back. It's part of the assignment, and the present."

"Oh." Eve turned it over, saw it was a two-sided frame. And as she skimmed the careful writing, felt her throat close.

"Would you read it?" Sinead asked, and looking up, Eve saw the movement had stopped, and everyone waited for her. "Would you read it to us, Eve?"

"I . . ."

"Why don't I do that?" Understanding, Roarke took the frame.

The person I'm most thankful for this Thanksgiving is Lieutenant Eve Dallas. She kept me safe when I was scared and I was sad. She took me to her house with Roarke and Summerset and Galahad so nobody could hurt me, not even the bad people who killed my family and my friend.

She told me the truth. She promised me she would find the bad people and make sure they were punished. And Roarke said she would never stop until she did that. He told me the truth, too.

She helped me find Richard and Elizabeth and Kevin. They're not my mother, my father, and my brother. But they're my family now, and I know it's okay to love them. It doesn't mean I don't love my mom and dad and my brother.

Dallas didn't treat me like a baby. She told me I was a survivor, and that's important. She worked hard, and she even got hurt, but she found the bad people, and she made sure they got punished.

She told me the truth. She kept her promise. So she is the person I'm most thankful for this Thanksgiving. Nixie Swisher.

"Well done, Nixie." Roarke bent over to kiss her cheek. "Well done."

"It's good?" she asked Eve.

"It's real good," Eve managed. "I'm . . . ah. I'm going to put it in my office, at Central. And it'll remind me to tell the truth and keep promises."

"Really?"

"I said so, didn't I?"

Nixie threw her arms around Eve's waist, then ran over to Elizabeth. "She liked it."

"Yes, she did." Elizabeth sent Eve a watery smile, then pressed her face to Nixie's hair.

"That was lovely, absolutely lovely." Sinead got to her feet. "And a perfect way to lead us to our feast, I'm thinking. Let's get a move on. With this lot of us, it'll take an hour just to settle."

"If I may?" Summerset offered Sinead his arm, gave Roarke the faintest nod before leading the horde out.

"I need a minute," Eve murmured.

Roarke just drew her in, kissed the top of her head. "She's a strong, graceful girl," he said. "You helped her believe the world could be right again."

"She lost everything, and look at her. She has heart and, yeah, grace and goddamn spine. Then you look at Reinhold. And you wonder why. You'll never have the answer, but you wonder."

Steadier, she drew back. "But Sinead's right. Fine and good right now's enough. You'd better grab onto that while you have it."

"And we do."

"We do. Let's go eat ourselves sick."

"I'm for it."

She took a moment to walk over, set the frame, sketch side out on the mantel above the applewood fire, between the flickering candles.

"I do look kick-ass."

"Darling Eve, you are kick-ass."

"You're not wrong."

She took his hand, went with him to join the family, the friends, the feast. And was thankful for the now.

ABOUT THE AUTHOR

J. D. Robb is the pseudonym for a number-one *New York Times*-bestselling author of more than two hundred novels, including the futuristic suspense In Death series. There are more than four hundred million copies of her books in print.